Danya

C. S. Jones

© 2017 C. S. Jones
All rights reserved.

ISBN: 1546336486
ISBN 13: 9781546336488
Library of Congress Control Number: 2017906995
CreateSpace Independent Publishing Platform
North Charleston, South Carolina

To my loving husband Rick for his constant encouragement and patient editing, and my faithful friend Luann who never gave up on me.

Prologue

UNDER THE EMANCIPATION Act of 1861, Alexander II announced that Jews possessing a Doctor of Medicine, a Magister (Master's degree), or a Candidate (PHD) can obtain careers in Russian commerce and industry and live outside the Jewish Pale of Settlement, located in the western provinces of the Ukraine. His conservative council argued that this move is unthinkable because it will encourage the Jews to pursue their illicit trades and harmful occupations on a larger scale throughout greater Russia, spreading "the plague" throughout the empire.

Alexander II had hoped that a gradual assimilation of the educated and talented Jews into Russian Society would bait the majority to convert. Over the next twenty years he issued several initiatives to accomplish his goal. In 1865, artisans who possessed a passport, a police certificate of citizen in good standing, and a trade union certificate were permitted to live outside the Pale if they sold only their handicraft. In 1879, he extended the law to allow all Jews with a higher education permission to live outside the Pale.

In spite of these increasing liberties, the broad masses of Jews still resisted Russification and fusing with the Christian society. Only the liberal, the enlightened, and the upper classes responded with enthusiasm. They also showed increasing indifference to the Jewish masses languishing inside the Pale, and a separation began to develop between the two groups. This aroused anger among the aristocracy and nourished the already present root of anti-Semitism.

However, Alexander's Jewish assimilation policies had constructed a far worse tinder-box around the Jewish masses, waiting for one major incident to ignite it. While the Tsar's policies sought to modernize and assimilate the Jews, he deliberately ignored the uneducated Russian peasant because the government felt that a liberal education would pervert their moral and religious devotion to their *Batiushka,* their little father, the Tsar.

When the long awaited Emancipation Act did not set the millions of serfs free from the medieval constraints under which they had labored, a new breed of radicals appeared accusing the Tsar of deceiving his people. These pioneers of liberation called themselves the *narodniki* expressing their devotion, not to their little father, but to the common people. They began to declare, "Go to the *narod* and tell them that they need land and liberty. The peasants, suspicious of change, rejected their message, and the movement dissolved into a handful of hardened terrorists dedicated to revolution and to each other; separated only by death. Known as the *Narodnaia Volia,* or the people's will, they had a single minded mission, to assassinate Alexander II. After a relentless pursuit over eighteen months, they finally trapped their prey

On March 1, 1881, the Tsar was on route to the winter palace in his new bomb proof carriage. As the horses turned onto the Catherine Canal Embankment, the carriage collided with a single grenade. Unharmed, Alexander foolishly stepped out of his protective compartment to inspect the damage and to comfort the people injured by the grenade. At that moment he was wounded by another grenade which severed both his legs. He died several hours later at the Winter Palace.

Immediately after the assassination, a state of emergency was declared by his son Alexander III. The new times paper, *Novoya Vremya* which was the semi-official voice of the Russian bureaucracy, insinuated that the Jews were responsible for the assassination. This triggered a series of imperial decrees to feed the aristocracy's anti-Semitic mania by inciting the beaten down Russian peasants to execute acts of violence against the Jews.

Chapter I

1882

THE VILLAGE HERDSMAN cracked his whip. Peasant women in long skirts hurried to drive their milk cows through wattle gates to join the gathering herd on the way to pasture. A *starushka* trudged up the road, stooped under a load of kindling tied to her back; the veins and muscles in her forearms strained when she gripped the binding straps. She passed Daniel Mendelev as though he did not exist.

Stone clenched faces and vacuous stares were not an unusual demeanor for men and women who labored as beasts. Today was different. Daniel noticed a strange presentiment among those peasants he passed, an unspoken tension.

He raced down the road to the old synagogue and leaped over the few dilapidating steps into the prayer house, reluctantly inhaling the rank odors of gingerbread, vodka, and candle wax. Around him men rocked and bobbed in prayer; his thoughts drifting in and out to their rhythmic chanting. He gazed at the ark, an ornate cabinet which contained the Holy Scrolls of the Torah. On the cornice, two lions held the twin tablets of the Ten Commandments reminding him of God speaking to Moses on Mount Sinai. *Who is this God that conceals himself in a mystery?* He wondered. He understood from the ancient texts that the God of Abraham, Isaac, and Jacob was not an incomprehensible idea to his fathers. He spoke to the patriarchs in a friendly, human sort of way, or so it was written. But every attempt Daniel made to understand this person of God, his thoughts butted against an invisible wall as dark and endless as the starry galaxies.

Today, his thoughts did not center on the person of God but on the Gentiles who shared the village of Lensk in the Russian Pale of Settlement. Those who patronized his father's dry goods store had intentionally averted their eyes instead of offering the usual nod of recognition. He could not possibly imagine what schemes may be fomenting within the hearts of these seemingly vague and docile people.

His daydreams disintegrated when he focused his attention on his father's book of the Prophets which lay on the high wooden reading table next to the Talmud. Out of boredom, he opened its well-worn pages and began to read from Isaiah;

"He was despised and rejected by men,
a man of sorrows, and familiar with suffering.
Like one from whom men hide their faces
he was despised, and we esteem him not."
(Isaiah 53:3 NIV)

Again his thoughts wandered. *Why do the Gentiles despise us? Why has our God left us drifting in perplexities...groping in a world so hostile to...our very existence. How long would it be before He redeems us and brings us back to Zion?* He took a deep breath and concluded that all the prayers of men were useless when God remains silent.

A sudden jab in the arm popped Daniel's reverie. In a momentary daze he glanced up at his father who appeared massive wrapped in his blue and white prayer shawl. The embroidered motif of silver thread at the neck of the *taleth* enhanced the thick brown curls which swirled about his *yarmulkah*. When he saw his father's eyes ablaze with disapproval beneath the black *tefillin* jetting out from his forehead, he quickly averted his attention to the prayer book with boy like obedience. Although at thirteen, he was now considered a full-fledged

Jew, a man, and eligible to participate in all the religious privileges of his gender.

But for him, repeating prayers from the siddur was more of a chore than a privilege. While his father swayed and chanted, Daniel stealthy pulled the book of Isaiah closer and began to read when he noticed a comment scribbled in the margin. These words cast a shadow over the scripture. He mused over them for a moment and then interrupted Nathan. "What do you mean by this *tahtuh*?" he asked pointing to the cryptic note in the margin. "To whom does the Prophet refer?"

Nathan looked at his son in surprise and then a profound quietness passed over him. The vague expression in his brown eyes revealed that he had allowed his own thoughts to wander for a moment.

Again with impatient curiosity, Daniel repeated, "*tahtuh*? To whom does the Prophet refer?"

Nathan snatched the book from under the boy's hand and gave him a double slap, one on each side of the face.

The chanting and rocking abruptly ceased. Eyes turned from prayer books. A pencil dropped. Someone's foot scraped. His grandfather, the Rabbi Adler, turned from his place along the eastern wall where he worshiped and arched one dark eyebrow towards his grandson. Chagrined and humiliated, Daniel quickly slipped out of the prayer house, his cheeks still stinging.

"Danya! Come back here," Nathan shouted. His voice seemed to resonate from the ceiling beams and blast over the synagogue yard.

Daniel's anger burned with resentment. Maybe he was wrong in asking a question during ritual prayers, but Nathan had no right to embarrass him with that kind of overt display in the shul in front of everyone. After all, it was his father's own question.

His elder brother Ezra followed him out of the prayer house. "What happened in there? Why'd *tahtuh* hit *ya*?"

"I don't know. I asked him something and he got angry. Like some bat…out of…nowhere."

Daniel glanced over his shoulder at Ezra, who stared intently at him through dark brown eyes beneath a shock of raven curls. He had chopped off his ear locks declaring himself a modern *Haskalah* man. His beard began to fill in, and he had developed the sturdy broad-boned shoulders of their father. Ezra always fished for information and this annoyed Daniel. He jammed his hands in his trouser pockets and kept on walking with a jaunty gate, the fringes of his *taleth-koten* jumping beneath his jacket.

"Oh...don't let him get you. He's always slapping me around for something."

The sweet aroma of bakery treats and the racy smell of salt-fish filled the air around the synagogue courtyard. The complex consisted not only of the three-hundred-year old synagogue, constructed in the form of a wooden fortress with small windows, and it's several study houses, but also the *hekdesh*, a single building where both the sick and the destitute gathered.

Ezra put his hand on Daniel's neck where his dark brown hair curled around his collar. "Come on kid, let's get a poppy seed cake, my treat."

Ezra poked Daniel in the back. "Hey look. Over there!" He pointed to a crowd which began to gather around Baranovitz's book stall. Eiss Kiegel, the only Jew in the shtetl who could read and write in Russian, mounted an empty chicken crate holding a newspaper. He adjusted his wire-rimmed spectacles under the curly *pe'ots* bobbing on his pale thin cheeks and began to read from the *Novoye Vremya*. Eiss was a meek young scholar who spent long hours instructing *cheder* boys. When he stood up before a crowd to read, something imminent was in the works.

Daniel and Ezra scooted over and pushed into the crowd. They craned their necks and weaved on tip toes behind the mass of long black kaftans, squeezing in to find a good spot where they could hear every word Eiss had to say. The men shuffled about, their faces tense.

The sour odor of clothing steeped in sweat permeated the atmosphere. Dust drifted upward in hazy morning sunlight.

"What's he saying?" Daniel asked the man standing beside him.

"He's reading from the editorial," he said quickly in a low voice so as not to miss a single word. "They're accusing us of bombing the Tsar…they're calling us enemies of the public order!"

Daniel gasped. "Enemies of the public order? What does that mean?"

"Trouble, my boy. Big trouble." Said a middle aged visitor attired in a cosmopolitan suit, advancing through the crowd towards Eiss.

Eiss stepped down from the crate and gave his place to the stranger as he seemed anxious to speak. The fashionably dressed merchant stepped up before the crowd and drew a deep breath to calm his nerves. "I saw youths getting on and off at the railroad stations in the South. Young men from Great Russia agitating the peasants, telling them that the Tsar has issued an Imperial Ukase calling for Russians to attack the Jews."

A rumble of alarm rolled over the crowd to the last man. They turned to one another in animated gestures, excitedly reviewing the news, kicking up dust. Apprehensive shouts rose up.

"Did he?"

"Is this true?"

"These railroad *katzaps* are Jew-baiting," Aaron Weinstein, the ritual slaughterer, blared out hoisting a chunky hand in the air. He turned his corpulent body one way and then the other, to command everyone's attention. "And that rag you read, Eiss, is a sounding board for the administration's policy. You can bet your life on it."

"But will the peasants listen to these men?" Eiss said.

"This I don't believe," Nathan said. "We get along fairly well with our goyim."

"Don't bet on it," added Aaron, lifting his cap to wipe the sweat from his balding head with his handkerchief. "There's always fanatics out there trying to make trouble for us. It's nothing new. Alexander's assassination is just the excuse they've been waiting for."

Daniel could not absorb the magnitude of what he heard. Although he had seen an isolated incident surface between Jew and Gentile, he could not imagine a mass persecution. As far as he could see, the Jews and Gentiles of Lensk got along well together, and the south of Russia was, after all, a long way off.

Ezra pushed forward through the crowd and sprang onto the crate. "If this is true, we have to organize a defense team to protect ourselves," he shouted over the black visor caps; his body poised in a fighting crouch; his fingers out spread.

Heated shouts swelled from the agitated crowd.

"These are just rumors."

"How do we know if anything will come of this?"

"If it does, will we have the police to protect us?"

"No, shouted Ezra, whipping a hand through the air. "We can't depend on the police. We can't wait for something to happen. We can't shut our eyes and pretend there's not trouble out there. Hasn't anyone noticed a tension between us and the peasants lately?"

Everyone spoke at once, recounting the past words and actions of "the other people" who shared the town. Which of these Gentile neighbors would likely cause trouble? Which ones would believe these lies?"

"We have to organize ourselves and be ready for them, just in case!" Ezra shouted.

"Ezra! Stop this nonsense at once and get down from there. Right now!" Nathan, using the full base of his voice, had no trouble making himself heard above the noisy crowd.

Ezra jumped off the crate while the men parted in Nathan's direction. He stood in front of his father and peeked at him through the lock of hair which persisted in falling over his right eye.

"Go with your brother. Now! And stay with him. I don't want him alone in that store. Not when there's trouble brewing."

Since Nathan delegated the management of his dry goods store to Daniel on his thirteenth birthday, he had more time to indulge in the scholarly pursuits which he enjoyed and to participate in the *Kehillah*, where he became active in community affairs. For Nathan to study was not only pleasure but an escape from the reality of the world. Each morning after prayer, he remained at the study house to ponder the Talmud, and the laws written around the Talmud, and the laws written around the laws.

His father's pursuit also delighted Daniel. He felt like a big shot running the store by himself. Recently, he even learned to manage an international deal. He bought lace curtains from Vienna for their best customer, Maria Kerenskaya, who was picking them up this morning.

Their store occupied a choice spot in the marketplace yard on the main street across from Kalmann Rosenfeld's saloon. The two story building was constructed of wood with carved shutters on the windows. Nathan had two apartments rented upstairs. Artisan shops encircled the yard. Along a wooden walk outside the stores, rag peddlers sat on benches beside their bundles of used clothing, chatting. Two goats stood nearby warming themselves in the sun, chewing their cud and waggling their beards. Everywhere, vendors began to crowd the market place, selling everything from broken down furniture and patched-up pots and pans which they salvaged from the junk heap, to notions and baked goods.

Shoppers had already jammed the center of the yard to pick out the best fruit and choice hens for their Sabbath meal. Women with patterned scarves pinned firmly over their marriage wigs, dressed in long dark skirts and high buttoned blouses haggled in Yiddish with vendors hawking from behind push carts. They pulled chickens from little pens, examined them from under and over, pinching their breasts for plumpness. Dealers, standing for hours on flat feet, spread baskets of produce over the ground and fish mongers packed live carp in tin tubs filled with water. Children weaved in and out freely. Aromatic breads and cakes mingled with the odors of poultry cages, over-ripened fruit and people who smelled of garlic and acrid well-worn clothing.

Here and there, men in full beards and long gabardine kaftans with black visor caps pulled over their yarmulkes gathered in small groups debating the news from Petersburg, gesturing with their hands and chattering in anxious voices. A cloud of dust rose and diffused the sunlight over the cluttered crowded market place.

"Hey, Ezra! Where's my poppy seed cake?" Daniel said picking a bagel off a long peg which poked up from the baker's basket. "The Jews will be back in Jerusalem before you ever spring for anything."

Ezra made no reply but was looking down at his boots which were encrusted with mud from the spring thaw.

"What's the matter, don't you want to eat something?" Daniel turned to a wooden trough and searched for an apple which didn't look rotten.

"No. I'm not hungry."

"Why? Think trouble may happen here?"

"No, not really. However, if these railroad preachers keep telling *them* dumb peasants to beat the Jews with the Tsar's beat regards, I wouldn't put anything past them…Na, it's not that."

"What is it then?" He said polishing his apple on the flap of his jacket. He gave the vendor a few kopecks.

Ezra paused a few minutes and spat in the dirt. "It's father. He really gets my goat sometimes. He talks to me like I'm dumb. I don't think it's a dumb idea to organize a defense group, do you?" He glanced at his brother for approval. "You know…be prepared…" he prodded for a positive response.

Daniel nodded his head while munching on his apple and bagel simultaneously.

"*Agh*, he never stops insulting us," Ezra added when he saw no support from his brother. "I mean, he's so damn backward. "He's still living in the dark ages. He still thinks the Messiah is going to charge through the Pale on his great white horse and gather all the Jews back to Jerusalem. "Ha! What a laugh. Can you imagine all the Jews in the world packed like sardines back in Jerusalem?"

He paused and thought a while. "*Ny*...nothing ever changes in this *stinkin* place. If we ever get to our homeland, it'll be by our own sweat, perseverance and hardship."

"Yeah, I feel the same way...I mean...he has no right to embarrass us the way he does in public."

———

Daniel unlocked the door to his father's store. Nathan had the finest shop of its kind in Pale. Everyone knew about it for miles around and moneyed folk traveled there to buy the latest imported fabrics, and the entire fashionable sundry that went with it.

Daniel kept Maria Kerenskaya's Austrian lace curtains in a special place under the long display counter. Behind, the shelves normally stacked bolts of fabric rising from floor to ceiling were nearly empty waiting for the new shipment to arrive. He took the curtains out and carefully spread them out on the counter to check them over, to be sure they were in perfect condition when she came in to pick them up. While he was examining the curtains, Maksim Palchinsky, the one Russian University student in town, walked into the shop.

"*Dobree den*, Maksim," Daniel said in Russian. "What can we do for you today?"

Maksim, a tall slender young man with strong shoulders, moved silently and deliberately around the shop, browsing, but not looking at any particular thing. His neatly trimmed thick straw colored hair framed a clean shaven chiseled face. As Daniel eyed him, he sensed something unusual, even foreboding, in his behavior. Or did he imagine this? Since this morning's scare in the newspaper, he found himself scrutinizing the actions and expressions of every Gentile he passed. However, he had nothing to fear from this young man. They were on fairly friendly terms, and his mother was a good customer.

"What's the latest news from Kiev University?" Daniel asked the usual question. He had set his sight on going there someday.

Maksim stood in front of the counter and narrowed his brown flecked eyes at Daniel. "Is it true that Jews spit on churches?" he asked abruptly.

"What?" Daniel's mouth fell open, but words eluded him.

"And call down curses on the heads of Christians?"

Ezra ran in from the stock room where he was opening a shipment of decorative ornamentations.

"What about the Passover blood?" Maksim demanded, "Where do you get it?"

"Passover blood?"

"You know…Passover…matzo?"

Daniel didn't know how to answer him. They had just celebrated Passover two weeks ago and the words of the prophet Moses popped into his head, who told his ancestors in Egypt to paint lamb's blood on their doorposts to ward off the death angel. But that happened thousands of years ago. Why would this goy want to know about Moses and the Passover blood? However, Daniel knew Maksim had not come in the store to discuss the Passover. "What do you mean?" he inquired raising his defenses.

"I heard there's a Jewish sect that uses the blood of Christian children for ritual purposes. What about it?"

Daniel gasped in astonishment when he perceived that it was not contempt that reflected in Maksim's expression, but perplexity, as well as indignation. His heart was pounding although he knew he had to appear calm and in control as Maksim's eyes burned into his. He tried to focus his thoughts and attempted to appeal to the former emotion, hoping to control the situation and peacefully head the young man off. "Maksim. You, an enlightened university student, do you actually believe these false accusations?" He was unaware that his brother Ezra was quietly moving into the picture and standing between them. He glanced at his brother and his blood chilled. Ezra's eyes blazed like two coals in a reddened face. His fists were clenched, and ready to go. Maksim ignored Daniel's reasoning and took Ezra's bait.

They poised, like two bantam roosters, ready to go at each other, when Maria Kerenskaya walked into the shop. Neither man budged.

"What are you boys doing?" she blasted. "Maksim! Don't you have anything better to do than to go around making trouble?"

Maksim reluctantly turned toward the pretty fashionable young woman standing inside the doorway.

"I'm sorry *Madam* Kerenskaya." He moved slowly toward the door, all the while with angry eyes set on Ezra.

Daniel sighed in relief and stood a few moments breathing deeply before showing his customer her beautiful lace curtains.

Chapter 2

MAKSIM'S STINGING WORDS shattered Daniel's theory that the South of Russia was a long way off. The *katzaps* were suddenly on the village doorstep. He wrapped his long dark kaftan against the raw wind blowing from the passing storm and trudged in ankle deep mud to the *shul* deliberately scrutinizing the faces of each Gentile who passed.

He couldn't tell with any certainty if the transactions with his customers were strained. Nothing out of the ordinary had shown on Maria Kerenskaya's friendly face. No, perhaps the incident with Maksim was isolated, he mused. After all, Tsar Alexander II had been assassinated for nearly six weeks and the problems in the big cities were quite different from those in the small towns.

The *shtetl* was buzzing over the autocracy's new wave of *Judaeophobia*. People speculated on everything from, "this kind of trouble can't possibly happen here," to an embellishment of every gory detail recalled from the pogrom of Odessa ten years before.

When Eiss Kiegel appeared in the synagogue courtyard with his copy of the *Novoye Vremya*, the men in long kaftans converged around him like a black cloud; anxious to hear the latest on what the editorials referred to as Jewish affairs. Eiss would then step up on his crate and adjust his wire-rimmed eyeglasses to read the hard-hitting acrimonious lies. But on this particular day, his emaciated face appeared ashen. He didn't read from the editorial as usual, but stood with his arms hanging at his sides, his hands lost in the drape of his coat which seemed a few sizes too large for his thin frame.

A hush fell over the men in the courtyard, each tossing the same tormenting questions in his mind. Daniel pressed closer into the crowd to hear. He felt the tension growing in the bodies closing in around him.

"They've hit Yelisavetgrad," Eiss said; his thin lips trembling in his sparse black beard.

The men opened their mouths to speak, but the words were stuck in their paralyzed throats. Finally, Daniel heard someone manage a hoarse whisper, "How bad was it?"

"The paper called it a petty street disorder," Eiss continued.

Suddenly, everyone talked at once.

"If that's all it was then we don't have to worry. Our police should take care of things if it comes here."

"Is this newspaper giving us the whole story?"

"Can we trust the police? How do we know they don't support this anti-Semitic mania?"

"That's right," several voices piped up.

"We can't trust any of them," Ezra stated. "I say we need to organize a defense group. If we don't protect ourselves, no one else will."

"May God help us. They hit a day before the Sabbath," said Nathan.

The men debated all through the morning and into the Friday afternoon *mikvah*. Inside the ritual bath, rows of step-like wooden benches rumbled under clomping feet while male voices rose in excitement. The bath attendant hurriedly poured buckets of water over hot coals until a cloud of vapor enveloped everyone.

Daniel sat down and rubbed his hands over his slender arms.

"This is nasty business Petersburg is playing with us," said the man sitting beside him staring straight ahead into the steam.

Daniel turned his head and glanced at Kopel Ullman, the matchmaker, who was combing his gray beard with his fingers.

"What do we do to them that they should pick on us?" Mottel Seltzer, the carpenter, said from behind. Daniel turned around. Mottel's complexion was flushed almost to the same shade as his red hair and beard. "We don't bother them, we obey their laws, we pay their unfair taxes...we even fight their wars. Why us?"

"I'll tell you why," Aaron shouted in his husky voice, brandishing a willow branch with which he had been hitting himself. "They're jealous, that's what. And ignorant. They can't hold a candle to us because our children study hard to make something of themselves, against all the obstacles they throw our way."

Daniel rested his elbows on his knees and listened to the words which intensified with the steam.

"True!" added Hirsch Goldiss, the tailor. "Why, Russian artisans can't even read or write. How can they make a pattern for a suit?" He moved around in his seat as a ghostly apparition below.

"Jealous or illiterate? What difference does it make if they're planning on beating our brains out?" Ezra said.

"But things are different down there in the South of Russia," Daniel said.

"*Whaddya* mean different?" You're a dreamer kid," Ezra said.

"I mean they have big port cities and they're always blaming the Jews for bad business down there. We have little *shtetls*. What would they want here with us?"

Kopel laughed at Daniel. "You have a lot to *live*, son. I heard some goy right here in Lensk blaming us for his business failure, already."

"Yes, it happened right here in my shop," said Hirsch. "He came by me yesterday and accused me of taking his customers away! Imagine! We work for chicken feed. They buy from us because they get their money's worth."

Nathan rubbed his hairy chest dripping with water. His loud voice boomed out above the sizzling steam. "I always thought we got along good together...as good as can be expected. A few years ago when the peasants had a crop failure they never dreamed of blaming us."

"Seems like they're setting us up, doesn't it?" Daniel said to Kopel.

Kopel shrugged. "So what else is new?"

Mottel ran his hands down his face and squeezed the water from his red beard. "I don't know about you people, but I've had enough."

Afterwards, on the way to synagogue, Daniel observed the powerful figure of his father plodding through the mud in his long gabardine *Shabbat* coat, belted in the middle to separate the upper spiritual body from the lower part. Its velvet collar matched his velvet yarmulke. Ezra would bring their mother, Este, later, as she was still preparing the last minute touches for the *Shabbas* meal.

"*Tahtuh?*" Daniel asked. "Why did God choose us from the rest of the people in the world?"

Nathan stopped briefly and glanced at his son, his eyes widened in surprise and then narrowed in agitation. "This is the wish of God and that's all," he said and pressed on trudging in the mud.

"We don't bother the goyim. Why do they want to make trouble for us? Why do they throw us in jail if we travel outside the Pale without a passport? Why...?"

His father stopped abruptly. "Why so many question from you?" At first he seemed annoyed. Then as quickly as his emotion had surged, it had subsided and he reflected for a long moment, stroking his dark beard. He gazed toward the late afternoon sun peeking through the dark clouds. The shadows had rolled away from the hillside, revealing a dusting of delicate greens, yellows, and pinks. The long afternoon rays of sun painted the village huts in blue, terra-cotta, yellow and white. A stork had nested on the chimney of the town hall and was tucking her chicks beneath her wings. Then he said, "God is trying out the people. Only when the people suffer can they begin to understand what life is about."

Daniel stood beside him through a long ensuing silence. His father's burly stature seemed to diminish as he bowed his head into his hand and wept.

On Friday evenings, jobless drifters were a common sight in the synagogue courtyard, but on this Sabbath many wayfarers began to appear from various southern towns. Several men had gathered around a wandering notions vendor who toted his wares on his back. He had seen every town along the way and recounted the horrors in all its detail.

"Every town, every *shtetl*, they hit," he said struggling to unbind himself of his merchandise. Nathan stepped forward to lend him a hand as he continued to speak, "when the peasants saw how incredibly easy it was to loot, like wild fire, they spread the word. In minutes, they made shambles."

"Where was the law?" Nathan asked him.

"What law?" The vendor gripped his back pack for support and laughed bitterly.

The color drained from Nathan's olive complexion. "How bad was the damage?"

"In my town they only destroyed the tavern," said one of the strangers.

"In mine, they ram-sacked homes and demolished shops," said a man of small stature. "Stole what little we had." He reluctantly extended a hand in a pleading gesture, apparently ashamed of what he had been forced to become. "Please, may God bless you."

Daniel gazed into his father's face looking to find strength when he saw his lips trembling beneath his thick beard and curly mustache. "May God help us," he whispered.

The men of Lensk stared at one another in gloomy silence. One thought blasted through their minds. "What if it happens here? To whom will we run for help? And worse, who will be left to help us?"

They filed solemnly into the synagogue and kissed the fringes of their prayer shawls before wrapping them around their shoulders. They fastened their *tefillin* in place, one over the forehead to remind them that they must always remember the laws of God, and the other on the left arm, to keep the commandments in their hearts. Then they quietly sat down inside while the women ascended the stairs to take their places behind a curtain.

"There is no peace for us," Nathan mumbled to himself as he took his seat between his two sons.

"What do you mean father?" Daniel asked. "Do you think it will be very bad? It seems we have always gotten along well here with the goyim."

Nathan shook his head. "That's superficial. The heart of the issue is that we are Jews. They hate us because we are not one of them."

Eiss lifted his eyes from his siddur to listen.

Nathan continued in a soft pensive tone. "The assassination of Alexander II is the opportunity they've been waiting for all along to make life so miserable for us that we will either want to convert or die."

"I say you more than that," Aaron squinted at Nathan. "They want us all out of here, that's want they want."

Eiss stared straight ahead pondering all the accusations that he had read over the few weeks, coupled with the recent news of violence. "Sometimes," he said, "I think, if you will pardon me, their hatred is as complicated and irrational in its origins as our stubbornness to retain our ancient culture."

Daniel gasped. Eiss, his first *cheder* teacher. Daniel loved Eiss. Whenever he was afraid to go to his father with his problems, he went to Eiss, a soft-spoken caring human being. How he and his family existed on the meager donations he received from poor parents, was a mystery. Reading that propaganda from The New Times everyday must have taken its toll on poor *ol'* Eiss.

Rabbi Adler entered the *shul* and had overheard every word. Everyone's attention turned to the rabbi. Though his hair was grey, his moustache and beard were streaked with black, reminiscent of the days when he was a younger man, but his dark eyes still sparkled behind his wire-rimmed spectacles.

"Eiss Kiegel," the rabbi said. "I will not pardon you! How can you entertain this noxious idea in the house of God, the house of prayer?

May His ear be closed to what you have said forever? To give up our ancient heritage is to give up life itself!"

"With all due respect, Rabbi, I didn't mean "convert" he shuddered when he spoke the word. "I meant modernized, dress like them, you know." He made a circular motion with his hand. "Which is better, to give up our tradition and grasp at some kind of life or to exist in this misery they have heaped on us?"

The rabbi smiled. "Would that make any difference to them? Would it make us like one of them? You know the answers, my son."

Eiss fixed his gaze on the Rabbi.

"Is it not better my friends," he looked around at everyone. "To keep on hoping, to keep on worshiping, to keep on believing in man because we trust in the God who created him?" Tears rolled down his cheeks into his beard. "We cannot give up the responsibility of our faith. The Lord our God told our father Abraham to go up into the land of Canaan. There I will make you into a great nation and will make you a blessing to the people of the world. The whole land of Canaan, I will give you as an everlasting possession, to you and your descendants after you, and I will be their God."

Then he lifted his face toward heaven. His moist black eyes sparkled as if he had seen a vision when he recited from Jeremiah (16:14-15) For behold, the days will come, says the Lord, that it shall no more be said, the Lord lives, that brought up the children of Israel out of the land of Egypt. But, the Lord lives, that brought up the children of Israel from the land of the north, and from all the lands where he had driven them. And I will bring them again unto their land that I gave their fathers. (23:5) I will raise unto David a righteous Branch; a King shall reign, and shall execute judgment and justice in the earth. His name shall be called The Lord our righteousness."

Daniel stared in awe at his grandfather. He marveled at his faith to keep on believing, to keep on hoping that God would send a redeemer to gather his people back to their homeland, back to Jerusalem. He wished he could acquire this strong faith.

The rabbi led the *Kiddush* in praise to God and the people repeated in unison.

"Deserving of praise are you, O Lord our God, ruler of the universe who chose us for your service from among all peoples and favored us by making us holy through your commandments. Out of love you gave us, O Lord our God; Sabbaths for rest, holidays for gladness, festivals and seasons for rejoicing, you granted us this Sabbath day and this day of the Feast of weeks, the season of the giving of our Torah as a holy gathering, recalling our liberation from Egypt. You chose us from among all peoples and hallowed us by giving us your holy Sabbath and Festivals as a joyful heritage. Deserving of praise are you, O Lord, who hallows the Sabbath Israel and the Festivals."

Afterward, in the courtyard, when everyone wished one another "Good *Shabbes*," his father invited three strangers home to share the Sabbath meal, according to tradition.

Este welcomed her family and guests at the door of her home wearing a stylish dress made of black imported fabric interwoven with golden threads and a black lace veil with golden spangles. She adorned herself with golden ear drops and a golden chain around her neck.

The faces of Nathan and his down trodden guests brightened when they saw her generous smile revealing even white teeth, and her large blue eyes glittering warmly. The aura of her floral perfume filled their presence.

Inside, the room sparkled of impeccable cleanliness and the brass candelabra over the table cast a Sabbath glow. For a moment, the pitiful men thought their arduous journey had ended in paradise. Este spread her graceful arms and beckoned everyone to her bountiful Sabbath table. "Come in," she said exuding grace and warmth. The mixed aroma from roasted goose, noodles in chicken broth, and gefilte fish, put a moment of Sabbath joy back into their heavy hearts. It was her desire to make this *Shabbas* as happy an occasion of celebration as possible, to somehow bring encouragement and lift the gloom from everyone's souls

When everyone was seated and the last vestige of sunlight faded, Este performed the rite of illumination and peace for her soul in this dark world. She lit the Sabbath candles and gracefully circled her palms over the flame. Then she placed her slender fingers over her eyes to shut out all the physical reminders of earthly life. Tears trickled down her cheeks and fell on the white linen table cloth as she softly prayed the Hebrew benediction to God.

Daniel raised his eyes to the pure, heart felt melody flowing from his mother's lips. The strain reminded him of a caged songbird longing to soar high above its terrestrial confines.

The four days succeeding the Sabbath had been strangely calm. Sunny spring days had dried the muddy furrows and the birds were singing their nesting songs. The meadows nearby were tilled and ready for planting. In the orchards, trees had burst forth into blossoms rejuvenating the village of ancient huts. The scent of musty black earth and the delicate perfume of the flowering trees drifted in balmy breezes. Daniel took long deep breaths to drink in a moment of happiness to sooth his troubled soul. He looked around, as he did each day, intently observing the peasants. Most saluted him with a nod as they always had on their way to work the earth with long wooden implements slung over their shoulders. Perhaps, he mused, the threat of violence had blown over and the prayers of the faithful had reached the ear of God.

However, the inhabitants of the *shtetl* went about their business beneath a bleak demeanor, as though all the glorious budding of nature had suddenly withered. In the *shul,* Hirsch Goldiss, a small, sturdy man, stood up nervously twisting the fringe of his prayer shawl.

"*Chawer,* mine friends," he said. His voice trembled. "Something terrible happened to me. I feel the need to tell you before we begin."

Every head snapped up.

"A goy customer came by mine tailor shop yesterday and said..." He bowed his head into his hand trying to compose himself.

"He said what?" Voices repeated. Some of the men quietly rose form their seats and inched forward. Someone's prayer book fell to the floor. Candles flickered. Suddenly in the death of silence, an elderly pauper wailed from behind the stove in back of the room. "May God have mercy! May God have mercy!"

Hirsch took a deep breath. He pushed his wire-rimmed eye glasses up the narrow bridge of his nose with his finger. "He, this customer, said he was looking forward to it."

The old pauper wailed louder.

Faces turned ashen, as dead men.

Hirsch continued in a meek voice. "He said that he had no personal animosity against the Jews. He just thought it would be a good sport to watch, that's all." Suddenly Hirsch exploded, like a coil which had sprung. "Imagine! A sport!" He repeated making large gestures with his hands.

Stunned, they all turned to one another. A flurry of voices swept over the room.

"No animosity? So this is supposed to comfort us?" said Aaron Weinstein.

"Why would he tell me this. Like a bar fly. Did he want to torment me? Yes, that's it. He wanted to torment me. He wanted that he should play his words in mine mind. Now every time a leaf shakes in the wind, I jump, thinking someone's sneaking up behind me. Mine head is spinning, mine children, mine wife. Where can we run to, with disaster coming down on our heads?"

"I didn't want to tell you this but I heard they burned and raped in Kiev. There were dead," Kopel said in almost a whisper.

Dread crept over the men. They stared at one another in silence. For the first time Daniel mirrored the fear which darkened the expressions of his elders. An icy chill of hatred sprang from deep within his heart and he shuttered. How could he look his gentile customers in the eye, smile and say, "*Zdrastvoyete*, how can I help you today?" When God only knew what heinous and malignant imaginations they harbored.

"It appears they're getting more violent with each hit," Mottel's blue eyes stared from a white face

"I read in yesterday's paper where soldiers and the police protected one *shtetl* from violence. Not too far from here," Eiss said in barely a whisper.

"You can't believe that rag," Aaron stated.

"What if what Hirsch says is true?" Nathan wiped beads of sweat from his brow beneath his *tefillin*. "And what if they do strike here? Should we defend ourselves? What can we do to protect our wives and daughters?"

Ezra leaned over behind his father and poked Daniel. "See he's coming around to my way of thinking. It's the only way that makes sense, kid."

The Rabbi leaned in Nathan's direction and glared at him through piercing black eyes. "Is violence the way to combat violence? Do two wrongs make a right?"

"So what are we to do? Stand by and allow ourselves to be persecuted by these superstitious, ignorant peasants?" Nathan protested.

"Remember my words, son," he warned his son-in-law. Then he turned to his congregation and said, "what each one of you does is between you and God. But today, I implore each one of you to fast and pray. Without His mercy, we are helpless."

The men fell to their knees and beseeched God. Tears streamed down their faces. They had no words, only their hearts cried out.

"We look for light, but all is darkness," said the Rabbi. "We walk in the shadows. We look for justice, but fine none."

They turned over benches and cried out from the first chapter of Lamentations, grieving for the destruction of the temple in Jerusalem, grieving for their homeland lost.

> How deserted lies the city,
> once so full of people!
> How like a widow is she,
> who once was great among the nations!

She who was queen among the provinces
has now become a slave.
² Bitterly she weeps at night,
tears are on her cheeks.
Among all her lovers
there is no one to comfort her.
All her friends have betrayed her;
they have become her enemies.
³ After affliction and harsh labor,
Judah has gone into exile.
She dwells among the nations;
she finds no resting place.
All who pursue her have overtaken her
in the midst of her distress.
⁴ The roads to Zion mourn,
for no one comes to her appointed festivals.
All her gateways are desolate,
her priests groan,
her young women grieve,
and she is in bitter anguish.
⁵ Her foes have become her masters;
her enemies are at ease.
The Lord has brought her grief
because of her many sins.
Her children have gone into exile,
captive before the foe.
(Lamentations 1:1-5)

"What have we done O' Lord to bring down your wrath?" they cried out and beat their breasts with their fists. "The heavens have sent blessings but we have blocked the channels of blessing. Our offenses testify against us." They implored Jeremiah to plead with the patriarchs and intercede with God on behalf of desolated Zion.

Chapter 3

Nathan took a sip of tea and said, "I don't think you should open the store today...too dangerous."

"In most towns they only hit the saloons." Daniel always tried to look on the bright side. "They didn't bother the people. Maybe they'll leave us alone. Besides, that goy implied it may happen, not that it would."

"It may; means it will. He didn't have the guts to tell the truth," Nathan said peeling an onion. He sandwiched in between two slices of dark bread and bit into it.

"Why? What makes you think so?"

"I know so. When you live here as long as I do, you'll know too. The Russians speak out of both sides of their mouths."

Daniel sat down on the bench next to his father. He leaned an elbow on the table and rested his head in his hand, gazing out the window. "It's a beautiful day out there," he said. "I can see the peasant women in the distance sowing the fields already. Everything looks normal."

Nathan waved a few flies off the loaf of bread and pushed it in front of his son. "Here eat," he said.

"No thanks, I already had two poppy seed cakes at the *shul.*"

Nathan's gaze moved slowly around the room. Copper pans hung on patterned wall paper beside the white clay stove which took up a good portion of the kitchen space. Usually the first person to rise would feed its dying flame to take the morning chill from the house. On a tin table under the cabinets, stood Este's *tzedakah* box in which she dropped a few kopecks each day for the poor along with the salt box containing the condiment she used to kosher her meat. Nathan's attention settled on the small opening to the loft under the roof. "We've been warned, I think we'd better get prepared for the worse, even if they don't hit us. We can bring our feather beds up to the loft."

Someone entered the hallway between the parlor and the kitchen. Nathan put his sandwich down and stood up when Ezra stomped in. He already had a powerful build, like his father's side of the family. He swung one leg over the bench, then the other and sat down. He took the loaf of bread and ripped off a chunk.

Nathan shot him an icy stare. "Wash your hands. Don't forget, you are a Jew."

Ezra popped up with a defiant shrug of his shoulders and went over to the counter beside the stove to wash his hands.

"Where were you?" His father asked brushing crumbs from his beard.

"Talking with friends." He poured some water into a basin from the pitcher.

"With who, that university David?"

"Yeah."

"So, what's to talk about so much?"

"We...ah...we're organizing a group to fight back in case there's trouble," he said coyly; his back turned toward his father.

"Organizing what? It's time you got off your high horse and help us get ready a place in the loft where we can hide just in case trouble comes."

"*Whaddya* mean hide?" He wheeled around and pointed over his head. "If they *wanna* get you in the loft, they'll get in there. You people have *gotta* wake up and listen. We've *gotta* organize ourselves. We can't let them have their way like in the other *shtetls* they've demolished."

"Don't get so excited everyone," Daniel interrupted. "Let's be calm and think. Kiev is a big city. We're a little *shtetl*. They only hit the little towns here and there, and mostly the saloons."

"We have a big town here, there's a lot for them to steal," Ezra said pushing away the lock of hair from his eyes. "Besides you don't know how many towns they hit. We don't get all the news."

"So it may not be as bad as you think. Why don't we hope for the best instead of fearing the worse?" said Daniel.

"You're *misuga*, kid. What kind of Jew are you…we may hope for the best but we know we can expect the worse. You can't sit around hoping. You've got to do something." He turned to Nathan. "Pop, get your friends together while we still have time. We need the cooperation of every man in the *shtetl*. And get whatever weapons we can find to defend ourselves."

Nathan burned with anger. Just as he opened his mouth to protest Este rushed in and put her hand on each side of her head and exclaimed. "Oy Vey!" she exclaimed. "May God preserve us! This is the day we get our big shipment from Minsk! I forgot about it with all this commotion. They're delivering our goods today. What shall we do? Nathan!"

"When it rains it pours. There's no peace for us," Nathan said. "I got to get to the station to meet that 12:35 train."

"Ma, don't worry so much," Daniel said, trying to comfort his mother. "It's a beautiful day and the peasants are out in the fields working. We can't sit around all day worrying when we're not sure. One day will turn into another and we'll lose business. Besides, if something does happen maybe our police are planning to protect us here."

"Oy, my child," she said. "You are so bright and at the same time so naïve. When they hit, they hit like a bolt of lightning. The peasants probably don't know the exact day themselves. Nathan, don't get that shipment today, listen to me!"

"The damn train only comes here once a month from Minsk. And it will be another month after that before they ship again. If they extend our credit."

"Don't risk your life for credit. If they attack and the goods are stolen, what difference will it make. Better they should go back on the train."

Nathan pounded his fist into his hand and paced back and forth for a few minutes. "Maybe Danya is right. The peasants are working. They only hit certain towns here and there. Maybe it won't be us. Maybe it will only be the saloon...maybe. Ezra! Go with your brother, just in case. I don't want him in the store alone, you hear? And don't go sneaking off with that university David." He waggled his finger. "Forget about this defense nonsense. I think your grandfather is right. If it hits we have to ride it out the best we can and hope." He raised his eyes in silence for a moment. "God knows we're trapped in this Pale. Maybe he'll spare us."

Este's blue eyes widened in terror. "Nathan! I have this terrible feeling. Please don't bring that shipment back to the store!"

Nathan put his arm around his wife to calm her. "Don't worry, I'll think of something," he said.

On the way out the door, Daniel and Ezra touched the mezuzah, a decorative tube tacked to the doorpost, which contained a parchment of scripture from Deuteronomy. They pressed the tips of their fingers to their lips and repeated the prayer, "May God watch over my going out and my coming in for now and evermore."

They closed the wattle gate in front of their home and started down the dirt road. "Look at these geese," Daniel said pointing to the white flocks waddling straight toward them; their long necks shooting up from plump bodies; their little heads bobbing from side to side. "They never cease to amaze me. Look how they strut in little units, like little soldiers; down the road to the river...each unit marching in precise distance behind the other."

Ezra looked up.

"Not one intrudes into the others territory. Why can't people respect one another like these animals?"

"Geese don't respect one another, *noodnick*. They have a pecking order. It's instinct."

"I'm not so sure about that, they seem to know something about life that we humans have missed. And don't call me a *noodnick*."

"As far as people go," continued Ezra. "They don't respect each other unless they are made to. Take the Aristocracy. They treat the peasant masses like crap. And in turn the peasants treat us like crap warmed over. Injustice keeps on going down the line unless someone does something to stop it."

Daniel eyed his brother. "Have you organized a defense team?"

Ezra grinned. "We're working on it," he said enthusiastically. "In all due respect to Eiss, going to the governor and asking for soldiers is ridiculous. They'll laugh at us. The only way to stop these goyim is to give 'em back a dose of their own medicine."

"Yeah, I suppose you're right about that." Daniel thought about his brother's words. In the past, he was told by the old folks that the *Kazaks* took every opportunity to amuse themselves by mocking Jews. Why would these soldiers suddenly change their minds and protect the Jews now?

Even before the brothers entered the market place, the aroma of oven-hot bread greeted them. A boy with a tray of rolls on his head darted across the yard from Ben-Zion's bakery. He exchanged greetings with the water carrier who carefully toted two large buckets strapped to a yolk around his neck. Some of the artisans who lived in flats above their shops were at work. Hirsch, at his sewing machine and Mottel pounding away in his furniture shop. However, the usual vendors and rag peddlers were missing.

"The square seems quiet today. Where are the vendors?" Daniel asked.

"It's early. They'll be here. Don't worry…ah…maybe they're thinking it over."

"Thinking what over?" Daniel gave Ezra a queer look. His brother's mouth was twitching below the growth of hair on his upper lip. He fidgeted for a few minutes in front of the shop, frowning, mulling something over in his mind. "Say, since things are slow this morning,

I'm going to take off for a while. There's a few people I need to talk to. I'll be back later."

"About what? The defense group?"

"About things. Be back later."

"Hey! Don't leave me here alone! Hey!" Daniel shouted after his brother who disappeared into the alleyway between the shops.

Ezra always had a shadowy side and it irritated Daniel. He unlocked the door to the shop, went in and sat down behind the counter. The absence of vendors and shoppers; the silence, gave him an eerie feeling. The street peddlers should have set up for business long ago. He got up and peeked out the window. A few scrawny men with greasy hair under their black caps stood in the street looking for work. One had a saw and axe slung over his shoulder; another a bag of tools. At the sight of a third man, his heart thumped down into his stomach like a hunk of lead. The jackal sat on the stone wall of the well in the middle of the courtyard, beside him rested a black sack filled with the clothing he bought at the expense of the dead. He always knew where to find business; he could smell death a *verst* away.

Daniel knew the jackal was not a psychic but a pragmatic man and his curiosity lead him to do something that would not enter the mind of an observant Jew. He ventured down the road into the Christian district to see if their shops were any busier.

What he saw set his brain spinning with simultaneous waves of consternation and anger. Someone had chalked large black crosses on the wattle gates of the Gentile huts. Icons were visible in their windows. The gates of his Jewish neighbors were unmarked.

His thoughts reeled in confusion. Nothing moved in the street except some dirty ducklings splashing in a mud puddle. He wiped the perspiration from his face with the back of his shirt sleeve. *Should I run to my father? No, I'd better find Ezra first. No, I'd better get back to the shop right away. All my father's money is tied up in inventory. If it's stolen, I'll never hear the end to it. Besides, he expects me to be there when he arrives with the stock.* He ran back to the shop. His heart pounded, sweat rolled from his head.

Nathan always kept a club hidden under the counter in case trouble broke out with the peasant boys. Daniel knelt down and pulled it out. He examined it a few moments and shoved it back. He went to the window. Mottel was gone. So was everyone.

I'd better run home before it's too late. He stepped outside on the walk way. *No, if I leave the inventory before father gets here, he'll kill me. I must be strong, strong and courageous, like Joshua.* He went back inside, dug out the club again and swung it around clobbering imaginary peasants on their heads. His anger elevated with each mighty blow. He was the brave warrior of Israel. He glanced out the window around the empty yard and trembled not with might, but with fear. He sat down and carefully leaned the stick beside his chair and waited. In his wildest imagination he had no idea what to expect.

The morning passed; there were no customers, no peddlers, not even a pedestrian. He repeatedly twisted his ear lock with sweaty fingers and nervously ran his fingertips over the fine hair that was beginning to appear on his upper lip. He kept glancing at the clock on the wall, tic...tic...tic... counting the seconds for the train to arrive. Every time it pinged, he jumped. He tried to recite from lamentations but couldn't. *Where's Ezra? Where the hell is Ezra! He and his friends should be here by now. Damn him. He always finds some excuse to shun responsibility. And who catches hell? Me. Damn him. Where the hell is he?*

The heck with him. I'm getting out of here too. Daniel rose abruptly. On his way to the door he peeked out the window. The yard was desolate. Not even a cat could be seen slipping into an alleyway. He glanced back at the clock, 1:15 already. *Where's father?* He sat down again. What to do now? Only a fool would be out there, he thought. He glanced at the rows of shelves behind him, almost empty of textiles now. He popped up to find a hiding place in there somewhere, when suddenly heavy booted feet thumped the porch outside. They stopped outside the door. He froze in consternation. He knew they came to get him.

Someone twisted the door knob. His knees buckled, his jaw trembled and he broke into a cold sweat. All at once the door flew open. It hit the wall with a violent thud.

He stared wide-eyed at the broad shouldered figure standing in the shadow of the door. He opened his mouth to yell, but no sound would vibrate from his paralyzed throat. He gagged and gasped for air.

Nathan screamed. "What the hell are you doing? Sitting here like a dumb quack ready to be picked off. Look! The door is wide open, here are the keys! In the lock!" He jingled them in the air. "Everyone else had locked up and taken cover. But you! What kind of a schlemiel are you!" He clomped over in a furry and yanked Daniel's ear-lock.

"But father! I was waiting for you...and the shipment."

"You were waiting for me?" Nathan asked, stunned. "I told Ezra to tell you to go home, hours ago. Where in hell is he?"

"D...did you get the material?"

Nathan exhaled in exasperation. "I left it by Piotr Dukov. I hope he's honest...come on, let's get *outta* here." He grabbed Daniel by the arm. Suddenly a loud whistle shot through the street and startled them. They peeked out the window across the yard. About forty youths had gathered outside Kalmann Rosenfeld's saloon. The commotion drew a few Gentile by-standers. A few policemen and several Kazaks also arrived on the scene. Their presence signaled to Nathan it was safe to go outside.

Daniel kept a few steps behind his father. Mottel, Hirsch, Ben-Zion and a few others peeked out their doorways.

Nathan stood beside one of the on-lookers and asked him what had happened.

The man glanced over his shoulder at Nathan. "A drunken fellow went into the saloon to stir up trouble. Rosenfeld threw him out." He replied with some reserve.

"Kalmann Rosenfeld is a decent respectable man. Surely, they won't harm him!"

"Yes, Rosenfeld is a decent man."

"Then why don't the police do something to stop these hoodlums from making trouble. Why are they standing over there...doing nothing?"

The man shrugged.

Nathan's brown eyes widened in astonishment and flashed in anger. "This is a set-up, isn't it? I saw several Moldavian thugs get off the train this afternoon. They're headed here to start trouble, aren't they?"

The by-stander turned away.

He scanned the rabble outside Kalmann's saloon. Young men, with big hands and grinning broad faces stood in groups smoking and chatting; exchanging dark sideward glances. He knew many of the youths. Their mothers patronized the store. They would trade poultry, butter, and eggs for yard goods while their worthless husbands gambled away the hard earned rubles. Their uneducated sons had little to do but drink and carouse. But he also noticed several crude muscular bruisers with unfamiliar faces, and fierce, angry eyes.

He was surprised to see Maksim Palchinsky appear among this ragged bunch of ignoramuses. He wore a bright red scarf tied around his arm, like some kind of clandestine signal.

The youths shouted, their tongues fired with vodka. "The Zhids are beating the Russians, the *Zhids* are beating the Russians." Some picked up stones and shattered the tavern windows. Others pushed inside. Within a few minutes, hundreds of rubles rained down on the noisy mob outside the saloon.

They scrambled over the ground, hunched like greedy vultures, bobbing up and down, plucking up the rubles and stuffing their pockets until the coins dropped out. Pavel Chernov, a Gentile who tended Kallmann's bar, pulled up behind the tavern in his empty hay wagon. He quickly helped the Rosenfeld family out the back door into his wagon and they disappeared into a cloud of dust.

Maybe this is it. Nathan reasoned. *Rosenfeld is a very rich man; maybe they only want his money.*

No sooner had the thought entered his mind when Maksim scrambled to the roof holding up a piece of meat he speared from the kitchen. "These are the remains of a Christian child found in the house of the wealthy Jew, Kallmann Rosenfeld," he said.

Nathan turned to some of the by-standers and said hoping to arouse their indignation. "This is a frame-up! Surely no one believes this!"

The police and soldiers glanced in Nathan's direction, grinning and chatting in the afternoon sunlight impervious to the happy hooligans staggering from the tavern with bottles of champagne tucked under their arms and pockets filled with rubbles. Some of the mob poured out the bubbling liquid into tall glasses and passed them out to the gendarmes.

Maksim hoisted his glass in the air, and shouted "Who runs every tavern? Jews! Wherever you turn, who do you run into? Jews! It is from the Jews we Ukrainian folk suffer most of all. It is he who exploits you. It is he who drinks the peasant's blood. In liberation of the Russian people, I propose this toast!" His red arm band blew in the wind like a banner, and his hair shown like a golden crown against the cobalt sky.

Daniel clenched his fists and quivered in rage, recalling the day Maksim came into the store firing accusations. He wanted to smash his head in. He looked around for his father. Nathan's face was turned to the eastern sky; his eyes squeezed shut; his lips moving. *Did he really think Messiah would appear from nowhere and gather his people back to their homeland?*

Suddenly one ruffian lifted his bottle of champagne like a war lance and bellowed. "Smash the Jews. Get the Jews." His words rang out like an Imperial Ukase.

The loathsome mob surged forward into a herd of stampeding beasts, their mouths twisted, their faces reddened with rage and drink.

Young savages snatched sticks and rocks and spilled out into the yard, racing in every direction. The spectators, both Jew and Gentile, scurried into the side streets and disappeared behind bolted doors. Others were knocked down and trampled. In a whirlwind of rising clouds of dust, and husky hooting, Daniel lost sight of his father.

He darted toward the small group of Kazaks standing in the street. His heart pounded. His fists clenched. He skidded in the dust, screaming. "Stop them. Why don't you stop them?"

The Kazaks grinned at each other, not with impudence, but with amusement at this young man's boldness. Rifles hung idly from straps slung over their shoulders and swords were tucked away in sheathes at their sides. "Look at this would *ya?*" said one laughing.

"Sorry boy, we have no orders," said another looking down at him through cool arrogant eyes, and at the same time trying to suppress his derision.

Daniel lunged one way and then the other, looking for his father in desperation, hoping he wouldn't be trampled to death. Clouds of feathers whirled around the yard like snowflakes. Window panes and doors went flying. Bolts of fabric fluttered in the air like banners over his father's shop. The mob roared and rioted. Wild whistles and shouts fused with bone piercing screams of anguish. Everywhere, broken dishes, furniture, and household utensils lay scattered about. Daniel wiped his face on his sleeve, sticky with sweat and dust.

Nearby, the rabble threw itself on the synagogue and yanked out the protective bars, locks and shutters. They stormed inside, heaved the Torah into the street and trampled it into the dirt with incredible passion.

Tears streamed down Daniel's cheeks. This act of violence was not against the Jews but against God, the creator of all people. In the dust and confusion, he spotted the police commissioner walking toward him in his brown uniform and official cap with the red band and gold button. Before Daniel opened his mouth to protest, the *Ispravnik* sneered at him. "Sly dogs. Tricksters! Tell you father and the others you're getting what you deserve. And tell them we won't do anything to stop it."

Daniel thought his world had come to an end. The hatred hidden in the hearts of his neighbors had overwhelmed him. Tears blinded his eyes. "How can you? We don't hurt you. Why don't you stop them?" he shouted back.

The *Ispravnik* smirked. "Stop them? Is that what you want?" he said.

Daniel's heart pounded. The inspector removed a large tobacco pouch from his pocket and said, "you are a brave little Jew boy, Daniel Mendelev." He took some tobacco and leisurely rolled it into a cigarette, lit it and took one long drag and exhaled smoke rings in the air. "Brave and forth-right. I have to respect you for that. You are not like the rest of your kind." He grinned and gazed at the white puffs of smoke enlarging like misty bagels and disintegrating into the air.

The agony in Daniel's heart momentarily lifted in hope by these complimentary words. "Please have mercy," he implored.

"Ah…mercy. Is that what you want? Mercy and justice. Don't we all." He looked at the cigarette between his fingers.

Daniel waited and wondered for what seemed to be an eternity. Would he relent?

Finally, he said, "the tillers of the soil are getting justice the only way they know how. Now get out of here Jew boy and tell that crowd of yours we won't do anything to stop it."

Trophies of destruction lay in the streets heaped to a man's waist. Ruffians emerged from the shops transformed from sinewy rabble into corpulent well-dressed gentlemen fattened by layers of clothing. They staggered, this time not from drink, but from loot teetering in their arms.

At last the mob seemed satisfied with its work. Their wild mania had ebbed. Daniel ran home leaping over smashed household articles and dodging broken furniture. He flew through the gate of his home, gasping for breath and pounded on the door. "Mama, Ma!" he shouted. "Let me in."

His father stepped outside the door yelling, "Danya! You had us worried sick. Where were you? Get up in that loft. A mob of looters are gathering in the church yard."

Daniel clutched the twine ladder and climbed the wooden rungs. Nathan followed him, pulled the twine ladder up and concealed the opening with a board. A thin ray of light streamed through a tiny window in the front gable and faintly illuminated chains of onions and garlic hanging from the rafters. They waited in silence.

All around them the roar from the pogrom kept swelling and falling like a tide until, when all at once, it sprung up around their house like a hell-fire. Windows rattled and shattered. The house shook. The mob thundered inside, hooting, whistling, and shouting. Daniel heard something rip from the ceiling.

Their booted feet thumped like cannon balls. China shattered. Furniture grated and thudded. Rochelle began to cry.

Someone stopped below the opening of the loft. Daniel's heart beat raced when he heard the heavy ragged breathing. A step. Then another. Closer. The heavy breathing continued under the trap door. Daniel was suffocating, gasping in terror. He waited senseless for the inevitable confrontation.

Then as quickly as the mob entered, it left. Daniel heard the terrifying shouts fan out across the fields. The family waited. Dead quiet.

All at once, laughter and excited chattering started up in the streets. Nathan crawled to the little attic window and poked his head out to see what was happening.

"Oy Vey!" he exclaimed. Ezra quickly crept to the window and Daniel followed. Astonished, they watched peasants loading their furniture into a hay wagon. They even pulled the brass candelabra from the ceiling and were fighting over it. Someone held up their samovar, showing it off to everyone. Their hearts sank when he saw their precious heirlooms, passed down from each generation, treated as trophies in the hands of goyim. And to add insult to injury, they laughed.

Slowly, the villagers drove their wagons away, creaking under the enormous weight. Some pushed cartloads, other dragged sacks behind them. Dusk fell over the *shtetl*. The family waited in silence. Strange sounds sprung up around them. Branches wrestled. Dried mud crunched under heavy boots. Doors stealthy grated open and slammed shut. Foul words spilled into the night. Suddenly one barbaric yell pierced their bones like a bullet sending simultaneous waves of ice through their blood.

"*Jhiddy*, we'll be back tomorrow, you hear?"

Chapter 4

A FEW DOZEN ruffians appeared in the early morning fog outside Rosenfeld's saloon. Within minutes, they swelled into a pulsating horde taking on a life of its own. Everyone who lived in nearby villages, from petty town clerks to peasants, came to loot and get his share of the booty.

"*Jhiddy!*" shouted one of the hired agitators from Moldavia. "We have orders from the Tsar to teach you a lesson you'll never forget!" He thrust his fist forward like a javelin. "Get the Jews. Drive them from Russia!"

They were met with about sixty men assembled in the yard to defend themselves and their families against the malignant mob of young thugs. Ezra's friend David Tournik was among them. He had a pistol in his hand.

Suddenly, Nathan pushed through the crowd and yelled at David. "Stop! Don't use that gun! There'll be blood shed for sure."

Nathan's words signaled an alarm and the bruisers surged forward with great passion, howling and hooting. David drew his revolver and fried. The bullets successfully dispersed the rabble. A few of them fell to the ground. Alerted by gun shots, the police magically appeared to defend the hooligans. They seized David Tournik and several others and arrested them. The complicity of authority unleashed the worst of human passions in the mob and turned it into a torrid river of flesh whose dam had broken.

Battle cries pierced the streets. "Smash the Jews! Get the Jews!" Like a tornado, they swarmed the streets with twisted faces, demolishing every house in its way and smashing every Jew that blocked their path.

Men, women and children fled from their homes into the streets. A living nightmare swirled around them. Screams from the tormented fused with jeers from their assailants, a madness from hell, a perpetuating frenzy feeding on itself.

A cold sweat of consternation broke out over Daniel's flesh. The mob swayed darkly, or was it his head? Hard bodies shoved against him and pushed him into a pile of broken furniture. Swirling feathers caused him to gag. When the commotion subsided, he pushed away the debris to free himself. He was about to get up when he witnessed Mottel Seltzer struggling with a leather scourge, trying to defend his work shop where women and children had taken refuge against a few savages who were determined to smash their way inside. Mottel's wife, watching from behind the door, darted out to assist her husband. She flung herself onto one of the thugs who contended against him. The brute thrust her back against the shed like a rag doll. She screamed hysterically as one bludgeoner snatched the knout from Mottel's hand while another clubbed his head. A hard blow to the stomach and Mottel crouched over in agony. A furious strike to the neck, and then the head. Like wild men, they lashed and clubbed until Mottel's deformed body slumped into a shapeless bleeding mass.

"*Tahtuh! Tahtuh.*" A young man lying prone with his face to the dust, lifted his head in reply to his child's pleas.

An adolescent voice rang across the yard. "Kiegel is still alive, Get him!"

"Eiss? NO!" Daniel cried out. Someone was moving near the broken furniture. "I heard someone shout around here, he said." Daniel's heart pounded. He lay motionless, like a dead man. A commotion diverted the brute's attention. He turned his head and saw a bludgeoner with a club in one hand and Mottel's knout wrapped around the other standing over Eiss.

"Oh...Eiss. Why did you lift your head?" Daniel moaned to himself. "But...can a father deny his own son?"

The killer screwed up his swarthy face. His white teeth flashed. With violent force, he thrust his filthy boot over Eiss' delicate face and squashed it like a pea.

The slaughters dragged the corpses of Mottel and Eiss through bloody streams to the middle of the yard. Once again, the tumultuous hooting and whistling sprang up as the rabble gathered in the square to gape. Two drunken women gathered up pillows and gave them to the thugs who, with their knives, ripped open their victim's stomachs and stuffed the pillows inside. Then they dumped feathers over the bloody bodies. The two women leaped on the corpses and howled and danced until their boots were washed in red.

Afterward, the savages prowled the *shtetl,* searching. These murders were but appetizers for them. Now they wanted women. Daniel remembered his mother alone in the house where he had thoughtlessly left her after his father ordered him to remain by her side. He had to get back. The mob was already vacating the yard, heading down the side streets when suddenly one of the drunken women cried out, "Look, up there. I heard a child cry." She pointed to the loft above Hirsch's shop.

Instantly the rabble swarmed over the building like rats. They ripped the roof open and disappeared inside. Two women leaped to the ground screaming hysterically. One escaped, the other fell into the snare of the bludgeoner. She struggled in vain against her killer. The other woman ran and clung to the knees of the *Ispravnik,* pleading and sobbing.

The police commissioner took a drag on his cigarette, crushed the butt between his fingers and flung it in the street. Then he kicked the woman off like a whimpering bitch. She struggled to her feet and fled for her life.

Tormenting screams and audacious laughter poured from the loft. *How much wickedness can live in a man's soul?* Daniel thought of that scumbag who stood under the loft last night, quiet as a snake. He had to get home to his mother and sister, somehow.

Several Kazaks rode through town on horseback, brandishing their sabers, disbursing the mob, but the rabble only moved on to terrorize another street. Daniel crawled through debris into an alley way between two artisan shops. He wondered about his father and brother. But he would think about that later. Now he had to get to his mother. The way was clear. He ran home slipping by pillagers unnoticed.

"Ma! Mama!" Daniel ran through the open door jam. His head throbbing, his heart pounding. "Mama. Are you there? Are you all right?"

Este looked down from the loft. She lowered the ladder. "We are still here," she whispered.

"Mama," Daniel said climbing the shaky twine ladder to the platform. "I'm sorry. I didn't mean to leave you. I didn't…I never thought." He heaved and gasped and fell into her arms. Tears fell from his eyes onto her bosom.

They embraced for a long silent moment and she pulled back smiling through her own tears. "You're safe!" They were both smiling.

Rochelle was squatting by the opening next to her mother. Daniel hugged and kissed her. They were both safe.

"Have you seen your father and Ezra?" Este whispered.

"No." Daniel shuttered. He stared into his mother's face. Even on the shadows he clearly saw the questions in her expression and the dread in her eyes because they mirrored his own. He gazed back through the opening, his thoughts in turmoil.

"Pull up the ladder," she said, "Hurry!"

No sooner had Daniel secured the board over the opening when he heard someone enter the house. He listened; the footsteps were not his fathers, nor Ezra's. They were light and slow like a prowling jackal.

Torrid imaginations raced through his mind. He decided he wasn't going to sit around like a scared rabbit. He had seen too much. His father kept some lumber in the attic. He saw a long flat board and quietly crawled over to reach for it. He carefully glided it back to the opening. The footsteps came closer. He knelt in the shadows holding the board in his hands. He heard the intruder pull up a bench. The attic board moved aside and a dark head rose through the opening. He was certain the youth could see the board shaking in the shadow and hear his excited breathing. He had only one chance to get him. He had to hit him squarely on the head with a single hard blow. He did it! The youth fell to the floor unconscious. Daniel gazed down at him, contemplating for a few moments. No, he couldn't do it.

He quickly lowered the ladder and helped Este and Rochelle down before their assailant revived. "We can hide in the raspberry thicket across the street," Daniel said. He picked Ronnie up and carried her across the room to the door, stepping over debris. A blood curdling whistle sounded in the street. It was too late. The thugs saw them. They ducked back into the house. Gun shots vibrated in their ears.

———◆———

The sun dipped behind the onion domed church and painted the yard and the mutilated corpses blood red. Drum beats rolled, the command rang through the streets. The cavalry mounted. They surrounded the scattered bands of hooligans and drove them off with the butt ends of their rifles. Here and there they shot and wounded a few of them. It was finished. Nathan was free to go home. His palms grew clammy with anxious longing when he thought of Este, Danya, Ronnie, and Ezra. He would not concede to his worse fears. He had to believe. Hope was all he had left.

He could see clearly that the pogrom had been planned, executed, and precisely terminated. But for how long? He knew how intensely passionate and unreasonable Russian peasants could become once they were incited, especially with the Tsar's best regards. Would they calm down as instantly as the turbulent wind after a violent summer thunder storm? He wondered.

He staggered home in the twilight. A few small boys sat barefoot in the dirt and threw stones at him, aping the adults. Dust drifted in the late afternoon sunlight, but Nathan was oblivious to the world around him. He grieved for what could have been. *Why, oh why did David use that gun. Why did I yell out to stop him?* When he saw the smashed houses on his street, his heart began to beat anxiously. Somehow he regained the strength to run home.

"Este, Este, Daniel, Ezra?" He stumbled over the door sash kicking up feathers. They swirled and dusted the floor like snow. Everything was ransacked, his precious volumes, the Torah, the Talmud, the commentaries, the books of the Prophet torn and trampled, doors hung open, cupboards stood gaping, crockery smashed, furniture broken and over turned, clothing scattered everywhere. But these were not his concern. He spotted the loft entrance open and the ladder pulled down. Slowly, he dragged his painful body half way up the ladder, just enough to see inside.

Este," he called weakly. "Este?" Someone was moaning in the bedroom. Then a thump. He broke out in a cold sweat of fear and descended the ladder. He crept to the bedroom and peered around the door. Retzel Kantor's goat stumbled from behind the bed stand chewing on the horse hair mattress. He slumped into a broken chair and groaned. He noticed Este's jewelry box was missing, and her silver candlesticks. The only heirlooms Ester had from her dear mother, stolen, along with the armoire where she kept them. Only the heavy oak bookcases which they couldn't lift stood intact. In pain he lifted himself. He had to go on. He had to find them. He searched the yard and the street.

A few disoriented hens dashed away. Near-by, in a field, he spotted the body of a youth. "Danya, my Danya." His boots felt like they were filled with lead as he dragged his painful feet through mounds of newly plowed dirt. Tears, blood, and sweat rolled down his face and dripped from his beard. He gazed down at the body. "Danya?" There was no movement. He knelt down beside him. Tears clouded his vision like a blinding torrent of rain. He put his trembling hands on the shoulders of the boy, afraid to turn him over, afraid to look. He couldn't bear any more, but he had to bravely go on. He had to know.

"Danya?" No, it wasn't Daniel. He felt the boy's pulse. His heart was beating. He was still breathing, badly wounded, but alive. He picked him up and carried him over his broad shoulders, straining from his own pain.

He hobbled to his neighbor's house and stood in the open door with the boy. Three little children gazed up at him with frightened eyes. Eyes that had witnessed the unspeakable.

"Mrs. Kantor, it's me Nathan Mendelev, your neighbor. Are you all right?"

She peered at him through swollen tear-filled eyes.

"Can you help this boy?"

She nodded. "You can leave him here."

"Have you seen my Este and my children?" he inquired eagerly.

She shook her head and began to cry, gasping between sobs. "It was horrible, Reb Mendelev. Horrible."

"What happened? Tell me."

"They took my Ben-Zion to *hekdesh*."

"Is he all-right?"

She nodded and lightly touched a swollen red and blue welt on her cheek. "Look at my house. What am I going to do? How will we live?" Nathan observed her torn blouse and twisted skirts. Poor woman, he thought, she, like everyone else, has to bear her own sorrows tonight, and who knows for how long? He slipped away silently.

Oh my God. What did you do with my Este? My children? He slid down the wall of his house where a bench had been. "Oh God," he sobbed. "Why us?" His throat was so dry, he thought he had swallowed fire. He gathered his strength and went to the well to drink.

His head reeled with the worse imaginations. *What if Este was mutilated, murdered, raped! He would...he didn't know what he would do.* "Oh my

God," he moaned. "Oh my God, no. Please!" *Hekdesh? Maybe they're at hekdesh. Maybe she's volunteering. Good ol' Este. She went to help the wounded, that's it.* The happy thought rejuvenated his strength. He trudged on to the community hospital in the settling darkness.

A throng had gathered in the synagogue courtyard outside the *hekdesh*; not only victims of the pogrom and their loved ones, but the homeless poor who needed a safe place to lie down and to eat a warm meal. Nathan pressed into the crowd. "Este! Este," he cried feebly, amidst the moaning and wailing of the wounded. "Este, where are you?"

Wagons brought those who didn't have the strength to walk. Most were victims of assault. Others were trembling half crazed women, violated by rapists. Those with broken and severed limbs were carried inside first. He couldn't bear the agony any longer. He slid down in the dust. Delirious, he turned to the old man squatting beside him gripping his face in his hands; blood seeping from between his fingers. "Have you seen my wife, Este Mendelevna?" he asked. The man moaned in great agony. He removed his hand to reveal a grotesque sight. "They accused me of looking upon a Gentile woman."

Nathan swooned. When he awoke someone was wiping his head with cool water. He gazed up into the tired eyes of a young volunteer. "You'll be all right with a little rest," she said.

He touched her arm. "Have you seen my Este? Este Mendelevna?" he asked weakly.

She shook her weary head. "We have so many, and we haven't been able to get all the names. Some are too badly beaten to speak."

He turned his head away. Moans and delirious screams rose like a sickening chorus all around him.

He became nauseated from the foul fetid odors of dried blood rags, perspiration, and antiseptic. He was lying on one of the many straw pallets which formed two tight rows of wounded thinking only of Este, Ronnie, Danya, and Ezra.

Chapter 5

EARLY THE NEXT morning, Maria Kerenskaya's husband, Nicolay Ilyaovich, and his comrades drove the women and children they had rescued to their homes. Maria gave each one a package of tea, bread, and cheese along with some apples.

Nicholay Ilyaovich, an artillery officer in the Imperial guards, was a formidable foe for any enemy, thought Daniel gazing at his handsome tanned face. Like the Tsar, he stood a good head over everyone else.

Nathan limped out of the house like an old man when he heard the wagon pull up to the door. Swollen red eyes peeked between his beard and a head bandage.

Este put her hands to her face. "Nathan! What happened? Are you all right?"

"I'm all right already. A few bruises, that's all."

Este threw her arms around his neck and chuckled. "Am I glad to see you in one piece. A little battered, but in one piece."

She pulled away and made a frown of concern. "Where's Ezra? Wasn't he with you?" When her husband did not answer, she shouted. "Where is he?"

"I don't know," he shouted back. "I haven't seen him since yesterday morning."

"May God help us!"

"Este, Este." Nathan whispered. He squeezed her to his bosom. "I was worried over you, and now you're back. I'm sure he'll be all right, too."

The two of them helped each other through what was left of the door. They stumbled over broken pieces of furniture, using each other as a crutch, scattering a few hens scratching through the shambles for crumbs. He looked around the room, pulled out a straight back chair from under the broken furniture, and sat her down.

Tears stood in Este's eyes. "Ezra may be lying near death in the hospital. We have to find him."

Nathan looked around for something to wipe her running nose. He reached down and lifted the apron from her skirt. "Here," he said and gave it to her. "He's not at *hekdesh*, I asked before I left."

"Good God!" She looked at Nathan, her eyes flashing with horror.

Daniel tried to recall if there were others besides Mottel and Eiss involved in yesterday's agonizing nightmare, but he could not. He tried to remember if there were more bodies lying under the broken debris but his memory blurred. The dead would be at *hekdesh*, laid out on a bare stone slab, side by side, in preparation for burial. What if Ezra was lying there beside them? He squeezed his eyes shut, and stumbled into a broken bench. "I can't bear to look at the dead again," he murmured.

Blood drained from his parents faces; they fell silent like two granite statues, with terror etched in their eyes.

"Dead?" Nathan said after a few moments. "How may? Who?"

"Mottel, Eiss, I don't know."

"Mottel, Eiss! My God! How many more? That means they are having the memorial prayers for the martyrs today, and the burial. If Ezra is there, why hasn't someone notified us?"

"May God help us? Maybe he's beyond recognition," Este replied and fainted.

Nathan gently laid her on the feather beds. "Danya, get a wet towel."

When she regained consciousness, Nathan whispered, "I'm going to the synagogue."

She sat up, dazed for a moment. "I'll go with you."

"No! You stay here."

"I'm all right." She stood up still shaking. "I'm going. I have to know."

"*Ny*...all right then. Danya take Ronnie next door to Mrs. Kantor."

"I'm not going, father."

"You're not going?" Nathan said. He took a deep breath, lowered his voice and said in a concerned tone. "Danya, look, I don't mean to be hard on you but you can't live with this in your mind. It isn't healthy. You have to face what happened yesterday. You have to let it out of you so you can have a healthy mind. If you try to block it out and pretend it never happened, it will torment you for the rest of your life. Besides, your brother..." his voice trailed off as his thoughts yielded to his worst fears.

As the family walked down the road to the synagogue, Daniel was in awe at his father's mental and physical stamina. Beaten up, stumbling along, yet he goes on with life as usual. He wished he could possess this kind of strength and courage.

Every heart in the *shtetl* was burdened with grief on this night, every eye washed in tears, not only because of the tragic deaths, but because their *shul* had been defiled and their Torah decimated. They gathered what was left of the scrolls which had been part of the synagogue for a few hundred years and buried them, along with their friends.

At the cemetery, Daniel stood among the people of the *shtetl* and listened but didn't really hear. They sang something and tried to express some thoughts to console the bereaved before lowering the bodies into the ground. The cold earth made a dull thud when it splattered on the coffins. A skinny little Jew scurried back and forth rattling coins in a cup crying, "charity saves from death." Everyone dropped in a few kopecks for good measure whether they believed it or not.

Somehow there was finality about death, Daniel thought as he walked home solemnly beside his parents. A great blackness, a nothingness, the final curtain. He couldn't imagine Eiss and Mottel still alive, laughing and sharing and hoping in some other dimension. Neither could he believe that they were simply a lifeless mass gone back to the dust of the earth. He would miss Eiss. Poor soul, he thought with tears filling his eyes again. Eiss spent his life in privation, devotedly instructing each *cheder* boy as though he were the only student in the *shtetl*. And Mottel, spirited Mottel with his carrot red hair, who created each piece of furniture with artistic pride. All the pieces they bought from him were stolen. Now anger mixed with his tears. His only memento's from Mottel were gone, stolen by some rotten goy who had the pieces in his hut. "Damn them."

He looked to his father as he always had in difficult times, hoping to grasp on to his great strength, but under the moonlit sky, his father had diminished into a broken old man. Nathan stopped for a moment and looked up into the heavens. "Why?" he cried. "Why?"

"Father," Daniel whispered. "Is there even a God up there listening? Or are we wasting our time praying so hard for his mercy, when there is none?"

Nathan gazed at his son with tears in his eyes. After a long silence, he answered in a low cracking voice.

"God hears the people's prayers, son. We may argue with God concerning the justice of death, but never-the-less it is he who gives and who takes away. We live in a world of injustice and sickness, sickness in the heart and sickness in the mind" Unable to bear the heavy burden any longer, he bowed his head and wept.

Daniel reached out and put his hand on his father's trembling shoulders. Nathan embraced him, this time the father leaning on the shoulders of his young son. Finally, he drew away, avoiding Daniel's searching gaze, and said, "the people are not to understand the ways of God, my son, but to trust." He paused for a long time. "To trust that

He will always be with us even when death comes." Then he turned away and sobbed openly.

Trust in someone he didn't know, or something he didn't understand? *How is this possible?* At least they were all alive and safe now, everyone except Ezra. His brother wasn't at the burial. No one saw him at *hekdesh*; no one remembered seeing him anywhere at all. He knew that Ezra maneuvered by his wit and that he would most likely turn up eventually…he hoped.

When they were a short distance from home, Daniel ran ahead of his parents and stood in the door. "Ezra?" he called, gazing into the silent darkness. An icy chill shot through his blood. "Ezra's not here," he said to his parents who were behind him now.

"He's not here?" Este exclaimed hysterically stumbling into the darkened house.

"Este, don't go in there." Nathan warned. "Danya, run next door and ask Mrs. Kantor for a candle…and get Ronnie."

Daniel hurried back with a candle burnt nearly to the wick. "This is all she had," he said.

"Let me have it. I found some candles yesterday and put them aside. Help your mother and sister inside while I look."

In the dim light, Daniel led Este around the broken furniture to the feather beds where she sat down trembling.

Daniel knelt down and put his arm around his mother's shoulders. "Maybe Ezra ran away," he said trying to guide his mother's thoughts away from her obvious fears as well as his own. "Maybe he ran away to get into some school. He's always hanging around with those university students."

"I wouldn't blame him," Nathan grumbled placing a candle here and there around the room. "So what's here? Shit! Cow shit! Horse shit! Goose shit! Can't put your foot down anywhere around this place without stepping in…"

"Nathan! Hold your tongue."

"Who'd want to stay here if he could get away." He persisted.

"Nathan! How can you at a time like this. We still don't know if he's alive."

Nathan sighed. "He must be alive, if he weren't, someone would have found him by this time."

"Well speak of the devil." Daniel said looking at the tall figure moving in the shadows beyond the door.

Ezra dragged in stepping over the threshold.

"Ezra?" Este bounded to the door and threw her arms around his shoulders. Ezra placed his hands on his mother's slender waist, lifted her in the air, and planted a kiss on her cheek. They both laughed.

"Here, let me make some hot tea," she said. "This is cause for celebration. We're all here now, we're all alive! I have a fresh loaf of bread, cheese and some apples. What more could we ask for?"

"Our samovar's gone," Daniel said.

"And the cheese isn't kosher," Nathan mumbled.

"It's all right this time, we have food and we are all together again. Thanks be to God! I'll boil the water in a pot. I saw a pot around here somewhere," she said searching through the clutter with a candle in her hand. "We have enough fire wood around this place to keep the stove hot for a year."

Ezra entered the parlor and stood in front of his father. Nathan gave him a lingering hug and patted him on the back.

"Come over here son and sit down," Nathan said propping up a broken bench with a piece of table. "So what happened to you? Where have you been?"

Daniel eyed his brother. He looked gaunt and tired, like he'd been in some kind of a mess.

"What's that in your hand?" his father inquired.

"It's a pamphlet, pop." His face lit up, eager to share with his father. "It's calling the Jewish working men of Russia to unite. Here, look. We had them printed up." He held it out to his father.

"What's this about?" Nathan snatched the pamphlet from Ezra's hand. "Where did you get this?" he said examining it on one side and then the other.

"David Tournik gave it to me."

"David Tournik?" He stood up and looked Ezra in the eye. "So that's where you've been, in jail!" He threw the pamphlet in Ezra's face and paced the room, running his hand through his curly hair. "Look son," he said. "I don't mean to be unreasonable but this David Tournik is a bad apple. He's been stirring up trouble ever since he started going to that university. I want you to stay away from him, you hear?"

"But pop!" Ezra stood up, taller than his father now. "What's wrong with asking for better working conditions? You know how bad it is in those factories. A worker is treated worse than a dog. Besides, England's passed laws. America's passed laws."

"This is not the only trouble he's made in this *shtetl* and you know it."

"What? You mean the defense group? But how were we to know?"

"I heard rumors that these rebel students are threatening to kill the new Tsar if he doesn't give in to their demands. Is this bunch taking part in that too?"

"Wha?...I"

"I don't want you to keep company with him, that's all!"

Ezra turned and stomped out the door.

Nathan followed him. "Where are you going now? If you have to go somewhere, then go to the store and start cleaning up."

Chapter 6

EVERYONE IN THE shtetl realized their struggle was not against peasant uprisings but against the Tsar himself. Alexander III would not yield in his determination to drive the Jews from Russia. With each Ukase, he tightened the screws of oppression, hoping to turn the Jews from their faith, which he believed to be an incubator of conspiracy against his Empire, and convert them to Orthodoxy. Everyone knew he wanted to gather all his subjects under the wings of the Imperial Eagle, and into the feathers of their *Batiushka*, their little father, the Tsar.

The Emperor forced both rich and poor Jews out of the Great Russian cities and into the overcrowded poverty stricken towns in the Pale. When the demand for charity became relentless, he prohibited the wealthy Jews of Petersburg and Moscow from donating so much as a kopek to relieve their suffering brothers.

New waves of terrorism broke out in towns across the Pale. This time, when the police and Kazaks moved swiftly to arrest the looters, the rift-raft set fire to hundreds of homes raining a deluge of new refugees on the little towns looking for food, work, and possessing only the clothes on their backs.

As summer days faded into autumn, Daniel observed his mother with deepening concern. She had taken on the job of chairing of the women's rehabilitation committee. He watched helplessly as her health began to fail. "Ma, please for our sake, take time out and rest." He insisted one evening after clearing the dinner table.

"I will, darling," she replied weakly. "But how can I rest when I see the faces of so many needy children staring at me each day. How can I sit at our table, with so much to eat, when there are so many who have gone without bread for days?"

"Trying to cure poverty in the *shtetl* is like trying to make a dying horse pull a wagon," he snapped. "You need your strength."

"My son, come here, sit down beside me. I've wanted to talk to you about something for a long time."

"Ma, you're not listening!"

"I am listening, darling, but I have something important to discuss with you. Come," she patted the seat beside her.

He sat down and gazed at his mother.

She smiled. "I know your heart is set on going to the university someday, but by the time you are ready, your chances of getting in will be next to impossible. Now, your grandfather is the rabbi of one of the finest Yeshivas around…"

Daniel unwittingly drew back.

"It would be his greatest privilege to teach you. There is nothing that would make him happier than to pass his mantle on to you, his grandson." She paused to examine his response. He made none.

"Ever since you were a little boy, you wanted to hear about Abraham and the prophets. At your bar-mitzvah, your Talmudic discourse won you praise throughout the whole *shtetl*. I think you would make a splendid rabbi. And our community desperately needs a strong-minded young man like you to lead them through these difficult times."

He sat quietly mincing his mother's words for a long time before he answered. "I know the Russians are closing the doors of education to us, and there is a quota…but how will I know if I can make it into the university if I don't try…actually my chances of getting into a gymnasium are pretty good. Then I can apply to Kiev University. "

Este backed away and looked at him incredulously. "Kiev University? Why they're hunting down Jews in Kiev like animals and throwing them back in the Pale. They've murdered them and burned their homes! My son, what do you want? To jump back into the ten plagues of Egypt?"

"I can live with uncle Sholem."

"Sholem? He's poorer than a synagogue mouse. He has barely enough to buy the Sabbath meal. Besides, he may not even be alive! I haven't heard a word from him in months."

"I'll get a job and help him. If I'm accepted in the university, they'll give me a passport! A passport out of here!"

"A passport? Are you *meshugine*? The Jews will be back in Jerusalem before you can get a passport now."

"And I'm even allowed two domestics."

"Domestics?' Este laughed until tears came to her eyes. "My son the dreamer," she said.

Daniel laughed too. He also had tears in his eyes to hear his mother laugh again after so long. "Ma, listen, seriously." He leaned forward and held his hand out to her. "The only way we can be accepted in this country as human beings is to earn a certificate from a Russian university," he paused and added with intensity. "I don't want to crawl in the ghettos all my life and tremble under the Russian boot."

"Do you really think you'll find a different world out there, with a piece of paper under your arm? The Russians will never accept you. Discrimination will follow you no matter where you go or what you do. At least if you are a rabbi, you will be revered by your own people as a scholar and a leader."

They both sat in silence. He absently pushed the dinner crumbs with his fingers into a little pile on the table. He had always thought that his mother's elegance and courage would match that of Queen Ester and that she shared the celebrated beauty of Rachel. He wanted to earn enough money to put her in the fine home she deserved, far away from this miserable Pale. His heart grieved when he took her thin rough hand in his, and looked into the blue eyes which once reflected enthusiasm for life.

"Mama," he whispered. "Look at you. Forget about all this stuff for a while and get some rest." He cupped her hand in both of his. "You've taken on more than you can handle. You're letting yourself get run down. Allocate the job to some other woman on the committee."

"I will, as soon as I finish stocking food for the winter. I have one more big purchase to make."

One day, on her way to the market, Este felt weak and began to swoon. Her world went black and she collapsed in the street. When she regained consciousness she saw Daniel standing over her, unpinning her marriage wig. He took it from her head, and ran his hand through her raven hair, now beginning to streak gray. Swollen dark rings circled her blue eyes and the old sparkle he had always known had dissipated into a dull gaze.

"I have the carriage waiting to take you home," he said. He lifted her up and carried her to the seat beside him.

"Danya," his mother said weakly. "Have you thought anymore about your future.

"Not really. I've been so occupied in the store that I haven't thought much about anything." Actually, he had thought about it nearly every day, to the exclusion of everything else. He worked hard to get the business in tip-top shape for his father and brother to take over when he went to the gymnasium. He even bought books and taught himself to read and write in the Russian language.

"My son, whatever you do with your life, where ever you go, I want you to remember, the greatest gift we can give our brothers is to demonstrate our love by feeding the hungry, assisting our neighbor to prevent his poverty, and give a hand to the wanderer groping in the shadows of life."

"Ma," Daniel snapped. "You've got to get over it. Now! Today… you'll never get rid of the poor. They're overwhelming us…sometimes, I think," he stopped.

"You think what?"

"I think," he hesitated… "I think you want to find a way to get out of this…." He wanted to say life, but said, "place." Although Daniel could see the desperation of the poor, he could also imagine their cunning. He blamed them for his mother deteriorating health. They demanded her time and energy. They had no pity for her needs. In his eyes, they could very well have executed her with a pistol and done the job quickly. It was all the same.

He turned his face away and saw the jackal by the roadside toting his black bag of rags. The jackal looked back at Daniel with a hollow stare in his eyes.

Chapter 7

1890

Countess Evgeniya Borisovna marveled over the vast fields of early wheat stretching to the horizons of Belozerkovka, one of her family's enormous estates; their golden heads like a luxurious carpet. She sat back in the carriage with Svetchin, the head grounds-keeper, perched atop the box set. He led Vaska into a full gallop causing clouds of dust to rise up in their wake.

The warm July breeze felt good brushing against her face. Today their liberal neighbor, Khishniakov, hosted the candidates running for the *zemstvo*, a district government board consisting of representatives from the noble class, the small land owners, merchants, tradesmen and peasants.

He was also about to unveil his two pieces of mechanical farming equipment from Germany and invited every landowner to view the new arrivals. He claimed this miracle of modern technology would guarantee an increase in grain production by fifty-fold while saving the peasants hours of back breaking labor. The young countess had used this marvel of technology as an excuse to go to Khishnaikov's affair. He always entertained the most interesting individuals with progressive new ideas in a world far from that of her archaic aristocratic family. Her father Count Boris Vasilivich Rostovsky, labeled Khishnaikov's open house parties a breeding ground for the revolutionary bacillus and forbade anyone in his household to set foot on the grounds of that *dacha,* but in this case he made an exception since Evgeniya would one day inherit Belozerkovka from her grandmother and he agreed that the antiquated farming methods on their estate undeniably needed overhauling.

With the approach of twentieth century industrialization, he had seen members of the old aristocracy forced to sell their estates to clever industrious overseers who better understood farm management. Although, far be it that her father would lose an estate. His acquisitions were enormous and included sugar factories in the south and a winery. He was president of the sugar trust, marshal of the aristocracy for the province of Kiev, and minister of the first European department in St. Petersburg.

Svetchin pulled up to the veranda and left Vasha in the care of a groom. The country manor was not particularly large and was built of wood with a stone foundation. Two wolf hounds lounged on a couch eyeing each arriving visitor. Khishnaikov and his wife stood on the veranda at the top of the stairs greeting their guests in the customary fashion, an embrace and a kiss on each cheek. Their faces beamed when they saw their noble visitor arriving from the Rostovsky estate.

"It is a great honor to have you as our guest today, Countess Borisovna," Khishniakov said bowing and kissing her white gloved hand. Her pastel cotton batiste dress fluttered in the breeze and her long chestnut hair was swept loosely up into a fashionable top-knot. Everyone said she was fortunate to have large eyes like her mother rather that the narrow scrutinizing ones which her unfortunate sisters inherited from the count. Although she was only seventeen, she already gave the impression of being a great beauty by the elegant grace with which she carried herself.

Khishnaikov was so flattered to have a representative of the aristocracy present at his party that he left his post and personally escorted her into the drawing room. Svetchin followed her and presented the hostess with a large bouquet of fresh flowers from the gardens and a basket of fancy pastries.

"How was your trip abroad this spring," asked the host. His words drifted elusively above Evgeniya's own thoughts of excitement as she entered the forbidden household. She was struck by the wood paneled walls decorated with family pictures and trivia, in contrast to their own drawing room, with the priceless paintings and ancestral armory. A peasant sat across the room among the gentry. She grimaced in disgust when he reached into the sugar bowl with a grimy finger and pulled out several sugar cubes, plunking them into his tea.

Khishniakov planted her in the company of another neighbor, Dmitry Alexeivich, who was an administrator in the Department of the Interior. "*Enchanté de faire votre connaissance, countess,*" Alexeivich said. He took her hand in his flaccid one and brushed a kiss upon it.

"How very nice to see you." She glanced at him politely but her attention had riveted on the peasant drinking tea and gobbling sweet rolls slathered in jam, the crumbs sticking in the hairs of his unkempt beard, like a pig. In fact, he looked like a pig with a round pink face and pug nose. "Despicable!" she thought and snapped her head away in disgust.

Alexeivich smiled and gazed at Evgeniya in part enchantment, part paternal homage, but mostly in curiosity. "We have a local member of the provincial council with us this afternoon, known as the Apostle of the soil."

"Yes, I know Prinkov," she said. She knew the old man as a member of the *zemstvo* and always suspected him to be underhanded. Khishniakov would use flattery to gain favor with influential peasants by inviting them to discuss their views on agriculture, education, and politics. She could almost read the thoughts behind his conning little eyes. "When we gain our liberties then the hour of your slaughter will come."

"Is it not unusual to see them at a landlord's party?"

"Yes," she quipped returning her gaze to Dmitry. He had a pale face, light brown eyes and a light brown mustache, sort of beige in appearance, she thought.

"And what brings a noble young lady to this party all alone? Certainly not peasants."

"I came to see the new farming equipment," she said sharply.

He opened his eyes in surprise. "Certainly a beautiful young woman must have more amusing interests than that of farming equipment, *nes pas?*"

"Dmitry Alexeivich, we care about our peasants at Belozerkovka. They will never go hungry because they cannot pay their taxes. My father provides for all their needs."

"So you care about your peasants needs, how nice."

After, when she realized she had been provoked by the savages in the corner, she regained her graceful countenance and lifted her aristocratic head. "I heard that the peasants who live on your estate may not be able store enough grain for themselves this winter."

"My peasants? What do you presume to know about my peasants?"

"How can they after paying such high taxes? I heard that the minister of finance has raised grain taxes again this year."

"Russia has now become a debt free nation. That is quite an accomplishment for an Empire as great and diversified as ours, don't you agree?"

She stared at him.

"Tightening the Imperial belt is never easy for the *narod*, but in the long run everyone will benefit from a strong economy." He narrowed his eyes and examined her for a few moments. "Tell me, I am still curious. Why do you want to see a piece of farming equipment?"

"I don't want my father to lose his estate because of outdated farming methods."

He laughed. "Quite admirable. But your father should not have to worry about losing anything with his vast enterprises, should he?"

She though a moment. "No…I guess not…I don't know."

"And why isn't your father here to see the new machine? Does he make a habit of sending his pretty young daughter out to do the job of running his estate?"

She blushed again and changed the subject. "Does the Tsar know what is happening to the *moujikii?*"

"Of course he does. He would like to see the landowners make reforms on their estates and raise their peasants living standard."

"What reforms?" Jeniya suddenly felt uneasy that she had entrenched herself under a hive of swarming liberals.

"For example, on our estate we have allotted the peasants land to work for themselves, built a school, a library, a day nursery for working mothers, and a co-operative store to initiate the peasants into the free enterprise system."

All these new ideas whirled in her head. "*Moujikii* are cunning and simple-minded, like silly children. We once had one co-op store in our village. One of the members stole the money from the till and gambled it away. Another member, who should have been watching, hated business. He only wanted to work outside in the fields. In less than a year, they couldn't pay their creditors and they lost their store. Peasants are incapable of conducting their own financial affairs."

"The *moujik* is cunning and simple minded because he is not educated. He has no incentive to better himself. Education coupled with the co-op system will not only enlighten him but will raise his moral, give him something to work for, something to live for."

"Education will not stop them from gambling and drinking away their rubles and that will be the end of your co-operatives. Peasants are slaves to their most primitive instincts. They live by passion and not by reason. They only have vodka and good times on their minds. Their women and children would have nothing if we, the elite, didn't look after them. Besides, sometimes, it's exasperating to make them understand what you want them to do."

"You under estimate people, countess. Sometimes peasants are not ambitious because they have no reason to be. The aristocracy still treats them as menial serf labor. They want to keep our *moujikii* humble and docile, by an antiquated system, not much better than when they were serfs. These poor people have no hope. Unless our backward masses are elevated culturally and economically, Russia will lose her eminent position as a great world power in the twentieth century."

"Don't you tell us how to manage our peasants, Dmitry Alexeivich. You don't understand peasants. Your plans will never work! Their families would suffer were it not for the good will of the landlords who look after them."

Evgeniya wheeled about in a flurry of temperament. She glanced around at the people in the room, looking for Svetchin. *Bunch of peasants. How can Khishniakov allow this half civilized low life in his home. My father is right. We don't belong in the company of those who are not of aristocratic blood, who are inferior in culture and social grace.* In a huff, she looked around for Svetchin.

"May I help you find someone, Miss...?"

Evgeniya glanced up at Daniel. His deep blue eyes sparkling beneath thick dark lashes had bewitched her. She only vaguely noticed the strong shoulders and the high color in his face.

"I didn't mean to startle you, but you look lost." He spoke in a voice that was golden in tone, melodious and inspiring.

"I was..." she wanted to say, leaving this circus of *gloopie moujikii*, but gazing into this gentleman's handsome face seemed to capture the very essence of her blooming womanhood, melting her resolve and causing her limbs to go weak. A flush rushed to her cheeks and blotted out all thoughts except for the image of this tall stranger. She made an awkward attempt to respond but at that moment she felt an unusual helplessness and could barely speak.

"My name is Daniel Nathanovich," he said.

"I'm Evgeniya Borisovna," she said awkwardly. "People I know call me Jeniya for short." They stared at each other in silence for a few moments. She spread out her hand fan and fluttered it to cool herself.

"It is warm in here," Daniel concurred. "Would you like to go out on the veranda? There's a breeze out there, a warm one, but better than nothing."

She regained her composure, and began to study him closely now. His dark wavy hair gleamed in the sunlight and he moved with the slender grace of an aristocrat. "Do you live nearby?"

"No, I'm a student at Kiev University."

"Oh?" She wondered why he had not gone to the polytech institute in Petersburg. Everyone who is anyone goes to Petersburg to be educated. But his classy appearance overshadowed her thoughts. At this moment it didn't matter who he was or to which society he belonged. She was basking the wonderful new sensation that seemed to envelop her in a dizzying cloud of pleasure.

"I was invited here by my friend Mikhail Khishniakov to see firsthand how they manage peasant affairs on the country estates," he said.

"Well, I can tell you first hand, Monsieur Nathanovich, that they don't know what they are talking about," she said matter-of-factly.

"Oh? Why is this so?"

By the half curious and half amused look on his face, she could tell he thought she didn't know what she was talking about. In a flurry of emotion, she tried to justify herself. "Just because I am a woman, it doesn't mean I don't know how to run an estate." She briskly fanned herself as she felt another flush rise up into her face.

"Is that so?" He was grinning at her now and admiring her glowing beauty.

"You think women have nothing better to do with their time than to lie around waiting for a husband, do you!"

"Did I say that?"

"No, but that's what you're thinking, isn't it! If you think I am one of those women, then you'd better think in another direction." She turned in a huff and started down the stairs. "Groom, fetch me my carriage."

She turned around at the bottom of the stairs and added. "If you want to see how to run an estate and manage peasants, then be at my father's party next Friday afternoon." She jumped into the carriage and started to charge Vaska into a gallop through the gate. "*Bosha moy.*

Mon Dieu," she said out loud, "I forgot Svetchin." She yanked on the reins and sat there not knowing what to do next. She turned and saw Daniel standing on the veranda laughing and Svetchin running down the stairs across the yard, yelling. "Mademoiselle. My lady Countess, stop! Where are you going without me?"

"I'm sorry, Svetchin, I must have lost my head."

"I saw the carriage from the window, and I ran outside."

"It's a good thing, because I don't know what I was thinking."

Chapter 8

DANIEL'S HAD BATTLED overwhelming odds to get into Kiev University. Only six Jews were chosen from the hundreds graduating top in their classes across the Pale. When he heard the minister of public instruction, Dyelanov, was lenient toward Jews, he wrote and asked him for a personal letter of recommendation.

He wasted no time in hunting for a job and landed one teaching at the Jewish Educational Foundation for children of the socially progressive Jews. Its founder, Reb Israel Brachmann, a short, robust and a somewhat corpulent individual, with a beard cropped and trimmed in the fashionable cosmopolitan Van Dyke style, was a commodities broker for the Ukrainian gentry.

"I started this foundation to find a common denominator between our culture and that of the Russians," he said. "Our intent is to encourage intellectual freedom among our young people, allowing them to gain a liberal understanding in the humanities and in western philosophy and theology. We want to revitalize Jewish life from within not compromise it. Otherwise we will have no choice but to leave our country and live as exiles in an unfamiliar nation or remain here and die of starvation…or God forbid, convert."

Brachmann would tell his followers. "In this society do as every other man. On the street, be a brother to your countryman, and at home a Jew. Speak Russian as your first language and in business stick to your original agreement. Don't give them any opportunity to accuse you of usury or label you as an exploiter."

Whether or not Daniel did the right thing by becoming involved in Brachmann's foundation in the light of the Talmud and its dissertation on the eternal value of suffering was irrelevant. That he did something to alleviate the intolerable weight of oppression under which the Jewish people lived couldn't be wrong. His mother spent her life laboring to relieve the misery of the destitute and it killed her. Could Brachmann's approach be any worse?

He had come a long way since he first arrived at this uncle Sholem's flat in Kiev four years ago dressed in a long black kaftan and yarmulke, bobbing pe'ots and a full beard. He felt ridiculous in those ugly side curls wearing a dark green school uniform with a double row of silver buttons and a gold braid around the collar.

He remembered his uncle's shock when he clipped his ear-locks and shaved his beard and announced that for the first time the students hadn't mocked him. "You don't know what it's like to be treated like an unwanted token Jew at the university," he said. "Like a dog, day after day, like a mangy rabid dog."

"I don't know what it's like?" Sholem stunned him with these sobering words.

As the days turned into months, and the months drew together into years, he was drawn deeper into the worldliness of academia. He became a frequent dinner guest in the homes of wealthy and influential Jews who had turned their back on tradition. Occasionally liberal young Russians would be included in these gatherings. There, at one of these affairs, he met Mikhail Khishniakov.

The stylish crowd to which Mikhail had introduced him was not hard to take. No matter what the Talmudic rabbis said, being a cosmopolitan about town was unquestionably better than being crushed in the ghetto like hens on the way to the market place. He remorsefully saw that deep within his heart he was happy to be accepted by the Gentile crowd. The crowd he had always hated. What is it in a man, he wondered, that likes to touch the unclean thing, that wants to wade in forbidden waters, that seeks be accepted by those powerful ones who are not his own, those whom he often regards with antipathy.

The rabbis may wait for their eternal rewards, but to Daniel, the rewards here on earth had become far more advantageous, until one day early in November, 1889, as he was about to complete his bar exams to practice law, his dream world shattered.

In the morning paper he read a dispatch from Petersburg; "Admission to the bar and to the profession of private attorney of persons of non-Christian faiths may be carried out only with the permission of the Minister of Justice."

He read and reread the article, changing the words around, looking for hope, but there was none. Permission from the Minister of Justice, what a laugh! There was no justice for the Jews among the ministers of Tsar Alexander III. He knew this was one more example of the autocracy's double talk to exclude them from entering Russian professional societies.

He wandered in the public gardens where he could clear his thoughts and assess his options. He already put four years of his life into studying law. What opportunities were open to him in Russian society now that the curtain of discrimination had fallen, crushing his hopes and dreams?

Squirrels scampered about gathering the ripe chestnuts which had fallen from the centennial trees and pigeons pecked around for crumbs in the brick walkways. In the distance a woodcock was whistling, he seemed to say "You'll get up tomorrow and the sun will shine again."

The university was a small town within itself consisting of several hundred students. The classic two story brick building, with a Parthenon like entrance, was painted in the ubiquitous red color of government institutions. Someone had told him that all the official government buildings were painted red to remind people in the futility of an insurrection against the Tsar. He decided to talk to his professor, Demchenko, a benevolent elderly man who knew all aspects of Russian Law, options and opportunities. He took out his watch and looked at the time; he had already missed his morning lecture.

Demchenko's door was open so he took the liberty to walk into his office. The professor sat behind a long desk piled with papers. He peered over his spectacles and said, "come in Daniel Nathanovich." His beard was also cropped and trimmed in the fashionable Van Dyke style.

Daniel looked around the rather large room with law books neatly arranged on shelves. The wood paneling on the walls appeared as though it hadn't been polished in years nor the dusty windows cleaned since the university was built.

Demchenko perceived the nervous hesitancy in his student and said, "I read the morning news, it must have come as a great blow to you."

Daniel nodded. He cut right to the point. "Your excellency, is it advisable for me to go on with law? What are my options?"

"*Ny*, you can become a lawyer in training or an assistant to an established member of the bar. Then, at the end of a five year's probationary period, if your work is exceptionally good and I have every confidence that you can meet that standard, the bar will present a recommendation to the Minister."

Daniel thought about these words. "In five years the number of exceptional Jewish lawyers in training to be recommended to the Minister may be myriad. Even so, I understand that only one Jew from that group may be admitted to the bar every two years!"

"It depends on whether they adhere to a strict literal interpretation of the law."

In a quandary, Daniel gazed at the scuffed wooden floor. New laws of discriminate seem to be popping up daily.

"While you may not conduct legal suits without admission to the bar, you may, under the law, be permitted to conduct the defense of civil cases."

"That is on the low paying side, isn't it? Arbitration for peasants, workers, charity cases?"

The professor gazed at the papers on his desk for a few moments then at Daniel. "Several of my colleagues and I discussed the possibility of keeping you on here at the university. Of course, we would send you abroad to prepare for a faculty position. But, it's too bad, it cannot be done."

Daniel stared at him, puzzled. "What do you mean?" He was dangling an exceedingly tempting carrot before him, a professor of law at one of the Empire's most prestigious universities and a European education! What was the catch?

Demchenko looked him in the eye. "By keeping you on as a colleague we would have to set a precedent unparalleled in the history of the law faculty here at the university. You understand that?" He paused and waited for a response from his candidate. Daniel's expression was frozen, partly in astonishment, but mostly in indignation at this double talk.

"Of course," the elderly man continued. "By taking the necessary step of converting, you would be joining the already rather numerous adherents of the Jewish enlightenment."

Daniel gasped, speechless. His uncle Sholem's admonition sprang into his thoughts. "You're tall, nice looking, refined, and intelligent. You have a good face, blue eyes. A Jew like you will be choice merchandise in their hands. There is no greater trophy for the Russians than to win over a smart young Jew and convert him." *It is all the same for us no matter where we go,* just as his mother had warned.

The old man chuckled. "We see great potential in your ability," he said, but the decision is up to you."

Chapter 9

SINCE THE CHANCE meeting with Daniel, Jeniya lay awake nights thinking of him, wondering if he would show up at the party. She knew nothing of Daniel's background, except that he was a student at the Kiev University, which was sure to make a hit with her father since, in his mind, the school was a well-known incubator for radicals and liberals.

The afternoon of the party, Jeniya relaxed in her bathtub calculating how she would introduce Daniel to her father. A maid stood by in the dressing room waiting to help her on with her petticoats, shoes and stockings. Outside in the dressing room, another maid waited with her dresses.

"No!" She said, standing in front of a triple mirror to view herself from all sides. "This one will not do. Get me the white dress with the blue ribbons." Each time she heard a carriage pull into the driveway, she ran to the window. From her second story bedroom she had a good view of the yard in front of the house. "Hurry, she said to the attendants. "Dress me."

She sat down at her vanity. "Galina, quick! Do my hair."

"Then keep your head still, my lady countess, or I shall never get your hair to stay on top of your head," snapped an irritated Galina, once her governess, now her lady's maid. She dropped the hair brush, placed her hands on her slender hips and heaved with a sigh of exasperation. "What's going on outside that window? What is so important that you cannot sit still for a few minutes? You still have strands of hair straggling around your neck."

"Leave them, I like the way they look." Jeniya said pulling at the strands of hair wistfully.

Galina held up a white panama hat with a frilly blue bow around the crown to match her dress. "Be sure and wear this if you go outside, or your face will get sunburn."

"No! I don't want to wear that hat."

"Take it and don't let your grandmother see you outside in the sun without it. And take this parasol too."

Jeniya grabbed the paraphernalia and ran out of her dressing room to the balcony overlooking a large circular anteroom. Footmen were standing on duty to take the luggage of the arriving guests and escort them to the washroom where they could freshen up after their long and dusty drives.

She hurried down the stairs and sat down on the portico wondering if Daniel Nathanovich had taken her invitation seriously? She was embarrassed by her behavior last week. Perhaps she had offended him? Did she speak too hastily or too vaguely? Did he think she was a silly female mouthing a bunch of meaningless words?

"Jenka!" cried Ekatrina, her younger sister, rushing outside." Everyone is looking all over for you. Why in heaven are you sitting out here by yourself? Mama wants you inside to take a rest before the ball tonight."

"I guess he's not coming," Jeniya said with a sigh. She was not relieved that he had not appeared. She had put too much effort into making his arrival a smooth event.

"Who's not coming?"

"No one. Probably the son of another ignorant *moujik* like the rest of them," she muttered to herself. Ekatrina gave her an odd look.

Through the trees and the high iron gates, Daniel saw an imposing empire style mansion sitting on a hill. At first he was excited about this adventure, but now he had second thoughts. He thought her family owned a simple country house, a dacha, like his friend Khishniakov. He ordered the *izvochtchik* to stop the carriage. The driver turned in his seat and said, "But sir we are still a good distance from the gate."

Daniel assessed the clean shaven cabbie wearing the standard heel length blue peasant coat with a high black belt just under the breast, and a black oilcloth hat with an upturned brim. "No, please drop me off right here, this will do fine."

"As you wish, sir." He got out and paid the driver.

A military band struck up a lively rhythm in the garden gazebo. He moved closer to see what was going on. This was no simple gathering like Mikhail's party.

He watched as a well healed society emerged from carriages with servants tagging behind, carting luggage. They ascended the wide stairs to the portico where one man enthusiastically greeted each guest with the customary embrace planting a kiss on each cheek. He wore a white military tunic and a broad clean shaven grin.

He perceived this tall, strong featured man to be Jeniya's father. He looked down at his own dark suit wondering if it were acceptable. He tugged at the high stiff collar of the new shirt he bought and meticulously straightened his tie. He took his handkerchief and blotted the sweat from his brow with a cold, clammy hand.

This is ridiculous, he thought. Even the grooms were lavishly attired in blowzy trousers tucked in high boots and silk *rubashkas* of various colors with matching caps adorned with feathers. He watched them unharness the horses and tug them toward the stables and run back again to fetch the next hitch. Boys in long red Kazak style *cherkesskas* weaved in and out of the great house baring silver trays laden with food and decorated with flowers. He watched each gentlemen guest choose a flower and present it to his lady before taking an hors d'oeuvre.

He decided to walk back to the nearby village and order a cab home. "How long does it take a *droshkii* to get here?" he asked the clerk.

"About an hour. They have to come from Kiev," said the stocky built peasant. He eyed the handsome young stranger dressed like he was going to a reception at the winter palace. "You're not from around here, are you?"

"No. I live in Kiev."

"Going to something special?"

"No."

"I hear Count Rostovsky is giving his annual spring shindig this weekend for the officials of the gubernatorial of Kiev."

"I was invited but I decided not to go," Daniel said.

The clerk lifted his brows and made round eyes. "Why not?"

"The invitation was vague."

"It could not have been that vague or you would not be all the way out here. You're all dress-up to kill. I would reconsider if I was you."

Daniel smiled and reconsidered. As much as he did not want to expose himself to a possible humiliation he might encounter at the party, curiosity as well as desire drew him toward the great manor.

The sun began to dip behind the gently rising banks of the Dnieper. The horizon faded from blue to gold, then to crimson and a deep purple. Little lights from bonfires popped up around a lake below. The sweet aroma of honeysuckle filled the night air. A familiar melody from the violins reminded him of his parents dancing at their anniversary party.

When he reached the colonnade, he saw several gentlemen chatting while servants filled their glasses with champagne. He decided to give up this nonsense and go home. Then he saw her emerge from the great house, laughing with several other girls, dressed in a rose pink party dress. A spray of tiny white rosebuds adorned her dark upswept hair.

She appeared not to have a care in the world. *Perhaps she didn't mean what she said. Her invitation was so vague, so capricious. Were they simply meaningless words that poured from her frivolous lips? Am I a fool or was she sincere?* There was only one way to find out. When the music started again and the girls went back inside, he meticulously straightened his tie and marched up the stairs passed the group of men on the veranda. Inside, he saw people milling around a lavish buffet of cold hors d'oeuvres. An elderly gentleman with silver hair and a smartly trimmed white beard stopped in front of a mirror to adjust his white bow tie before proceeding up the stairs to the ballroom.

Again he hesitated, checking his own modest attire. Before he could change his mind and retreat, a footman in a black waist coat and white gloves greeted him, "*Bon soir.* Would the master like to step inside and refresh himself tonight?" He wore a bland expression and neatly trimmed side whiskers, English style.

"Excuse me?"

The servant repeated the question.

Daniel nodded yes, then no. He froze when he heard three young ladies giggling about some poor fellow who had faltered in his French. His own knowledge of the language spoken by the Russian aristocracy was limited. He turned around and headed toward the exit. The footman stood like a guard dog staring back at him. He decided he must proceed.

Upstairs, the guests hovered around the entrance of the ballroom like a swarm of bees. They all appeared to know one another well, glancing about, gossiping. Young men decked out in colorful officer's uniforms and white gloves did their best to charm the young women dressed in satin and lace. Matrons paraded in dazzling jewels, enough to knock a poor man's eyeballs out. The heavy aroma of perfume permeated the air.

In the shadow of the eminent crowd, he felt like the loneliest and most conspicuous man in the world, certain he would be detected as an outsider, although he knew he could stand up intellectually to anyone of these people whom he considered to be shallow. Conflicting emotions began to assail him, ones that he could not understand, nor that he wanted to confront. He felt a combination of anger, indignation, contempt, hatred and envy. How could these people be so flippant, so unconcerned, when human beings, their own kind, Russian peasants, as well as Jews, were oppressed? Maybe he was judging them unfairly, but the matrons could barely stand up and walk under the weight of the precious gemstones that hung from their necks, arms, and fingers. For the first time he empathized with Ezra's revolutionary zeal, and this troubled him.

He searched for Evgeniya, scanning groups of men and women gathered around the ball room near tall windows draped in blue velvet and tied with golden cords. When the musicians sat down in their places and took up their instruments, Daniel understood why the familiar strains of music conjured up pictures of the past. They were Jews. Impoverished Jewish musicians playing for the aristocracy for kopecks no doubt.

He decided to leave when someone called out, *"une valse, s'l vous plait."* Then he saw her gliding onto the polished dance floor, her hand in the arm of a tall young officer. He wore a blue military tunic with a red mandarin collar and moved in the haughty swagger peculiar to the Kazaks. How could he ever forget the Kazak's jaunty arrogant gate as they paraded in front of Rosenfeld's saloon enjoying the pogrom as though it were some kind of a carnival side show? The young man's features were almost primitively chiseled, with high cheek bones. He had a steely expression in his eyes, judicious but at the same time flirtatious. Jeniya glanced at him fondly.

Daniel's eyes were riveted on the two of them whirling in three step time, she in rose and he in blue, she in the arms of that Kazak or whatever he was. The music stopped. A cloud of adoring young officers descended upon her, anxious to sign her card for subsequent dances. He had seen enough. Schlimazel, what makes you think a count's daughter would give you a thought. His father often warned him that his eyes were too big in this world, that he was a dreamer and lacked practical sense. However, he considered himself to be fairly prudent at the age of twenty-one. His brother Ezra was far more the dreamer than he'd ever be.

A footman offered him refreshments from a tray of drinks. He took a cold lemonade and belted it down. He looked around for a place to put the glass when he spotted her coming straight toward him, her cheeks flushed and pink, her face glowing. He was dazed.

"Daniel Nathanovich?" she said brightly. "I'm delighted to see you here this evening." His blood shot to the top of his head. His knees went weak. The strands of dark hair that fell about her delicate face were damp. His gaze drifted from the pearls which graced her smooth throat to her creamy bare shoulders and high rounded bosom throbbing beneath her silk satin dress, which aroused a lusty desire in him and a flashing moment of fantasy which he could not control.

She pulled her silk stole up around her shoulders.

He lowered his gaze.

"Have you been enjoying the dance?" She said awkwardly knowing that he was not at the party.

"Yes, very much," he replied nervously looking again into her face. She did not return his gaze. She was searching for words just as he was. She fluttered her fan with quick, sharp motions.

"It's quite warm in here, isn't it," she said.

"Yes, it is."

"Would you like to walk in the garden?"

Daniel followed her like a puppy dog outside into the formal rose garden. They strode down a path of hanging jasmine. He couldn't tell if the sweet perfume was hers or from the abundant flora. He thought he had arrived in heaven, a world so far from the cluttered ghetto streets outside his uncle's flat, and the outhouses stinking in summer heat.

"You said you were attending Kiev University?"

"Yes, I'm in law school."

"You must be clever to study law."

Except for an occasional glance, their eyes were fixed straight ahead. He thought he detected a slight frown on her face. Something had troubled her thoughts. Had he become offensive to her?

"I heard there is some kind of radical movement going on at the university," she said. "I think they call them Marxist study groups. Do you know anything about this?" She gave him a sideward glance.

"I don't care for the Marxist philosophies," he said. "And I don't feel these groups are a threat to anyone. They are a puny bunch of disorganized rabble that are vaguely idealistic, but they cannot come to any concrete conclusions."

"Oh?" She stopped and stared at him with a puzzled face and then smiled. "Well, I'm glad to hear you are not involved. I wondered if you may have been a spy from some kind of liberal group when I first met you at the Khishniakov party. I knew you were not a land owner from a main line family."

He was bewildered by her last statement, then he realized that the landowners of the great estates throughout Russia must have been a closer knit group than he suspected.

"Where are you from?" she asked.

"I live in Kiev."

"You don't speak like a native of Kiev."

"I'm originally from a little town called Lensk."

"Where is that?"

"It's west of here." He felt reluctant at first to tell her the exact location of his hometown because of the concentrated number of Jews who live in that area. But he couldn't hide his true self. If she rejected him, then so be it.

"I'm not familiar with the area west of Kiev," she replied. "I've spent most of my life in boarding schools in Petersburg."

The music started again. "Oh. I'm sorry. I've already promised all my dances. I didn't think you were coming."

"That's very good."

She looked at him with an odd expression.

What a dumb thing to say, he thought. He couldn't tell her he didn't dance very well. "I mean, don't worry about it. I am not offended. I should have been here earlier, and I would have had the privilege of signing your card."

She listened to the beginning strains of the music for a moment. "It's the quadrille," she said happily. "You may still have the privilege of being my dancing partner because I haven't promised this dance to anyone. Come on!" She took his hand and led him back to the ballroom. He was completely unaware that her family was staring at him from the sidelines, or that her two sisters were casting inquisitive glances his way.

Some of the men drifted into the ballroom from smaller rooms where they played cards and gambled to watch the younger dancers maneuver the complicated steps of the quadrille.

"Do you mind if I sit this one out?" he said. He was sure to make an impression on her now, not that it mattered much in the long run.

"If you wish..." she said with a questioning tone. "Oh, don't tell papa that we met at the Khishniakov party. Promise me?" When he opened his mouth to ask why, she was already leading him to meet the family. By the anxious expressions on her parent's faces, they must have been watching him for some time.

"Father, mother, grandmother, I would like to present to you Daniel Nathanovich Mendelev. The women held out white gloved hands and Daniel took each one and kissed them. He resented kissing the hands of the aristocracy who held the Russian masses under their boot and the Jews under their bayonets. Once again feelings of anxiety and anger passed over him. One thing he disliked was an appeasing individual, and if he were to mingle in this society for too long, he feared he might become one. "It is my pleasure to meet your Excellences," he said.

"Excuse me, but I will leave you in my parent's care for the moment," Jeniya said when a young officer appeared to take his dance.

Mortified, Daniel fixed a grin on his face. At least Jeniya had the tact to introduce him in the Russian language. She seemed to be aware that he was an ordinary fellow from their brief conversation in the garden.

"Please sit down, *gaspaja* Mendelev," said the count. He gestured to an uncomfortable looking antique chair.

"Thank you, your Excellency." He sat stiffly on the edge of the chair. The three of them eyeballed his every move without the hint of expression. The count scrutinized him through shrewd narrow eyes, a carbon-copy of his mother who sat in the chair beside him. The countess, a fair woman dressed in a mint green silk gown to enhance the color of her large eyes, held her handsome face high. Daniel perceived her vague countenance harbored a critical spirit that had launched itself on him. He felt increasingly uncomfortable, knowing he was the object of their collective curiosity, until a woman interrupted searching for a morsel of gossip. He sprang to his feet.

"Ah. *Et qui est celui-ci?*" she said smiling.

Jeniya's mother did not volunteer any information but simply introduced him. Before the woman could give him her hand, the countess artfully averted the matron's attention by engaging her in an avid conversation about someone or other. The dowager countess followed suit, and the threesome went off together.

Daniel was not relieved. He could scarcely breathe from the mounting tension, much less speak to the count who had fixed his eyes on him. A footman approached holding a tray of wine sparkling in fine Bohemian crystal stemware.

"Please sit down, young man," the count said. "Would you care for a glass of wine? It's from my own vineyards."

"Thank you," he said lifting a glass from the tray held by the servant. He tried not to spill it, he was shaking so.

The count also took a glass of wine in his strong hand and held it up. "*Za zdaroviye*," he said in a firm dominating tone. Daniel repeated the toast and lifted his glass and they drank.

"How do you find the wine?"

"Very good, Your Excellency."

"My wine took first place at the convention in Paris for two years in a row." The count's thick, dark auburn hair was combed back, enhancing the high color in his face. Beneath his elegant and formidable looking features, behind those small eyes, Daniel suspected he had a sense of humor. When he smiled, his cheeks became round and revealed dimples. His blue eyes twinkled mischievously.

"It's very good, Your Excellency." Daniel made an expression that he was genuinely impressed which he was. Through previous inquiries, he discovered that the count had been an officer in the prestigious Preobrazhensky guards, and an aid de camp to Alexander II, served as Ambassador to France and is currently Marshall of the Aristocracy for the province of Kiev. However, none of these titles intimidated him, only that he was Jeniya's father.

"Daniel Nathanovich Mendelev? Is that a Russian name?" the count questioned raising one bushy eyebrow from his narrow gaze, pronouncing each word deliberately. A row of metals decorated his white military tunic, each one representative of his eminent service to the Tsar.

"Yes, Your Excellency."

Rostovsky stared at him obliquely for a long moment, making him feel uncomfortable then abruptly changed the subject. "Rumor has it that the tsarevich Nicholas II is about to take a German wife. How do you feel about that?"

A strange question? Daniel wondered if he were testing his allegiance to Russia.

"I believe the Tsar would make a positive move to unify the country if he took a wife from the Russian nobility, Your Excellency."

The count lifted both eyebrows in surprise. "Yes, you are quite right. I whole heartily agree with you. Where are you from, young man?"

"Lensk, a town in the Western Ukraine."

"The Western Ukraine has a large Jewish population, doesn't it? Can't make a transaction anywhere in Russia these days without first going through a damn Jew, eh? Can never trust them, every ruble goes through their filthy hands."

Now, Daniel realized the count was playing a game, baiting him, trying to provoke him to see if he would wince. Again his eyes pierced him for a long moment as if he were dissecting him, looking for something that annoyed him, like his Jewishness, as if that were a tangible object that can be found in a man.

"I once knew a Polish family named Mendelev. He was an overseer on one of the great estates. Any relation?"

Daniel shook his head. "No, Your Excellency. I don't believe so. My father is a textile merchant."

"That so? He owns a mill, then, eh?"

Daniel thought the heat from his face would burn through his shirt collar. "If I tell him my father has a dry goods shop, he'll know for certain. If I lead him to believe he owns a mill...." Daniel simply smiled. He couldn't tell if the count was looking for ways to trap him or if he was simply making conversation to get acquainted.

"Where did you meet my daughter?"

"We met at...at..." As he stumbled for words, Rostovsky's attention wandered off to several gentlemen who had gathered nearby.

"Please excuse me young man," he said rising to his tall sturdy height. Daniel jumped up from his seat. The count made a pretentious smile showing straight white teeth, "Nice to see you, young man," he said and walked away.

The women were still in a cluster gossiping, along with a few more and Daniel was able to conveniently slip away. He knew he should leave immediately and forever, because he was gambling for a sweetheart in the wrong house. The deck was stacked against him and the stakes could be life threatening.

But he wanted to see the young countess once more, to carry her memory away with him for the rest of his life and to reminisce when he was once her guest in the great manor. After all, how many Russian Jews were allowed to mingle in the inner circle of the aristocracy, among the members of the Emperor's own court? He could think of only one, Anton Rubinstein, the great musical talent who gave Russia their esteemed conservatories of Petersburg and Moscow, but he had to convert in order to get there!

He stood in a dream and didn't notice that the music had stopped and Jeniya was on the way over to him.

"Thank you so much for waiting, but I did promise a dance with another gentleman, and if I didn't keep my promise, everybody would talk. You don't know how these people pick up on every stupid little thing that happens around here and beat it like a dead horse." She threw up her hands. "Actually they have little else to do than to meddle in everyone else's business."

All his agonizing suddenly vanished in her presence including the not so subtle meaning behind her heedless words. He was so bewitched by the magical spell she seemed to cast on him that he did not comprehend a word she had said. "I can very well imagine," he said smiling.

"All the young people are going down to the lake to sit by the bonfires. Do you want to join us?"

He looked into her wide smoky-green eyes, the pupils large and dark, sparkling in the candlelight. She was not only lovely, she was warm and exuded magnanimity. No wonder all the fellows fought to have a dance with her.

"Yes, I would." He bowed and taking her hand, kissed it. This time he meant it with all his heart.

She let her hand rest in his for a few moments, returning his gaze. He was smiling. She lowered her eyes, glanced about the room and blushed pulling her hand away. "Ah, come on then," she said. "Let's go."

She twirled her shawl around her slender shoulders, and the two of them strode down the great stairway.

In the moonlight, swarms of gulls appeared like white specks on the sandbanks of the great Dnieper river. Stars sprinkled the cloudless sky and bonfires glowed in the dark around the lake.

Jeniya took a deep breath and said, "I love the sweet, delicious smell of freshly cut hay."

"So do I." Daniel was so spellbound, he had not a word to add to the conversation. Of all the dashing young officers decked out in full military dress, she had chosen to spend the evening with him. The stinking smells of ghetto life were now a galaxy away and he wouldn't dare reveal this meager world with her. He felt she was as able to comprehend his life and background as a delicate rose was able to bloom by a hot dusty highway.

They stopped beside the lake. A mist hung over the water. Shade trees loomed on the banks like giants beneath great black cloaks.

"Let's go sit near the fire," Jeniya said pulling her thin wrap close around her shoulders.

He wanted to put his arms around her and warm her next to his own body but he was afraid. "Do you want my jacket?" he asked. He wondered if she had the same feelings for him as he had for her.

"No, it's all right. It's warm by the fire."

Some of the younger boys were weaving around the bonfire with giggling girls clutching their arms while others stood in groups laughing and clapping.

"What are those silly children doing?" exclaimed Daniel.

Jeniya laughed. "They want to see how close they can get to the flame without searing the girl's skirts. But don't worry about them, the boys are having fun teasing the girls." She glanced up at him and smiled.

Her face glowed by the fire's light and the innocent sparkle in her eyes invited and tempted him. Heat rushed through the loins of his body and he held his hand out to her. She took it nervously.

"There is one boat left. Do you want to take it and join the others across the lake?"

Her words popped his fantasies. He knew he had to get back home at a reasonable hour as he didn't tell his uncle where he was going. "It'll be cool and damp out there," he said.

"You're right. We can go boating tomorrow." She turned again to him, "You are staying overnight, aren't you?"

"I wasn't planning…"

"Oh yes, please do. We have so many things planned, a picnic, tennis. Do you play tennis?"

He smiled. He wanted nothing more in the world at this moment than to accept her invitation, although he didn't know if he could handle another day under the eyes of the count.

"Oh look," she said gazing up at the many sparkling colors fanning out in the night sky like hundreds of tiny stars. A group of boys on the other side of the lake had lit fire crackers and were throwing them over the water.

He gently reached over to touch her face with his hand. Her smooth skin was softer than the rose petals in her father's garden. He lifted her face and brushed his lips to hers. She raised her hands to his chest in defense for a moment and then slowly released herself into his arms allowing her hands to glide around his neck and touch the back of his silky hair. He kissed her gently.

She pushed him away and lowered her eyes. He could feel the warm flush rising in her face.

"I'm sorry," he said taking a deep breath.

"No, there is nothing to be sorry for, it's just that…"

"That what?"

"It's nothing," she said without looking at him. She ran her hand over her falling hair trying to straighten it out. "I have to go, let's go and see what the others are doing." She turned to lead him back up the path.

Her admirer in the blue tunic stepped forward to meet her as though he were waiting and watching all along. "Jenka! he said. What happened to you. Everyone is asking."

"Nothing," she said shaking her head but not looking directly at him.

He stared at her with questions in his eyes until he spotted Daniel walking up the path behind her. The two men exchanged icy glares. Daniel bowed to the young countess and left.

She started after him, "Daniel," she called reaching out with her hand as if to grab him back.

"Who is he, Jenka?" Vadim called from behind.

She turned and looked back at Vadim and then at Daniel as he vanished into the darkness.

"Who is he?" Vadim repeated catching up to her.

"He is a friend of mine."

"What kind of a friend? Do you know his background, his family?" He said with the fluency of an investigator.

She shook her head.

"Where did you meet him?"

"At a party."

"Jenka!" He took her arms and affectionately drew her close to his chest. His body was conditioned like steel. "He could be a spy for the underground revolutionary movement."

"No! He's not a spy," she pushed him away.

"How do you know? You cannot go around these days picking up people at public gatherings. This man could be dangerous."

She looked away frowning.

"We also have our spies, you know. The Okhrana has discovered several infiltrators slipping into society and some of them can be violent. These people have no scruples. They are dedicated to overthrowing our government."

"No! He is not like that! Sometime I think you are always finding a revolutionary under every bush Vadim!"

"And you Jenka, are a very intelligent young lady, but you do not use your common sense. You can see a bunch of liberals in the park carrying hand grenades and think they are out on a Sunday afternoon picnic."

She stared at him wide-eyed. She knew everything he said could be true, but she couldn't comprehend his words while she still tasted Daniel's kiss on her lips. Her new friend may not be of the landed gentry, but she was certain he did not belong to the revolutionary underground. In her eyes he was a fine, sensitive, intelligent young man working his way up in the world, and she had great respect for him. His handsome face and refreshing viewpoint perked up the stale boring circles in which she traveled.

Vadim put his arm around her shoulder. "*Allons, mademoiselle,* they are waiting on you for supper."

Chapter 10

Daniel climbed up the path from the lake to the road that led back to the village. He lied, not only to Rostovsky, but to himself and to God. Now the count thinks he is the son of a textile manufacturer. He hated liars and cowards and he imagined God didn't have much use for them either.

Israel Brachmann had repeatedly told his students, "do not give them any reason to affirm their notion that we Jews are the liars they believe us to be." Now Daniel clearly understood how a man can become the person he hates, simply to survive.

Scenes of the party flashed through his mind; the dazzle, the glamor, the free flowing champagne, goblets of vodka, tables of canapés, and caviar. Her father lifting glass after glass of vodka, each time calling on his friends to propose a toast, Jeniya dancing in her daring pink evening dress, the taste of her kisses on his lips and the fragrance of her perfume still on his shirt collar. For one brief moment there was neither Russian nor Jew, only two people who had found their first love. He smiled.

As the days passed, her image lodged in his mind, haunted him through restless nights, and followed him to class and home again; the smoky green eyes that mirrored a carefree life, one that defied sorrow. When he lay down at night, he envisioned her young body next to his, felt her warm embrace and her soft lips.

He struggled against these foolish imaginations, but could not release her memory. He knew any kind of relationship with her would be hopeless because she belonged to the privileged class, the titled aristocracy. Still, he could not rest knowing there was once the possibility of love between them.

He was sitting under a shady tree outside one of the many cafes along the wide boulevard sipping coffee, oblivious to the noisy commotion in the street. Peasants as well as Jews in brimmed black caps, home spun shirts and felt boots haggled from behind pushcarts as shoppers rummaged through the merchandise. A Tartar set up his display of colorful *burnous'* and a vendor poured hot tea from a large copper tea pot into glasses set in slots around a flat semicircular wooden surface secured over his shoulder by a wide strap. Artisans carried the tools of their trade and sold their services on the spot, and *izvochtchiks* sat in carriages waiting for passengers. A crowd had gathered to watch an itinerant veterinarian. He secured the head of a howling cat into an apparatus hanging from his belt and castrated him while the owner stood by continuously crossing himself.

Daniel paid for his lunch and headed into the market place, winding around shoppers and vendors. A poster pasted in a shabby store front window caught his attention. Dr. James Worthington of the London Missionary Society will lecture on Isaiah 53 at 3PM. All are welcome. He stood in front of the poster for a long time and pondered. The Evangelical Society of Protestants of Petersburg was written over the entrance doors.

When he opened the door and stepped inside a pungent odor of sour cabbage overtook him. Beneath the portraits of the Tsar and Tsaritsa, he found a sign which pointed the way to the meeting room. He continued down a hallway and peeked inside an open door. A few dozen people sat scattered on long benches.

At that moment the speaker appeared in the hallway and was about to enter the room.

"Please come in and sit down," he said to Daniel extending his hand in a gracious manner. "We are about to begin."

Daniel cautiously slithered inside and sat on the end of the last bench in the rear of the room, watching as Dr. Worthington went to the front of the room and opened his Bible. "Perhaps you will agree with me," he began. "That man has managed to get this world into a terrible predicament and his wisdom has failed to settle the issues that are plaguing our society today." He looked over the little gathering of souls. They were mostly men between the ages of twenty and fifty, probably laid-off workers in clothing that appeared to have been bought from rag vendors. A few women sat here and there in dark attire with scarves wrapped around their heads. "In Isaiah chapter 52: verse 13," he began. "The lord says;

> "Behold; My servant shall prosper,
> he shall be exalted and lifted up, and shall be very high.
> But many have wondered about you,
> How marred his appearance is from that of a man,
> and his features from that of people.'
> So shall he cast down many nations;
> Kings shall shut their mouths because of him,
> for what had not been told to them they shall see,
> and that which they had not heard they shall consider."

"The prophet tells us that a mystery hidden throughout the ages will be revealed. A righteous servant will come who will be high and lifted up. But before this he would endure sorrow, suffering and death on a cross, not for himself as he was sinless and sent of God, but for the iniquities of all mankind. The sight was so appalling that God put a mantle of darkness over the land, so no one could gape at his intense agony. When the sun lifted again, he did not look human. He was beyond recognition.

Someday in the future, kings shall shut their mouths in astonishment when they see that this man who died as a common criminal on a cross will be exalted on high where he will have the power to raise and cast down nations."

Daniel shuffled in his seat and groaned. *I should have known.*

Worthington fixed his eyes on Daniel squirming in his seat, making gestures to get up and leave when the preacher caught his attention with the question that had plagued him ever since his father slapped his face in the synagogue.

"Now, in Isaiah 53 we are asked to consider this question, who has believed our report, and to whom is the arm of the lord revealed?"

"We understand that God spoke and the heavens and earth and all that is within them came into existence. This was an easy task for Him to accomplish. But when He sacrificed his son from the throne of heaven to redeem man it required His own right arm to work salvation for Him or in other words, He gave it all he had. He gave His only son who sits at his right hand. It was not easy for the Father, nor was it easy for the Son to come here and be hunted, persecuted, and left to die an agonizing death on a Roman cross."

The speaker continued to read.

"And he came up like a sapling before it,
and like a root from dry ground he had neither form nor comeliness,
and we saw him that he had no appearance that we should have desired him.
Despised and forsaken by men, a man of pains and accustomed to illness;
and as one who hides his face from us; despised, and we esteemed him not.
Indeed, he bore our illnesses, and our pains he carried them,
yet we accounted him as plagued, smitten by God and oppressed.
But he was pained for our transgressions, crushed for our iniquities,
the chastisement of our welfare was upon him, and with his wounds we were healed.
We all went astray like sheep, we have turned, each one on his own way,
and the Lord accepted his prayers for the iniquity of all of us."

Before he explained his text, Worthington gazed across the faces of his audience and observed that Daniel was listening. "It was a time of great spiritual drought and oppression for the people of Israel. The spirit of God had been silent for four hundred years, until his anointed servant appeared. He grew up as an ordinary man. He taught the people the word of God and healed the sick. He cast out demons and raised the dead, but many accused him of being of the devil. They despised and rejected him when he did not fit their concept as a mighty king who would deliver them from their Roman oppressors as Moses had delivered them from Egypt. They esteemed him not as a man sent of God, but as an impostor smitten by God. They did not want to be numbered with him, so they turned their faces and fled, fearing for the approval of man rather than the favor of God. They did not understand that he had come to release them, not from Roman oppression which was temporary, but from the curse of death experienced by all mankind, and give them eternal life in return with his Father in Heaven."

"No!" Daniel said to himself. *This man Jesus cannot be! He's got that all wrong.* His thoughts began to reel in rebuttal. The smashed and bloodied face of Eiss Kegal flashed through Daniel's mind. He saw Mottel's mangled corpse, his blood squirting out over the dirt, the bludgeoners pounding him until he became dismembered and unrecognizable. *Mottel was crushed and persecuted on account of the sins of his Gentile neighbors. He bore the sorrow and pain along with the afflicted and despised people of Israel.*

Worthington's gazed penetrated Daniel. "The prophet writes in chapter 64: 6-7."

> "All our righteous acts are like filthy rags;
> we all shrivel up like a leaf, and like the wind, our sins sweep us away.
> No one calls on your name or strives to lay hold of you;
> for you have hidden your face from us."

Daniel recalled the night before that dreadful day when the Jews beat their breasts with their fists and cried out to God. *Why did He hide his face when they begged through the night for mercy and there was none? Why?*

The preachers explained, "We have all departed from the righteous ways of God and went our own way, seeking our own truth. Because of our rebellion, we have all nailed God's righteous servant to the cross, but on that terrible day, he prayed, Father, forgive them for they know not what they do. And the Father accepted his prayer on our behalf, so that by faith in Christ's sacrifice on the cross, and by the power of the Holy Spirit, we can turn from our rebellion and begin our journey back to God, back to the Father and unto the resurrection."

How can he attribute this absurdity to one man when it is we Jews who are despised and rejected of men. It is we who were stricken by God to carry the transgressions of this intolerant world. The Gentiles blame us for everything from plagues to economic woes and insurrection. We are the scapegoats of the world's injustice.

Worthington went on. "This is the mystery of the ages; that God reached down into history of mankind with his own right arm of salvation in Christ, and reconciled the hopeless human race, bent on war and destruction, to himself and to the eternal life for which we were originally created."

And Daniel's thoughts whirled in his head. *We are the descendants who were cut off from the land of the living, cast out of our homeland and force to wander about like dried chaff, begging the bread of mercy from one alien nation to another. Our graves lie scattered among the strangers of the world. This teacher is crazy to attribute a single solution to all our woes in one man who was an impostor at best. This man Jesus, the Jew, like Eise and Mottel was crushed because of the sins of his assailants.*

Suddenly Daniel jumped up in indignation. Just as he was about to turn and stomp out of the room, he heard Worthington say, "suppose the cross is God's remedy for your earthly sorrows and you go on rejecting him. Do you think he will do anything more for you in this life or the next, when he gave all the love he had in sending his Son to die as your atonement, and now is patiently waiting for you to come to him, so he can bless you with his presence? It is no light thing to turn down God's love for you. If He so punished his son who knew no sin, what do you think he will do with you?"

Daniel stepped toward the door with his back toward the preacher.

Worthington eyed him and said, "The same spirit which raised Christ from the dead wants to work in you, to make you into a new man, a free man. He is not asking anything in return but that you simply believe. For without faith in Christ and in his resurrection, there is no hope for mankind, only death."

Daniel slipped out of the room.

On Sunday morning, he would use the quiet time to study for his final exams. He sat at his writing desk, pencil in hand, staring out the window, lost in the glamorous world of Belozerkovka, oblivious to the children playing in the streets and the idle men and women sitting on benches, chatting with animated gestures. He threw his pencil down, got up and decided to go outside and get some air. It was too beautiful a morning to sit in a little room studying. He did not know how long he walked lost in thoughts of Jeniya or conversations with the count but he soon found himself in one of Kiev's many beautiful parks with flowers arranged in symmetrical designs around the fountains ablaze in color.

The homes outside the ghetto exhibited a mixture of architecture, some of Mediterranean style painted in pastel colors with lacy iron balconies, some traditional Russian wooden structures with elaborately carved window shutters, and others Victorian. From the hill above the great Dnieper River, he saw what must have been thousands of devout peasants disembarking river steamers. They flocked to worship in the ornate cathedrals of Kiev, decked out in their finest festive clothing, the women adorned in billowy sleeved blouses under embroidered vests and full skirts over which they wore aprons of lavish needlework, and girls in crowns of flowers with brightly flowing ribbons. Men also wore embroidered *rubashkas*. Richer peasants had leather boots while the poorer wore bast sandals crafted from birch bark tied over thick stockings with twine.

He wandered down a narrow crooked street in the shadow of St. Andrews Cathedral curiously browsing through the books, post cards, trinkets, souvenirs, and even colorful feathers which were supposed to have been plucked from the tail of the Holy Spirit. Unscrupulous monks waiting to fleece the flock, sold everything from bottles containing the imperishable parts of some saint to the milk of the Virgin Mary, as well as the usual icons, holy pictures, charms and amulets of every sort which the people hung around their necks to ward off evil spirits.

He wondered if this was the religion of the Christians? This holy merchandising repulsed him, like trivializing the incomprehensible and Holy God. The one who determines the number of stars and calls them each by name, and who stretches out the heavens like a canopy so that no one will ever discover its end. The one who holds life and death in his hands. Has the Russian clergy sunk so low that their only concern is extorting rubles from these ignorant pilgrims? Whatever credibility Dr. Worthington may have presented concerning the Christian faith, or whatever tempting biddings his professor, Demchenko, had put forth, had now tumbled into a farce.

He continued to wander down the line of tables set out like a holy flea market into the cobblestone square below the Cathedral where an immense crowd of pilgrims had gathered. Above, rose an imperious pale blue Cathedral with white pillars supporting green onion domes outlined in golden beads. The crowd pushed him like a strong current upward toward the cathedral courtyard where he found the one and only place to stand, just outside the entrance doors. From there, he had an excellent view of the golden pillars which framed an ornate red iconostasis containing stylistic images of what… gods, holy men, saints? Immediately, several people frowned and made angry gestures with their hands for him to step aside. He was puzzled at first, then he saw a large icon of a mother and Child on a stand laden with fresh flowers. Holy ground, he thought which reminded him of something Mikhail had once told him. Icons to the Russian people are not saints but the spirits of all the ancestors who had gone before and were now watching over them, guiding and helping them. He lowered his head in respect and moved aside, careful not to push anyone. From inside the Cathedral, a great chorus of a cappella voices rose in a soul wrenching crescendo, and poured out through the courtyard. The passion, the hope, the suffering, and the soul of the Russian spirit longing to find liberation, however temporary, reflected in their musical liturgy.

He gazed over the mass of people, noting for the first time their lined faces and furrowed brows, revealing their heavy souls and in many, pain in their bodies. A *stariik* stood next to him, with silver hair and beard, dressed in a crisp, clean pinstripe *rubashka* belted over wide pants stuffed into his polished but worn boots. His piety intent, his aquamarine eyes lifted heavenward, shinning as clear crystals beneath the rays of morning sunlight, like those of an icon, embodying the soul of all Russia.

Daniel turned to leaved and saw a *starushka* wearing black rags and leaning on a younger man for support to stand on swollen deformed arthritic feet. Tears streamed down her face, no doubt beseeching God for relief from pain and poverty. He dropped some rubles in her hand and she lowered her head, either too proud or too humiliated to look up. When he turned and walked away, he saw her open her twisted rheumatic hand to see how much.

The crowd began to part and several orthodox priests carried someone down the steps in a wheel chair. They placed a horribly deformed woman, a giant with crippled limbs, and a huge hideous face, in the courtyard. She carried a stack of paper icons of the Holy Virgin in her enormous hands and passed them out to the people who took one and bowed. When she noticed Daniel staring, she gazed at him through dark knowing eyes that pierced strangely into his soul, in a way he couldn't explain. Could she see that he thought her to be grotesque, weird, aberrant? Or did she connect to something inside him and see his destiny.

Jeniya waived some flies out of the bread basket and secured a napkin over it with the salt shaker. On warm Sunday afternoons after church the Rostovsky clan enjoyed picnicking outside under the trees overlooking the Dnieper. The servants blanketed the ground and brought out chairs and tables and set them under large shade umbrellas.

"Are you going to see that handsome fellow again, Jenka? The one you invited to the party?" Ekatrina asked. She had always been envious of her older sister's beauty and charm in captivating the attention of men.

Somehow, Jeniya could not mention Daniel's name. Although she was dying to innumerate all the wonderful attributes of her new love, at the same time she hesitated, thinking that she may have been duped by this handsome stranger looking to gain something. Was it Vadim's warnings that had alerted her, or because of her vulnerability and impulsiveness, she did not know. Jeniya pretended to pay no attention, hoping the matter would vanish. When her father latched on to the subject, the lavish assortment of fresh and smoked fish suddenly became unappetizing.

"Which one was that?" the count asked breaking bread.

I believe his name was Daniel Nathanovich," her mother, Zinaida replied. "Jenka introduced him to us at the party, darling, don't you remember?"

"Ah…yes! I remember. He said something about his father owning a textile mill." The count washed the bread and fish down with a gulp of vodka.

"A textile mill?" The women all chimed together.

Jeniya's pulse quickened.

"Mills are generally owned by ambitious peasants or Jews," said the dowager countess.

"Yes mother," the count snapped. "And they have more damn money than these aristocratic sponges of yours I am supporting on this estate." Although he said it loud enough for those relatives sitting at the other tables to hear, his comment did not warrant more than a glance as none of them had any illusions concerning their welcome.

The old countess winced. "Speaking of Jews, Jenka's young man did rather resemble a Jew, and the name. What do you think?"

Jeniya felt heat rush to her face. She reached for her fan. The arrow meant for Daniel pierced her own heart.

"I rather thought that at first," replied the count. "But he didn't behave like one or talk like one, however, he did mention that his family came from the Western Ukraine."

"*Ny*, there you are," the old countess said.

No one was eating except the count. Everyone's attention had riveted around the word "Jew".

"How could a Jew slip into our party?" said Zinaida. "Besides, Jenka mentioned that he was about to take his examinations for the bar. If he is a Jew, he'd have to be crazy. The new law prohibits Jews from admission to the bar, except by special permission from the Ministry of Justice, which we all know isn't going to happen."

Jeniya felt slightly sick to her stomach. She wanted to leave but she wanted to hear this, so she sat like a good soldier and took the blows.

"I rather liked the young man," said the count. "He seemed to be a nice fellow, whatever he is." He pushed the remainder of the fish on the bread and finished it, chasing with vodka. "Sergei." His eye now on his reprobate cousin at the next table. "Didn't a clever peasant pick up your estate for taxes?"

Jeniya was relieved the conversation had changed and that her father had unwittingly come to her defense. The footman brought out terrines of chicken soup and she took some.

"There are many enterprising peasants watching for an opportunity to pick up bankrupt estates. Nothing new," Sergei remarked, shrugging.

"If you had listened to me and invested your inheritance instead of squandering your money on that Parisian show girl, you wouldn't be living here off of me."

Everyone was silent until Zinaida recovered the subject at hand. "Our Jenka would never bring a Jew into this house, rich or not." She turned to her daughter. "Would you dear."

Jeniya stared into her bowl of soup. Ripping Daniel apart was also tearing at her. She had already given him a part of herself.

"I noticed he had an eye for you, Jenka," said her father. "I hope you're not getting any ideas. You are about to make your debut into Petersburg society this season. Not that I wouldn't marry you off before that…if I found a suitable gentleman who wanted your hand, I'd give you away tomorrow." He looked around in exasperation at his three daughters staring back at him. "God knows I've got to get rid of one of you sometime…soon. But I want you all to know this…you will be old maids before I give you away to one of those liberals, be he Russian or Jew."

"What about Vadim?" asked Ekatrina? "I like him best because he teaches us how to do tricks with our horses."

Vadim, thought Jeniya. She had been infatuated with him ever since he first winked at her from beneath his white astrakhan hat, when he rode beside the Tsar in the St. Petersburg military review. He was decked out in his magnificent fire red *cherkesska,* with a dagger secured on his belt and a line of silver cartridges slanting across his broad chest. His stallion, the shade of the desert sand in moonlight, arched his graceful neck and waived his black main, prancing at his master's slightest touch. Vadim was truly master of the horse. He was also an excellent sharpshooter and could hit a target while his stallion galloped at full speed. But the most exciting intrigue was that he offered her a glimpse into the forbidden titan world of the Kazaks.

"And what about Vadim?" repeated Yelisaveta, her eldest sister, popping Jeniya's reverie? "Do you like him?"

"Why Vetka? Would you like him for yourself?"

"I like Vadim," said the count. "He's a brave young man. Intelligent. A great asset to the Empire. Keeps me informed. But, he's a descendent of those wild-eyed rebellious herdsmen, and I'll hear no more of this nonsense."

Jeniya excused herself from the family clan and went for a walk in the gardens to sort through the derogatory comments as well as the events that had taken place over the past week. She had no knowledge of Daniel's background. He said his father owned a textile mill. He could have said anything and she would have fallen for it until her family chopped and diced him.

He seemed like a good man…he dressed meticulously and conducted himself in the way of a true nobleman, a gentleman of the finest caliber. Kindness shown on his face and compassion in his eyes, not that insipid expression she saw on so many of the faces among the bored and arrogant nobility. She would like to see him again… get to know him better, but she was certain he would never return to Belozerkovka, not after the incident with Vadim. Maybe she could organize a little dinner party…with friends…and invite him.

Chapter II

DANIEL PICKED UP his book of the prophets and flipped the pages to Isaiah 53, trying to understand how Worthington arrived at his illogical assertion. He understood that the ancient rabbis believed a Messiah would appear in Israel about 2,000 years ago and bring peace into the world. However, this man Jesus did not bring peace to the world, but division, hatred, and war. He also understood that the prophets spoke of a time when Messiah would come with great power and glory and defeat the enemies of the Jewish people bringing them into a time of prosperity and blessing in their promise land. At that time the entire world know that He is the God who keeps his promise to his people, to Abraham, Isaac, and Jacob. To believe and accept an ordinary man as that Messiah, a man who died like all men, a man who is worshiped by the goyim, who had and the Imperial family formed a procession signaling the commencement of the ball become the symbol of persecution and death to the very people he was supposed to deliver, revolted him.

He sat at his desk in a quandary, absently staring out the open window looking out on a line of two story wooden tenements. The afternoon was hot and hazy with no breezes, and the stench from the out houses simmering in the summer heat rose in the air. After living in the ghetto for so many months he became accustomed to its odors.

"Danya!" Golda's thin voice broke into his reverie.

"Yes, tanta Golda? What is it?"

"I've called you three times already for dinner." She paused outside the door. "What's wrong, *tattela*? What is so important in this world that is driving you like this? You *schlep* your nose along your books like a little mole."

He dropped the pencil in his hand, got up and opened the door. "Tanta Golda, you know I have to study for the State Judicial examination." Golda always wore a little frown between her large blue eyes which came from years of perpetual worry.

"*Ny*. Your dinner is getting dried up already. I've been keeping it warm on the stove for so long. Sholem and I ate hours ago." He followed her from the bedroom through the dining room to the kitchen and sat down at a small metal table by the sink. He watched, as she opened the lid of each pot warming on the back of the iron stove. She carefully ladled out huge portions of beef, potatoes and green beans, and set the dish down before him. "Come *tattella*, eat," she said. "I made your favorite."

He gobbled the food like an automaton. Eating and drinking became a mechanical motion, and interlude to his studies. Afterwards, he put his hands on the table, about to get up and returned to his room, when Golda interrupted him.

"Danya, my goodness." The freckles on her fair skin became as one, when she flushed with indignation. "How can you taste your food? How do you even know what I cooked? You gobble your dinner down these days. What's bothering you so much that you cannot sit and relax?" She paused waiting for a response. "So say something."

"It tastes good, *tanta* Golda. Very good"

"I try so hard to prepare what you like. What's to become of you?" she mumbled removing the empty dishes from his place.

"I may go home for a while," he said.

"It's none of my business." She shrugged, waiting to hear why.

"I don't know for how long, maybe only a week or two."

Daniel went back to his room and flipped through the books of the prophets to Zachariah 9:9. "See, your king comes to you, righteous and having salvation, gentle and riding on a donkey." The picture the prophet describes is not that of a mighty King coming in great glory to save Israel from her enemies and rule over the earth form Jerusalem. He flipped back again to Isaiah 53. This passage does seem to describe one man, a suffering servant, a type of redeemer, rather than a nation but how can this be? If this describes one who comes as a suffering servant, how can it be attributed to one who will come as a mighty king? Are there two Messiahs? An old parable came to his mind about a rabbi who heard that Messiah said he was coming today. So he set out to find Him. Afterward, when he could not find Him, the rabbi decided to see the Prophet Elijah to find out what Messiah meant when he said that he was coming today. And Elijah replied, "By the word 'today' he meant if you but hear his voice."

And what does this mean, hear his voice? Daniel wondered. He had gone around one great circle, only to arrive back to where he had been on page one of his search so many years ago.

He heard the front door slam and then hushed tones seeping through the thin walls from the dining room. He sensed that his aunt and uncle were discussing him and he strained to hear their conversation. "What is he doing in his room every night like a hermit? Maybe you should go and find out," he heard Golda say.

Immediately, Daniel closed his books and set them aside on his desk. He couldn't share his problems. Sholem would not understand.

"Daniel, I want to talk to you about something." Sholem said knocking on the door. He came in, sat down on the edge of the bed, unbuttoned his black vest and loosened the top buttons of his shirt. "Your aunt Golda and I have been concerned about you sitting here, night after night, even into the small hours of the morning, studying, when school's out for summer recess. Your final examination cannot be this tedious, so tell me what's troubling you so much?"

"You know I only have a few months to prepare."

A shadow of deep concern crept over Sholem's face. "Tell me something, are you seeing a girl?"

Daniel nodded. He rested his arm on the back of his chair. He was happy that his uncle was unaware of the immediate problem. But not relieved because he had put his finger on a more sensitive issue. "How did you know I was seeing someone?"

"Anyone can see that you are infatuated with someone by the way you've been acting around here this past month. One of the finest things that can happen to a man is to love a woman." He knitted his dark eyebrows. "But tell the truth, is this girl a *shiksa*?"

"What makes you think I am seeing a gentile woman?" Daniel was amazed and curious at the same time.

"I suspected it all along, when you came home around dawn one night, upset, and especially when you darted out of here early one Sunday morning. Actually, this past month you have said little as to where you are going and what you are doing. This is not like you." He peered at him through wire-framed eyeglasses, his expression politely demanding to know the details, but too much of a gentleman to pry.

"I wasn't trying to hide it. I was just uncertain as to what to do."

"Does she know you are a Jew?"

Daniel turned away and murmured, "No."

Sholem took a deep breath and ran his hand over his head, his thick hair had receded nearly to his *yarmulka*. "Look," he said. "You need to quit this relationship. I know it's hard, especially when you're young and you think you've found love. But you are on the road to heartache if you don't stop this, now!"

Daniel turned and gazed out the window.

Sholem said, "Golda tells me you are going home for a few weeks."

"I thought about it, it's been several months."

"You are at the age now when you need to take a wife, one from our own people. Always, I have tried not to meddle in your affairs, but when I saw you slipping out of here these past few weeks, I took the liberty to write your father about this matter. While you are there, you and your father need to talk about this."

Daniel stared at him. In his head he knew he had to heed his uncle's advice, but his heart remained a light year away.

Sholem said as if reading his mind. "This love thing, at your age it is mostly infatuation. As soon as the marital troubles come it will flee like a Jew from a Kazak. And that will be your fate if you marry this *shiksa*. On top of that, you are setting yourself up for unbearable heartbreak, you know what I mean."

His words shocked Daniel. They wouldn't cut him off, not Rochelle, not Golda, and Sholem...and his father?

"Listen to me, I beg you...in your future...in dealings with all the goyim, tell them the truth...you should be proud of your heritage. I'm sure Reb Brachmann will agree with me." He got up and put his hand on Daniel's shoulder to comfort him in a paternal way.

Jewish traders and merchants heading westward into the crowded ghettos of the Pale jammed the third class compartments of the train. Daniel took off his jacket, neatly folded it and carefully laid it over his satchel in the overhead rack. He rolled up his shirt sleeves and sat with his shoulders pressed up against the window frosted with grey dust. Passengers squeezed themselves into the seat beside him. The overflow of people sat on the floor in the isles outside the compartments and some stood against the car wall, with arms leaning on open windows. The train slowly rolled away from the platform and Daniel glanced around at the other passengers who shared his compartment. "Do you mind," he asked, "If I open the window?"

The corpulent man sitting next to him grinned. Large teeth peeked from beneath his untrimmed black mustache and beard, and his fat arm pressed into Daniel's side. "Please, please," he nodded amiably wiping his forehead with a handkerchief. His breath smelled of garlic.

Animated conversation soon enlivened the passengers and they stank with perspiration. Daniel rested his elbow on the dusty windowsill leaning his head on his fist, allowing the summer wind to caress his face and toss his hair. His body language clearly implied, "I want to be left alone."

The train clacked across the metropolis with the speed of a snail and lingered at every little station taking aboard and unloading passengers. "Brovary, Bobrovitsa, Bobrik," the conductor called. It finally picked up steam when it entered the flat open countryside blending peasant huts, grazing cattle and vast fields of grain into a picture in motion. The rattling of metal wheels jostled the cars, and the hissing rhythm of steam blotted out the conversations of his neighbors. Eventually, the droning undercurrent of conversation and the repetition of the train put everyone to sleep until the conductor called out "Leeensk," in that peculiar language of train conductors. The engine came to an abrupt halt and jolted him awake.

The little station of Lensk was not more than a *verst* from the center of the village and he decided to walk, breathing in the fresh country air and the sweet scent of freshly cut summer hay. He opened his arms to embrace the gentle breeze, letting it cool his body after sweltering all day on the train.

Even though he was perplexed by many problems, he felt happy because he saw the generosity of God in His creation. Everyone seemed happy on this beautiful day. Peasants laughed and chattered, bouncing along atop their hay carts as they passed him.

He went down to the river and stopped to reflect in the moment. Emerald leaves sparkled against an azure sky and sunbeams danced off the water. A gypsy girl tended the enormous flocks of geese that dotted the grassy riverbank like white specks on a green canvas and women washed their clothes in the quiet current. The river raft filled with peasant women on their way home after laboring all day in the fields. They carried flax on their backs to the thrashing barn. During the long cold winter months, they would weave the fibers into linen.

One woman toted an infant on her back, bound to a board with colorful embroidered wrappings. A clever custom, he thought. No wonder the peasants grew up with strong, straight backs and never seem to complain of back pain in spite of years of strenuous work.

The oarsman pushed off the little dock with a long pole and ferried the raft to the other side. For the moment all his troubles seemed to dissolve in the clear water as he idly gazed at the peasants drifting across the river. He wondered how his sister looked, now that she was growing up into a young lady.

He ambled along the rutted dirt road past wattle fences which framed the yards in front of the huts to the familiar town square dominated by a large onion domed orthodox church and then onto the street which lead to the Jewish quarter.

Inside the yard, everything looked the same except for one glaring change. Mottel's carpenter shop was conspicuously missing and in its place had grown a patch of wild flowers. A flurry of activity from butterflies, bees, insects, and birds, testified as a memorial to the martyrs who were once so filled with life.

The door to his father's shop was open and he stood outside for a few moments to observe Rochelle. She had taken his place behind the counter and was busy tallying the day's sales. She had grown into a majestic beauty like her mother. Her long dark hair was brushed back and pinned with one of the pretty hair ornaments which she sold in the shop.

"Ronnie," he said softly, smiling. She looked up and shrieked with joy.

"Danya, what are you doing here?" She darted out from behind the counter and threw her arms around his neck. He laughed with his sister and they hugged each other. He swung her around in the air, as though she were still the baby of the family.

"And you Ronnie. The most beautiful girl in Lensk?" he said holding her at arms distance to admire her beauty. "The boys must be standing in line to ask for your hand."

"And what about you? Father told me he had orders to find you a bride and soon!"

"I know." his smile turned to a frown.

Ronnie gave him a puzzled look. "Aren't you excited about the possibility...?"

"I have a surprise for you," he said evading the subject. He handed her a small package.

"Oh, what is this?" She took the present and smiled, admiring the pretty blue bow and decorative ornament. "Oh, it's wrapped so beautifully, I want to save it just as it is...thank you Danya."

He smiled, enjoying her pleasure in receiving his gift. She carefully unwrapped the package and took a large cameo pinned to a dark blue velvet ribbon from a silken red tufted box. "Oh, Danya, it's beautiful!"

"All the city girls are wearing them now."

"I know," she laughed. She allowed Daniel to tie the ribbon around her slender neck and went to the long standing mirror to admire the brooch.

"Now you are the most beautiful girl in Lensk," he said.

"Oh, how can I thank you?" She turned back to looked at him and said, "how long are you staying with us?"

"I don't know, maybe a week, maybe less if father starts advertising that I am in the marriage market. Right now I need to see grandfather. I have to talk to him about something. I'll see father later." He hugged her and kissed both her cheeks.

Chapter 12

OUTSIDE THE RABBI'S house, Daniel stood on the stoop a few moments reflecting on his problems before he knocked on the door. Last minute jitters cautioned him to reconsider. What would his grandfather's reactions be to his radical ideas? Maybe he would be understanding and then, maybe not.

He kissed his fingers, touched them to the mezuzah, and said his prayer before he knocked. Through the little window to the left of the entrance, he saw a dark figure dart by. His grandfather always wanted everything tidy before visitors entered.

The rabbi opened the door and a broad grin lit up his face. "Danya, my child!" He laughed with delight. "What brings you here?" He reached for his grandson and clung to him tightly for a long moment, in the way of elderly people. For all he knew, this may be the last time he would embrace his beloved grandson.

Daniel immediately noticed that his grandfather had aged and it saddened him to see this one he loved so dearly growing near to the end of his days. His sleek black hair had become completely white and his once erect frame had stooped somewhat. He walked with some effort as he led Daniel through the small hallway to the parlor.

"Grandfather," Daniel said slowly following the long black figure. "Why don't you move in with father, and let him take care of you?"

Rabbi Adler turned and looked at him, his shining dark eyes may have faded a bit over puffy little pouches but they still pierced right through a man.

"Are you a big shot now who tells your elders how they must live?" The initial joy on the rabbi's face had faded to a look of deep concern. He was scrutinizing Daniel's clean shaven face. "I have heard things about you from Sholem that are not flattering."

"Like what?"

Daniel heard the familiar quavering hum of the samovar. The rabbi always kept the water boiling, ready to serve a fresh pot of tea.

"Come," said his grandfather gesturing toward a comfortable chair. "Sit. We'll talk."

Daniel sat down and gazed at him while he went over to a long mahogany table and picked his wire frame spectacles off the white bureau scarf. He put fresh tea leaves in a china tea pot along with hot water and sat it atop the samovar to brew. Then he sat down in his favorite arm chair and examined Daniel who remained silent.

"So what is bothering you or have you come this long distance just to sit?"

Daniel perceived his grandfather was not going to be open-minded about the matter he wished to discuss. Something told him to quit now.

"You don't want to talk? Then we won't talk." The rabbi got up from his chair, went to the samovar and poured strong tea in two engraved glasses which were set in silver holders. Then he diluted it with hot water from the samovar. He placed them on a small table between their two chairs along with a dish of egg cookies.

Daniel gazed at the long figure in a black gabardine kaftan, the full white beard which fanned slightly at the corners. His demeanor was that of an ancient sage and Daniel had confidence in his wisdom. Perhaps he might understand his dilemma after all.

"I've been troubled, grandfather," he began. "In my studies of the ancient texts," he would never divulge that he had gone to hear an evangelist. "I've read where some rabbis have interpreted the one of whom Isaiah speaks of in chapter 53 as a Messiah, a suffering servant who came to bear mankind's iniquities."

"This is not new, my son. Many rabbis throughout the ages have pondered the fifty-third chapter of the prophet Isaiah. Is that all that's bothering you?"

"Well, I've been wondering, suppose this chapter does refer one man. Suppose our Messiah had already come and we missed him?"

"Don't trouble yourself, we have not missed our Messiah. He will come in glory as a mighty king just before a great battle to defeat the enemies of Israel. He will break the oppression of Gentile power over us and restore the scattered Israel to her homeland. From Jerusalem, he will bring peace to the world. This man, this Gentile god to whom I suppose you are referring, did not bring peace, but every kind of religious intolerance, hatred, persecution, murder and war. We could never accept this man as our Messiah because he did not do what the Messiah is supposed to do."

He put a cube of sugar between his teeth and sipped his tea scrutinizing his grandson who was fidgeting with a piece of paper in his hand.

He put his glass of tea down and said. "First of all, the servant of which our prophet Isaiah speaks always refers to Israel. There is no scripture in the text that describes Messiah as suffering. You must read the surrounding chapters to understand about whom the prophet is writing. Isaiah 53 is part of the servant songs, which begins in chapter 41. When you come to this passage, you must ask the question, who is speaking here." The rabbi paused and gazed at his grandson who was listening intently. "Now I ask you, who do you think is speaking?"

Daniel thought for a few moments and considered the possibilities. "God? Isaiah? I don't know."

"No, you don't know. There is much you don't know. These are the Gentile kings of the nations who are living at the end of this age when the Messianic age unfolds. They will be shocked when they discover that which is about to be revealed. When Messiah comes and they see it is not this Jesus, they will be astonished. They will see what they were not told and understand what they have not heard, that the

Jewish people have been chosen by God to be the suffering servant for mankind. Therefore, we must not only bear our own transgressions while we are in exile, but also those of the people in this world who have afflicted us with suffering. Never-the-less we must pray for our oppressors because this is right in the sight of God, and He will accept our prayer."

The rabbi lifted his eyes heavenward and recited as an ancient who is reminiscing and at the same time with a deep longing as one who has seen too many years.

"We were afflicted, forgotten, forsaken, and despised of men, and they turned away. Just as we have received a double portion of tribulation so we shall receive a double portion of blessing when Messiah comes. In that day, all the nations who despised and rejected the Jewish people shall come to serve them in Zion. She will no longer bear the shame of their iniquities." His dark eyes penetrated into the eyes of his grandson, probing. "This is why God has separated us and instructed us not to follow other religions so we will not miss out on these blessings. We want to be accepted by others in this world, this is only natural, everyone does, but to receive the blessings promised of God we must endure. Now you must understand that not all Jews will come into this blessing, but only a remnant, those who are faithful to the word of God. Therefore, we must continue to endure...." His voice trailed off. He lowered his white head as a man who has seen many sorrows, and sought to strengthen himself to go on.

Daniel had enough common sense to know that he should end the discussion there in respect to the elderly sage, but his youthful impetuosity demanded that he press on. He had to have the answers to his questions. "Grandfather, I have a few more questions I would like to ask you, if I may."

The rabbi nodded. "Go ahead."

"Why did Isaiah call Israel a sinful nation in the first chapter, and then later speak of them as the chastisement for the people's sins?

What if Isaiah is referring to one Holy man sent of God to bear the iniquities of mankind?"

The rabbi peered over his spectacles. "Where did you get this notion? *Ny,* so this is what happens when you associate with these Gentiles. Now you have not only exposed yourself to their worldliness, but to their pagan myths as well, and you think you know everything."

"First of all, only God can forgive sin. This doctrine of one man taking on another man's sins allows the believer of this dogma to act irresponsibly. As long as one man will absorb another man's evil deeds, the latter is free to go about and murder, steal, rape, anything he chooses. You see how unspeakably cruel some of our Russian neighbors behave toward us. Then they go to church on Sunday morning and think no more of it. And it is no wonder, with doctrines such as these. And you, an honor student, give credence to this foolishness? You know better. No man can justify another man's sins. The prophet is correct, we are all sinful men and must stand before God to declare our own transgressions."

Daniel frowned. He hesitated wondering if he should press this issue any further. He gazed at the deep red oriental carpet, the shelves rising nearly to the ceiling stuffed with well used tomes, the Menorah on the table and before it the *Tenach*. He opened the piece of paper in his hand and said, "may I ask one more thing? Rabbi Moshe Kohen Ibn Crispin said, Isaiah 53 was given of God as a description of the Messiah. He must mean a suffering Messiah, not a glorified one."

"I know what he means. It is just as I told you"

Daniel fumbled with the piece of paper in his hand, considering whether or not to ask the next question, until finally he said, "Rabbi Elijah de Vidas said, and I quote. 'Since the Messiah bears our iniquities, which produce the effect of his being bruised, it follows that whoso will not admit that the Messiah thus suffers for our iniquities must endure and suffer for them himself '."

"What he says is correct, each one of us are responsible before God for his own transgressions. To quote Crispin and Vidas and imagine that they would consider belief in Yeshua as our Messiah is absurd.

They never did and they never would." He leaned forward in his chair and took another sip of tea.

"But why...?"

"Why, why, why!" Stop this nonsense at once! What's wrong with you? Have you become mad over this religion? Are you trying to justify a ridiculous argument by pulling a scripture here, a verse there? What's wrong with you? Tell me the truth," he waggled his finger. "Are you searching the scriptures, looking for an excuse to escape the hardship of being a Jew?"

"No grandfather, not at all." He opened his hands to the rabbi. "I just wanted some clarification on these contradictory scriptures. That's all."

The rabbi put his hand to his head and swayed. Daniel jumped up to help him. "I'm sorry," he said.

"My son," the elderly man said still shaken. He leaned back into his chair for a few moments. "I can understand you're longing for the Messiah to come and deliver us from our oppression, even as we always have, from the ancient of days. You are not the first to come here and discuss this matter."

He placed his slender hand, the knuckles thick from arthritis, on the young man's strong forearm. "Many times someone would come to me and try to justify this Christ as our deliverer. Sometimes he wanted to marry a *shiksa*." Daniel flinched. The rabbi sensed the young man's tension and silently gazed at him for a few moments before he continued. "Others wanted to take a position in Russian society. You know the Russians give converts the best jobs in the bureaucracy in order to tantalize the rest of us to convert. He spoke his words carefully all the while assessing Daniel's reactions. "No, my son," he shook his head. "You are not the first."

Daniel drew away and sat back in his chair and both men sat in silence for a while.

"My son, to try and correlate our prophetic scriptures with the gentile god is stretching the words of the prophets too far. Anyone can pull a verse here and there from the *Tenach* to justify his argument. But it takes many years of study to understand its meaning. The *Tenach* was written by men who were under great suffering and persecution just as we are, here in Russia. They wrote about their own hope for deliverance. It is unreasonable to dwell on a scripture written by one man and say this means a certain inerrant dogma."

Daniel quietly considered his grandfather's words. He was not comforted by the rabbi's logic, but confused. Everything made sense, and nothing made sense. The concept of God remained one big mystery. "Would you like another glass of tea, grandfather?" he said rising to pour himself another one.

The old rabbi nodded. "Please."

Daniel handed him a glass of tea and another cube of sugar.

"You see son, the men of old were men of faith. They didn't wake up one morning and talk to God. God sought them out because they were faithful and obeyed His commandments. And it is our duty to remain faithful, so that one day, God will call us to our promised land, just as he did our father Abraham, and then he will vindicate our sufferings."

Daniel reflected on all these arguments for a while, especially dwelling on the rabbi's last remark.

The rabbi narrowed his eyes. "Not to change the subject," he said. "But I have heard that you are associating with a liberal sect of Jews, and even number among your associations, gentiles. Is this true?"

"This is true, but these Jews are not strange heretics like uncle Sholem thinks."

"I have been worried about you for some time. You must put these strange liberal ideas out of your head. They can only lead you into trouble. These new Jewish friends of yours claim they have the answers to our problems, but in truth, they are standing at a junction where they must choose a road on which to travel." He leaned forward in his chair and lifted a finger to enhance his parable. "The first road leads the eternal people homeward. But, along the way they will encounter suffering and persecution. The second road leads to assimilation with the gentiles. Along this road they will be torn from their roots and blown about with every new doctrine. Its destination is a wasteland, and those pitiful men who travel along its way will drag their Judaism behind them, like a galley slave drags his ball and chain. They will never find peace because they are always compromising."

Daniel gasped, gripped by a sudden siege of guilt. He took a deep breath. His grandfather had cast a shadow on his conviction that dialogue and the pursuit of a common ground between Jew and Russian would create a brighter future for the Jewish people.

The rabbi paused and scrutinized his grandson before he continued. "The third road leads, God forbid, to the unspeakable baptismal font. A convert is a man who has been uprooted and planted in foreign soil. He is a man without a people, a man who has lost the eternal vision.

The Russian people tell us they want us to convert to their Orthodoxy and share in their society. But to them, we will always be Jews." The old man put the sugar cube between his teeth and sipped his tea and they sat silently for a while.

"They tell us that Anton Rubinstein our celebrated artist and founder of the famous conservatories of Petersburg and Moscow, has converted. You know that."

Daniel nodded.

"He is decorated by the Tsar, the delight of Petersburg society. But he once said remorsefully, 'the Jews regard me as a Christian, and the Christians, a Jew.' The rabbi leaned forward and stared straight into Daniel's face. "Now, my son, let me ask you a question. Which would you call him?"

Daniel shook his head. "I don't know."

"Then I will tell you, like the salmon who returns to his birthplace to spawn, so we Jews must also return to the heritage which has been given to us through the patriarchs, no matter where the road of life leads. And this, my son, can be the source of great and terrible conflict in the heart of a convert." He paused. "Let me ask you something personal. Have you fallen in love with a *shiksa?*"

Daniel shifted his gaze from his grandfather to the glass of tea on the table.

"Ah ha, I suspected as much," the rabbi said. "I know a certain poet, Constantine Shapiro, who married a Christian woman and for her, he went to the baptismal font. Later he said in a letter to a mutual friend, 'if you knew how great is my love for my people, you would laugh. For indeed a man deserves to be ridiculed if he exchanges his religious dignity for no good reason, while his former dignity is still alive within him. But what can I do? My heart cries out to my people. Can I tear out my heart and replace it by a stone?' Hear the voices of these converts that cry out to you my son. Once you walk down the third road, you can never return to your people, although you may want to. Then you will understand the words of Isaiah in the 53 chapter; when you will be afflicted and pierced many times."

"I know all these things, grandfather. I've tossed them around in my mind one thousand and one times. But I've fallen in love with this woman, and I don't know how to tear away my heart's desire for her. When I look into the face of another girl, I see her face and I feel an empty ache. But when I am with her I feel complete, like I have everything I always wanted in life."

"This *shiksa* has bewitched you."

"If you could see her grandfather, she is a free spirit. When I am with her I feel light hearted, like I can do anything, be anything on this earth which is possible."

"Like going to the moon?" the rabbi smiled.

"Yes, that's it. The moon and the stars, nothing is too great."

"That's very nice, but this is the illusion of infatuation, not reality."

Daniel frowned. "But reality keeps us common people down, living in fear of the police today and of the Tsar tomorrow. Jeniya invited me to a party at her home, a great manor in the country. She introduced me to her parents, Count and Countess Rostovsky." He happily carried on, so anxious to talk of his love and share his adventures with the Imperial society that he was unaware of his grandfather blinking his eyes in alarm. "Her father and I sat down and talked. We even toasted and drank wine together. His own wine from his own vineyards. And all the while I was cowering and imagining that he was looking down on me, but, he wasn't. He regarded me as nothing more or less than simply a young man."

"Oy vey! OY VEY!" The rabbi put his fingers to his temple and shook his head. "And I thought you were smart. I have been bragging to everyone about my intelligent grandson. He goes to the university? So why?" He kept shaking his head. "I can't believe this what I am hearing!" He looked wildly into Daniel's eyes. "And did you tell them you are a Jew?"

"My best friend Mikhail Kishniakov comes from the landed gentry. He knows I am a Jew, and it doesn't matter to him. He has bought me tickets to operas, concerts, and the ballet. We go all over together."

The rabbi looked at him incredulously. "That is not the question. Did you tell this count and his family that you are a Jew?"

The word stuck in Daniel's throat.

"You didn't, did you." He raised his eyes and threw his arms in the air in the manner of prayer. "May the Lord our God have mercy on this house!" He turned back to Daniel. "Don't you know that you could bring down the wrath of this count if he finds out you have deliberately deceived him?"

Daniel was speechless. Inside he recoiled in agony.

The rabbi sat in silence for a while, his head bent down, and his hands over his eyes.

"I will tell them, grandpa. I know you are right," Daniel insisted.

The rabbi took a deep breath. "You are charmed and elated because the gentry have accepted you. But stay away from them. You do not belong in their company. They may seem gracious, but inside they are diabolical and skilled in the art of manipulation. They have no concept of what it means to be poor, struggling and persecuted. They have too much of everything, too much money, too many servants, too many homes, too many good times. You are nothing more than a new play toy for this young woman. And when she is no longer amused by you, she will throw you out like last week's garbage," he sighed shaking his head.

"Of all my grandchildren, I have always favored you. Perhaps it is because you remind me so much of my only daughter, may she enjoy paradise forever." He squeezed his eyes shut to prevent the tears from streaming down his cheeks. "I'm sorry, I seem to cry so easily these days. She was such a talent, so bright, but like you she lacked good common sense. She believed too much in the goodness of people. But people are not all good and you have taken on the most treacherous of all, the aristocracy.

Please, my child, listen to your old grandfather who has seen many sorrows. Terminate your associations with these people before you are surrounded by a hellfire from which you cannot escape."

Stunned, Daniel sat in silence, overcome with disappointment.

The rabbi sat quietly and stared straight ahead for a while sipping his tea through the sugar cube. "Sholem has written me to help your father find a nice bride for you. It is time you took a wife, like your brother Ezra."

———

Daniel left his grandfather's house disturbed and perplexed. His grandfather's wise admonition sifted through his brain until one cog remained, the desire he could not release, Jeniya. Would she be content to elope with him, he wondered? If men like Rubenstien, Shapio, and Poliakov, the railroad king, and even Israel Brachmann could make it in Russian Society why couldn't he? He decided to put the whole mess behind him. On his way back to the yard he heard quickening footsteps approaching from behind.

"Hey kid! *Whaddaya* doing here in town? Did they kick *ya* out of school?" Ezra caught up with him and was walking beside him. He had a big grin on his face.

"No, I just came by for a visit. How's Leinha and the family?"

"She has one every year. What about you? When are you *gonna* get a wife and start giving pa some grandkids?"

"Sounds like you're doing fine for both of us." They stopped in front of their father's store.

"Say kid." Ezra cocked his head and frowned in the same way he had from boyhood when he was conniving. The same lock of curly black hair fell over his brow. "How's chances of me staying with you and uncle Sholem for a while?"

"What? Why do you want to stay with him?"

Ezra stood to his full six feet one inches and enthusiastically said, "I heard there's an active league of Jewish working men in Kiev. I'd like to check it out."

"What about Leinha and the kids?"

"*Agh,* her folks adore the kids. She's always over there anyway. She'll be glad to get rid of me for a while. It'll give her a break. You know what I mean." He laughed.

"Can you take off, just like that, at the drop of a hat?" Daniel snapped his fingers in the air.

"Sure, Ronnie can tend the store better than I can. You should see her now. A real beauty. Pa's hunting for a husband to suit her, but she's hard to please. He gives in to her every whim. Not like me, just slap some girl on *ya* out of the clear blue. But, we get along good. The old man made a good choice. Hey, *wanna* meet the family, come on."

Chapter 13

By the end of the week, Ezra had finagled his way to Kiev and into his uncle's home. He bought a cot and was squeezing it under the window of Daniel's room where his desk had been.

"Hey, what are you doing to me?" Daniel protested when he saw that another bed could not fit in the room comfortably. "This room is the size of a closet already. It's not big enough for both of us," Daniel protested.

Ezra was broader in the shoulder and chest than Daniel, and taller. He stood up and glanced at his brother. "Aw kid, I'm not going to be here very long, only a few weeks, until I find a place to stay and a job." He pushed Daniel's armoire and desk together on the wall at the foot of the two beds with barely enough room for a person to pass by.

"Hey, I can't even pull my chair out now! Daniel yelled. "The bed's in the way."

"So sit on the bed."

A few days later, after one of his meetings, Ezra came in and flopped down on his bed, placing his large hands under his head. "Hey, Danya, what ever happened to those meetings you were going to at that dandy's house?" He said thoughtfully, gazing from the side of his eye toward his brother. "I thought you were finally beginning to see the light when you started going to those meetings to discuss political reform and all that. What happened to that group anyway? Haven't heard much about 'em lately."

Daniel turned around annoyed that his brother had interrupted his studies. "I still go occasionally."

"Listen kid, you need to get out of yourself. Get your face out of those books." He slid down to the edge of his bed and snatched a book off Daniel's desk. "What's this, a religious book?" he said flipping it on his brother's bed. He pulled the rest of the books over to examine them. "Commentaries on Isaiah, Ezekiel? What are you reading in there so much, anyhow? Think you're studying to become a rabbi or something?"

Daniel gathered the books from his bed and piled them neatly back together on his desk. "And what about you?" he said. "Your nose is not in a book? He reached over with his foot and kicked over a stack of leaflets, scattering them on the small patch of floor in front of the door beside his own bed. "You even drink tea in a book. Look at all those dirty tea glasses on the floor by your bed. You are so preoccupied you can't even pick up your dirty underwear." He pointed to the pile on the floor near the end of Ezra's bed beside his desk. "When was the last time you washed them?"

Ezra looked around. He took a cigarette off the windowsill and lit it.

"Not in here, you don't." Daniel protested. "Outside."

"What's the matter? You smoke, don't *ya*?"

"No more, I quit."

"All right, all right," he butted his cigarette. Ezra widened his dominate dark eyes and slid around to sit on the side of his bed to face his brother. "Why don't you forget about them countesses and come with me to one of our study groups. Everyone shares as one spirit, Jew and goyim, alike. And bring that friend of yours, what's his name?"

"What's this? A study group with the goyim? I thought you were going to meetings of the Jewish Bund?"

"One thing leads to another; you know how it is." He brushed the persistent lock of hair from his face.

"What do you mean? Is this a revolutionary group?"

Ezra shrugged. "No, we're not a militant group. We're a study group." He stared pensively across the room at no particular thing and began to recite, "for us the world's not made up of different nationalities and races, but only two kinds of people, rich and poor, comrades and foes, laborers and those who oppress them. Russian, Jew, German, French, whoever he is, as long as he labors under oppression to make someone else rich, he belongs to the great invincible brotherhood of workingmen. Brothers in spirit are we…forever." He raised his hand in the air, made a fist and punched the air. "We are molding the future of Russia. Not only Russia, but all the Empires across Europe." He swept his arm in a wide arch. "We are dedicated to building a new society where men and women, Jew and goyim, can work without oppression and live together in harmony."

"A lofty and noble concept." Daniel said sarcastically, still irate at his brother's intrusion into his privacy.

"You may sneer at us now, but one day the socialists of the world will unite, you'll see."

"Socialists? Is that what you call yourselves? And how do you know the working men in Western Europe are of one mind with your dismal crowd?"

"We write letters to each other, encourage each other, share our pains, joys and victories, you know. We all have one goal, and that is to build a new world, Jew and goyim alike."

"You talk like a nut! In the first place how can a Jew live in harmony with the goyim? You know how the Russians hate us. How they are trying to destroy our culture, forcing us to convert or get out. How can your bunch reconcile religious differences when no one in history has been able to accomplish that?"

"It will happen." He pointed his finger at Daniel. "And you'll live to see it!" We are *gonn*a create a new order of things, where everyone will want to have a part in building this new society because they will live in peace, justice and equality.

In our new world, there will be no more cruelty and injustice of man against man. A world where every man, woman, and child will breathe free from the tyranny of the capitalist and of the priest. Where everyone will work for the common happiness of all and at the same time be free to pursue his own happiness." Ezra did not tell his brother that he had forsaken his faith. That he saw religion as an instrument to divide and enslave people, to keep them ignorant, and that all forms of it must be destroyed.

"You talk like an idiot, Ezra, like one of those crazy leaflets you pass out. Who writes this stuff, anyway?" He picked one up off the floor and examined it. "How can a man labor for someone else's welfare and at the same time work to pursue his own goals? Isn't that a kind of contradiction?"

"It will work if people are free from competing with each other, and grabbing for themselves in order to have something in this life."

"No, that's not possible. People have different levels of ambition, different hopes, aspirations, dreams. Besides, if there are fifty percent of the people who want to contribute to the peace and harmony of all, then there will be fifty percent who want to use these generous souls for personal gain."

"Can't you see? People just need to be re-educated. They have to learn to think of the common good and to serve for the advancement of all. Not just what they can get for their selfish selves. Then we can have peace and harmony between people and nations." Ezra opened his hands to his brother. "By sharing, all people will have a chance to find individual fulfillment and not just a few. Why don't you come to one of our meetings, then your eyes will be opened to something."

Chapter 14

EZRA PLANTED HIMSELF in Kuznetsov's textile mill. He thought it was a hornet's nest ready to sting with anti-government propaganda, but instead, he found insurmountable barriers against his intension. First, he lied when the foreman, a man of stocky structure with a barrel chest, asked if he knew how to operate the spinning jennies. He figured that what he didn't know he could learn in one day, since even simple minded peasants are able to operate this equipment. The foreman gave him a notebook to tally his work record, some brief instructions and told him to go to work.

Down the center of a long warehouse, two lines of looms reached from floor to ceiling illuminated by daylight streaming from large windows. Two people sat on a wooden bench in front of each loom and operated the machinery with its many wheels and threads. Another group of operators stood on the other side and maneuvered the fabric into large bolts of material that workers would haul into the stock room on their backs.

Ezra took his place at the loom and studied the weaver next to him trying to imitate his dexterous actions with his own clumsy fingers, but the machine spun faster than he could handle the thread. He repeatedly asked his neighbor for help, each time shouting louder over the clatter of the gear wheels and driving belts, but the man ignored him. Finally, his neighbor turned to him and said, "Look here you, we keep to ourselves here. We are fined for everything and anything, even while talking on the job…see that poor devil over there?" Ezra leaned back and gawked past the row of weavers. He saw the foreman berating a poor woman while jotting remarks in her notebook. "She's getting a warning for coming in late. Next time she's out."

Ezra thought for a few moments and seized the opportunity to ask questions. "How can I make this thing go slower?" The man obliged to help him while keeping one eye on the boss.

Ezra never worked a hard day in his life. Now that he saw how relentlessly his boss hunted for even the smallest error, he became anxious for his job. Besides, he concealed another matter, his Jewish identity. In Alexander's latest assortment of decrees in his war against Jews, he prohibited them from joining the Russian labor force. However, Ezra noticed Jews working in the mill, but he decided to avoid them. He felt for his fellow Jews but he wouldn't share with them, not yet. When the time came, they would fall in easily.

In the monotony of the relentless clacking machines, he began to think of new schemes. How could a member of the beaten down hated race approach an inferior class of peasants and preach to them about freedom from tyranny?

The whistle blew at 9PM announcing quitting time. Exhausted and starved, Ezra was about to file into the mess hall when his neighbor called him. "Hey you. You have to clean your machine before you go. No one else does it for you around here." Ezra wearily turned around. This was his chance to ask all he needed to know in operating his equipment.

He learned that the man was called Ivanovich. He was older than the others and had an intelligent clean shaven face, a brush mustache and trimmed hair. He also learned that he lived in the village.

Ezra completed his chores and dragged himself into the noisy mess hall, dimly lit by a few light bulbs attached to cords hanging from the ceiling. The putrid odor of cabbage seeped into the air outside. He looked at his grimy hands, but was too tired and too hungry to find the latrine. He laughed to himself thinking how far he had strayed from his strict upbringing. He stood in line and waited for the one and only thing on the menu, borscht, and yesterday's stale bread from the village bakery. A stocky woman stood behind a huge black iron pot, ladling the steaming liquid in large tin bowls.

Ezra stared at the repulsive liquid sloshing around in his bowl and said to the woman, "Aren't there any potatoes in here?"

"*Kartufflee?*" One of the workers standing behind jested, "You may not see *kartufflee* until Christmas."

"We are the potatoes!" someone else said. "If they do not eat us this winter, then they'll plant us in the spring." They all grunted bitterly.

"Ezra took his meal to one of the long wooden tables and sat down on the bench with the others. "How much do they charge for these here slops?" he asked randomly. Even though no cash passed hands, he already knew that meals were jotted down in his tally book and deducted from wages, eaten or not.

"This costs us twice as much as we pay in town," someone said.

"Then why don't you eat in town?"

"The son-of-a-bitch pays us here four times a year...If we get paid at all!"

"*Whaddya* mean, paid at all?" Ezra inquired.

"They deduct every kopek we earn for something."

Within minutes the men had finished their grub and were up shuffling from the wooden benches and stomping into the barracks where they flopped into their bunks exhausted.

The stench in the dining area was so nauseous that Ezra left without finishing his meal. Outside, he took a few good breaths of fresh air, rolled a cigarette and lit it. *These workers are ripe for revolutionary harvest.* He had to work quickly. He didn't want to remain in this forsaken place any longer than he had to.

Ezra went back to the mill to find a place in the barracks to sleep. When he opened the door, a foul stench of perspiring bodies, unwashed bed rags, and liquored breaths assaulted him along with the discordant rhythm of snoring, snorting and wheezing. These accommodations were beyond meager, they were downright sordid.

Moonlight seeped through the tiny windows, enough for him to make out two rows of bodies stretched across the dormitory, lying head to head on partitioned planked platforms. *Smells like a damn stable!* He found an empty slot and crawled onto a greasy smelling sheep skin thrown over a straw mattress. Although he was exhausted, he couldn't sleep. His flesh itched from something crawling, a mosquito was singing over his head, and his stomach growled from hunger. He finally dozed off when a foul smelling sot dropped his dead weight on top of him.

"*Schto eto?*" he grunted, driveling vodka soaked saliva in Ezra's face. "*Kto vee?*"

Ezra slid out from under the drunken man's sprawling arms and legs and found a place to sleep on the floor under an open window.

Promptly a 4AM, the mill whistle's shrill blast jolted him awake. Bodies rumbled, men groaned, and boots began clomping around his head. "What the hell, it's the damn middle of the night." He grumbled to the air above him. "What the hell time is it?"

"4AM. Time to get up and get to work," someone said.

Ezra staggered to his feet and bumped into a wooden beam. "Son-of-a-bitch," he mumbled disoriented, looking around at the scrambling men. He scratched himself under his clothing and when he lifted his shirt and examined his stomach, red welts glared back at him. He wanted to flop back down in someone else's bed, but he thought of the late fine and he couldn't afford that on his second day at work.

The next day, after supper he went out for a smoke and to be alone with his thoughts. The victorious imaginations he harbored yesterday had now collapsed. *Gray robots grinding all day and into the night. Can't talk on the job, no time in the stinkin mess hall, no time in the barracks.* He wondered how his comrades would smuggle the Marxist literature to him through the factory gates under watchful eyes everywhere. He flipped his cigarette butt. He couldn't bear that *stinkin* barracks another night, but he hoped that after a few more days of backbreaking labor in the noisy mill, he would be able to get a little sleep, even on a *stinkin* wooden plank. On his way to the barracks he noticed a long sliver of a man lying on the ground, his head propped up on a folded jacket, reading a book by candle light.

Ezra knelt on one knee beside him and said, "*skajeete minya, tovareesh*. What are you reading?"

The young man turned from his book startled. "It's a book about adventures in the American West," he said.

"Is it good?"

He rolled over on his side and leaned on his elbow. "Yes! I love stories about the American West. I love all stories that take me on adventures across the world, away from this dismal place." His tired eyes began to show a tiny spark of life when he spoke of his bedtime travels.

Ezra knew immediately, this was the fellow he was looking for. He sat down beside him and proceeded carefully. "I would like to go places too, travel, see things. I wonder if I will live long enough to do that?" he said probing.

"I don't know but that's why I read."

"Why do we working people allow ourselves to become slaves to the *bourjuis* factory lords I wonder? Did you ever think about that?"

"Yes, I think about that all the time."

The young man's words were music to his ears and fodder to feed his plans. He continued to probe, this time adding a little fuel to the fire. "Why are the working people so fearful of their mill lords, when we out number them by tens of thousands. You'd think that with so many more workers, they would unite and fight for better working conditions…wouldn't you think?"

"Are you new here?" He eyed Ezra cautiously.

"Why do you ask?"

"*Ny*, I'm sure you understand that if we lose our jobs at the plant we will be tossed out in the streets with beggars and thieves, with nowhere to go for help. We can't go home because our families barely have enough grain to feed their children through the winter." The young man sat up and rested his lanky arms on his knees. "It's not that we wouldn't like to organize, but we're tired, sick and weak...and ignorant. Besides there is always more coming from the countryside, maybe hundreds, maybe even thousands every day. If we are not adept at our job, the barons will find someone else to take our place. They don't care. You'll find out."

"*Poniimyou, tovareesh*," Ezra said in agreement.

Ezra thought for a while gazing at the moon lit barracks. It was time to add a little more fuel. "There is something that puzzles me," he said. "While a man is still young and strong, why do so many smash their brains out with vodka? When they could...like you...think and read and learn and maybe get a group together...to...study...to encourage one another to fight for what belongs to him...his human dignity."

The young man gazed in amazement at Ezra's words and energy. "What good will it do? The lords are stronger than us. They have the money and the power. They don't need guns and Kazaks, they can smash a thousand of us with two words. You're fired. At least the drink numbs our senses so we can survive another day in this hole."

The moon had hidden its light and they both sat quietly staring absently into the blackness of night.

"Actually, we are afraid of change," said the young man. "We are born into despair and raised without hope...slaves to the gentry. We view any change as life threatening, be it for the better or for the worse because it encumbers us with heavier burdens. Life is cruel enough as it is, a curse that carries us along like a current to the grave. We work, we eat. We work, we sleep, and what's left. In effect, we are all marching to the grave, it awaits with anxious arms. The mill barons feed on our fear of death...no work, no food. They can treat us worse than cattle and we take it. At least a farmer feels sorry for his cattle because they're worth money. But who feels sorry for the workers? We don't even feel sorry for ourselves."

Ezra saw he had a greater barrier to overcome. The beaten down Russian worker would not embrace his message of liberation with open arms, but rather, they would regard him as a meddlesome stranger speaking with lofty impractical ideas. However, it was not in his nature to give up. "We are not beasts," he said. "We are human beings. We have dignity. We do not work just to eat and sleep and die, but to make a decent life for ourselves and our families, and live as human beings should."

The young man laughed and shook his head.

"By the way, I'm Ezra Nathanovich, what's your name?"

The young man clasped Ezra's outstretched hand, "Pyotr Antonevich." He made a little salute. "*Tovareesh*," he said.

When Ezra lumbered into the mill the next morning, he was horrified when he noticed children darting in and out from between the looms replacing spindles of thread and oiling gears, sometimes while the machines were still clattering. Even he feared to touch a spool when the jenny's enormous wheels were spinning. He glanced around at the workers faces hoping to find his new friend, Pyotr, when he saw a woman slump down over her loom.

"Poor devil," said Ivanovich, stopping his machine for a few minutes in respect to the newest causality of the mill. "She had her baby here not long ago. Gave birth by her loom, she did. The baby died and she hasn't been the same since."

Ezra also stopped his machine and looked. "Is she dead?"

Ivanovich shrugged.

"You. Get a bucket of water," the foreman said to the woman sitting beside the unfortunate victim. She sprang to her feet in fright, fetched the water and splashed it over her neighbor.

"Now get rid of her," the boss shouted when the victim revived, motioning with a strong arm, not only to display his intent but to instill fear in the others. "What's the matter with the rest of you?" he said looking around the room. "You're not paid to gawk. Get back to work or I'll fine the pack of you for sloth on the job."

"What will become of her?" Ezra asked.

"Who knows? Some become beggars, some prostitutes. None of them last long. Too bad. A heavy fine she must pay for heartbreak. Indeed, must we all."

Ezra nervously applied his fingers to the loom with the little knowledge he acquired in the past few days, hoping his boss wouldn't make him the next victim.

After work, the young man Antonevich sought Ezra, and brought along a friend. "This is Marka," he said in a low tone. "Marka Stefanova."

A girl stood in the shadows outside the mill trembling.

"She lives here in the village. Would you like to walk with us before dinner?"

"Sure," said Ezra wondering.

After they walked a good distance from the mill, Antonevich said softly, "Marka said we could meet together in her home, to talk."

"When?"

"Tonight?"

"What made you change your mind about this?" Ezra asked.

"The incident today."

They walked in silence for a while, Antonevich gazing straight ahead, his large eyes clear. "Actually, everyone who labors thinks of revolt, but privately, to himself," he said. "Sometimes I lie awake all night thinking...my thoughts wandering like dumb sheep without a shepherd...and then I say, what's the use of all this thinking, I need to get some sleep...but...if I don't think and live like a beast to work and eat...then my existence is purposeless...and if I do think...well...it's still purposeless. Maybe, Ezra, you will be our shepherd."

Marka's hut was small, but clean and neat. From behind the large clay stove an older woman bowed silently and disappeared. Three younger children were asleep above the oven to keep warm. An oppressive stillness filled the hut, broken only by the humming of the samovar.

"Please sit down," Marka said, extending her hand toward a bench by the table. "Won't you have some supper with me?"

She went to the stove and ladled soup into three bowls, then sat down wearily at the table. Before she ate, she pushed back the straggling hair which had fallen from her top knot over her pale thin face. Ezra was staring at her in the dim light. She glanced up at him. "Working at the mill has added to my age."

He lowered his eyes.

"Sometimes I just want to run away from everything and everyone," she said. "And not look back, ever. Life here is like a long tunnel with a black hole at the end, with no future...just a long tunnel of despair."

"Like marching to the grave," Pyotr interjected.

"*Da*. I guess that's it," she said.

Ezra made a little nod in agreement. He glanced around the room. "Aren't your parents *gonna* eat with us?"

"My mother had already eaten with the children. My father died of consumption, working in the mill."

Ezra lowered his head. "I'm sorry," he said. A strong wind buzzed through the straw roof and rain began to patter on the window panes.

"Who are the pigs that own the mill?" Ezra asked.

"It is one pig," Antonevich commented. "We have never seen him. We do all our business with the foreman. He's our boss."

"Why is he so ugly?"

"Kuznetsov, the pig, is always looking for more profits to support his obscene life-style. To get those profits, the foreman accuses the workers of drinking on the job and stealing parts from the machines so he can levy hefty fines. In turn, Kuznetsov supplies him with cheap whores."

"Why does the owner allow this to go on?"

"He doesn't care. He keeps his own high class whores in mansions. All he cares about is rubbles."

Ezra shook his head in disgust.

Soon several more workers joined the evening meetings at Marka's home. Pyotr Antonevich, Marka, and Ezra taught them to read from the leaflets calling for workers to unite. Ivanovich, the senior member, joined them at risk of his family's livelihood.

From time to time, Ezra would build them up with hope. "I thought the first thing we could do, is draw up a petition asking for tolerable working conditions." When he saw that resistance cross their faces, like a dark cloud in a clear sky, he said, "We don't have to present our petition to the mill boss right away."

"He'd laugh at us, rip it up and fire us, he would," Ivanovich said.

"I think you're right," Ezra conceded. "But we still need to draw it up and put it on a back burner to simmer, while we increase our numbers." *Let it marinate so it will smell real-good to these beaten down souls.*

"We can never increase our numbers enough," said Antonevich.

"Maybe, but we can no longer sit by and expect the Tsar to help us, or anyone else. We need to help ourselves by learning to read and write. If we had a large organization of dedicated men and women teaching people in factories all over this Empire to read and write, opening their eyes to life, freedom, and human dignity, then we can unite into one band of workers struggling for our human rights." He raised his fist and said, "Liberation to the people of Russia!" They all joined in. "Power to the people! Power to the *narod!*"

A battle cry was the encouragement they needed to draft a petition. They eagerly got down to work and requested an eight-hour workday, overtime pay, and hours lost due to illness not be deducted from their wages. They wanted the right to clean their machines during working time rather than after hours without pay, and to restore the holidays which had been abolished. They surreptitiously passed the document on to those whom they could trust. They also agreed to abstain from vodka and set a moral example to the other workers.

While the workers supported their cause, they did not respond enthusiastically. Survival was greater than sacrifice. Ezra saw that it was not an easy task to convince these men and women that their lives could be made a bit easier if they would join together and take a firm stand for their rights, and that their greatest fear of someone taking their jobs could be put to rest if new applicants could be persuaded to stand with them and strike if their requests were not met.

The next morning a small group of men and women huddled around an announcement nailed to the door. They murmured excitedly to one another as Ivanovich tried to read it to them out loud. He pointed to each word and read slowly, syllable by syllable, as he had been taught at the evening meetings.

"Ezra, *smotriite!*" Ivanovich called when he spotted him walking down the path to work. "Look, over here! It says the manager is going to deduct another kopek from every ruble for a new tax." He said, pointing to the document.

"A tax for what?" Ezra inquired.

"The new day center. They say it's the law."

A woman approached Ezra and addressed him with a title of esteem. "Before you came, Pan Mendelev, they collected a tax from us to build a day care center for the children of the mothers who work here. That was two years ago and still we are paying this tax and have not seen the day care center." She flicked away the tears filling her eyes with her fingers. "Now my child is old enough to work at the mill, even though he has seen only seven summers of life and they are collecting taxes from him. How have they come so low as to suck the blood from our children? Please, Pan Mendelev, help us."

"Where is our day care center?" said the workers who had gathered around Ezra. "*E gdea nac rubblee?*"

"You are a knowing man among us Ezra," said one who recently attended the meetings. "You have a brother who defends the poor. He knows the law. Will he help us?"

Ezra frowned, perplexed and overwhelmed.

"That's not all," continued Antonevich. "The clerks and foreman are exempted from paying this new tax!"

The pleas from the people stunned Ezra and their pain aroused his anger as well as his pity. He wondered if this was the break he had hoped for.

When the whistle blew calling the people to work, they scattered to their looms, like ants whose hill had been smashed by the imperious boot, all except Ezra, Ivanovich and Antonevich. They were prepared for a confrontation of reason according to the request they had drawn up. The three men marched into the mill to find the foreman.

"What's going on here?" snarled the pocked faced foreman approaching them.

"We demand to see the manager of the mill or we will not go back to work," Ezra belted back impetuously, unable to separate the people's desperate pleas from his own furry. "We want to talk to the manager or we strike!"

The foreman's chunky face broadened into a grin. What was left of his teeth were chipped and broken. "See your strike," he pointed to the workers assiduously separating and winding threads, getting their looms ready to weave.

"Where are the rubbles you collected for the day care center? What did Kuznetsov spend them on? Whores?"

Everyone ceased their activity and riveted their gaze on Ezra who stood alone now. Ivanovich and Antonevich had distanced themselves, winching from his audacity. This was not the approach they had in mind. The foreman's face inflamed with anger.

"You and your kind will not get away with this when the workers learn the truth," Ezra continued. "When they understand their human rights. Then they will strike and they will refuse to pay your unfair taxes!" Ezra shook his fist at the foreman.

The foreman flung his fist in an attempt to strike his face, but Ezra, who was quick, jumped out of the way.

"You scumbag. I suspected you all along. A *narodniikii*. An infiltrator. An agitator. You get out of this town, and if I ever see you again, I'll have you arrested as a terrorist." He raised his fist in the air.

Ezra was not a drinking man. After he gathered his things he went straight to the local dive, stood at the wooden bar stand and belted a couple of vodkas. When he came to the mill, he knew conditions were bad, but he hadn't realized the extent of it, nor could he understand the reluctance of the workers to get involved. How much lower could they go, he wondered, before they stood in solidarity for their rights. He lit a cigarette and guzzled a few more drinks, until the vodka and close air in the room made him woozy. He stumbled over the dirt floor to the corner of the room where he slid down the rough wooden wall boards on a bench and fell asleep. The bartender said nothing. He was used to seeing a lot worse.

The shrill blast of the factory whistle spilled forth workers from their prison into the tavern. The sour smell of spilt vodka and beer mingled with body odor and the place came alive with weary workers looking forward to their drunken evening respite.

Ezra awoke and found two men sitting beside him. One wheezed and mumbled into his drink. "Why do they torture me?" he said.

"Look at him," said an old man grinning at Ezra and showing stained rotten stubs of teeth above a bushy grey beard. "It's the same thing every day."

Ezra lit up a cigarette. "Maybe the man has his reasons." He could tell the inebriated man was not much older than himself, although he resembled a corpse.

"*Nuh*, go ahead, look at me." The young man gazed through red rimmed eyes, one wider that the other from drink, trying to focus on Ezra. "I have become a freak. I bend into a stoop, like an old man. I have only twenty-nine summers and already I am dying." He inclined his head toward the old man. "I should live like you Misha, to seventy summers, but they have robbed me of those forty summers."

"I have fifty-two," said the old man.

"Have either one of you heard about the new tax at the mill?" Ezra asked.

"The young man laughed bitterly. "Everyone knows Kuznetsov keeps a prima Dona. Bought her a golden wash basin, solid gold. That is where our tax money goes." He pointed down to the dirt floor. "My blood was spilled out for that golden basin."

"Grisha!" said the older man. "Don't be so morbid. We have a guest tonight."

"Who is morbid? I was once so strong and healthy...I thought I would live forever." Beads of clammy sweat broke out on his pale forehead. "Not too long ago, I could lift five bolts of fabric on my back. That is how I became to be this freak." He coughed and sipped some vodka to clear his throat. "And now I am just another bolt on a long shelf... like expendable merchandise, a jot in their cash receipts. His head swayed slightly from side to side; his breath sour with sickness.

The old man took out a pouch of tobacco and offered some to Ezra. They rolled it in paper, lit up and squinted as they took a drag. The little trio sat in silence. Ezra gazed vacuously at a fly circling the old man's beer glass.

Someone came in with an accordion, sat down and began to play. Soon others joined him, attempting to sing making a doleful, monotonous noise.

"Look at them," said Grisha. "Poor devils. They drink to gain some pleasure in this life, but inside they are seething with a rage they do not understand, a rage they willfully ignore. But their rage demands an outlet so they drink."

Ezra belted a few more glasses of the cheap biting liquid, burning on the way down. He grimaced and exhaled the fire. "I did stir up hope in the people, didn't I?" he said. "They began to come to me for direction. They pleaded with me to help them."

"*Nuh*, that you did. I was there. Did you know I was there?" The old man belched. "Look, there's the son-of-a-bitch now.

"What? Who?" Ezra looked around.

"Over there, he comes in here every night, has a few drinks and leaves. He don't dare make any ruckus in here."

Ezra saw the foreman standing in the corner at the bar, leaning over his drink, his head down. He sprang up from the bench, as though someone had lit a fire under his rear, and shouted loud enough so the boss could hear. "That tax was unfair, I tell you! Unfair!"

People turned around. The accordion player ceased his noisy squeezing. The foreman of the mill swaggered over to him. "You scumbag. "I thought I told you to get out of town."

Ezra stood up to him, taller in height, "Who are you to order women like dogs! You give them beggars wages and take it back in taxes and fines." He pointed to the prostitutes working the room. "These poor women were once employees of the Kuznetsov mill, earning an honorable wage. But you extracted their blood-earned kopeks in taxes and fines forcing them into the streets."

"Son-of-a-bitch. And who slept under the porch with your mother, you black ass." The mill boss braced his feet firmly on the floor and took a deep breath increasing the width of his barrel-chest. His hands were curled in fists by his sides.

Ezra flew into a rage and lurched at him, screaming. "How dare you curse my mother?"

The foreman hurled a huge fist square to the center of Ezra's face and sent him sailing across the room. The staring faces blurred and the room darkened. He tasted his own warm blood trickle down from his nose over his lips. He defied the distorted images spinning in his head, lifted himself with one arm on the table and staggered toward his opponent with clenched fists, possessed with some kind of hideous fury, like a demon beast.

The foreman took another swing at Ezra, but Ezra was quick even in his inebriated state. He dodged the swing and dealt the foreman a powerful blow to the stomach and slammed him in the jaw. The man's head snapped backward and hit the sharp corner of the wooden table. He fell unconscious. Ezra looked around. The room whirled; faces blurred. He careened toward the door. Everyone's attention had riveted to the limp body lying on the dirty floor, the head bleeding profusely from a large gash to the left side.

"Don't move him," someone cried bending over the body. "Rinse some clean towels and bring them, quick. Get a doctor! Hurry!"

Chapter 15

"Hey, one of us has got to get out of here," Daniel complained one night picking Ezra's underwear and stockings off the floor, exactly where he had stepped out of them the night before. "This space is not big enough for the two of us."

"What's wrong with you now? We always got along growing up?" Ezra said, stretched out on his bed, peering at his brother from behind a book he was reading.

"You live like a damn pig." He threw the underwear at Ezra's face.

Ezra pushed the things off, rolled to one side of the bed and leaned on his arm. "You strut around here like a damn smart ass, complain about everything, living in your pampered little world. You should only have to work from day break to dusk everyday like them poor peasants. You don't know what it's like out there."

"There's no excuse for sloppiness. I've never had a wife to pick up after me."

"Maybe if you get you mind off that countess." Ezra stuck his nose in the air, "floozy, you could find one. I can't understand why you get so excited about these hoity-toity people. They don't care about you… eventually they'll spit you out like a piece of stinky meat." He opened his fingers in a sharp gesture. "Anyway, you're wasting your time." He laid back down and gazed up at the ceiling.

"Well, you might as well forget about 'em." He added thoughtfully. "The new order of Russian people is about to dawn and a democratic republic is about to be born." He flung his fist toward the ceiling.

"Then the working men of Russia will rise up to rule over them counts and gentry. We'll confiscate the land and wealth they stole from the peasants and everyone will get a share!"

Daniel sat down on his bed by his desk. He had to remove the chair for lack of space. "You and your dirty bunch of renegades are pretty arrogant to think that you can penetrate the aristocracy and take away their land."

Ezra laughed. "You know what your problem is?" He whirled his solid legs around and sat on the edge of his bed facing his brother. "You need to get out and get interested in something else besides yourself. Why don't you use that law degree to plead on the behalf of the poor mill workers? They are desperate for someone to defend their rights as human beings. But no…you're miserable because you have become mesmerized by this capitalist society. You see, you want, but you cannot have. And you are miserable. You think it's easy for me to live with you moping around here love sick over some *shikse*."

Daniel stared at Ezra who appeared like a bull in the small room with his dominant dark eyes and a mop of curly dark hair. Even though he had a wife and four children, he probably never knew love. Maybe he was being unfair, but he never saw his brother show any kind of tenderness toward Leinha. He left her to flounder on her own, and if there were problems in the marriage he let her parents solve them. I bet Aron Weinstein regretted the day he did business with his father, he mused.

"Hey, maybe if you get me a job in that school where you're teaching, I'll have time to learn to be a gentleman!"

"You'd like that wouldn't you, so you can contaminate young minds with your foolish ideas."

"I am working hard to help the poor miserable people of Russia, groaning under the oppression of poverty and unfair levies. What good are you anyway? Running around with some countess. Sooner or later you're *gonna* bring ruin down on your uncle's household with them Jew-baiting counts, you'll see."

"And with your lawless underground activity, you will surely bring disaster to this household when you are discovered. And you will be!" he said pointing his finger at Ezra.

"If they crush us in one place, we'll spring up in another. We are the new Russian Democratic Socialist Society and we will prevail over this rotting regime because in our new world everyone will share all things in common. No man or woman will go hungry so some fat pig can sit in obscene comfort.

We, the socialists of Russia will be a glowing example to all the capitalist swine in the world. They'll see what we can achieve when we work together, and they'll shake in their boots. The miserable masses only need a little push and they'll prevail against those fat pigs, the aristocracy and the petty *bourjuis* who feed on the blood and sweat of their workers."

"That what?"

"The *bourjuis*. Those bloodsuckers who turn a blind eye to families left to die of hunger and sickness...it's a new word from France. The Frenchmen pronounce it *boosh-wee*."

Daniel thought for a moment. "I can understand your animosity toward the aristocracy. They have amassed insane wealth. Wealth that could give the people schools and hospitals. But why are you targeting the middle-class artisan who works hard to make a better life for himself and his family? Why the middle-class entrepreneur who supplies jobs? Why are you going after the professional who tend to the people's needs? Bourgeois simply means middle-class and it's pronounced boosh-wah."

"Capitalist greed doesn't make life better for anyone no matter what the class of people. Money rots a man's soul. It causes him to build a wall and separate himself from the common folk. But, he can't separate himself forever. One day the workers will rise up and say, down with private property! Power to all the people. Unto everyone his fair share!"

He gazed upward and thought for a few moments. "There is a place in our new order for everyone, doctors, lawyers, teachers, and factory workers, everyone who is willing to work together for the common good."

"Come on, Ezra. And who will pay the people's wages when everyone is working for the common good?"

"Your study of the old order is history. You wasted your time in that university. In our new people's socialist republic everyone will share all things in common. All the money earned from the production of goods will go directly to the collective who will supply everyone's needs."

"And who will work their tails off to give their hard earned money to the collective who will give it to someone who doesn't work?"

"The people." Ezra looked at Daniel incredulously. "Who do you think? Besides everyone will work and contribute to the people's democratic government which will sell the people's products and pay their wages. Simple as pie. Look, instead of sitting around being so opinionated, why don't you come to one of our meetings and open your eyes to the real world. We are forming small socialist groups until one day we will unite with the struggling workers of the world to achieve universal human rights. The entire enlightened world is marching toward the new order of the future and it is up to us to pave the way.

We have dedicated men who are behind us. Men like Presnakov and Ulinov and Martov. Brilliant men who have dedicated their lives to the new economics, and the overthrow of capitalism. Our team leader is Mark Natanson, a Jew who is known as the gatherer of Russian lands. No more separation of Jews and Gentiles, Orthodox and Catholics. We are working to obliterate cruelty and injustice where everyone will live in peace and harmony with his neighbor.

One day when we gain control of the estates, we will give the land back into the hands of the peasants who work it and the factories to the workers who slave in the sweat shops. Land and liberty to the people!

That's our slogan." He raised his fist. "Someday soon your aristocracy will be beneath us, licking our boots!"

Daniel gasped at his brother's words in astonishment. "And how is this new utopian society supposed to happen?"

"We have sympathetic listeners among the factory workers, they will lead our revolution and the peasants will fall in easily because they are by nature socialistic."

"The peasants. Socialistic?" Daniel laughed. "What makes you think these peasants will listen to you and your bunch? They are suspicious of everything and resent anyone who disturbs them with new ideas. Besides, they are loyal to their little father, the Tsar, and to their Panii, the landowners."

"That's where you're wrong." He pointed his finger at Daniel. You don't know those stupid people. They are seething inside with revenge toward the gentry who sit on their necks and whip them like beasts. All we need to do is tap into that resentment and turn it against Russian authority."

"No, you've picked the wrong candidates to usher in you new world. The peasants resent anyone who has anything of value because they are greedy themselves," said Daniel. "Haven't you lived among them long enough to know what they are like? Don't you remember the pogroms when they grabbed everything they could get their hands on? You saw how they looted everything we had. They will never understand your euphemisms. I cannot see how you can mobilize a half civilized mass to work for the common good of mankind.

And what about these petty bourgeois, are they going to put their hard earned rubbles in your dirty little hands and share equally with the greedy masses. How does your crowd plan to redistribute the wealth of the middle-class working people in this Empire, short of snatching it away by violence and bloodshed?"

"Once the peasant opens his eyes, he'll perform great executions to avenge his masters who grind him up and suck out his life's blood."

Daniel looked at his brother in alarm. He saw something in his face that he had not seen before or perhaps he had denied it.

Ezra continued, elevating his tone. "We will purge the whole structure of this *stinkin* society. The time will come when we will squash the *bourjuis* like insects…the worms that they are. All the *bourjuis* constitutions and agreements in the world will not stop us. One day our cause will overtake the world. It will continue to grow until the hour of victory, when we have vanquished all deceit, evil and greed. The day is coming when the people will lift up their heads and declare enough! We want no more. And then the power of the greedy rich will crumble and vanish from Russia, from Germany, and from all the nations."

The person inside his brother's body had suddenly become a stranger to Daniel. He spoke like someone who had been indoctrinated. "If this is your attitude and that of your comrades, then I am afraid for you, my brother. You have gotten yourself involved in the wrong crowd. Anyone who advocates violence to solve the problems of society will not find a satisfactory solution, nor will you find peace."

Ezra jumped to his feet shouting. "And I declare to you, my brother, don't be left out of our great movement, or I shall fear for you!"

Sholem pushed the door open, his eyes wide in astonishment. "I am horrified by what I am hearing. I had no idea I was harboring a rebel. You are both shouting loud enough for the whole neighborhood to hear. And look," he pointed. "The window is wide open. Daniel shut that window!"

Sholem turned to Ezra. "If I knew for one moment that you came here for the sole purpose of hunting out a nest of rebels, I would never have had you set foot in my home. You are a disgrace to your father's house and to that of your father-in-law. And you, Daniel. How long have you known about this?"

Daniel and Ezra exchanged glances. "Ezra has always been interested in liberating the poor people of Russia," he said.

"What a commendable and lofty attitude," Sholem said sarcastically. "For both of you. I want you out of here. Now! This minute!" He pointed to the door with one hand and with the other grabbed Ezra by the collar, pulling at his large fame.

Ezra started toward the door and Sholem's gaze followed him. "I suppose you don't have a passport either," he said. Ezra stood with his back toward his uncle, facing the door, his head down. "The Okhrana is always hunt for Jews without passports on the high holy days which are less than a month away now. You won't get away with this forever. They will discover your hiding place eventually."

"What about him?" Ezra turned and nodded his head in his brother's direction.

"You are both a torment to me with your new and liberal ways. I want you both out of my house." Sholem said remorsefully stroking his fingers through what was left of his hair. He turned and left the room in disgust.

Ezra got his straw satchel from under the bed and threw his things in it while Daniel began to neatly organize his books and papers. Later when Ezra left, Sholem came back into the room and said, "You know, I love Ezra as much as I love you, but I fear for him. He means well. He has a big heart for people, but he cannot seem to get his priorities in order. He is too idealistic, too quick, too young. He doesn't understand that he must get his own personal life straightened out before he can help someone else." Sholem sat down on the corner of the bed and stared at his nephew. "But…perhaps you are the one for whom I should fear most?"

Daniel studied his uncle's tired, drawn face, and for the first time he appeared much older. He wondered what he was driving at.

Sholem reached into his vest pocket and pulled out an envelope. "This looks like an invitation. It bears the name of Count Rostovsky."

Daniel gasped and his heart raced as though the golden sealed envelope contained a treasure.

"I want you to decline this invitation, whatever it is."

He could only think of Jeniya, and his thoughts must have reflected in his expression because his uncle said, "What business do you have with this count? You know he is a notorious Jew hunter and supports all the Emperor's anti-Semitic policies." Daniel turned his eyes away and did not answer. "Ah ha, I see. The girl you like is his daughter. Now I understand."

"Just because he is a member of court society, doesn't mean he's like them." Daniel tried to justify his actions. "He tries to be fair and open minded to different kinds of people. He donates to the university, the arts, schools and hospitals, which is unusual for men in his society, don't you think?"

Sholem stared at him incredulously. "I thought you were an intelligent young man. How can you be so blind? Does this family know you are a Jew?"

Daniel shook his head.

"Oy Vey!" He slapped his forehead with his palm. "Sometimes I think I am talking to a deaf and dumb man. Even a deaf and dumb man has some kind of common sense, but you!" He took a deep breath in exasperation, stood up, put his hands on his nephew's shoulders, and faced him gazing into his eyes. "You are as my own son, you know that. I am begging you this time, pleading with you, cut your ties with these people, do not bring disgrace to this house and to that of your father. If you decline this invitation now, today, it won't matter what you've told them. But if you deceive them, they will accuse you of tricking them and you will play right into their hands. These kinds of people thrive on this sort of thing, to ferret out another tricky Jew in order to confirm their prejudice."

Daniel averted his penetrating gaze, a sudden fear came over him, he wondered if Jeniya knew where he lived. "How did you get this invitation?" he asked.

"It was sent to the university and they forwarded it here. *Ny*, here is your invitation." He went toward the door, then turned and said, "Ezra is fool-hearty, but you my son, I hope you are not the fool."

Daniel gazed at the envelope and its seal for a few moments weighing his uncle's words. He thought of those last moments he spent at

Belozerkovka. Jeniya's soft kisses and warm embrace had entered his dreams and had continuously invaded his thoughts. He knew he was treading on dangerous ground and his uncle had been extremely lenient with him, but he had to see her one last time. Then he could tell her before she left for St. Petersburg and was lost to him forever. He eagerly ripped the invitation open and read it.

Chapter 16

A GREAT CHESTNUT tree stood as a sentinel near the entrance of what the Rostovskys called their "*petite maison*". Its limbs embraced a cherub motif above the portico. A footman dressed in formal attire appeared and asked him to sign a calling card which he gave to Jeniya. His heart pounded when he ascended the staircase behind the servant. He could visualize her face, waiting for arriving guests. Waiting, along with whom else? That savage looking character, what did she call him? The servant led him through the great white paneled doors into the drawing room.

Jeniya, her sister and two other young women sat on French provincial settees on each side of the fireplace. They reminded him of a Renoir painting in their pastel dresses. Jeniya wore a light blue silk dress with yellow rosebuds at the scooped neckline, and her sister, a green print dress with ruffles over the sleeves. Three young men, two in white military tunics and one in a dark suit like himself, completed the serene picture. Before the servant announced his name, all heads turned and all eyes fixed themselves upon him. He interpreted their silent gaze as critical and condescending, but in truth they regarded him with curiosity. Everyone who was anyone knew everyone else in Kiev as well as in Petersburg and they simply wondered who this newcomer was.

Jeniya immediately arose from her circle of friends, as light as a mist in her pale blue dress and held out her arms to Daniel. She linked her arm into his leading him to the eminent group. Her green eyes sparkled with pride when she introduced him to each person. Daniel felt awkward, separated by class, rank and money but at the same time, he savored the thrill of moving into high society. He had discovered through his friend Mikhail that the Rostovsky family liked to include various people from the academic and professional community at their social affairs, as long as they had something of interest to contribute to their otherwise banal company. Mikhail had also warned him that although the count prided himself as being open minded, not to over step his bounds.

The tall young man who dressed in a stylish dark suit and vest took a special interest in Daniel. Jeniya introduced him as Prince Dmitri Petrovich. He had a slight build and moved gracefully. While the two officers began to converse about military affairs in their division of the Imperial guards, the prince drew Daniel aside and looking him over through light blue eyes, confided in French, "I hate Russia, and I hate the Russian language." A footman approached offering champagne and anther with a tray of hors d'oeuvres. "I really can't wait to leave this place," he said taking a canapé in his long fingers. "Count Rostovsky is helping me to prepare for a diplomatic position in France. He knows everyone who is anyone in Paris." He took a bite of the tidbit. "Divine. I could live forever on champagne and caviar, especially these," he said admiring the work of culinary art between his fingers. "Will you have one?"

Daniel took one and stood with it in his hand, too excited to eat as Jeniya stood by him smiling.

"Did you know that Count Rostovsky has one of the best chefs in the Empire? I understand he took him from one of the finest clubs in Paris, isn't that right, Jenka?" He glanced in her direction.

Daniel nodded politely and smiled. He had only gathered about half of what the prince had said. Someone was playing Rimsky-Korsakov's Scheherazade on the piano. He looked around the room but saw no one, then he realized the melody must have come from an adjoining parlor. The music, along with everything about the room created a soothing ambiance. Impressionist paintings hung on blue Wedgwood paneled walls and the oriental carpets had peach and cream floral patterns. Someone must have an affinity for blues and creamy whites because the colors predominated both homes and were exquisitely coordinated.

A footman appeared at the great white paneled doors and three more guests entered the room. Everyone smiled and greeted them enthusiastically. The young man, Anatole Konstantinovich Urassov proudly wore the uniform of the prestigious Preobrazhensky regiment and the two striking young women beside him, were evidently well known by this group and well liked. The tall officer had large deep set brown eyes and a prominent classic nose. The dark green uniform with the wide white belt and double row of gold buttons as well as the erect manner in which he carried himself made him appear handsome. Somewhere Daniel had remembered seeing a picture of Alexander I wearing the same uniform after his triumph over Napoleon. Jeniya received the trio graciously and from the fondness in their eyes, he perceived that she and the young man were well acquainted. One of the young women at Anatole's side, whom he surmised to be his sister, had the same large dark eyes and long nose, and carried herself as a great beauty. She tossed a coquettish glance in his direction. He also noticed that Jeniya saw it.

The conversation around the fireside took on an easy, friendly tone but Daniel could not relax observing Jeniya and Anatole standing aside laughing together. Another young officer swaggered into the room. He was strikingly handsome and at the same time homely. His Mongolian ancestry was evident in the wide cheek bones and piercing grey eyes which had a hard mocking gaze that could send daggers through a man. His dark wavy hair fell just above his collar. Everyone smiled and greeted him, not in the same easy way as Anatole, but rather in awe. He sauntered around the group in a merry disposition until he spotted Daniel and his grin faded. He expressed neither a look of rivalry, nor contempt, nor even familiarity, but Daniel would never forget his face.

His eyes hid deep mysterious thoughts, and at the same time a flirtatious charm which he directed to the ladies, especially Jeniya.

Neither would he forget the uniform, the blue jacket with a red mandarin collar and the dark blue trousers with a single red strip down each leg, symbolizing democracy. Daniel laughed to himself at the irony. The Kazaks bargained away their freedom to serve the oppressive Romanov monarchy in exchange for land and wealth. Yes, it was him all right. Vadim had come to the party after all.

Vadim didn't dwell on Daniel for long. He was quickly drawn into a debate with the other officers as to which regiment was the greatest in the Empire. They made fun of the Chevalier-guard's massive silver helmets surmounted with a golden eagle which they wore at formal affaires. "But you must remember gentlemen, that we are hand-picked of the Tsar," said one of the officers of high noble birth.

Yelizaveta smiled and said to the young men. "If I knew you *chellevekii* would be jealous of one another, I would have invited all Preobrazhensky guards." She gave Anatole a flirtatious wink and then one to Vadim. "Or maybe Kazaks?"

"Ah, but there is no contest," said one of the guards, his eyes twinkling at her. "We already have them out numbered." They all laughed.

"Those Kazaks just think they're the best of the Tsar's regiments but they really have no class. Don't you agree?" said the prince inclining his head to Daniel.

Daniel began to wonder if he were playing the fool's game as his uncle suggested. Was Jeniya toying with his heart as a seasonal amusement to be discarded when she went off to those Petersburg parties? Were her vows of love nothing more than the fantasies of an adolescent romantic and as unpredictable as the autumn weather? Were they all just spoiled rich kids as Mikhail suggested, playing with some new and interesting toy to perk up their summertime ennui? His grandfather's alarming words sprang into his mind. *They will use you and throw you out, like last week's garbage.*

He looked at the prince who tossed him a salacious glance. In less than two hours he climbed the ladder of society from the count to a relative of the legendary Tsar Alexander III, a giant who some say could crush a man's skull in his great fist, although his inner sense told him the prince had devious motives behind his lily white hand of friendship. *I have to be out of my mind. This is mishuga!*

The footmen offered another round of drinks and canapés. Vadim took a goblet of vodka from the silver tray and raised it for a toast.

"I raise a toast to the most beautiful women in all the Empire."

"I'll drink to that," chimed the men in agreement, each taking a goblet. They all lifted their drinks and said, "*Za zdaroviye.*"

Vadim gulped the fiery liquid down and sauntered over to Daniel.

"*Dobre vecher*, I am Vadim Pavelovich Rodzianko."

"*Kak pazhiivayete*, Daniel Nathanovich Mendelev."

"Mendelov?" The Kazak paused, his gaze never leaving Daniel. "The name sounds familiar. Have I met you before?"

"Possibly, I saw you at Count Rostovsky's party."

"Ah, yes. Now I remember you." Vadim said without showing any emotion at having discovered a past rival. Nor did he display any expression of hostility or jealousy in remembering the occasion. He simply frowned showing little lines between his brows, as trying to recall something else from the past. Not being able to congeal his thoughts nor refresh his memory, he added in a slightly arrogant tone. "I hear you are a student at Kiev University."

Daniel could not detect if the glare in his gray eyes was his normal expression. He finally decided that his attitude was not one so much of haughtiness but of the natural male supremacy over another male when competing for the female of choice, like the dominating cock defending his hens.

"Yes, I am about to take my final exams for admission to the bar."

Vadim raised his eye brows. He seemed impressed. But then he frowned and scrutinized Daniel all the more. "I hear that only extremely bright fellows or those with political pull get into law school at Kiev University."

Daniel smiled. He made no attempt to announce his intellectual prowess before this man with a war-like countenance.

Jeniya walked toward them. Both gentlemen bowed. She slipped her arm into Daniel's and drew him to her side. If she was uneasy she did not show it.

They were about to take a seat, when a female voice rose to a sudden high pitch. "Yes, it's true! I'm certain it's true," said a young woman who had been defending herself while the men laughed.

"What's true?" Jeniya injected.

"Our head housekeeper's niece was mute and she had been healed at the icon of the weeping Virgin," Nadia explained. The petite girl with pretty round eyes and buck teeth had developed an out-going personality to compensate for her one physical misfortune.

"She believes that stuff," laughed one of the guards.

"Well," Nadia continued, "I also doubted it at first, so I asked the housekeeper to invite her niece for tea so I could ask her for myself. And she told me that she hadn't spoken since she was a child."

"You actually had tea with a servant girl?" the prince interrupted. "My, my. What is this world coming to?"

"Yes!" Nadia answered emphatically. "Why anyone could see this girl was telling the truth, she exhibited so much exuberance and happiness. She told me she touched the tears of the Virgin and rubbed them on her throat, and from that instant on she could speak!"

The men laughed. "That's impossible!" said one of the guards. "The priests perform all sorts of magic to fleece the gullible peasants. One of these unscrupulous monks sold our coachmen an amulet containing the tooth of St. Joachim, and he paid a month's wage for it."

"I once saw a priest selling the colored tail feathers of the Holy Ghost," said Daniel. Why do people spend their hard earned rubbles on such things?"

"The feathers are supposed to chase away the evil spirits," Anatole said chuckling.

"You people are terrible," Nadia said. "Suppose one of you were mute or crippled?"

"If I were mute," replied one of the guards. "I wouldn't have to salute a colonel every time I met one on the street and say, certainly so, Your Shining High Well Born, or bow to a commander and say, in no wise so, Your Becoming Brighter Super Excellency."

The girls were not impressed, but the officers laughed themselves to tears.

"No doubt she was telling the truth." All eyes turned to Daniel. "As she saw it. She may have suffered from a trauma early in her life and lost her voice. It is not unusual for people to temporarily lose their ability to speak under some great stress." A young woman came to his mind who had become mute after being brutally raped during the pogrom. "Later," he explained. "In a more relaxed atmosphere or under the spell of a deeply touching spiritual experience, as no doubt was the case of this servant girl, the person will regain the ability to speak."

The others gazed at him, greatly impressed with his eloquence and knowledge.

When the footman announced dinner, Jeniya looked proudly at Daniel and took his arm. Everyone else paired off and proceeded into the dining room where a large Austrian crystal chandelier hung over the center of the table. Jeniya wisely sat Vadim at the other end of the table from Daniel whom she placed between herself and the prince, but Anatole sat opposite and his eyes never left Daniel or Jeniya.

Daniel marveled over the elegant supper. It seemed like a battalion of footman swarmed over the table serving each masterpiece of culinary art on Danish Flora Danica china. The wine Stuart poured wine and vodka into blue and gold Bohemian crystal.

"Do you know anything about the recent murder in Kuznetsov's mill?" Anatole asked Vadim.

"No more than you do. I'm not working on that case. I have been investigating the infiltration of Marxist tutors into the estates. Seems to becoming quite a problem."

"*Mon Dieu!*" cried Nadia with alarm in her eyes. "My father just hired a new tutor for my two younger brothers."

"Don't fret you pretty self over it," said Vadim. "Reports have been spotty. So far we have only uncovered two suspects. But we'll put a tracer on him, if you'd like. Right now we are advising people not to be upset but to keep close supervision over their children's servants."

"The pheasant is divine," said the prince, poking and pushing the beautiful creation with his fork, trying to decipher the ingredients. "I must have this recipe for our cook."

"How can we tell whether or not a tutor is a Marxist socialist?" asked Nadia.

"Get an English tutor," replied the prince.

"These days everyone is suspect," said Vadim. "These people will not be wearing their political persuasions on their shirt sleeves. They will be extremely congenial to the opinions of their employers. The time has come when we can no longer turn our eyes and simply trust our servants or our employees."

It took Daniel a while to connect Kuznetsov's mill…murder…and Ezra suddenly leaving his job without an explanation, but when he put it together, he felt someone had pierced him with an arrow. "Was this man a new employee at the factory?" he said.

The conversation ceased, and everyone's eyes riveted on him. He didn't realize his comment was out of context with the sequence of the conversation; so intent was he to discover if Ezra was the killer.

From that moment on the Kazak's trained eye was on him.

"Was the murder an isolated incident or was it part of a planned organization?" asked Anatole's sister in defense of Daniel.

"I don't think it was isolated," replied Vadim gazing at Daniel. "We know there is a violent revolutionary group working here in the city but they move their meetings from place to place and we cannot get our hands on them."

"Does anyone know who they are?" asked Anatole. "They say the Jews are in back of this."

"They are," said Vadim. "Both Jew and Russian. But the Jews are the instigators."

Daniel blanched. The glorious desert with swirls of raspberry sauce around fresh peaches and ice cream, nauseated him. He hoped it was not Ezra, but in his heart he knew.

Vadim jotted Daniel's name down on his little note pad. It bothered him that the name stood out in his mind and he could not rest until he discovered why. Early the next morning he went to the bureau of the Okhrana and searched their files.

"Ah ha! There it is!" he said to himself. "Mendelev, Ezra Nathanovich...wanted for murder...the foreman at Kuznetsov's mill. Race, Jewish." His address was given at the mill. He was also accused of being an illegal alien in the city of Kiev as well as a populist terrorist. There was nothing on Daniel in the files, neither was there anything more written on Ezra except his description.

Vadim's curiosity was killing him now. He had a hunch. He went from the police station to the department of immigration and searched their files.

"Yes! There it is! Mendelev, Daniel Nathanovich. Immigration permit no. 7014. Race, Jewish. Reason for entry, student at Kiev University." His domicile was given as well as the address of the academy where he worked.

So, Vadim thought, grinning to himself. "He is a Jew! An infiltrator! Why that dirty dog!"

He immediately went to the general of the gendarmes with his information.

Chapter 17

A SWEET PERFUME drifted from the gardens. No impressionist painter could have captured the living colors of the roses, carnations, marigolds, sweet alyssum and purple verbena. In the distance, the domes of the Lavra Monastery and great bell tower dominated the skyline and glistened like golden sugar drops above the Dnieper. Here and there timber rafts appeared as floating brown specks in the wide river.

Jeniya found a seat under a chestnut tree, folded her umbrella and gazed at the fountain, allowing the hypnotic tapping of the water soothe her anxious heart, hoping that Daniel would show up. The ornate sand colored houses with hipped roofs and black iron balconies reminded her of the fashionable addresses in Paris. She wondered if Daniel had an apartment in one of those classic two story homes, or did his father, the textile merchant?

Pigeons gathered around her bench on the winding red brick walk, tilting their heads, eyeing her. "No, she said, I don't have anything for you to eat." She wistfully gazed at students from the university, strolling through the park, some hand in hand with their sweethearts, laughing and enjoying the beautiful afternoon.

She had accompanied her parents to the city that afternoon. Her mother thought the walls of their St. Petersburg home filled with family portraits and classical paintings needed a splash of bold color from the new avant-garde works of Matisse and Toulouse-Lautrec so the Count took his wife and his pocketbook along to a traveling art auction from Paris. Actually, it was an excuse for him to give his city friends a dinner party at their *petite maison* in Kiev.

"*Bonjour, mademoiselle.*"

Jeniya looked up, startled. Her heart leaped. A sudden flash of heat rushed to her face.

"Is your family still at the auction?" Daniel said awkwardly.

"Yes, I thought it would give us an opportunity to do something together this afternoon."

"You look as though you could have stepped out of an impressionist painting yourself," he said gazing at her pretty face beneath a white hat tilted slightly on her forehead. Lilacs adorned the crown and complemented the high buttoned bodice of her lavender dress belted at her small waist.

She lowered her eyes and smiled.

A shadow of concern fell over Daniel's happy encounter. Finally, he said, "who is Vadim?"

"Vadim?" The image of Vadim popped up like a dead fly floating in her favorite soup.

"Is he your boyfriend?"

"Ah him." She gazed down at the little pattern in the fabric of her skirt. "He's just a good friend of the family. None of us would ever consider him as an appropriate suitor. My father would never approve… ah." She gazed up at Daniel and realized that in her clumsy attempt to explain, she made a blunder when she detected a look of rejection in his eyes.

"Why wouldn't your father approve?"

"He's a Kazak, a military man from a military family, dedicated to defending Russia and the Tsar. Their wives and children come second." She could not tell what thoughts were running through his mind from the frown between his brows. She wondered what women he had been with. "Do you have a girl friend?" she asked.

He smiled. "I don't have anyone."

A tension began to grow between them, both from excitement and from insecurity.

"Would you like to go for a walk?" he suggested.

She grinned and nodded.

"What would your father say if he knew you were walking off with a stranger?"

She smiled. "I don't consider you a stranger, although in a way I suppose you are."

They strolled quietly beneath the shady branches of the chestnut trees as though the slightest sound might shatter the fragile new love that had taken root in their hearts.

"Look," he said pointing toward the *Chateau de Fleurs*. "A carousel." They listened for the faint music in the distance. "Would you like to take a ride?"

"Yes!" she said with child-like laughter in her voice. "You know, when I was little, papa used to take my sisters and me to this park and he would ride the carousel with us. We all wanted to sit on his lap."

"Come on then, when we get to the carousel you can sit on my lap."

"All right." She giggled.

He gave the man a kopeck and took her hand to help her up onto the platform. After he sat comfortably on the gaily painted horse, he held her waist with both hands and lifted her onto his lap, holding her in his arms. She felt the magical pleasure that compels two lovers to become one, as though nothing more was needed to live in this world. She gazed down at his hand gently pressing her body to his own and placed her hand over it, feeling his protective strength. The scent of his cologne spelled handsome. She thought neither of the longings of yesterday nor the uncertainties of tomorrow, but only wanted to laugh and live in that joyful musical moment forever.

When the carousel stopped, they walked hand in hand lost in happiness until the mid-afternoon chimes of the city's cathedrals jolted Jeniya's dream world back into the reality of her obligations. "I have to go," she said suddenly. "My family will be calling the Okhrana to search for me."

"They'll what?"

"I am not joking!"

"Then let me walk you back to the auction house."

"All right, but we must hurry."

On the way back she invited him to her father's dinner party tonight. When he declined, she invited him to the estate to celebrate the annual harvest festival with the peasants. "Please come and be my escort, this is a very special occasion for us and I know you will enjoy it."

The carriage hastened along the dirt road ahead of a cloud of dust, Daniel's heart beat accelerated until it kept time with the trotting horses. He looked out over the vast fields of wheat that had been harvested and tied into sheaves cutting stark lines across the many golden fields, and marveled at the wealth of one family. Above the meadows, pale clouds swelled into the hazy August sky.

His palms grew sweaty thinking about the aristocrats who lived there, but families are part of the deal and one must recon with them. With his grandfather's dire words still lingering in his head, he had resolved to tell Jeniya, the truth about himself. However, when he stood below the white Doric pillars on the veranda of the stately mansion, apprehension loomed over his resolution.

I must be a crazy man. Tell these people I am a Jew. A Jew has come to court your daughter, Mister Count, gaspaja Ambassador to France, your Excellency, Grand Marshall of the Aristocracy? I must tell her good-by. Today!

A sweat broke out on his forehead. The air hung heavy and still in the summer heat. He ascended the stone steps of the portico, brushed the dust from his new white jacket and ran a hand over his hair to smooth it down. It took all his courage to stand before the great carved double doors, slip his fingers into one of the large solid brass rings and knock. Almost immediately, the footman opened the door and told him he would find the countess Jeniya near the stables. He pointed the way.

Daniel descended the hill through the meticulously maintained grounds leading to the stables. On the way, under a clump of shade trees, he saw men and women in a flurry of activity. Matrons wearing full skirts and gingham blouses, with colorful scarves wrapped around their heads, were busy slicing tomatoes and cucumbers and arranging platters of prune and poppy seed cakes. *Starushkii* dressed in the tradition of their ancestors, with long dark skirts, hand woven hemp blouses and black boots sat in groups gossiping. They untied their dark babushkas and left them open to cool their gray heads.

The matrons worked quietly with sober faces, but every now and then someone would make a comment and the others would laugh light heartedly, flashing semi-toothless grins. The maidens celebrated the tradition by weaving floral wreaths which they would place on their heads for the festive ceremony. Their hair was combed back into long braids with colorful satin bows tied at the end.

The men hammered trestles together over which they placed large flat planks to be used as tables and benches. Others brought in large wooden barrels. He knew the count liked his vodka, but he couldn't imagine any group of people drinking that much at a picnic. He also thought it a peculiar place to entertain his guests.

He saw that the peasants paid no attention, so continued down the hill to the stables and found Jeniya inside dressed in a high buttoned white blouse with leg-o-mouton sleeves, riding boots and a long dark skirt. Her brown hair was loosely braided in the same fashion as the peasant girls. She was stroking a sleek chestnut mare. The animals coat gleamed as though it had been polished into a high gloss. She didn't see him come in.

"Jeniya?" he called.

"*Zdrastvooyte?*" she called back turning to see who was there. A broad smile brightened her face. "Daniel! she said. "I am so happy to see you. I didn't know if you would come so I decided to take Vasha out for some exercise."

"Doesn't your battalion of grooms take care of that?" he asked stepping closer.

"What?"

He stood beside her and admired her beauty. A beam of sunlight streamed through the small window and lit her large eyes rendering them emerald green.

"Oh," she said, turning nervously from his gaze to the horse and stroked Vasha's velvety muzzle. "She loves affection. Here, pet her nose, see how soft it is."

Daniel lifted his hand to touch Vasha's muzzle. With a start, the horse jerked her head backward revealing her teeth and the whites of her dark eyes. Daniel simultaneously snapped his hand back in fear of the majestic animal.

While Daniel was dealing with the horse, Jeniya was dealing with her own emotions. Before she knew it he was staring into her eyes. She tried to ignore the dizzy, overcoming weakness. "Would you like to go riding this afternoon?" she asked.

He lifted her face and brushed his lips softly to hers. "Do you?" he whispered "Have a gentle horse?"

"N…ah…I think…" Her body began to respond in ways she had not known. She felt his hard slender thigh move against hers. She cautiously raised her hands to his neck, fearing the faint desire that was rising up within her body, and slowly released herself into his arms. He kissed her gently.

"My lady countess," called a husky voice from the entrance of the stable. Jeniya lurched backward, pushing Daniel away. The head housekeeper, Georgiana Ivanova's bulky frame blocked the view from the partially opened door and her broad boned face was in the shadows, but Jeniya could see the shock and indignation in her expression as though she was standing in the bright sunlight.

"Yes? What is it?" she said brushing some dangling strands of hair back with her hand.

"I saw you enter the barn, but you didn't come out. I wanted to see if something was wrong." Her wily tone indicated that she knew exactly what was going on. Georgina Ivanova's eyes were everywhere and she never missed anything that went on around the estate.

"No, Georgiana, nothing's wrong." She glanced up at Daniel. Vasha had nuzzled up to him and was resting her long face on his broad shoulder. "See, she likes you after all." She whispered to her friend.

Georgiana stood there a few moments with her hands on her hips before she went back outside.

"What are the peasants doing out there?" he asked.

"They are setting up for the festival this afternoon." She took a deep breath to regain her composure.

"Festival?"

"Yes, today is the festival of the harvest. I thought it would be interesting for you to share a bit of country life with us." She smiled.

He was also smiling. "I'm delighted that you thought of me this afternoon."

"And I am so glad you could come. I've missed you…" she murmured looking at him, hoping he would give her some indication that he missed seeing her as much as she missed him.

Daniel knew what she wanted to hear. He wanted to tell her of his dilemma and how much he agonized over their relationship, or how the precious time they shared together in Kiev had occupied his thoughts for the past two weeks.

She was staring at him intensely. But when he gazed back into the wide searching green eyes, he was grasping for words to tell her the truth about himself. He took a deep breath to relieve the building tension and said, "I care for you very much, Jeniya, more than you know. There hasn't been a day that has gone by that I have not thought of you," he said sincerely. "But our worlds are so different, I wonder if you can understand that, if you could accept that?"

"Oh yes, Daniel. I fully understand, but that shouldn't matter. We can find a way together. Love always finds a way..." She blushed. "Ah...I...ah." She quickly changed the subject. "We have the whole day to spend together, what would you like to do?" When he hesitated to respond, she said, "we can do whatever you wish."

She blushed again. "Ah, I mean like boating on the lake, tennis, horseback riding?"

"Where is your family? Aren't they hosting this festival?"

"Where is your family? Aren't they hosting this festival?"

"My father is away on business at one of his sugar mills and my sisters and their dates are wandering around somewhere."

"I thought it was beneath the gentry to become involved in industrial matters."

She laughed. "Yes, many believe this, but my father says that is why they are losing their estates as well as their fortunes to clever enterprising peasants."

Hmm...he has reason here. No wonder the count is the most powerful man in the province.

"Well what would you like to do?"

He didn't know how to play tennis, and he had never ridden a horse. He considered his new spotlessly white jacket. "Why don't we take a walk?"

"Walk? Only peasants walk around here. Why don't we go riding?"

"Boat riding?"

She smiled. They gazed at each other, flirtatiously yet shyly, their eyes locked and lost in time until all thoughts had vanished, save the melding pleasure of their closeness. Daniel reached for her hand and held it gently and protectively in his own strong hand.

Together they walked up the hill, hand in hand, reveling in the fragile tenderness, careful not to project beyond the moment, lest it be shattered. They strode through the woodlands. Daniel pointed to the hundreds of mushrooms growing in the cool moss. "I have never seen so many," he said in amazement.

"They are ready for picking," Jeniya said. "Sometime soon we will have a mushroom picking party, before the peasant girls sneak in here and pick them all for themselves. More than once we've caught them with their baskets full, cleaning out the crop."

"What's wrong with letting peasant girls pick your mushrooms? There are enough in these woods to feed the whole city of Kiev."

"That's not the point," she said. "You give them license in a small matter and soon they'll have no respect for your property. Next thing you know they'll be bringing their animals to graze on our best pastures"

He looked at her incredulously. "There are ample meadows here to graze the Emperor's cavalry, and no one would notice them."

She flashed her eyes at him. "That's not the point. You don't understand how it is here, because you come from the city. We have to draw lines of discipline. You cannot imagine how we have to contend with these people and their clever schemes to take advantage of us."

He saw that this conversation had hit a sore spot. It had to happen sooner or later, the insane breach between rich and poor. No wonder Ezra's crowd was filled with vengeance. It came from frustration. Could it ever be resolved in this Empire? A life of wealth and ease appealed to him but not with the price of injustice. Even though this incident amounted to not more than a drop, he began to fear the gap between them may be broader than an ocean. He thought they had shared a kindred spirit, but for the first time he saw that her opinions were not only opposite from his, but unreasonable as well.

"Why did you go the Kishnaikov's party?" He was curious to know what someone with her antiquated biased opinions was doing at a progressive meeting.

"I wanted to see the new machine," she replied in a questioning tone.

He raised his dark eyebrows. "A beautiful young woman like you interested in farm machinery? Truly?"

"Yes! And why not?" She frowned. "And...why did you go to Kishnaikov's party?"

"Mikhail is my good friend."

"Well, he and his crowd certainly don't know a thing about the nature of peasants or running a large estate. We don thing the old way here, the right way. Not like those nouveau rich landlords who rent land to the *moujikii* and then let them fend for themselves."

"And become one of those nouveau rich enterprising peasants?"

She scrutinized him with a sudden suspicious look. "You don't understand. We look after all their needs. We buy their farming tools, supply material to sew their clothing, and many other things. The Kishnaikov's and their kind think we have tied our peasants to serfdom while they are liberating theirs. But in truth, their *moujikii* are worse off than ours, especially with taxes on grain going up every year. And if there is a bad year, which sometimes happens here, our peasants will have bread to eat, they will not have to use their last ruble to pay taxes because we pay it all. If we can increase our grain production, our peasants will be better off than anyone's. That is why I went to see the machine. Besides, the *moujikii* are not bound to us, they can do as they wish, but they do not leave because they know they are well off here, since we do everything for them."

"Your family is truly benevolent."

She glared at him with a hard opinionated expression, and at the same time she appeared so young and naïve. He couldn't help but smile. He admired her courage, her audacity, in discovering her fledging independence, and especially her strong will.

"Why do you take such an interest in this place? It's not customary for young noble women to be so absorbed in the business of an estate, is it?"

"Ah hah, you think I should be out husband hunting, don't you? Well, my grandmother owns this estate...and she runs it! She loves it and so do I."

Jeniya quietly gazed over the meadows to the river. Her voice softened as she spoke of Belozerkovka. "I love these green hills along the river. In the spring when it rains and the snow melts, the river swells so wide in some places it seems impossible for a gull to fly across it. The poet, Gogol, once wrote; 'there is no bird that can fly across the great Dnieper.' And in the autumn, when the rains cease, I love to see the long white sandy beaches." Sometimes, the flat bottom barges get stuck in the sand for days until the boatmen drag them loose. She paused and thought for a moment. "In Petersburg, the land is flat and swampy, not like this. The days are dreary and the people are somber. Here it is sunny. When you walk down the streets of Kiev, the people tip their hats and smile. In the north a person will smile because he has recalled something pleasant, but here in the south, people smile because they feel like it. Oh, Petersburg is all right for a change but I have never really liked it there."

"So, will you be going to Petersburg for the winter?"

"Yes, my coming out party will be in January. Would you like to attend? It will be at the Winter Palace."

Daniel was speechless. The Palace of Tsar Alexander III. When he did not answer, she went on. "I can get you an invitation. It will be wonderful." She laughed in sharing her big day with him. "The Winter Palace is the biggest and most beautiful palace in all the world. And its walls are covered with the greatest art in all the world. I would love for you to be there and see it."

As the afternoon shadows began to grow, they heard a chorus of men and women singing in the distance. Daniel looked around inquisitively.

"The peasants are coming to celebrate the feast of the harvest wreath. Come on, hurry. My grandmother will kill me if I'm not there to meet them when they come into the gate."

They ran up the path to the mansion until they were both out of breath. They saw that everyone had assembled on the expansive front lawn, and were shifting about to take their places. Jeniya took a deep sigh of relief that the ceremony hadn't started. She told Daniel to stand on the sidelines with the other guests, and members of the extended family. She went to the front of the house and stood on the portico next to her mother, grandmother, and two sisters. From under her parasol, Zinaida scanned her daughter's appearance with a look of disapproval and the dowager countess shot a glance of indignation of what she considered to be a spectacle. Her two sisters whispered to one another, their pastel dresses blowing slightly in the summer breeze, their faces alight with query and whim, expressing the desire to have spent the afternoon in Jeniya's shoes.

In a few minutes they heard a chorus of voices in the distance. About eighty men and women appeared walking up the roadway lined by evergreens and shade trees. They entered the open gates and a delegation of several peasant women stepped forward into the yard and stood in front of two white Corinthian pillars. They wore white blouses with red embroidery and long royal blue skirts embellished in elaborate needlework of floral designs, with red sashes tied at their waists. Garlands woven of corn husks, fresh poppies, and cornflowers adorned the younger women's heads and they all held sheaves of wheat in their arms which they presented to the family. The men were also decked out in festive white *rubashkas* embroidered in red patterns, and full dark blue trousers tucked into their best black leather boots.

The Rostovsky family advanced to meet the peasants in the yard as the men and women sang another chorus. Svetchin, the overseer of the estate, stepped forward and stood in front of the family holding a wreath woven from dried ears of corn, paper flowers and ribbons. In song, he asked for good health to the masters of the household and for prosperity in the next year's harvest. Then all the peasants knelt before Jeniya's grandmother, the grand matriarch of Belozerkovka. She dressed in the traditional style of an elderly Russian widow, with a black jacket pleated at the waist and buttoned to the neck, over a long black skirt. Small golden loop earrings adorned her ears. Svetchin then presented her with the wreath.

She accepted the gift and kissed him on one cheek, then the other, and again. She gave the wreath to a servant who brought it inside and laid it on a special table in the dining room where it would remain until next April, when an orthodox priest would then consecrate it in the fields.

The procession of peasants and the sight of the harvest wreath provoked painful memories for Daniel. It happened on the day he decided to deliver Maria Kerenskaya's lace curtains. He saw her walking in the fields behind a priest in full liturgical vestments. He carried an ornate cross and she held the wreath. The family followed, and behind them, the peasants who served on the estate. Suddenly, everything began to flash through his mind in an instant, Maria beating the wreath until the kernels of corn fell to the ground where it would be the first seed to be planted, the horrible nightmare in the days that followed, the black crosses painted on the fence posts. His thoughts reeled in a daze until he saw silver coins gleaming in the afternoon sunlight and it jolted him back to Belozerkovka. Jeniya's grandmother had put a coin in each peasant's hand. Afterwards, the family and guests remained behind and the dowager countess led the procession down to the celebration feast.

"Jenka," her mother scolded. "Why didn't you and your young man join us for tea this afternoon?" Her eyes critically scanning Daniel.

"I forgot mama. I went riding and then we walked to the lake and the time completely slipped away."

"I had hoped you would have been more thoughtful of your family. We all wanted to meet your young man today." She forced a smile toward Daniel.

"I'm sorry mama." She paused. "You remember Daniel Nathanovich from the dance."

"Yes, of course I do," she smiled politely. "Did you have a nice day with us, Daniel?"

"Yes, my lady countess, very nice. Thank you for your kind invitation."

She nodded graciously and turned toward the house.

Daniel shuttered. The warnings of his uncle had now lodged in his mind.

"We can do whatever we like now, until dinner. I think my sister Yelizaveta and her boyfriend are playing tennis this afternoon, would you like to join them?"

"No, not really."

Jeniya thought for a few moments. "Would you like to come down to the park and watch the rest of the ceremony, I think you would really enjoy it as it only happens once a year."

He nodded. His good instinct told him he should pay his respects and run, but instead he followed her behind the procession still dazed from all that had happened.

The succulent aroma of smoked meat pervaded the atmosphere and triggered his hunger. He saw a long table amply laden with loafs of bread shaped like large brown platters, fruit, freshly chopped cucumbers and tomatoes, cabbage and potato salad, pinwheels of smoked bacon, ham and plump sausages, sauerkraut, barrels of beer, and one of vodka.

"We can sit here and watch," Jeniya said. They sat down on the hill above the festivities.

The men, women and children gathered around the old countess who stood at the center table. She raised a glass of vodka and proposed a toast for everyone's good health and prosperity. The peasants did the same, lifting their glasses to return the toast and to wish her another productive harvest.

"Za zdaroviye." The old countess replied in acceptance, sealing her pleasure by drinking the glass of vodka.

"Za zdaroviye." They all said in unison and drank. She made the sign of the cross and excused herself.

"Why doesn't anyone else in your family join the festivities?"

"We never associate with the peasantry, never. This party is given in their honor."

"Doesn't Christ teach that all people are to be treated equal and not to exclude someone because he is of a lesser class?"

She tucked her knees up to her chest, wrapped her arms around them, and gazed at him with an odd expression "Are you Orthodox?" she asked with a hint of suspicion.

She had him on the spot. *Now is the time to tell her.* The Divine had opened the way and led him into it. What did she think of Jewish people, he suddenly wondered? After what he had just been through with her mother, he didn't want to know. He couldn't think anymore. The day's heat wore on him and he took out his handkerchief and wiped his brow.

She was staring at him, puzzled, waiting for an answer but he made none.

Just then a roar went up from the party. Three gypsy musicians had arrived, two fiddlers and a man with an accordion, a homely threesome with swarthy pocked and marred skin. When they struck up a lively *csárdás*, some of the younger men got up and began to dance, mimicking the Kazaks with difficult whirling and leaping movements, while the elders sat along the side lines clapping and whistling.

"Look," said Jeniya. "They're good."

Daniel was happy she had a short attention span but he was only half interested in the entertainment. In silence, he watched the sun go down behind the river, transforming it into a wide silver ribbon. He twisted a blade of grass between his fingers, tossing his grandfather's words in his mind. *You must tell her who you are or cut your ties...cut your ties.* Finally, he said rising, "Jeniya, I've got to leave you now."

She gazed up at him. "Oh, no! You mustn't leave now. The evening is just starting. Besides you haven't met my sisters yet and we have nice things planned for this evening. You can leave tomorrow morning, after breakfast."

"No Jeniya, it's a long way back to Kiev." She appeared as sweet and fragrant after a long sultry day as when she had just stepped out of her morning bath.

"Wouldn't it be better to travel in the morning?" Besides, our chef is preparing a wonderful supper."

"As much as I would like to stay, I need to go home this evening."

She turned away and stared into the night. "Well…" she said coolly with a tone of rejection. "I hope you enjoyed the day…At least let me get you a sandwich to take with you."

He saw that she could not conceal the feelings of love she had for him, nor could she hide her disappointment. He felt lower than a schlemiel. He sat down and put his arm around her shoulders, drawing her to his side and kissed her on the forehead. "Believe me," he said. "I want to stay more than anything, but…." Now was his opening, all he had to do was tell her, then he could stay, and in the morning he could tell his uncle the good news, or…maybe the wrath of her family would fall on his head causing him to leave in humiliation. He would either win her or lose her forever.

"But?"

He searched her longing gaze and his heart ached. She was so vulnerable sitting there in the moonlight. Although, he was also exploding with passion, he didn't want to betray her trust. The risk of the family's wrath would be beyond his imagination. He thought of his beautiful sister, Rochelle. He believed he would kill any man who violated her. Even if the secret were concealed, the marriage bed would be inspected on the wedding night and the truth would be revealed. The bride would be returned to her father's house in disgrace, where she would be forced to live in humiliation as a spinster for the rest of her life. As he would want a man to honor his sister, then he needed respect the woman he loved.

"Jeniya, I love you. You are my first and only love." He said struggling to find the words he so desperately wanted to share with her to relieve the agony pulling at his heart, and do what was right by her family and his.

She looked into his eyes and whispered, "I love you too." She slipped her arms around his neck and trembled as his mouth came down on hers with a hunger that matched her own.

Chapter 18

IN A DREAMY stupor Daniel heard the jingle of spurs outside his window, the midnight alarm which instilled dread in every Jew who lived in the Kiev ghetto.

He heard his uncle say in a cracked uneven tone. "Who is there?"

"Open up Jew," came the course reply.

A raid! Daniel's heart pounded. *What did the authorities want? Everyone's papers were in order here. Certainly, they had not come to snatch away his uncle. Sholem was careful to keep his nose meticulously clean. Were they looking for Ezra? That renegade was long gone. Or was someone else behind this? Jeniya? Count Rostovsky? What had he done to them?*

He knew the authorities were after him. He grabbed a shirt and stumbled into his trousers on his way into the dining room. He would turn himself over to his interrogators and suffer the consequences, in order to spare his uncle any more trouble.

A tall gray figure tumultuously pushed his bulk through the doorway, followed by the odor of wet wool and two gendarmes, the typically nondescript lackeys, except that they made a big presence in the small room. "No one you expected, eh?" sneered the district police commissioner. Daniel had identified him from the red insignia on his lamb's wool hat.

Sholem's voice quivered in an attempt to rebuke them. "This is an outrage! You break into a man's home in the middle of the night when everyone's asleep. What do you want here?"

The police commissioner swaggered toward Sholem and squared his large shoulders to emphasize his intimidation. "Stop grumbling you old Jew," he said. "Can't you see this is a round-up. I have to make a search of your house." He scanned the room with protruding eyes beneath thick brows and saw Daniel standing in the doorway. "Which one of you is Ezra Mendelev?"

No one made a sound.

"I asked which one of you is Ezra Mendelev? Does anyone have ears?"

"I am his brother," Daniel replied trembling inside.

"Let's see your residency papers. Come on, move!"

The commissioner's spurs jingled and his heavy booted tread resounded on the floorboards as he followed Daniel to his room.

One of the lackeys worked quickly, seizing Sholem's books from the shelves. He flipped through the leaves, shook each one and with the dexterity of his boney wrist, flung them on the floor.

"Why are you looking through my books? What do you want? Must you throw them on the floor?" Sholem shouted as he bent over to pick them up.

The other flunky, a muscular blond bruiser, kicked the books from Sholem's hands scattering them on the floor again. "Where are the criminal proclamations and propaganda pamphlets Ezra Mendelev distributed at Kuznetsov's mill?" He snapped.

"Pamphlets? I don't know anything about this," said Sholem. "I assure you there are no pamphlets or any other kind of propaganda in this house." Although he shook from rage and dread, he stood tall and held himself with the dignity of a true gentleman.

The commissioner screwed up his brown eyes, raised his hand and smacked Sholem across the face knocking his spectacles off. "You're a liar! We know this is the residence of the criminal Mendelev. Where is he hiding?"

"He is not here, I tell you."

"You're lying! Where are your residency papers?"

Sholem trembled visibly, in a state of semi-shock.

"Are you deaf, old Jew? I'll knock your ears off so you'll never hear and rip out your tongue too, so you'll never lie. I said, get your residency papers! Move!"

The boney one threw cushions from the chairs and looked underneath furniture. He looked through cabinets sweeping things on the floor with his hands all the while, his spurs jingling.

"There are no pamphlets here," Sholem clamored. "Ezra does not live here?"

"Who's in those rooms?" said the commissioner marching through the bedroom doors.

Golda sat up in bed clutching her nightgown with a small white trembling hand, shrieking and sobbing.

"*Teeho*, old woman, stop your blubbering!" His eyes budged with contempt. "Do you think that by clutching your nightie, it would stop me if I wanted?" He let out a scornful laugh.

Sholem lurched into the bedroom and screamed, "Stop! Leave my wife alone." He thrust forth his arm and fanned his fingers in an attempt to grab the large figure tormenting Golda. Fury burned in his dark eyes.

The commissioner glared back at him, spat on the floor, and said, "Don't worry you old Jew, I wouldn't take that dog." He went to the bed, seized Golda's arm, and tugged. She struggled against him. "Get up old woman," he growled.

Sholem grabbed the man's other arm with both his hands and pulled as he would at the root of a nasty weed. "Stop! Leave my wife alone." The commissioner flicked him off like a fly.

"Get up, I said." He yanked Golda once more and she wobbled onto her feet. He signaled with a jerk of his head and the blond officer came in, stripped the bed and threw the mattress over.

"All right, old woman, get your passport and be quick about it."

"Don't shout!" She flung her hand toward him.

Sholem caressed her trembling shoulders, guided her to a chair near his writing desk, and said, "Try to calm yourself, Golda." He turned on a lamp, bent over and fumbled through the papers scattered on the floor until he found both passports and handed them to the commissioner.

The commissioner glanced over the papers, then gazed annoyingly at Golda shivering, with her arms folded over her bosom. Tears tumbled from her eyes.

"You're bawling ahead of time, Misses Jew," he warned. "Look out or you won't have tears left for the future."

"I have too many tears," she gasped. "Too many."

Sholem handed her his handkerchief.

The tall thin police officer materialized. "There is no one hiding in the yard, I searched everywhere."

"Well of course not," derided the commissioner. "I knew it all along! We are working with experienced criminals here, eh? It goes without saying. Someone get me my briefcase." The commissioner opened his briefcase, dropped the residency papers inside, pulled out some more papers and said, "I place you, Daniel Mendelev and Sholem Adler under arrest."

Golda shrieked and swooned. Daniel tried to help her revive.

"What is the meaning of this?" retorted Sholem. "Why are you arresting us? We have our proper immigration documents. What do you want?"

The commissioner blinked his right eye and rubbed it with a grimy hand. With a mixture of impudence and weary reiteration, he read methodically from a document which he raised to his face by the light. The only words that resounded were, "the accused Sholem Adler and Daniel Mendelev are found guilty of conspiracy with the criminal Ezra Mendelev. Then he flung the papers on his briefcase and said, "Here, sign."

"I will not sign," protested Sholem, his black eyes flashed in defiance. "This is an outrage. You cannot accuse someone without evidence...without an explanation as to what we have conspired."

"This is the domicile of the accused criminal, Ezra Mendelev. We have evidence of your complicity with the accused. You will get an explanation later. Sign, I said."

Daniel made an attempt to reach for the pen.

"Daniel! Don't you sign anything until we are read our rights." Sholem burned with indignation. "Why do you arrest decent law abiding citizens in the middle of the night like a pack of petty burglars who are afraid to be seen in the light? We have our passports, our residency papers, we have broken no laws."

The inspector stood with his arms crossed over his broad chest, waiting as Sholem vented his anger. He knew it was going nowhere. Then he said, "Your rights? Jews have no rights here in Kiev. You are all aliens." The gendarmes laughed and the blond said, "you are wasting our time, old Jew, now sign!"

"It's no use uncle Sholem; there is nothing we can do." Daniel knew it was useless to protest since Kiev was only geographically located outside the Russian Pale of Settlement, but still remained ideologically inside. Another awkward attempt made by the Russians to sweep its large Jewish population under the Empire's carpet.

Besides, these kinds of people have no understanding, it is their job to stun people, to jar them senseless, and instill the fear of the Tsar's secret police in them. They are indoctrinated instruments of the government, the wheels that turn the autocracy. They do what they are told without reason, without understanding, without mercy or pity. Their hearts were filled with contempt, not only for others but for themselves as well. How could they be otherwise when they regard people as dogs?

Sholem bowed his head as a man standing in the shadow of the gallows, a man whose blood had ceased to flow through his veins. He numbly took the pen with a shaking hand, and signed the papers. The commissioner hastily stuffed the papers into his briefcase and motioned to his lackeys, "get these dogs out of here."

Golda wanted to cry, but her eyes were scratchy and dry, the pink lids were like thick puffy clouds that could not produce rain. "Why are you taking my Sholem?" she said hoarsely. "Why do you snatch people from their homes without an explanation? What kind of animals are you?"

"*Teeho*, old woman, this does not concern you," snapped the blond one.

"Then at least let me get their coats, its cold outside," she said sarcastically.

The boney one rolled his eyes impatiently toward the commissioner. "How independent these Jews are."

"An impudent pack!" said the commissioner.

"March!" commanded the blond officer. The long gray coats flanked Sholem and Daniel as they disappeared out the door, and the last thing that resounded in Golda's ears was the jingle of their spurs.

The first blast of Artic air had enveloped the city and stung their faces as they stepped from their warm apartment and cozy beds into the cold. The gendarmes seized their arms and hurled them into the street like trash where men and women of all ages had been rounded up from other tenements. A grey wall of great coats surrounded them and drove them like cattle to the Prechistensky police station.

The frosty ground crackled under the heavy tread of boots and the people huddled together shivering. Women quietly sobbed. Lonely gas lights randomly blinked over the streets. They seemed to say, "If we cannot shed light on what is true and noble, then why bother at all."

"Why are you here?" Sholem asked the man walking next to him.

"We have no passports," he mumbled in a thin voice trembling from both cold and fear.

Sholem turned to his nephew. "What did you do? For four years you glided through the university with honors, one of two Jews to be admitted into law school. What have you done?" His voice elevated in anger. Daniel had never heard this kind of outburst from his uncle, and he knew it was justified, maybe long in coming.

"It was Ezra."

"Don't blame Ezra. You are well aware that they don't accuse one man for another man's felony, even as hateful as they are."

"I don't know."

"What do you mean you don't know? You must have done something, said something, to provoke their suspicions. You must have done something terrible to deserve this!" Every eye was turned on them. The women stopped their sobbing.

Daniel wrapped the collar of his overcoat around his neck and chest against the damp cold. He didn't look at his uncle. He felt no remorse or even fear. He felt nothing. That same hollow portent that swallowed him on the afternoon before the pogrom paralyzed his thoughts and feelings. "I don't know why they want me and that's all!" he snapped.

"You know all right. Down deep in your heart you know. It is your association with Count Rostovsky's daughter. They are accusing you of criminal infiltration into their home."

Daniel bit his lip shut. Except for the sniveling from the women, the accused walked in silence, occasionally accompanied by jeers from the officers.

Inside the noisy police station, drunks rounded up off the icy streets were beaten mercilessly and dumped into a large cage, they called the "drunk box". The boozers leaned like chimpanzees, with arms dangling through the bars, slurring incoherent words at the guards who sat around complaining incessantly about their jobs being nothing but a pack of trouble. Some of the officers dozed in their chairs and upon awakening, coughed, spat on the floor and joined their grumbling cronies.

A prison guard escorted Daniel into security headquarters and commanded. "*Sooda, seedeet!*" The prisoner sat in front of a white panel. A face with a small goiter beneath the chin popped up from behind a curtain of a large black camera. "Head a little higher," said the photographer. "Now the profile."

Chapter 19

GOLDA STRUGGLED WITH the mattress, trying to put it back onto the bed springs. Overcome with both mental and physical exhaustion, she sank to her knees beside the bed and sobbed until her tears formed little puddles like rain on the bare mattress.

Think Golda, you must think. But she could not. Each thought fled like a leaf driven away by the wind. She slid down on the rumpled bed clothes and slept deeply until the shrill of a nearby factory whistle invaded her subconscious. Then she realized her nightmare was not a dream.

She gazed across the room. The chaos, the broken china, pieces of glass everywhere, every personal item strewn from one end of the apartment to the other. This great indignation would break the spirit of the strongest individual, but fear of what horrendous fate may await her men in prison gave her the determination to go on.

I have to move quickly. I have to find Shalom and Daniel. I have to know where they are. They must be vindicated from this terrible injustice. But what to do? Who will listen? Who can I turn to for help? Money, that's what they want, money. How much.

In agony she lifted her body from the floor, stiff from arthritic pain. She could barely stand up to find the drawer where Sholem had hidden his rainy day cash.

She knew that those who could not raise the ransom to bribe their way out of jail were dispatched to the transport prison, that iron fortress where the doomed awaited trial, where no one was found innocent.

The fortunate were convicted to a life of hard labor in Siberia and the rest...she could not speak of it.

"The drawer? Where is the drawer?" She repeated to herself as she searched through the debris. She found her purse and some warm clothing she could wear, but where was the drawer? Did they take the money? She could not remember. She threw the things about the room in a dizzying blur. She began to perspire from fear and shivered with chills at the same time. She needed the money. She bowed her head and prayed. Through the grey dawn seeping through the windows, she saw the desk drawers on the floor of the parlor and found the one with the false wooden bottom. The brown paper envelop was still stiffly jammed underneath and the money was there. She sighed in relief and thanked God. *At least those devils hadn't found it in the raid.*

She took it all and put it into a small purse which she dropped into her handbag, dressed herself and went outside into the bitter cold. Sleet spit out of a misty sky and stung the fair skin on her face. She wrapped her woolen shawl to protect her face and doggedly trudged along the slippery streets until she found a line of taxies waiting for customers.

"*Izvochtchik*," she called waving her hand. When no one responded, she shouted up into the deeply wrinkled face of one driver asleep in his cab. "*Izvochtchik!*"

The driver opened his eyes, yawned and scratched his beard white with hoar frost. Then he stretched his arms in the air and hammered on his well-padded breast like an ape to stimulate his circulation. He pulled a bottle of vodka from under his seat and drank, grunting in satisfaction.

"Where to madam?" he said peering down at her.

"To the police station."

"That will be a half rubble."

"A half rubble to go a few blocks? That's an outrageous fare."

"The price of oats has gone up."

"The price of oats is always going up. I will pay you twenty kopecks and not a kopeck more."

"Very well," he grumbled. "But an extra ten on the oats would help."

"All right, twenty-five," she said and the matter was settled. Golda climbed into the back seat of the carriage and covered herself with the blanket inside the cab. The lift across town seemed to take forever. She could walk faster than this old horse, and she would have, but her feet were too painful from the damp cold. Suddenly the driver jerked his rein to the right to avoid colliding with a carriage pulled by a great stallion clipping along at a gallop. Golda toppled to the floor. She lifted her painful body back to the seat. "Woe is me," she said. "This trip will take forever."

When she arrived at the police station, the doors were still locked so she wrapped herself in her shawl and huddled against the wall inside the entrance to shield herself from the sleet and cold. Her warm breath made tiny ice crystals along the rim of her stole. A few others gathered inside but said nothing. Finally, a guard opened the door and with a jerk of his head, said, "Inside."

She went inside and sat in a dingy grey waiting room under the watchful eye of Alexander III, gazing from a portrait hanging on the empty wall above the wooden benches. A cockroach peered from behind the picture and looked around, his antennae quivering, probing.

People came and people went. Some stared idly, others prattled in words laced with sarcasm, about everything, about nothing. Each wanting to share the miseries of his life, and to complain about how bad things are in the Empire.

"The price of bread has gone up again," said a bearded peasant in an agitated voice. "Twice now and my wages haven't risen a kopek."

"*Pravda*," said another. "And when someone rises in protest they slam him in here."

"Injustice to the people," said a young man alerting the attention of the guard who made a little motion to get up but then settled back into his lethargy.

A plump rosy-faced peasant woman balancing a large tote-bag on her lap ran her eyes up and down Golda who sat next to her. "Soon they'll be sending all the decent working people to Siberia." She widened her round eyes and probed for a response. "I hear they are already rounding up innocent people with mistaken identities and throwing them in here."

Golda anxiously worked her hands on the handle of her purse, thinking of Daniel and Sholem rotting in prison with these half-civilized *moujiks*.

"Who are you visiting?" the woman finally asked outright.

"A friend," she quipped.

"Oh?" said the woman. "Once they spend more than a week in this place, they never see the light of day until they get to Siberia."

A widow dressed in black, held her head high and said. "My son has been here for ten days, tomorrow he goes to transport prison. Soon the prisons will not be able to hold all the courageous young lads. Then you will see something."

"Soon they'll put us all in prison, said the bearded man. The people cannot endure forever."

"May power come to the people," said the young man.

A stout woman opened a napkin and took out some sausage and bread and ate. Golda stared unwittingly, she had not previously thought about her hunger. The woman made a sideward glance and shifted herself further down on the bench. Golda could not bear any more humiliation. She got up and went to the guard sitting behind a desk shuffling papers. "When can I see the general of gendarmes?" she said in a voice shanking with indignation. "I've been waiting already six hours. It is past lunch time already."

"Sit down, please, misses Jew," he said. "The general is busy. He will call you when he is ready to see you."

The minutes passed into hours and the day was nearly over. A few bureaucrats appeared in their overcoats and left the building. Then

Golda saw the general of gendarmes emerge from his office wearing his coat and hat. "Sir." She stood up and said looking ruefully into his long pale face. "Please."

The middle aged man gazed at her standing alone in the room, not with insolent eyes but with the tired, vacuous gaze of an overworked bureaucrat. He said nothing and continued toward the door.

Feeling every bit as tired, painful, and hungry, she gathered all her strength and rushed to intersect him before he reached the door. "Sir, sir, your excellency, please wait. Please, your excellency, my husband and nephew are in this jail and I don't know why they arrested them."

"I'm sure madam, there must be a good reason. We do not put people in jail for no good reason."

"Sir, they haven't done anything wrong. We've lived here legally in Kiev for nearly twenty- five years."

The general ignored her and headed to the door. Golda got up and followed him. "Please sir, your Excellency; I must know why they have arrested them. My husband teaches in the gymnasium. My nephew is studying at the law school; at Kiev University. Always, we have tried to do everything the right way." She clung to his sleeve with both hands pulling him away from the door.

The general screwed up his basset eyes and looked down on her, this time not with pity but with contempt. He jerked his arm tying to loosen her grip.

"Please!" she pleaded still clinging to his overcoat, nearly pulling off the sleeve.

He freed himself and relented to her request. "*Preehodeet*." He said and gestured with a nod of his head toward his office and opened the door to a cluttered, stuffy over heated room. He took off his hat, unbuttoned his overcoat, and agitatedly fanned his face with a leaflet. When he felt more relaxed, he took out his wire rimmed spectacles, wound them around his ears and opened his brief case. "What are their names?"

Golda sat eagerly on a straight backed chair with her purse resting on her knees and her hands wrapped tightly around the handle as if clinging to the last branch of safety in a frightful storm. "Sholem Adler and Daniel Mendelev," she replied with renewed hope.

He stared at her for a moment before shuffling through his papers. "Not here," he said at last.

She gasped and her voice quivered in shock and disbelief. "But... sir...they have to be here! They were taken only last night...at midnight. They must be here...somewhere!"

While she chattered, he went to the file cabinet and opened the drawer. Dust drifted in the air. "When did you say they were arrested?"

"Only last night, your Excellency," she repeated. She slipped to the edge of her chair and hunched over her purse like a feline ready to pounce on its prey. Her pulse quickened.

The general pulled a paper from the file. First he read it to himself, and then to Golda.

"It says here that they are accused of conspiracy with the revolutionary activist Ezra Mendelev, brother of the prisoner Daniel Mendelev who has also been found guilty of infiltration into the home of Count Rostovsky, Marshal of the Aristocracy for the government of Kiev." He peered at Golda through his round wire rimmed glasses. "Do you know what that means, Misses Jew?"

She recoiled and gasped. "Guilty?" She felt herself swaying.

"It means they have infiltrated to the very top," he pronounced each word deliberately to be sure she understood. "They now have personal information on Count Rostovsky, his family, his home, and God knows...the state files."

She blanched in horror and swayed. The general stood quietly by the cabinet for a few minutes while she regained her senses. Then he put the file back in the drawer and quickly gathered the papers in his briefcase.

She put her hands to her face and sobbed loudly. "Woe is me," she said softly and took a handkerchief from her purse. With tears streaming down her cheeks she glared directly into his face and repeated. "Guilty. Guilty!" Suddenly she jumped up in a burning rage with a vigor she didn't know she had. "How have you found them guilty without even a trial? This is injustice. This is wrong!"

His sad basset eyes turned harsh. He put his hat and coat on and headed for the door.

"Please, please, sir...your Excellency. Please, I'm begging you. I know they're innocent. Why don't they get a trial? Please help me." She bewailed loudly. "This is unfair. Where is the justice?"

The man looked at her sternly for a few moments. He knew the sentence was unfair and that trials for insurrectionists were already rigged against them, but with Jews, they simply skipped the protocol.

"Look, mister, sir," she said in a last attempt to rescue her loved ones. "I have money...cash...to pay for their release!" She opened her handbag and took out the little purse. "Look!"

"Keep your money, Misses Jew. It won't do you any good now. Your husband and nephew are no longer here. They have been dispatched to armory prison this morning and Ezra Mendelev has vanished. He is wanted for the murder of a foreman at the Kuznetsov mills. There were witnesses."

Golda stood paralyzed in body and mind, as though someone had sealed her in cement.

"Perhaps you can tell us where he is hiding," he said without malice, even with a touch of sympathy in his drooping eyes. "Then he can testify as to whether or not your husband and nephew are innocent."

In a daze, she wobbled outside and sat down on a bench to regain her strength. She gazed at one of the city's many beautiful onion-domed churches and it provoked in her bitter thoughts. *"Kiev, the city of churches. The city of piety, honor and justice.* A tale of horror popped into her thoughts concerning her neighbor's brother, a poor artisan, who rotted to death shackled in wooden handcuffs while awaiting his trial in the Moscow transport prison. His only crime was residing in the city without a passport.

But they were not awaiting trial; they may be waiting to be shipped off to Siberia. Maybe they were on their way now. And suppose, God forbid, they never ship them to Siberia but just leave them there to rot. She thought of the last words spoken by the general of the gendarmes. Find Ezra. She had no idea where to look, not a clue to the names of his acquaintances or where these revolutionary groups were hiding? Certainly someone must know. But if the Okhrana couldn't find them, who could? *"I will find that devil, even if this old woman has to join up with the insurrectionists."*

Chapter 20

"She will be magnificent, madam. *Le colour et perfect.* We will complete the look with a tiara of pearls and diamonds, *nes pas?*" said the great dressmaker from Moscow, famous for her fashion design.

Zinaida smiled, pleased that her beautiful daughter would be presented to Petersburg society. It was time to make a fine match with a gentleman of her own class and the day would not come too soon.

Jeniya was not pleased. Two seamstresses hovered about her. One crawled on all fours around the long skirt of the gown with a mouth filled with pins, and the other pinched, pulled and draped a champagne slipper satin around her waist. A maid served petite sandwiches and cakes while another refreshed the tea.

Jeniya did not know how she would survive Petersburg without the man she loved. The haughty, braggadocios sons of the laconic aristocracy would be returning from commissions throughout the Empire, after deflowering peasant girls in every hut, romping in every brothel, and gambling in every club, to be primed for the rite of match making.

Suddenly a great roar came from downstairs. "Zinaida! Where's that daughter of yours? Tell her to come down here this minute."

Zinaida scurried to the landing outside the apartments. Jeniya jerked her skirts from the fitters and with pins flying, ran out behind her mother. The maids and seamstresses followed like shadows. Count Rostovsky was pacing around the rotunda with the agitation of a caged lion. Jeniya turned and saw her lady's maid standing just behind her mother. "Galina," she whispered. "You go down and see what he wants."

"But, my lady countess…"

"You can calm him down better than I can. You'd think I'd killed someone by the way he is acting."

"Boris Vasilevich," Zinaida called down. "Jenka isn't dressed, she is still being fitted for her gown."

"Fitted for a gown? My God woman! What's this world coming to? I didn't ask for an explanation, I ask for Evgeniya to come down here this minute…and if she doesn't turn from her foolish escapades, she may never get to wear that gown."

"Boris you are an embarrassment. Can't you see we have an honored guest with us?"

"Women!" he shouted from the center of the rotunda, brandishing his hands in the air above his head muttering, "They drive me nuts! They drive me nuts!" Then he straightened to his full six feet one inches. He cut an imposing figure attired in his khaki military tunic. Beneath the wavy hair there was no detection of a smile in his dimpled cheeks nor the hint of a twinkle in his blue eyes. He ordered the women as though he were still a commander in the Preobrazhensky guards. "Get going. Every one of you! Out of my sight! I called Evgeniya."

Not one woman budged in compliance to his command, but stood on the stairs like porcelain dolls staring through expressionless faces. By this time Jeniya had shed her gown, put on a simple dark blue velvet dress and came running down the stairs, lifting her skirt in both of her hands.

Zinaida ran down the stairs after her. "Boris," she said, her voice trembling. "I am her mother and your wife. I want to know what is going on here."

"Indeed madam, as her mother you do need to know what is going on with your daughter!"

The count sighed in exasperation and opened the door of his study for the two women to enter. Neither one sat down, both were shaken. He slammed the door behind him. Boris Vasilevich only roared when some terrible deed had been rendered.

He went to his mahogany desk and poured himself a brandy from a crystal decanter and belted it down. "I have just received some very grave news. Something dreadful has happened to this family."

An immense collection of books jammed the bookcases. On one wall he proudly displayed his collection of guns, swords and sabers. Snap shots, family photographs, trivial souvenirs, and knick-knacks collected from his travels abroad cluttered the table tops. In one corner was an ornately carved shelf for his icons, one of which he bragged belonged to Prince Vladimir, who first brought Christianity to Russia a thousand years ago.

Zinaida remained silent but she put her hand to her throat and twisted her necklace, a habit she had when she became anxious. "Has something happened to the dowager countess?" she said.

"No! This is not about my mother! She is a lady in every tradition. This is about your daughter, Evgeniya" he said evenly trying to control his anger.

"What papa, what did I do wrong?"

"Evgeniya, were you aware that you brought a common Jew as a guest into this household?"

"I never brought a Jew in here," she protested. "Who?"

"Who? You have no idea who?"

She flinched, a flood of confused emotions washed her speechless. She turned to her mother who looked on in horror. "Daniel?" she said.

Her father glared; his normal jovial expression hardened.

Now that she knew the mystery of Daniel's true identity, she was forced to acknowledge something she was not willing to admit, something she had wondered about ever since the evening of the harvest festival when he did not answer after she asked if he was Orthodox. She often thought it strange that he never spoke of his family and how he insisted on leaving before the evening had begun, when he knew she had invited him to be her escort. She remembered the hurt she felt, but still she invited him to meet her friends at a dinner party. She invited him to her home, to the intimate family gatherings, and gave him her love. Why then did he shield his identity from her. Didn't he have enough trust in her affection and open generosity to tell the truth about himself? Moreover, she was disappointed that he did not stand up for truth and be the man she thought he was, regardless of the consequences. She wondered if he had intended all along of slipping out of her life before she discovered his secret.

"Since when has being a Jew been such a grave matter?" She said not in defense of Daniel, but to justify her own gullibility.

The count narrowed his eyes. "This Daniel whom you loved and trusted…is a terrorist! A conspirator with the revolutionary underground."

"No, that's impossible. He is a refined gentleman and he has graduated top in his class. Why would he…?"

"Impossible? And who else would they send to case my estate, only the best of them, the smartest, the most industrious and diligent. I received this message from the general of the gendarmerie today. Look!" He held the letter up in their faces. "It says this man, this Daniel Mendelev of yours, has been conspiring with his brother who is wanted for the murder of a foreman at the Kuznetsov's mill." He rattled the paper and threw it at their faces. It fluttered down to the hems of their dresses.

Jeniya winced back in horror and fell down on the settee behind her.

Zinaida stared at her daughter, her hazel-green eyes large in astonishment, moaning. *"Mon Dieu, mon Dieu,* may God help us. She sat down beside her daughter, repeatedly making the sign of the cross over her chest with a trembling hand.

"You could have had us killed!" exclaimed Rostovsky.

"May God help us." Zinaida repeated, making the sign of the cross over her chest again.

The rosy color had drained from Jeniya's cheeks and she began to swoon with a sickening feeling of nausea. The room began to fade and swim. She had fallen for the accomplice of a cold blooded killer. Fear, anger, and even embarrassment assailed her thoughts as she tried to regain her composure and to think clearly. She put her head down on her mother's lap until the dizziness subsided and her head cleared, then she lifted herself limply and asked, barely able to form the words on her trembling lips. "Where is he now?" Despite everything, she had to know.

"He has been dispatched to the armory prison where he belongs along with the rest of the scoundrels who are conspiring against the Empire!" Rostovsky didn't notice his daughter swoon back into her mother's arms. He was gazing past them out the long elegant windows into the gardens. "Now he knows every entrance into this house, our whereabouts…our habits. God only knows if he has informed his brother who is still at large, and his pack of revolutionary scum. I've informed the Okhrana. I will warn the servants to be on the lookout while we are in Petersburg. Hah!" he busted out. "The servants. Can we even trust them these days? I've seen their greedy eyes on us, waiting for the opportune time. Today they plunder the Jews, tomorrow it will be us."

"Boris, don't speak of such things," Zinaida moaned weakly.

The count turned around, glanced at his wife and saw his daughter crying in her mother's arms.

"What's wrong with her now?" He poured himself another brandy. "She goes around here like the mistress of this mansion. Prances around town like Catherine the Great, mistress of all the Russias." He fixed his gaze on his daughter who was struggling desperately to compose herself. "Don't you know you could have had yourself killed? Whose daughter are you anyway. Sometimes I wonder if you even belong to this family."

Zinaida gasped, "Boris!" she protested angrily. "She is every bit your daughter, impossible, strong willed, and high tempered. Don't be so hard on her. She is still a child, who has been beguiled by this cunning Jew. She doesn't understand yet that this is in their nature. She is yet to learn the ways of this world.

"Don't be so hard on her!" he bellowed pacing with his brandy in hand. "Do you realize what she's done? She has exposed us to the underground terrorist movement through her liberal associations. Now they know everything about us." He brandished one arm in the air. "We could be targeted right now. We could be dead tomorrow!"

"Boris! Maybe you are overstating this issue. If his brother is bad it doesn't mean that this young man is bad. After all he worked his way up against overwhelming odds to receive his Juris Utriusque Doctor and with top honors from a prestigious law school. He is to be commended for that." She paused for a moment and added. "He seemed to be a refined, charming young man even if he is a Jew." Jeniya was lying on her mother's breast while Zinaida stroked her temple.

"Don't tell me you have also been bewitched by his charm and good looks. May the devil take him!" Vasilevich flipped his hand as if to swat away an insect. "And the university? That is nothing more than a hatching ground for insurrectionists these days, and the Jews are the instigators. I say get rid of every last Jew from Russian soil. Don't give them the opportunity for education…keep them bound to their queer religion and let them leave Russia. Give them an inch and they run off with a mile."

He paced rapidly now as his words became more vehement; his thick brows pinched in anger. He stopped by the window, took a deep breath and gazed at the gardens for a few moments to calm himself while the woman sat rigidly waiting for his next move.

"I tried to believe in becoming more liberal. I listened to those who say we need change…we have to bring Russia into the modern age. But now I say damn this age of enlightenment, it will be the destruction of us yet. The nobility is cut from a different fabric. The ignorant masses belong where they are! And there is reason for it. Divine providence has given us the task of governing over the ignorant masses to keep them civilized."

He turned and went back to pour himself another brandy. "Jenka, you exasperate me. You cause me nothing but problems. Why can't you be like your sisters and be interested in young men of your own class. In my day this would never have happened. We were told who to marry and that ended the argument. Now young women want to go out into the world and choose their own husbands. They want liberation, next the peasants will be storming for liberation, liberation from this, liberation from that. Liberation will be the death of us yet!" He threw up his hands and left the room.

"Mama," Jeniya said sobbing and wiping her nose in her handkerchief. "Do you think he used me to get to us?"

"Darling, your father does dramatize things. His brother may be involved in the revolutionary movement. But I cannot understand why a young man, and a Jewish fellow at that, who has worked so hard to get through law school, which is so difficult, would jeopardize his future and involve himself in that dirty, petty underground movement." She made a face of disgust.

"Mama, do you think he used me?"

"Yes dear, he no doubt did use you, but to advance his own interest."

Jeniya cried all the more. "He did use me! Oh mama, how could I have been so dumb, so gullible, so naive and childish?" She jumped up, grabbed a pillow and hurled it across the room. "I hate him, I hate everybody, and I will never trust another man again. He took my love and my trust and I believed in him." She paced the room clenching her fists. She picked up another pillow and threw it. "I believed in him and he bewitched me like a devil. No human being deserves this kind of treatment...this should not happen to a dog! And I fell for him! Oh why, oh why! I never want to see another man." She sat down and sobbed. Zinaida gave her another handkerchief. She wiped her tears and looked across the room at no particular thing. "But how was I to know, he never told me. He pretended to be something he is not." she said thoughtfully. "Oh, how could I. How could I." She clenched her fists. "I hate men. They are no good. They just want to use us to get their own selfish pleasure. The old women in the village are right!

Men just use us! I hate them, the lot of them." She pounded her fist on the sofa.

"Don't worry my darling, you are still very young." She put her arms around her daughter, held her to her bosom, and stroked her hair as she would a child. "You are feeling abused and rejected now but it is not your fault. Because you have been targeted by one scoundrel, that doesn't mean all men are this way. Soon you'll forget this and one day you will meet a good man, one who will love you and care for you as you deserve, as a man should. None of this lawyer nonsense but a man from a noble family with estates and land like your father. That is why it is so important for you to court young men from your own class. Otherwise you will never know if you are loved for yourself or for your inheritance, which one day will be great from your dear babushka. She plans to give you Belozerkovka." Zinaida tried to sound cheerful and encouraging. Jeniya looked up with tears standing in her puffy eyes. "She is? Really?" She thought for a moment. "Then I shall not need any man, I will make Belozerkovka the envy of all the land owners!"

Zinaida smiled. "Next week we will be in Petersburg. And you will go to lots of parties in beautiful dresses and have many admirers seeking your hand. This will be one of the best years of your life."

Chapter 21

JENIYA TOSSED THROUGH sleepless nights trying to justify Daniel's actions coupled with the love he had declared for her. She had a hard time coming to grips with his perfidy, and the consequential hurt and anger. The anticipation of the long awaited social season in Petersburg could not remove the pain of being used and rejected by the man she loved, a man to whom she opened her heart, and worst, the man she loved sitting in prison chained to those dreadful wooden hand cuffs.

She had to talk to someone. Her parents had already made up their minds and her sisters would not understand. Galina, once her governess and now her lady's maid had always been there for her, through growing pains, adventures and achievements. She watched her young mistress's first love unfold and shared her joy. She listened as Jeniya enthusiastically enumerated Daniel's many merits. She also knew all the torrid details of the scandal since it ripped through the servant's quarters faster than the Moscow dressmaker had time to pack her belongings.

"Galina?" Jeniya said one morning when her confidant came in to prepare her toilette. "Do you think Daniel used me to gather information about our family for the underground revolutionaries?"

"I can't say, my lady countess. What would his motive be?"

"He could have been angry over the new law prohibiting Jews from entering the bar and wanted to get retribution against those who govern."

"From what I have seen, I can't imagine he would be that kind of a person. He was too much of a gentleman in every sense of the word." she said picking up a brush from the vanity to groom her young mistress's long hair. "And he seemed to be kind, thoughtful and understanding, as least from what you told me."

"Then do you think he used me to advance his career?"

"All he would have to do to advance his career is convert to Christianity, whether he believed in it or not. You know, they give the best jobs to those who do."

"Galina? Suppose he is innocent...then I should never forgive myself."

"Forgive yourself for what?"

"I don't know...in a way I feel guilty."

"Why should you feel guilty?"

"I think I may have gotten him into this mess by leading him on. He didn't chase me, I chased him. He kept trying to tell me that his world and mine were so different, but I wouldn't listen. I was so caught up in my own desires, I continued to invite him to parties and insisted he stay when he knew he must leave. He had reason to hide his identity, he knew he was in a place where he was not welcome. He knew my father was a fierce anti-Semite with lots of power in the province of Kiev. He must have known then that a lasting relationship was impossible. Maybe he had intended to tell me all along, but was afraid of hurting me."

"Or maybe he loved you and didn't want to lose you."

Jeniya looked at Galina, longing to hear more, looking for confirmation of Daniel's final words of devotion. "He did say on the last night we were together that he would always love me no matter what happened. He must have loved me." She put a hand to her brow and shook her head. "I am so confused right now. If he is sitting in prison because of my selfishness...oh Galina, what should I do?"

"If you are asking my advice, my lady countess, I think you need to go to him and see if his love is true. I cannot say what is in his heart but if he is innocent of these crimes, then you need to go to him and find out."

Love was not supposed to happen like this. Love was supposed to be magical. One of her friends sailed away from her society debut into the arms of a young man who had a prominent future in the administration. Everyone cried at the wedding and the bride was radiant. Now, they have a baby, and the adoring family swirls around the young couple like the stars swirl around the universe.

And what of deception? A girl could marry into a good family never know for certain what her husband did when he went to the fashionable men's clubs. These exclusive establishments all had poker tables and enough liquor to drown an elephant…and God knows what else.

She thought of the first evening she and Daniel spent together walking in the moonlight, the sweet kisses, and the sadness in his eyes on the day of the harvest when he told her he would always love her no matter what happens. He had the most promising future of any young man she knew and she pictured herself living happily within it. She didn't think of asking questions or insisting on answers, she was in love. A proverb from Pascal popped into her mind. "The heart has its reasons of which reason knows not."

Jeniya didn't find much comfort in the morning walk through a snowy wonderland with ice coated trees dazzling like diamonds in the sunshine.

In the distance she saw a blue onion dome rising above the village and the gold cross on top gleaming in the sunlight. *Pan Zukov. That's it. Maybe he can help me.* Whenever anyone had a problem they always consulted the village priest who usually had the answer and knew exactly what to do.

As she approached the church, several men and woman stood begging outside the entrance, not an uncommon sight to every church in Russia. No one passed by them without dropping a kopek or two into their hands. She gave them each a rubble.

The door was unlocked so she stepped inside closing it quietly behind her. Light seeped down from four long windows in the cupola and from a long candelabra which hung from the ceiling. Pews were unknown inside the Orthodox sanctuary except for a few long benches on each side of the door where the elderly and the lame could sit. The iconostasis had none of the golden ornate pillars and frames of the great cathedrals, but only four icons; that of a highly stylized mother and child, one of an angel, and one each of the apostles St. John and St. Peter. Two golden candlesticks stood on the floor on each side of the images.

She lit a candle and knelt to pray. When she arose, the priest greeted her with a warm smile, "Good morning, my lady countess, what brings you here today? I thought you would be leaving for St. Petersburg by now." His long black cassock billowed slightly as he ambled through the sanctuary. A long golden chain hung around his neck with a cross of semi-precious stones.

"Pan Zukov, do you have some time to talk with me?"

"Of course I have time for you. My goodness, child. You must be thinking of your season in St. Petersburg now." He frowned. "Do I see tears?"

She lowered her gaze.

"Come with me," he said. He led her to a small room and motioned with his hand to sit down. "Tell me, what great problem is troubling your heart today," he said smiling. "Is it love?"

She looked into his face, the lines around his kind eyes crinkled above his grey bearded cheeks when he smiled. She bowed her head not knowing how to begin her story. Finally, she blurted out. "Do you... do you know anything about Jews?"

"Jews?" His happy face changed into a peculiar expression of inquiry. This was not the usual story of romance he had expected to pour from the heart of a young girl. "That covers a lot of ground. What is it you want to know about Jews?"

"I was wondering…why don't we accept them into our world?"

"Well my dear, it's not that we do not accept them, it is that they will not accept us. They have a strange religion, a strange culture, and strange customs that causes them to shut themselves off from others who do not share the same tradition. Why, their peculiar dietary laws do not even allow them to eat at our table, shop in our markets or partake in our social events. How can one expect to live with such a people? No, we have not separated ourselves from them, they have separated themselves from the people of Russia."

He reflected for a moment. "It would be nice if they would convert to us, but we understand that is not always possible. Conversion is a necessary step in order to have unity in the Empire. And if they were willing to convert, we would willingly offer them the best positions in the Empire to show there is no animosity, but still they refuse." He shook his head, indicating perplexity, and then he said. "Is that all that is bothering you?"

"Well…not exactly," she said mulling through his descriptions of the Jewish people which seemed so strange, searching for words to describe her dilemma. "You see, I…think I am in love with a Jewish man."

He stared at her, but not in shock. She was not the first to seek his advice on these matters of an interfaith relationship. "Are you considering marriage to this man?"

"I…I don't know."

"Is he willing to convert for you?"

"Convert?" She began to wonder why he did not speak of conversion to her faith if he loved her? The little seeds of doubt began to creep in again.

"Have you spoken with your family about this?"

"No, they only found out that he was Jewish today."

"You mean you never told them?"

"No, he never told me. He had hidden this. He led me to believe he was Christian. I only found out today along with my family."

"And you are still in love with him?"

She nodded, she was gazing down at her hands which she held together rigidly. She still didn't know how to reveal that he is incarcerated as a criminal.

Pan Zukov stroked his long beard, nodding his head indicating his understanding. "I see. Well, my advice to you would be to forget him and go to St. Petersburg and enjoy your young life. In time you will meet a nice young man of your own faith and you will forget all about this man."

"But Pan, you don't understand. I must see him again before I leave for Petersburg!"

"Why must you see him again? Doesn't it bother you that he has deceived you?"

"Yes, it did at first. He is a very fine man, and I still love him. He must have had a reason for not telling me. Maybe he feared my father." She looked at him. "You know how he is."

He smiled but left the subject of her father alone and pursued his point. "My dear, if he has deceitfully concealed his true identity, and was not willing to convert for you, then he had no intension of ever marrying you."

These words sent a cold chill through her heart. Maybe she had misinterpreted his feelings and was foolishly imagining a loving relationship all along. "Then...he didn't love me," she said.

"No, my dear, I have no doubt that he does love you. But...you see...actually he did have a reason for not wanting to marry you. If he became a Christian for you, then he would be cut off from his family and his people forever. He would be considered as dead to them. No man should have to make this decision, it is too painful, even for love."

"But why? I don't understand."

"None of us do, but that's the way it is. Perhaps this is one of the greatest oddities of their religion. Now my dear, I suggest that you forget him. Besides when love begins on deception, in the end it will only die."

She sat in silence for a long while clutching her clammy hands. Now that she saw the whole picture, she was convinced that his love for her was real, and she felt all the more responsible for leading him on. "Pan Zukov, I can accept your advice, but…there is something else I need to tell you, something far worse."

"Yes?" He looked concerned now, fearing what seemed to be an inevitable result of a first young love.

Perceiving his thoughts, she blurted out quickly. "His brother is an underground revolutionary who murdered the foreman of a factory, and they have accused Daniel of collusion with these people, for infiltrating into our home, and gathering intelligence. Now his brother is on the run and Daniel will be left to rot in prison. All his ambitions and his dreams are destroyed because he was falsely incarcerated for something that his brother did."

"How do you know he is innocent?"

"I can't imagine otherwise. He is one of the finest young men I have ever met. He has worked hard, and graduated top in his class from Kiev University. He was in the middle of his exams to receive his license to practice law when his life was cut short. He was even offered a teaching position at the university upon his graduation…and a European education! He would have to be crazy to conspire with his brother in such petty affairs when he had such a brilliant future!"

The priest stared into her pleading eyes and knitted his grey brows together showing his concern for both the girl and the young man. "Now I understand your anguish. Do your parents know about this?"

"My father told us today. You see, in a way I feel responsible for his trouble. He didn't come after me, it was I who went after him and invited him to our house because I fell in love with him. And now I must tell him I'm sorry and to find some way to encourage him…to help him. Can you help me?"

"Your father would be the one who could exonerate him. Have you talked to him?"

"No, Pan, I cannot. He will not listen."

"Do you want me to talk to him?"

"No, he will not listen, he hates Jews now."

"What do you want me to do?"

"Can you arrange a meeting for me at the prison?"

"I can do that, but I will have to talk to your parents first. You cannot go all the way to Kiev without telling them why."

"Well, I thought Yelizaveta and I could meet with our friends to say good-by, and stay overnight at our city house. I know my parents wouldn't mind that."

Jeniya winced in shock when Daniel appeared behind the guard, with wrists and ankles clamped in wooden cuffs. He dragged along peering through dead eyes, seemingly resigned to his destiny. His handsome face had become dull, drawn, and the outline of his jaw stubbled and unkempt. Tears streamed from her eyes.

The prisoner disappeared into another room behind closed doors and the guard returned and bowed his head. "My lady Countess," he said. "Come, follow me." He led her into a small empty room behind the doors, where the prisoner stood staring at the wall. Gray light crept through the film of dirt on the window exposing black street dust, paint chips and the brittle bodies of dried insects along the sill. The guard sat in the only chair and raised his arm to look at his watch. "You may begin," he said.

"Danya?" She whispered. She felt hesitant, confused, guilty.

He turned slowly to face her, "Jenka?" he said with a distant and impenetrable gaze, like that of a dreamer.

"Danya," she said sobbing, "I'm sorry, I'm so sorry."

"You had nothing to do with it, Jenka," he replied tenderly.

She opened her arms to embrace him.

"Halt! Move away from the prisoner!"

Daniel's kind expression did not show vindication or blame or even a justified anger. He lifted a chained hand to touch hers.

"Ahem..." grunted the guard, frowning. "Suppose you two move away from each other a bit. Let there be some distance between you."

Daniel stared at her for a long time with a million questions in his eyes. Then he said, "do you...know the whole story?"

She couldn't stop the tears from flowing. She knew now without a doubt of his innocence and felt a horrible pain. "I love you...I...did this to you, didn't I...I shouldn't blame you if..."

The guard sat up and listened intently. Such an intimate morsel of gossip from the nobility rarely crossed the prison doors.

"You had nothing to do with it. I brought this calamity on myself. You are the most beautiful thing that ever happened to me. I'm guilty of messing up my own life. I should never have gone to your home the night of the dance. I knew it was wrong from the very beginning."

"Why was it wrong? We loved each other from the very beginning. Didn't we?"

"I've loved you from the first time I saw you on the porch at Khishnaikov party." He smiled. "You were so upset."

"I was upset because you thought I was a dumb woman." They both made a little laugh. She took her handkerchief and wiped her tears.

"I knew you weren't a dumb woman. I knew you were daring and brave...that deep inside you had a heart for people. You want to help the peasants and I admired that in you."

She turned her eyes away from his gaze which pricked at her heart. Until now, she had no intention of helping anyone but herself.

He continued, "I knew you were not an ordinary woman and I loved you, even then. And I'll always love you no matter where this life leads."

She had a nasty presentiment that this would be their last meeting. "What do you mean? When you get out of here we'll be together, won't we?"

He shook his head. He looked so mature, gallant and in control of his fate, no longer the starry-eyed student, but a man who had passed through that world of dreams into one of cold reality. They were moving apart then, and she knew it but she said, "I have to get you out of here."

"How can you get me out of here?" he replied softly. "They have already determined my guilt. And who is there to plead my innocence? If I could somehow reach the outside world, I would ask my old law school professor to help me." He paused and considered what may be his only option, though he hesitated to ask at first. "Would you go to him for me? His name is professor Dunchencho."

She wasn't listening to a word he said, her head was spinning with her own solutions. "My father...I'll ask him. He can free you."

"Are you serious? I am accused of infiltrating into your father's house, of plotting revolutionary activity against him!" he raised his voice.

"It is forbidden to talk about this subject," interrupted the guard afraid they would mention the Count's name and someone would overhear.

"I can persuade my father." She went on hurriedly paying no attention to the guard who began to show signs of agitation. "He'll listen to me."

"I told you, this subject is forbidden, it's not allowed. You may talk only of family matters."

Jeniya whirled about to face him. He had a round face and the buttons on his jacket pulled over his belly. "This is my family's matter." she said.

"I don't mean to offend you, my lady countess, but I am here to look after your safety, and the safety of your family. You may only talk about your boy-friend's wash, his underwear, and his food. Nothing else."

She glared at him incredulously and persisted in a hushed tone. "We can live in Paris. I have lots of friends there."

Daniel declined. "We would live like refugees, outcasts. I would ruin your life and you would hate me someday."

"Again, on the subject. I tell you it is forbidden!" the warden demanded. "He is charged with treason against your father and here you are, plotting for his freedom. What is this?" he said but his expression was one of great interest.

Jeniya gave the guard an annoying glance. She had to convince Daniel that she could be happy with him anywhere, even in Siberia. She had to encourage him and keep his heart from sinking into despair.

The guard looked at his pocket watch. "Time's up. Take your leave." He leaned back, stretched out both his arms and made a wide yawn.

"Danya," Jeniya whispered, "when I get you out of here we can start a new life together, anywhere. Amerika!"

"Separate, I said. Time is up."

He leaned over and kissed her on the cheek. "God be with you," he said. "Remember, no matter what happens to me, to us, I shall always love you."

The tears began to stream down her face again when the guard took her arm and led her away. She turned back to gaze one more time at Daniel. Their eyes searched each other, both wondering if this would be the last time they would meet.

Chapter 22

A POWERFUL CLOUT over the right ear introduced Daniel to the new regime. "Off with your trousers!" Two gendarmes searched his clothing. For a moment he was dazed and when he came to his senses he was staring into the face of a crimson nosed warden who led him to the cell.

"You *politicals* are always such bright lads. As for me, I like you all, Socialist Revolutionaries, Social Democrats, the lot of you."

Daniel's new home was a single large cell, one brawling animal house. The Socialist revolutionaries and the Social Democrats were in a heated argument espousing their various revolutionary creeds and plans for a new Russia.

"Revolution by force. Now or never," shouted the revolutionaries.

"No," advocated the Democrats, "Revolution by constitution. We must first penetrate the working class and its weight will topple the autocracy."

A few were singing revolutionary songs at the top of their lungs. The prison warden stood and listened for a while. His smile indicated that he was enjoying the pandemonium. "My, how you politicals like to fight. But I like you all. You are clever young men and you have good reason to challenge the aristocracy, but what is to become of Russia? Only the Lord God knows." He shook his head.

"Welcome to paradise, *tovareesh*," said one young man, offering his hand in camaraderie. "Which group are you in, Democrats or Revolutionaries?"

Daniel gave him an empty stare. Then someone yelled, "cut out that incessant noise, it is impossible to read."

"Cheer up, *tovareesh*. We have elected an elder. See that one over there, the bespectacled Jew." He pointed to the young man behind the voice. "His name is Ira, he has declared that between 9AM and noon, noise is forbidden."

Daniel glanced in Ira's direction. He had the face that only a mother could love. None-the-less, there would be no relief from the commotion. At exactly 9AM, three anarchists who had no respect for rules, prattled like popinjays. "Let the red banner signify the triumph of the Soviet!" they sang.

That evening, Daniel found a narrow opening on one of the two wooden planks which projected from opposite walls and laid down to rest his weary body. There may have been straw mattresses and blankets but he would not touch the filthy things. However, he could not escape the sour odor of perspiring unwashed bodies and the damp smell of mold climbing the walls. Two little windows above the bunks were not enough to circulate the stale air.

His thoughts whirled. Thrown out of the university after almost four years, his residency papers confiscated, banished from Kiev, banished from life! But this ignominy was the final blow. His whole future crushed, as well as his hope. And now what? Siberia? Execution? All because of that insect, Ezra, and his grandiose insane ideas for a new society. Or was it Ezra? Was it count Rostovsky? His word was law in the province of Kiev. One stroke of his pen finished a man. Could he blame the count and his family for his troubles? No, they reacted predictably. For all they knew he was conspiring with Ezra and his rotten crowd. What reason would they have to believe otherwise? They opened their home to him, their table, and their hospitality, all in good pleasure. They even allowed his friendship with their daughter.

No, he recounted. They did the predictable thing. He really had no one to blame but himself. He knew the kind of people he was dealing with from the beginning. He knew he was mingling with people where he had no business, among a society to which he did not belong. Was he so arrogant and puffed up with himself that he thought he could fool them and gain their respect at the same time? His grandfather's admonitions haunted him. "They will turn on you and you will bring great sorrow upon yourself and upon your father's house."

He groaned and rolled over on his side, poking his neighbor with his elbow. His sleepless eyes stared at the lad's back. He would deal with whatever dire consequences were to be heaped upon him, but he could not deal with the grief he caused to his father's household and that of uncle Sholem. He wished he could be given another chance to undo all the transgressions he caused against those he loved.

The filthy common cell resembled an insane asylum. In time, the arguments between the social Democrats and the Socialist revolutionaries became more strident as new arrivals from the underground came in.

"Overthrow the autocracy now," said the revolutionaries.

"No! It will create civil war."

"What difference does it make how many people die in a war. Be done with it."

The warden who had once amused himself by their arguments had become intimidated by their rampages. His gravest threat was only, "look here, you are over doing this, aren't you?"

As with all insane asylums this one was not without its truly mad. A socialist revolutionary awaiting his execution for taking part in armed raids was either faking insanity hoping to postpone his execution or he had truly lost his mind. Regardless, he drove everyone frantic day and night with wild bird screams and incoherent babble, occasionally injected with a hideous laughter.

Permission to receive visitors was not allowed by the warden unless he was paid in rubles of which Daniel had none. Prisoners were allowed to receive packages but only after they were first examined by the warden who took whatever he fancied, especially chocolates and Brandy. Only Golda wrote Daniel letters and sent him packages. She told him of Sholem's release from jail after a few days. Daniel insisted that they tell no one in his family of his incarceration as he would deal with the situation himself as the fate of his future unfolded. He wondered if Jeniya still thought of him, or was she so caught up in the glitter of court society that he had simply become a memory. He wondered if the warden had informed her of the transfer or had the family shielded the information.

After a few months a colonel of the gendarmerie had been assigned to review his case. On the day of his appointment two armed guards drove him to the police headquarters for a hearing. He looked forward to this excursion not only to find relief from "Paradise" and to defend his innocence, but to see normal city life again.

Daniel told the colonel the whole story. He had no reason to hedge, he was just as interested in finding Ezra and his revolutionary cell as his interrogator, in order to prove his innocence. From what he could see, the officer seemed to believe his plea, but there was no indication of release.

A few more months went by and he had not heard from the colonel. Some of his inmates awaited trial, some had been sent off to the work camps in Siberia, and some were carried off to solitary confinement where they would rot. A few went to their death beds in the infirmary, and one, the bird-man to his execution.

Daniel decided that unless he took control of his situation, nothing would be done. Using his knowledge of the law, he composed a strategy in his mind for his vindication. First, he had to gain the favor of the warden, a curious fellow who would occasionally sit in the cell with the prisoners looking for a bit of excitement to pass his boredom. Daniel decided to entertain him with stories. One day, he asked for some paper and a pencil.

"How many rubbles is it worth to you?" asked the warden.

"You know I don't have rubbles."

"Why do you want paper?"

"I want to draw up a petition for my release."

"Your release?" The warden laughed and laughed until tears fell from his eyes, and Daniel laughed too.

"That's the funniest story you've told."

"I am going to send it to the general of the gendarmerie."

"The general?" He blinked his bloodshot eyes and laughed some more until his round cheeks and bulbous nose turned cherry red.

"Do you know what I am going to tell them?"

"What?" He inclined his round face closer. Daniel flinched from the puff of his liquored breath.

"I Daniel Mendelev, confined to the Kiev transport prison no longer wants to sit behind bars, but he wishes to be released at once!"

Now the warden howled with laughter. "I like you, you are a very clever lad, maybe the brightest one in here. And you are a good lad, you keep to yourself and do not get involved in arguments." He wiped the tears from his eyes and blinked. "I have not had such a good laugh in weeks. It is worth the price of rubbles. I will bring your paper. I should like to see what becomes of you."

True to his word, the warden brought in a few sheets of paper and a pencil. Daniel wrote his intended words and added, "If it is your objective to deprive me of my life when I have not been found guilty of the crime for which I am accused, or to deny me a fair trial which is my right as a citizen of the Empire, then I wish to be informed of the reasons." The warden delivered the petition anxious for a little drama in his otherwise miserable existence. It was duly numbered and put on file.

Weeks passed, and still no word came from the gendarmerie or the warden, so Daniel had resigned himself to his fate, and would wait for his probable deportation to Siberia. Actually, he had no idea of what they had planned for him. Except for the new arrivals, everyone was thin, pale, and bearded.

"Daniel Mendelev!"

He jumped up terrified one afternoon when he saw a police guard standing at the door of the cell with a sword at his side. They do not call a man's name in such a harsh manner unless they intend to remove him to solitary confinement or God forbid, to his execution.

"Daniel Mendelev!"

"I, your Excellency."

"Get your things and follow me."

The gendarmerie led him to a small grey cell containing a desk, took a piece of paper from the drawer and placed it on the table in front of him. "Sign here!" he demanded.

Daniel took a pen in his trembling hand. It was difficult to read what he was signing in the dim light, but he saw the words printed at the top, Petition for Release. He gasped but did not want to show his delight, in case he was mistaken.

"You must leave the district of Kiev without delay and proceed to your hometown of Lensk in the Pale, where you will await your pending trial," said the guard. "You will be under strict police surveillance. Is that clearly understood?"

Daniel nodded.

"Here is your ticket." Another guard came in with his suitcase. Golda, the good heart that she is, packed his things to take on his journey.

Prison was a hard master. It taught him patience and gave him time to consider matters that had not previously occurred to him. He pondered on life's simple pleasures lost in the daily routine of existence; the crow of a rooster as the fog lifts from the meadows and the world comes to life, the fragrance of spring and the beauty of autumn, sitting in busy cafes watching preoccupied people scurry to and fro. It seemed that the average man goes through his life almost oblivious to these precious gifts, and worse, not understanding the price of freedom to enjoy them.

He bought a cup of tea at the train station and stood by one of the small round tables in the cafeteria to drink it. Sweet cakes dusted in soot were displayed under a glass rack and corpulent attendants in soiled white uniforms dished out *shaslisck*, boiled potatoes and gravy from behind the counter. A shriek erupted from the kitchen and a stray cat lumbered around under the tables. The room reeked of tobacco smoke.

Several soldiers stood around another table laughing boisterously, while stuffing smoked fish in their mouths and washing it down with Vodka. Occasionally they shot a sideward glance around the room. At the table beside him, Jewish tradesman debated with animated faces and busy hands, drinking tea and smoking cigarettes. He couldn't help but to overhear their conversation.

"The police smashed down doors, searched every bedroom. The people weren't even allowed to pack their belongings. Just dragged them off without mercy in the dead of night, half naked into the bitter cold, and marched them to the police stations. Everyone, including infants, ...even those on their sick beds could not postpone their deportation."

"What have we done to offend God so much that He allows so much suffering? Wouldn't you think He would look down from heaven and cry a little?"

"The rabbis tell us we are born to suffer. But why? By what divine rule?"

"Excuse me," Daniel said. "I couldn't help but to hear your conversation. What has happened?"

"Haven't you heard the news?"

"No."

"The Tsar appointed his brother, Grand Duke Sergius, to replace old Prince Dolgoruki as the new governor of Moscow. But before his uncle would set foot in the city, it had to be purged of its thousands of Jewish residents. Everyone...from those without residency papers to those who owned business establishments were transported to the Pale of Settlement. Even those born and raised in Moscow who nobly served in the army under Alexander II were forced to evacuate."

A young man wearing a fedora and a long black kaftan joined the conversation "The only hope for us is to return to our homeland, Eretz Yisroel." He shook his head and his ear-locks jumped. His eyes reflected sadness, not only because of the wretched situation of the Jews in Russia, but also in their shape. From his soft and scholarly diction, Daniel surmised he may have been a yeshiva student.

"Our status is not only shaky here in the land of darkness but also in Germany, the seat of science and reason. In every land where we settle. We are regarded as the ghosts of a dead nation, refusing to disappear…wandering about within the Gentile societies and it creates in these people a certain fear. I say it's time for us to stop becoming the scapegoat for the transgressions of these nations and promote migration to our historic homeland in an effort to form a Jewish state, where no one will be able to defeat our determination to live as free men on our own soil and die peacefully in our own homes!"

Chapter 23

DANIEL BOARDED THE train and despairingly stared out the window into a misty grey landscape. The distressing state of affairs in the Pale had only compounded the inevitable and dreaded confrontation with his father concerning the events that had transpired over the past few months.

On the way home he stopped by the store to see Rochelle but the door was locked. When he reached the wattle fence outside his father's house, he took a deep breath, wiped the sweat from his face, and stood for a few moments. His heart pounded from both excitement and vigorous exercise after so long a confinement. He went to the door, touched the mezuzah and asked God's blessing. The hour of confession to his family had come and he needed to fortify himself against all the obstacles that may be thrown his way before he gave an explanation for this little holiday at home.

Nathan smiled when he opened the door. "Danya! What brings you here?"

Daniel gave his father a cordial smile.

"Come in, come in," Nathan said, giving his son a welcoming pat on the back. "So, can I now brag about my son the lawyer?"

Rochelle was sitting in the parlor mending clothes, when she heard her brother's voice at the door. She ran out to meet him and threw her arms around his neck. "Danya! What are you doing here?" she said happy to see him. They both laughed and he lifted her into a strong hug. This was the first happy moment he had in weeks.

"And you Ronnie?" He put her down and held her at arms distance, looking her over. "Aren't you married yet? The most beautiful girl in all of Lensk?" Her dark hair was knotted into a dowager's bun and she felt like a feather in his arms.

"She should have been married long ago," Nathan interrupted. "I've had every eligible young man in here…from every town around to see her."

"What's the matter, Ronnie?"

"Oh, I don't know. I guess I'm in no hurry to take on the miseries of married life."

"You'd better not wait too long or you'll be an old maid and all the good men will be taken." He gazed sadly upon his beautiful young sister, in her long dark skirt. Instead of the joy of anticipating a new life with a young husband, she had taken on the countenance of a matron who has buried her spouse.

Rochelle smiled to mask her hurt at her brother's well-meaning but inappropriate words. "You are still available, I see," She rebuked him with a hint of sarcasm.

He smiled, sensing her pain but choosing to ignore it. "But you are still young," he said wishing to lift her spirit. "One day you will have a good husband." He felt badly that the simple innocence and pure beauty which radiated from within her person was hidden under a cover of duty to her father. He took her in his arms again and held her tightly for a long time. He could feel the warm tears on her cheek next to his and the trembling shoulders, like a little bird.

Had he been so enamored, not only by Jeniya, but by the insulated dazzling world of high society, that he had forgotten there was another world occupied by the forgotten people, the world in which his father lived with his dear beautiful sister, more elegant than any society's unremarkable princesses.

When he let her go, she led him to the kitchen. "I made some borsht, are you hungry?"

"Mm, very hungry," seeing his sister's gracious manner brought back warm memories of his mother and his happy childhood home. He noticed that his father was not the bull of a man he used to be and that he began to acquire the downcast countenance of a man who had been beaten by unfortunate circumstances. His curly brown hair and ear-locks were flecked with grey now.

Rochelle quickly brought out another place setting and a basket with a few slices of bread while the men went to wash their hands before they sat down at the table to eat. A few minutes later she dutifully brought two hot bowls of soup, placed one in front of each man, and returned to the stove where she sat alone as was the custom of an old *babbeh* after she served her family and guests. *She has become like a little servant girl, devoting herself to her father.*

His father blessed the food, broke some bread and began to eat. "Have you heard about the tragedy in Moscow?" Nathan asked noticing Daniel's reluctance to take one of the slices of bread. "Not only in Moscow but all the cities across great Russia."

Daniel shook his head. "Yes," he said.

"It is causing hardship for everyone in the Pale, no jobs, not enough grain for bread. The peasants had to sell most of what they planted to the government to pay higher grain taxes. They have little left to sell us this year."

Then Daniel remembered hearing talk on the train about the ministry selling all of Russia's grain to Europe to pay off the bloated government debt. There was also talk of peasants going without enough grain to last the winter. Suddenly, the image of Ezra popped into his head working like a devil to incite the hungry working peasants to revolt. Not that he didn't see the justice in his brother's pursuit to liberate the oppressed, but it was his devious and volatile ways that angered him, especially since Ezra's actions had destroyed his good name, his future, and all the years of hard work he sacrificed to get out of this retched, desperate, poverty stricken pale only to be thrown back into it with a criminal record to boot. *Ezra, that dog!* "Has anyone seen Ezra?" he cried out in a flash of impetuous anger.

"Ezra? I thought he was with you in Kiev," his father quipped as if he had been taken by a sudden storm.

Daniel gasped as if to gulp back his words when he realized that Golda and Sholem had kept his secret and told Nathan nothing of the murder, nor his imprisonment and his expulsion from school. He had hoped to let the truth slide out slowly in time, in a civil manner, if at all. Now his troubles were compounded. Nathan stared at his son trying to connect words with events. In the next few moments of agonizing silence, Daniel began to fear his father's reaction. He knew him well enough to see it coming.

"Where is Ezra?" Nathan asked not with concern, but with that familiar tone of accusation he used when he wanted to extract certain information.

"I don't know," Daniel rebutted with sudden reserve.

"In his last letter he said he got a job in Kuznetsov's mill. He said he may move Leinha and the kids to Kiev. What happened?"

Daniel stared at the soup and the spoon lying beside the bowl. The moment he dreaded had arrived sooner than he thought. "He left Kiev." He said quietly, hoping not to elevate the tension that began to fill the air.

"He left Kiev? Why? What happened?"

"I don't know why." Daniel blurted out in defense.

"And you? Why have you left Kiev?" Nathan persisted. "To what do I owe the pleasure of this unexpected visit?"

Daniel's gut tied into a knot. He could get up and walk out, avoiding further confrontation. But he could not avoid the guilt that would follow him, knowing that he had left his father in a broken state.

"Don't lie to your father."

These words stung Daniel like a poison dart. In the past, he had managed to slide by with alibis but this time he knew he had to face the truth as Nathan would make it his business to find out the entire horrid story from Sholem.

"There was a riot in a saloon near the mill where he was working. The foreman was killed. They are looking for Ezra in connection with the murder."

Nathan's mouth flew open and Daniel saw a million questions spinning in his father's horror struck eyes.

Daniel hesitated. "They thought I was his accomplice."

When Nathan recovered from the initial shock and fully comprehended what had happened, he said. "Why did they suspect you of being his accomplice, what did you do to arouse their suspicions?"

"I had nothing to do with Ezra." Daniel's ordered thoughts unraveled under his father's accusing glare. "They arrested me because I was his brother, that's all."

The muscles in Nathan's face froze as a man about to suffer a stroke. "May God help us." Nathan said weakly after a long silence; his lips quivering above his beard.

"I wasn't guilty, father, I had nothing to do with Ezra."

Nathan arose and put both hands on the table to brace his trembling body.

A sudden fear gripped Daniel when his father began to sway. He jumped up and held out his hand to help.

Nathan pushed him away. After a few minutes, he said, "you must have done something to arouse their suspicions. They just don't arrest someone who keeps his nose clean, I don't care if you are a Jew."

"No! They knew Ezra and I were both living with uncle Sholem, that's why they came after me."

"Don't tell me no and shovel your foolish tricks off on Ezra. He wasn't living with Sholem when you were arrested, or they would have taken him too. They arrested you because of your connection with Count Rostovsky's daughter, that's what!" He pointed a finger of accusation. "You were in his home, pursuing his daughter. The murder was just the alibi they needed to get rid of you. You are so smart and yet so dumb...I never will understand you."

"How did you know about her?"

"Sholem wrote me."

"What else did he tell you?"

"There's something else?"

Ronnie approached from behind and gently wrapped her slender arms around Daniel's shoulders to comfort him. She fully understood his unfortunate circumstances. "A terrible injustice has come to you," she whispered. He put his hand over hers and said to Nathan. "I'm sorry father. You wanted the truth..." He bowed his head. "I shouldn't have come home...I have no home."

Without looking at his children, Nathan went to his room and slammed the door. Shortly after, Daniel heard his father sobbing while reciting the familiar prayers from the Destruction of the Temple in Lamentations. Now he had caused a greater misery to come upon his father than he had upon himself. In time he would overcome his troubles. He was young, had a good education, and could still carve out a life for himself. He saw how easy it was to mingle with the Russians right to the top of the social ladder. Although it wouldn't be easy to start again, it may take time, even years, but his troubles at home were not yet over. Nathan still did not know that he was under police surveillance for his pending trial nor that he had been expelled from school before he received his degree to practice law.

The next few days were impossible. Nathan went about his business in silence except for an occasional sarcastic dig, but it was better than dead silence and Daniel hoped that by maintaining a calm and helpful presence their relationship would improve. Then he could talk to him reasonably about his entire situation. He decided to see Maria Kerenskaya. She and her husband were warm generous people and he always felt comfortable in their home. Perhaps she could help him find an experienced lawyer to defend his innocence. He knew they had many acquaintances across the Empire and had always held out a helping hand.

———◆———

The faithful old servant dutifully answered the door and gazed blankly, but Daniel immediately recognized him even though he had grown old. His dark beard had become long and grey and his bright eyes had dimmed, but he still stood tall with a straight back and broad shoulders, emphasized all the more in a home spun *rubashka* belted at his waist. The peasant custom of wrapping their infants onto a board even had its rewards in old age. "Feodorchenko!" he said.

The old man squinted for a few minutes searching Daniel's face but then he lit up in both surprise and delight. "I remember you! You are Mendelev boy. *Poiihodiite*," he said ushering him into the parlor. "*Seedeete*." He pointed to a comfortable cushiony sofa.

"Panii Kerenskaya is not here, but she will be back soon." He pointed to an assortment of liquors and jams around the samovar. "*Pashalusta*, help yourself. I'll be back with white rolls, I remember how you liked them," he said with a chuckle.

The elegant room was just as he had remembered with the tall blue and white stove in one corner, and the long windows dressed in the lace curtains he purchased from Minsk. How he would always remember those curtains. She still had flowers and potted plants arranged artistically in front of sunny windowsills. He smiled to himself. The quiet hum of the samovar ready to offer a cup of tea made a visitor feel relaxed and welcome. He took some homemade raspberry jam, mixed it in a glass of tea and sat down on the large cozy sofa. While he waited he noticed an open book on the tea table. He picked it up and examined the cover. *The Holy Bible*. He flipped the pages to Matthew 5: 3 and read;

"Blessed are the poor in spirit:
for theirs is the kingdom of heaven.
Blessed are they that mourn:
for they shall be comforted.
Blessed are the meek:
for they shall inherit the earth.
Blessed are they which do hunger
and thirst after righteousness:
for they shall be filled.
Blessed are the merciful:
for they shall obtain mercy.
Blessed are the pure in heart:
for they shall see God.
Blessed are the peacemakers:
for they shall be called the children of God.
Blessed are they which are persecuted
for righteousness' sake:
for theirs is the kingdom of heaven.
Blessed are ye when men shall revile you,
and persecute you, and shall say all manner
of evil against you falsely, for my sake.
Rejoice, and be exceedingly glad:
for great is your reward in heaven:
for so they persecuted the prophets which were before you."
(Matt. 5: 3-12 King James Version)

He was astounded to see these words in their Bible, for he had always been taught that only through suffering could a man understand life and bring his soul closer to the heart of God. But he also thought that the rabbis made this idea up to console the beaten-down eternal people. Curiously, he read on;

> "Ye are the salt of the earth: but if the salt
> have lost its savor, wherewith shall it be salted?
> It is thenceforth good for nothing, but to be cast out,
> and to be trodden underfoot of men." (Matt. 5:13)

He would never forget his grandfather's words, "If you try to escape from who you are you will wander in life's shadows and never find peace."

While he was mulling over these verses, the old servant brought a basket full of fresh hot rolls. "I see you make yourself at home, *harasho*." He nodded approvingly. Then he took a watch from a pocket hidden in his puffy trousers and glanced at it. *Panii* should be home soon."

Daniel smiled. "It's all right, I'm in no hurry."

The old man nodded and quietly left the room. Daniel put some butter and jam on the roll and devoured it, he could not remember when he ate anything so good. He took the book back to his lap and read on;

> "Think not that I am come to destroy the law, or the prophets:
> I am not come to destroy, but to fulfill." (Matt. 5: 17)

He thought to himself. This man Jesus is teaching as one of our rabbis, a Jew to Jews: this man they worship as God, and at the same time in whose name they persecute us, how peculiar. As he continued to read he was astounded to see this forbidden book expounding the Torah, explaining the laws of Moses and he became interested. He knew the Christians had a Bible of sorts, but he didn't know it contained a commentary on the laws of Moses. He became so absorbed in his reading that when he looked up to take another roll, he saw Maria Kerenskaya standing in front of him. He snapped the book shut and sprang to his feet.

"Madam Kerenskaya," he said, "how are you?"

"Danya!" she said taking both his hands in hers and looking him over, pleased to see that he had grown into a handsome young man. "How nice to see you. How long has it been? Why you were just a boy."

He smiled.

"Please, won't you sit down?"

She sat in a chair facing him while the old servant fixed a glass of tea and brought it to her. The years had transformed her youthful beauty into a gracious noble woman. Her upswept chestnut hair was still dark and luxurious but with an elegant streak of grey at the temple.

"What brings you to Lensk? Your father tells me you are about to get your degree to practice law."

"It over," he said abruptly. "I made a horrible mistake and…a…I'm sorry." He caught his words and was embarrassed over his outburst in front of the one woman he hoped to impress.

She gazed at him through wide brown eyes. An expression of deep concern fell over her face indicating she knew something was terribly wrong. She waited patiently to see if he wanted to confide his troubles. She was also the one person who did not intimidate him, who allowed him to relax, open up and be himself.

"Madam," he leaned forward on the sofa. "I don't wish to inconvenience you, but I am in deep trouble and I need help. I have yet to tell my father everything because I have already brought too much heartbreak to his house." He related the whole story to her and said, "my father cut me off when he learned that I was accused of revolutionary activity along with my brother. Now I am here under police surveillance until a trial can be arranged. I need a lawyer to defend my case and I had hoped that you knew of one."

She was frowning as she listened deep in thought. "My goodness, this is a terrible thing that has happened to you. I will try my best to help you. Perhaps we may be able to work this out."

Daniel thanked her.

"You understand I cannot promise you."

"I understand," he said, his hopeful spirit deflated.

"And what will you do now that you have been so cruelly deprived of you law degree? Will you work with your sister in the store?"

"No! I cannot do that. I cannot go back!" he said shaking his head. "I will look for work elsewhere." He paused and thought for a moment. "Do you…know of any family who may need a tutor for their children or perhaps a teaching position opening up in a gymnasium?"

She thought for a while and then concluded, "Right now, it is next to impossible to get a teaching job around here." When she observed the despair on his face, she said, "Daniel, your world has not come to an end because of these things which have happened to you. The end of one thing is always the beginning of another. There is nothing you cannot do if you believe that you can do it."

"I used to think that and it got me into all my troubles. Now I see my future as a struggle for survival like everyone else. The quiet desperation of the masses, as they say."

"If you trust in God and walk in his word, then He will be there to guide your path through the unknown future. Your life need not be one of quiet desperation but one of meaning and purpose. This is what your faith teaches doesn't it?"

Daniel stared at her. So simply stated, so easy to say but there were too many contradictions that reached beyond mortal understanding. In their quest to trust God and walk in His commandments the eternal people have only heaped sorrows upon themselves. She cannot begin to understand what it is like, especially coming from the privileged class.

"But it doesn't work that way," he replied.

They were both silent for a while. She was staring at the Bible which had been opened to the beatitudes and was now lying shut on the tea table. Finally, she said, "I have a small new testament you can have if you would like to read it."

"Madam, I would like to ask you a question if I may. Something which had troubled me ever since I was a boy."

"Yes, what is it?"

"How can you people call this person Jesus a god when he was clearly a man? So far, what I've read in that book," he pointed to the Bible on the table, "is about a Jewish teacher expounding on the laws of Moses. There is only one God and He is spirit. Besides, the church is filled with hypocrisy and atrocities which they do in the name of their god. How can they….?" He excitedly opened his hands to her. "Do what they do?"

She shook her head, "I don't know, I can only offer a feeble explanation, and I say this with deep sorrow in my heart. The Church of Russia had been defiled. The Tsar has become the state arm of the church. The church is like the sun and the Tsar like the moon who reflects church doctrine to the people. His crest is the double eagle which holds the state in one talon and the church in the other."

He stared at her in amazement. Now it had become clear to him why the illiterate peasants mindlessly follow every edict signed by their little father, the Tsar.

"The true Church follows the teachings of Christ," Kerenskaya continued. "It tends to the welfare of the poor, not to exploit them for gold or keep them ignorant with religious dogma. It tells the good news of God's grace and mercy toward anyone who will believe in the words of his son Jesus Christ."

He gazed at her perplexed.

She reflected for a moment. "The road to spiritual maturity is long and difficult as we battle with our own fears, doubts and self-interests. Your father Abraham trusted God's promises and God Blessed him… Daniel, do you believe God loves you?"

He stared at the oriental carpet in the middle of the room. "I don't know," he said.

She rose from her chair and said, "excuse me. I'll be right back." She left the room and after several minutes returned with a faded sheet of paper. "One time when my father was on holiday in England he encountered one of their great missionary preachers who gave him this list of prophetic scriptures comparing the first and second coming of the Messiah. It also has reference to those which have already been fulfilled."

He took the paper and thoughtfully examined it.

"You are welcome to take it to the desk and make a copy if you like. I will get to work on your trial right away." As she was about to leave the room, she turned and added, "Sophie will be serving dinner in about an hour. Why don't you join us?"

"Thank you very much, I would like to."

"Good. Then we will see you later at dinner."

Daniel opened the door, walked in and looked around. No one was there. "Father?" he called. "Ronnie? Is anyone home?" Ronnie had cabbage and potatoes prepared and warming on the clay stove. On many nights they ate cabbage and potatoes prepared in one form or another. Ronnie was reluctant to discuss the business with him, and each time he inquired, it was always, "business is good, everything is fine." Nathan had nothing to say, he spent his days at the *Kehillah* and at the study house, buried in books.

He sat down on the kitchen bench. His mind, body, and soul were weary as though he had lived through two life times. He wondered if someone, a person, a man, a Messiah had walked the road of suffering before him to pave a path of hope. He remembered a verse in Isaiah 30:21. "And thine ears shall hear a word behind thee, saying, this is the way, walk ye in it". He wished someone would speak to him and show him the way through this insanity called life.

Nathan clomped into the room without looking at his son, washed his hands in the basin before he went over to the stove where the borsht and potatoes were warming. He scooped out a dish full for himself and took his bowl to the table. "I waited for you," he said. "Go ahead and help yourself. There's enough." Then he said the blessing and broke some bread, sopped it into the liquid and began to eat. That his father offered dinner was at least a positive sign that he still welcomed him into his home.

"What's the matter?" he said. "Not hungry?"

"I ate a big dinner at the Kerensky's."

Nathan lifted his head and raised his eye brows partly in surprise, partly in curiosity, and stared at him.

Daniel hated that stare, it bore right through a person, pealing him apart, dissecting him to the bone. "I went there to see if she knew of anyone who needed a teacher or a tutor," he explained. "I need a job."

Nathan shifted his attention back to his meal. He broke another piece of bread and dipped it. "*Ny*, so how did you make out over there? Did they find a job for you?"

"No, there's nothing around here."

Over the next several weeks, while he anxiously awaited news on his trial, he went to help Rochelle in the store to take his mind off of his tribulations, but there was to be no relief. Each morning the same police guard sat on the bench outside the shop reading a newspaper. These people made no attempt to conceal their presence, he thought. Perhaps it was part of the intimidation process to remind him that he is not a free man.

As the days dragged on, he became edgy and could no longer focus on the business. He stayed home and tried to read to relax by researching the study sheet Maria had given him but he could not concentrate. One afternoon while he was sitting at the table scribbling notes, he heard a persistent heavy-handed knock at the door. He peeked outside the window and saw a large man wearing that fearsome official brown uniform and the red banded cap with its official insignia. Apprehensively, he slipped off the bench and opened the door. The officer inquired of his name, his prison identification number, and handed him a telegram.

Daniel ripped it open with shaking hands. "You have been granted full pardon." It was from the office of the general of the gendarmerie. He ran out the door and sprinted to the Kerensky home. Maria laughed and embraced him like her own son. Then she informed him that it was not she who obtained his release but his old professor Demchenko, who was now dean of the law school.

While he was away his father came home and tidied up the papers scattered around the table to make room for the evening meal when he discovered a new testament and the list of Messianic scriptures. All this study may not have made sense to Daniel but to Nathan it was clear, especially since he knew that the Kerenskys belonged to a denomination called the old believers; dissidents of the state run, Tsar dominated Orthodoxy. They were a closely knit society, who fiercely defended their ancient Slav heritage as much as the Jew defended his tradition. They were the soul of old Russia, the Moscow merchants who had become the titans of the Empire's commerce, banking, industry and railroads, whose wealth dwarfed that of the aristocracy.

Chapter 24

THE EVE OF the great famine of Russia had begun and it affected workers everywhere in the Empire. Jobs were non-existent for peasants migrating from the drought stricken black earth region of the Volga and impossible for the ever increasing Jewish destitute deported from the cities of Great Russia. No one needed an arbitrator or a teacher or a tutor. They wanted bread.

Daniel soon learned that the administration had artificially set low grain prices in order to balance the Imperial budget by assessing a head tax on the peasants forcing them to sell their autumn grain futures for kopeks. They then shipped the grain to drought stricken Germany for immense profits. Adding fuel to an already critical situation, corrupt brokers gambling on the world's commodities market, deliberately failed to report the growing famine to Alexander III. When the Tsar finally learned of the tragic circumstances, he declared a moratorium on grain shipments abroad, but these profiteers continued to ship even more grain underhandedly for a few more months.

With even meager jobs unavailable, Daniel took what rubbles he had and purchased a train ticket to the German port of Hamburg, where he could board a steam ship to America, but at the German border, he discovered something else to compound his misfortune forcing him to turn back. A cholera epidemic had broken out in the port city and was blamed on the Russian immigrants, closing all German borders to Russians, even to those who held tickets to travel to Hamburg.

He then decided to go to the port of Odessa where he could get a job on a ship sailing to anywhere as long as it led away from Russia. He had two choices of transportation, the train or the river steamer which was cheaper but due to the severe drought the boats ran sporadically. If and when they did sail, they were caught on sandbars for days waiting for the boatmen to haul them off. Either way he did not have enough rubbles for transportation so he decided to hitch-hike.

The terrible drought which had devastated the black region along the Volga had spread southward toward the Black Sea. The closer he got to Odessa, he found the fields of winter wheat withered and the dark people of Russia who inhabited dirt floor huts going about their chores in a listless stupor. They would stop and stare at him with dumbfounded expressions on their faces. He could not hitch a ride on a hay wagon because there was no wheat to be harvested and most of the animals had been sold to buy food or perished.

Bread became scarce and dear. Daniel had just enough money to buy one loaf and make it last for the next few days until he reached the port of Odessa, if he could find one. As the sun was setting, he made his bed in a dried up grain field. He puffed up his bundle of clothing, tucked it under his head for a pillow and stretched out on the hard ground.

Usually the chirping of the insects would lull him to sleep, but tonight his mind was racing with thoughts of that worm Ezra, and his band of hoodlums. He hadn't seen many of them around in the countryside these days. *Well, what would they do here? Hungry peasants do not care about philosophical euphemisms. On the other hand, why aren't they here with bread and medicine, they are so good at preaching a utopian world of unity, justice, and happy times for all. Now, where are these champions of the beaten down hungry masses desperate for a slice bread. They were probably hiding in some underground bistro, eating and drinking, while the people they pledged to liberate starve.* No, he commiserated, they were most likely scattered among the dark masses of Russia, striving along with the rest of them against hunger.

He grew increasingly sympathetic toward their movement, and increasingly hateful toward the greedy aristocracy as well as the corrupt money changers who never seem to have enough. If he met up with a band of insurrectionists, he had seriously thought about joining their ranks. But their philosophical view of life troubled him. They boldly proclaimed that there is no God, and that only man, by his will could stamp out greed and injustice and create a new world of unity and peace. *Maybe they were right,* he concluded. *Maybe there is no God and the direction of our destiny does lie in our own hands.*

His people had always looked to a God, a Messianic figure, who would deliver them from the crushing ghettos, and the more they looked, the worse their situation became. *So where is this God and why doesn't he make himself known. Why doesn't he alter the circumstances not only for 'the chosen' but all people who are suffering in this unfair world.* Only the greedy rich find peace and solace and comfort. Still the rabbis continue to indoctrinate each generation that suffering is necessary to understand life. That suffering is the heart of Jewishness, everything revolves around suffering, and they call this tradition.

But they speak to a God without ears. He rolled over on his side. *Ah,* he said to himself, *what does it matter whether or not there is a God. It's all the same down here, hunger, desperation, greed, and injustice. While the Jews keep clinging to hope. The word on the street these days is Revolution!* "Revolution now or never!" he said and raised his fist in the air. He flipped again onto his back and stared at the stars which swept the night sky in milky swirls. *But...there must be a God,* he thought. *If there is no God, then who put the stars in the sky and keeps them all in their place? These ancient constellations defy the greatest minds of man.* He concluded it was useless to philosophize under the unimaginable order of this vast universe.

He lay there gazing at the silent beauty and incredible wonder in the clear night sky. *Well, what does the concept of a God have to do with me? Anyway, who cares,* he thought and drifted into a deep sleep. Suddenly, he awoke. "Know there is God." Daniel sat up and looked around startled and saw no one. "There is none in the universe like God. One day, and all the works of man will be burnt up and dissolve like dust, and no one will remember only as in a dream."

He shook with fear. The night had become dead quiet, not even the sound of a cricket.

When he awoke in the morning, he was still rattled, but he had to move on with his plan, time was shrinking between starvation and Odessa.

He picked up his little sack and pressed on toward his goal, stopping in the nearest town to buy a loaf of bread with his last few kopecks. He paid dear for this stale old loaf as few were for sale in the bakeries. He sat down on a bench and divided the loaf with his eyes, calculating how many chunks he would need until he reached Odessa. Then he broke off the end and began to eat, chewing slowly to make it last and feign his hunger, when he heard a child cry. He looked up and saw a woman about his own age with a young boy approaching.

"*Pashalusta*, please kind sir, can you spare some bread for my child?"

She must have at one time been strikingly beautiful, even so in her emaciated state. She moved toward him with the flowing grace of an aristocrat. The child was also handsome with large intelligent eyes, like pale blue crystals. He stared at Daniel as a person of physic insight, almost metaphysical.

"Please sir, just a little for my child," the woman pleaded. "May you be blessed."

Normally he would not hesitate to give his bread, but this was all he had left. She gazed at him. "May you be blessed, my lord." She held out a slender hand and swayed slightly on her feet. Her yellowish grey complexion had the tell-tail sign of someone surviving on *goludny Kleb*, a foul smelling, famine bread made from the stubborn toxic goosefoot weed milled with a bit of rye flour.

Daniel did not look at her pitiful bloated face, but only at his loaf. *Would one slice keep them from inevitable death...they will soon die anyway.*

"Give your loaf of bread to this woman and her child, and I will give you the bread of life, so you will never hunger." Daniel turned around to see who was speaking behind him, and again he saw no one. He looked up at the woman. She gave no indication that she heard someone speaking, as she continued to plead silently through blue eyes under drooping puffy lids. He shook his head. Had hunger now made him so delirious that he was hearing voices? Or was his mother speaking to him from beyond the grave? She would often say, "Blessed is the man who gives to the poor, who cares for the widow and the orphan, for God shall pay the dividends." Was his mind playing tricks, reminding him of the religion that had been so firmly indoctrinated in his head since childhood. There was one loaf between death and Odessa, between *goludny kleb* and liberation from this land of misery, between these voices and whatever trouble may be waiting tomorrow. If he gave his bread to this woman and her child, then the dust of the earth may be his last meal. What did it matter now, he reasoned, to the dust of the earth we all are eventually gathered, or as he often overheard the despairing peasants say, "we are all marching to the grave."

He handed the loaf to the woman and her child, not from compassion for he desperately wanted that bread to end the gnawing in his stomach. Neither because of his mother's dying wish to care for the poor and the needy, but because he believed that these voices may be from God or something beyond and he was afraid.

The woman knelt down kissing his hands and weeping. "*Slava Bogu*," she repeated, "Glory to God. May you be blessed."

Daniel gazed at her blankly, not fully able to comprehend all that had happened, as she disappeared from his sight like an apparition… with his bread.

"God help me," he said out loud. "I cannot think anymore. I cannot see the day ahead. I cannot plan. Everything is dark, the heavens are dark, and the world is a pit from which I can see no way out." He combed his fingers through his hair, everything spun around for a moment. "I must be going mad."

He arose and listlessly picked up his sack, when all his belongings tumbled onto the ground. The New Testament which Maria had given him was lying in the dust with its pages open. He still carried it, God only knew why, as he could not bear to look at it since he left Lensk. He almost threw it away as a bad omen, but could not desecrate a holy book, even theirs. He bent over to pick it up and the words from John, chapter 6, jumped out at him.

"I am the bread of life; he that comes to me shall never hunger, and he that believes in me shall never thirst...Your fathers did eat manna in the wilderness and are dead...if any man eat this bread, he shall live forever..."

What kind of nonsense is this? What prophet in his right mind would say such a thing, and what kind of idiots would follow him? He stared at the page and pondered. But these events are too uncanny; twice in the last twelve hours, it cannot all be coincidence. He looked up at the sky. If indeed, this word was from God then he wanted His divine presence in his life more than he wanted life itself, for life had now become worthless.

He gathered his things and stuffed them back into the sack. He would press toward his goal while he still had the strength. His stomach growled and his mouth was dry from thirst. Here and there he saw the old and weak lying outside their huts waiting to die of typhus, the famine disease carried by infected lice and rats. No one would touch them except the flies that crawled on the bloated bodies.

Soon he would arrive on the outskirts of Odessa where a large Jewish population resided. There he hoped to find a *hekdesh* where he could eat a meal. He often told himself that he would never beg outside the poorhouse or take bread from mouths of mothers and their children as the Russian government provided no subsidies for the Jewish destitute whose population was now exploding within the Pale. What miserable pittance the *Kehillah* received to feed the starving came from the housewife's mite, as she would often deprive her family of a few kopecks each week to assist the needy. But after weeks on the road, the will to survive had hardened him to suffering and sickness.

When he arrived in the community, the sight before him was more catastrophic than the pogroms of 1882. He found throngs of emaciated men, women and children camped in the streets around the poorhouse, not only victims of famine and the scourge of the Tsar, but also the prohibitively inflated cost of available grain.

He sank down by the roadside and supporting his elbows on his knees, hung his head limply to the dust and wept. Death was mocking, waiting to swallow him into the grave.

Chapter 25

GRAY PEOPLE WRAPPED in dark clothing rushed about in the stinging cold on the broad Nevsky Prospekt. No one strolled or gazed into shop windows or stopped to exchange a few words. They passed each other straight on, looking through one another, around one another, but never at one another. Rows of imposing buildings were constructed with uniform symmetry along the arrow straight avenues. When the sun peeked through the fog, it gave an oblique blue-green light which reflected on the sand colored facades creating an illusion of sunshine. Darkness descended by 4PM.

Petersburg's wintery gloom had settled in Jeniya's heart. The parties, receptions, dances, and frolicking lovers in sleighs gliding through snowy streets to the sound of jingling bells, only intensified her longing for the magical times she and Daniel spent together under the blue skies and starry nights of the Ukrainian summer. She tried to relive those moments, but as time passed, they too faded into winter's gloom.

As soon as she settled in the city, she wrote letters to encourage Daniel, but they were returned. She badgered her father to write the necessary document of acquittal, but he remained adamant in his decision. "Let him stay in prison where he belongs. It will keep him from stirring up more trouble." No amount of reason could persuade him otherwise. His understanding should have been above that of the half-civilized, uneducated peasants, but in reality she saw little difference. He had the inflexible determination of the Slavs. Once they had taken something in their heads, the argument was over. Each day she checked with Yaroslav, the first footman to see if there were any letters and he continuously replied, "No, my lady countess." His manner remained ambiguous but she saw the sadness in his eyes and believed he told the truth. To comfort her aching soul, she would order the coachman to take her to the islands skiing where the snow drifts piled so high she could almost glide to the tops of the fir trees.

Meanwhile, the unconcerned Rostovsky family was busy making plans for their daughter. One of society's most eligible young bachelors had shown more than a passing interest. Anatole Konstantinovich Urassov had been making frequent visits to the family's mansion. When a young man was seen at a house where there were marriageable daughters, it was proper for him to declare his intentions. Brought up in the strictest of etiquette, Anatole performed his duty and asked Count Rostovsky for Jeniya's hand to begin a formal courtship. Zinaida was delighted, as he more than satisfied all the requirements for a son-in-law; rich, high born, with the promise of a brilliant career. His strong bones, height, and erect posture, a prerequisite for joining the Tsar's elite Preobrazhensky regiment, cut an imposing handsome figure. Both families had decided they had made the perfect match since their darlings had played together from childhood. Zinaida announced the news proudly to her closest friends knowing that this choice tidbit would rush through all the glamorous salons to be discussed in all its details. As far as mother was concerned, the match was sealed.

Jeniya would make her entrance into the Petersburg society at the fairy tale setting of Emperor's State Ball, after she had been formally presented to the Empress and made her debut. Before sunrise on the morning of the big event, she jumped out of bed, pushed aside one heavy curtain and peeked outside at the softly falling snow blanketing the city with fresh white powder. She watched by the window until she saw the appearance of the *Skorokhod* moving in a quick running like walk to deliver the invitations ahead of the Tsar's coach which glided silently through the snowy streets. The messenger wore knee breeches, a short green coat with gold lace above a red collar, and a green cap adorned with a bundle of black ostrich plumes falling to one side. As soon as the coach disappeared into the morning mist, she ran to get the invitation, a command of duty to the court and its ministers that demanded precedence over all other previous engagements.

The Imperial event came as no surprise to the members of society. Everyone eagerly anticipated the yearly festivity, especially the ladies as it gave them a chance to display their priceless gems. Even before the new year began the aristocracy had already prepared their finest regalia.

While the household slept, Jeniya ran her hand over the soft slipper satin of her gown. Hand embroidered lace and pearls embellished the low cut bodice and elbow length bell shaped sleeves. The skirt had a short train with more embroidered lace that she wore over a petticoat of fine ruffled tulle.

The day went by quickly and the maids had drawn Jeniya's hot bath and perfumed it with verbena. She slipped in the delicious scented water and relaxed, thinking of the exciting evening ahead and of dear Anatole...tall, dark and handsome...Tolya, as she affectionately called him. What girl wouldn't be thrilled in his company. Sometimes pleasure, almost tenderness filled her heart recalling their youth together in the country. It all drifted through in her memory like a dream. She let her fingers glide through the rose petals floating in the bath water watching them part and circle around. He had always been agreeable, simple, and open in contrast to Daniel who concealed his identity. She could not begin to imagine what it would be like to be in Daniel's shoes. Until a few months ago, the desperate circumstances under which the Jews were forced to live were totally alien to her understanding. And even more so, their peculiar ways. Still, she painfully longed for his wit and charm, his astute intellect, and the winsome ways in which he surprised her and made her laugh.

When the water began to cool she stepped from her bath to her dressing room where a maid waited by baskets lined in rose satin containing cambric linens bordered in French lace. She helped the young mistress into her undergarments and tied her corset. Another maid ordered her petticoats, shoes and matching stockings, and finally, Galina helped her into the champagne silk satin gown. The hairdresser swept her hair up in the popular Grecian style. She attached two long curls which fell to the shoulders and pinned three white ostrich feathers at the crown. Jeniya opened a drawer and took out a small compact of rouge she bought from a traveling gypsy peddler for the occasion, but Galina snatched it out of her hand. "Painted faces are not allowed." she said. Lastly Jeniya wiggled her hands into the long white gloves which were made to order for the occasion. Ekatrina, a year Jeniya's junior, fastened the three buttons at the wrist in silence, her eyes dark with envy, not because her sister was going to the Emperor's ball but because she was going with Anatole, whom she had always fancied for herself. Her job was to go to the jewel cabinets in her mother's bedroom and fetch the gems her sister had chosen from an array that would rival that of any jeweler. Jeniya chose to wear pearls, a ruby and diamond brooch, diamond ear bobs and two diamond bracelets.

When she entered the drawing room, Anatole's eyes lit up with the delight of a groom when his bride appears. He quickly arose, clicked his heals together and kissed her gloved hand. He had always admired her and was happy when the two families had long ago entertained the possibility of a match. Zinaida, sitting in a majestic gown of royal blue silk brocade, beamed with a blaze that matched the sapphires and diamonds on her neck and wrists, thinking of a wedding made in heaven.

Anatole wore the dress uniform of the Preobrazhensky guards; fitted white leather pants, a black jacket with a red double-breasted insert, gold buttons, and trimmed with a red collar and cuffs. The hat which he held in his white gloved hand was decorated with the emblem of the golden eagle, a long narrow plume extending from the top. Her father wore his court dress uniform, a navy tunic with a laced-pattern of gold embroidered down the front. Metals denoting his service to Alexander II as well as his office, minister of foreign affairs, were pinned on his breast. Around his right shoulder swirled the golden robes of an aid-de-camp. The lady's maids wrapped Zinaida and Jeniya in sable coats as Ekantria stood at the top of the stairs and watched them file out the door.

The coachmen shook the servant girls dozing under fur blankets to warm up the seats in the two sleighs before the ladies stepped inside. "Off with you," he said when they opened their sleepy eyes. Except for the tinkling of bells, the sleighs glided silently to the palace under a lightly falling snow. Jenyia visually drank in every moment of this magical wonderland.

In the center of the great Palace Square, stood the Alexander column, signifying Russia's victory over Napoleon. It rose fifty feet from a huge monolith base carved in a bas-relief and was topped with an angel holding the cross. Tonight it became the gathering place for attending coachmen who warmed themselves around large braziers of burning coals while they waited through the night for their masters.

The Palace windows blazed with lights for the special occasion. Illustrious passengers stepped from sleighs and carriages into the main entrance of the Winter Palace where footmen came forward to usher them inside and take their furs. Several thousand courtiers, officers of various regiments, statesmen in court uniforms, foreign ambassadors, ladies drowning in jewels, and Oriental Kings in white turbans passed through the long corridor to the Grand Jordan staircase carpeted in red. They filed up the stairs past the troopers of the Chevalier Guards who stood motionless with swords in white gloved hands. Silver breast plates decked their white tunics and silver helmets surmounted by the golden double-headed Imperial Eagle made these men of the nobility, already chosen for their height, appear gigantic. Kazak Life Guards with glossy black mustaches were posted by the great lapis lazuli columns above the staircase. They wore long fire-red *cherkesskas* adorned with silver cartridge holders across their chests and imposing engraved silver daggers on their black waist belts. Jeniya gasped when Vadim locked her gaze as she passed into the great Nicholas hall. His grey eyes burned into hers. She quickly snapped her head away. *What is he doing here? How did he wiggle himself into this esteemed position of the proud and privileged elite of the Tsar's Imperial Guard, the flower of the Kasatchevo who patrolled Tsarskoye Selo day and night, galloping at intervals of fifty meters.*

The enormous rooms of the Winter Palace had ceilings so high that they disappeared from one's view like the sky. Floral scented air drifted throughout the chambers magically transforming them into a tropical paradise decorated with orchids and other rare tropical flowers brought from the Imperial hothouses. Endless rows of palm trees were placed along the main stairway and along the hall of mirrors that reached to the ceiling. In the great Nicholas Hall of high arched windows and marble columns, a dream world of lights radiated from large majestic crystal chandeliers and danced off the sparkling diamond diadems, sapphire necklaces, the emerald bracelets, and ruby brooches worn by the great ladies of court. The inner circle of statesmen and courtiers, along with bishops and archimandrites wearing red and gold brocaded robes studded in sparkling jewels, gathered outside the Malachite room for the anticipated moment. Court Arabs, the name given to gigantic Ethiopians in white turbans and brightly colored silk tunics belted over baggy silk trousers, stood as majestic statues in front of the massive doors that led to the Tsar's inner apartments and waited for their cue.

A hush fell over the crowd when the grand master of ceremonies appeared adorned like a peacock in a blue frock coat stiff with gold braided embroidery and gave three taps on the floor with his ivory-handled ebony staff decorated with the ribbons of St. Andrew. "The Emperor and Empress," he announced upon the arrival of their Imperial Majesties. The court Arabs then threw open the heavy doors and the courtiers gaped in awe when the mighty giant, Tsar Alexander III, autocrat of iron will, stood on the threshold looming over his guests larger than his legend. Over dark trousers, he wore a scarlet military tunic, decorative metals, and the blue sash of St. Andrew across his chest under looped golden braids. The Empress Marie, glittering in a diamond studded gown and diadem with ropes of pearls around her neck, appeared as a child at his side. The courtiers bowed. The tall, slender grand dukes and grand duchesses followed the Tsar in order of priority and the Imperial family formed a procession. The orchestra struck the first cords of Glinka's polonaise. Six chamberlains stepped forward to led the royal entourage through the halls of the palace three times, to announce the commencement of the ball. When the Tsar passed by Jeniya, she was struck by his steely blue gaze, sometimes threatening, even frightening. The eyes of a man who wielded power above all others in the world and who carried a monstrous burden.

Anatole took Jeniya's hand for the first dance of the evening, the mazurka. The guests gathered in the great hall to watch the young officers with their girls run and hop and twirl in quick steps across the floor. Suddenly, the gentleman would stop and fall to one knee holding his lady's hand while she danced around him like a doll, after which, they swung into a waltz. Dresses of lace and satin opened and swirled like many colored blossoms scattered over the elaborately inlaid floors that gleamed like polished amber in a glittering surreal world.

"Tolya, I think this is the most beautiful evening of my life," Jeniya said when they waltzed throughout the chambers of the palace. "I could never have imagined anything like it. The imperial court of Alexander III must be the most splendid in all the world and I shall always cherish this memory."

"I am honored to share this beautiful evening with you," he said smiling.

Vadim wasted no time claiming the second dance, the waltz. "Jenka," he said. "May I?" He bowed, kissed her white gloved hand, and held her at arms-length admiring how she had blossomed into a beauty, the hour-glass figure pinched in by a corset, the full bosom beneath the lace bodice of her dress. "You look ravishing tonight," he said.

She brushed off what she regarded as a mundane compliment without a word and put her hand on his shoulder.

He drew her into the dance position and said in a rich baritone voice, "like a bride."

She glared at him.

"All of Petersburg is talking about the brilliant match."

"How do you know that?" she said in surprise.

"Standing at the entrance to the ball room I hear everything. The socialites cannot live without gossip. They can't wait to exchange the latest. Their mouths start up as soon as they enter the palace, and you, *ma chere*, are on the tip of everyone's tongue tonight." He emphasized everyone with a certain mockery. Then with a force of power he gripped her close and whisked her off in three step time.

She felt the raw animal magnetism in the strength in his grip and the steely thighs touching hers. She hated him and all he stood for, and all that he came from. At the same time, she was intrigued. She changed the subject. "So I see you are in the Escort of Tsar's Konvoy? How did you happen to wiggle yourself into the elites of the Imperial guards?"

"I don't need to wiggle myself into anywhere, my dear Jeniya."

"You don't think much of yourself, do you."

"*Au contraire*. I think a great deal of myself. I earned this appointment. I made a succession of important arrests. Evidently my work with the Okhrana gained the attention from the Tsar's advisors."

She immediately thought of Daniel. "And how many innocent people did you arrest and leave to rot in prison," she said in an accusing tone.

"As far as I know, none. Everyone I arrested was part of a well-organized revolutionary cell. Despite the strong arm policies of Alexander, there are rebel informants everywhere. You never know who your enemy is these days. It may be the butler serving your coffee in the morning, or the maid tending your wardrobe. Do you know what their slogan is?"

She listened now, wide-eyed.

"Revolution now or never! I know it sounds far-fetched, but it's happening. We feel that the Jews are the main instigators in this rebellion."

"But Russians won't listen to Jews?"

"Speaking of Jews, I saw your friend, what was his name?" A slight smirk crossed his lips. Like a fox, his sharp grey eyes probed her reaction.

Her heart leaped against her chest causing her to tremble. "Who?" she said anxiously.

"Who?" He laughed showing perfect white teeth. "Did you forget his name already. Glad to hear it!"

"Where?"

"Aha, so you are interested after all. How you women do carry on after weak, loathsome men I will never understand."

"Where did you see him!"

"He was among that rabble they transport from the prison to the gendarmerie for interrogation."

She was silent for a long while trying to assuage her anger. "Was he all right?"

"He was sitting upright in the carriage looking around. Maybe he was looking for you?" He laughed again.

A chill swept to her bones and she yanked herself free from his embrace. "You are lower than a worm…did they release him?"

"I don't know. I left service with the police to take up my new appointment here in Petersburg."

Jeniya was happy to hear that Daniel was well, but the news that he may still be in prison disturbed her. She wondered why he had not written.

At midnight the dancing ceased and the Sovereigns led the procession in the same order as before to the supper-tables, preceded by the Master of Ceremonies and the Chamberlains. Of all the guest in attendance, only a privileged four hundred were invited to dine with the Imperial family. According to etiquette the Emperor and Empress remained standing until all the guests were seated at two rows of round tables with an empty chair provided at each for the Tsar. When he sat down at her father's table, Jeniya's beauty caught his eye. Before he departed, he smiled and took her slender hand in his great one and said, "now take care of yourself, dear one." She then saw that the coldness in his bright crystal blue eyes could also radiate a fatherly warmth and a simple openness. Besides her first palace ball, she would always cherish the moment when the mighty Tsar of all the Russias took her hand and wished her well.

Footmen in red waistcoats served eight courses of delicacies beginning with vodka, blini and Beluga caviar, then borsch with little *pirogies*. The main courses consisted of sturgeon, partridges, venison, and endless bottles of French wine, champagne and an assortment of liquors. In between courses footmen brought sorbet and jeweled boxes containing slender yellow cigarettes. A chorus of the best artists from the Imperial Opera House presented a program of beautiful but mournful Russian arias chasing the cheerful smile from the Emperor's face.

Everyone observed that Alexander began to show fatigue in his cumbersome gate. He tried to conceal the terrific strain under which he labored each day in directing his Empire by assuming a pleasant demeanor at the ball. But people became concerned when they noticed the minister of internal affairs, Ivan Durnovo leaving the room frequently and each time returning to exchange a few words with the Tsar. Ever since the assassination attempt on his life in 1887 by Alexander Ulyanov, the elder brother of the revolutionary who would one day call himself Lenin, the Tsar took extraordinary measures to protect the palace. He knew he may have enemies planted among anyone of the many employed for this occasion. Alexander III may have been feared by everyone, even admired by some, but not well liked because he was distant, inflexible and ruled with an unyielding fist.

After protocol, the Sovereigns left early and the guests continued to feast on Beluga caviar, fruits, sorbets, tiers of chocolates, pastries and cakes. They devoured bottles of champagne cooling in huge blocks of hollowed out ice contained in silver tubs. They danced until dawn. After the last waltz the *Skorokhods* ushered them to the palace entrances.

Heavy snow was falling when Jeniya and Anatole emerged from the palace entrance into the waiting sleigh. They glided home in a silent world snuggled under a pile of furs recalling every detail of this eventful evening.

After her parents said good night, Anatole sat down next to Jeniya and took her hand. "Jenka," he said gazing into her face. She was still radiantly beautiful as when he escorted her to the ball early in the evening. "I've asked your father if we could begin a courtship and he agreed…that is with your consent."

"I know," she said lowering her gaze presenting the image of a shy maiden, but she was thinking Daniel in prison, and all the uncertainty surrounding their relationship, if indeed there still remained a relationship. She looked up. Anatole's eyes were large and brown like those of a yearning puppy dog. She couldn't say no. Not tonight. "Yes…I think so."

He leaned toward her and kissed her lightly on the lips. "I am so happy," he said. "I think this has been the best evening of my life."

She smiled. "Yes, it has been absolutely wonderful."

"Well…I think I had better go and let you get some rest." He lingered a bit not knowing quite what to do next. She got up and they slowly walked to the front door arm in arm.

Chapter 26

ANATOLE BEGAN HIS courtship at the Rostovsky mansion in the presence of her parents and several other guests. They drank tea, ate little sandwiches and cakes and played cards. Since he knew Jeniya loved the outdoors and the countryside, he invited her for an afternoon of ice skating. It turned out to be a sunny afternoon, a rare day after a succession of depressing overcast weather. His coachman picked her up the next afternoon and they drove by forests surrounding immense summer villas along the waterfront. The dim light of the early afternoon sun peeked from between the evergreen trees casting long blue shadows over the silvery snow. They laughed and slipped down deeper under a bundle of fur.

The skating ring was a common meeting-ground for the well healed of Petersburg society where both young and old, with cheeks glowing from the cold, came to skate. A group of musicians played waltzes from the pavilion as ladies with hands in muffs and their gentleman glided arm and arm over the ice like synchronous dancing partners. Novices stumbled along in awkward contortions until they fell shrieking in laughter and girls clinging to the sides of chairs with metal runners screamed in fear while young officers swirled them around on the lake. Echoes of laughter and light hearted shouts drifted from the ice over the powdery snow banks.

Jeniya sat down on a bench while Anatole tied up her skates.

"How does that feel?" he said.

She stood up and wiggled her ankle. The fit was snug. "Good," she said.

She waited while he tied his own skates and the two of them wobbled hand in hand down the path to the lake trying to maintain their balance. Jeniya broke his grip and glided over the ice swishing around. "Look at me," she shouted. "I'm skating backwards!"

"Can you do this?" he shouted back making figure eights. She followed him carefully putting one foot in front of the other, looking down over the crackled hair-like patterns in the smooth ice.

Anatole saw several friends playing a game of ice tag. "Konstantinovich!" they shouted, "come and join us!" They were all good skaters and raced around after each other teasing and shouting. Jeniya flew over the ice like a bird when the chase began. Anatole caught up with her and swirled her around until they both fell on the ice laughing.

They lay there for a moment gazing into each other's eyes. As he came close to kiss her, she turned her lips away. Suddenly she felt an icy chill enter her heart. She put her frozen hands inside her muff and said, "Tolya, please lets go inside to warm-up." He got up and lifted her from the ice.

On the way to the pavilion, she gazed at the sun setting on the horizon like a fiery circle emitting a strange polar light over the Gulf of Finland. Inside, they sat down near a warm fire and listened to the waltzes. The combination of cold air, warm fire and music, melted Jeniya into a serene state of relaxation, but Anatole sat erect, his mind working with intent.

"Jenka," he said after the waiter placed two mugs of hot chocolate on the table. "You and I have known each other since we were children." She sat up and looked at him. Instead of distracting from his looks his dominate nose added a certain air of nobility to his character. She could visualize him one day as commanding general of the Tsar's armies, but she could not see herself fitting into the military lifestyle. His beautiful large eyes were somehow missing that spontaneous flirtatious spark.

"You know my feelings toward you," he said. "I have always admired you. Do you remember how I would follow you around like a puppy dog when we were young?" She smiled and her eyes sparkled in the fire's light. "Even then I had thought of you as my wife and nothing has changed."

She gazed down at her hot chocolate, and cupped it to warm her hands. She knew this moment would come but was still uncertain of how she would respond, moreover, how she would evade his question and drag him along while she waited and wondered if she would ever hear from Daniel again. Anatole had the patience of a saint but this was no longer a game as much as she wished.

"I have always liked you too and had also entertained the idea of marrying you one day but...right now I am not ready to make the decision to marry." She looked into his eyes, intently absorbing his every nuance. "Can you understand?"

He nodded and put his arm around her. She leaned her head on his chest knowing in all fairness to him and the anticipating families, she would have to make her decision soon. Not that Anatole demanded it but her mother and aunts were breathing down her neck pushing with impossible probes and it made her anxious and unsettled.

"I understand," he said. "I have waited this long to have you as my wife and I will continue to wait."

They were both quiet in the coach going home snuggled down in fur, each drowsy from the vigorous workout in the cold, each sifting through the actions and words of the afternoon. *He is a magnificent escort. Well respected and liked by everyone. No doubt he would make a devoted husband and father as well as a good provider for his family. I had so much fun skating with him this afternoon and the Emperor's ball was a dream. Perhaps the spark isn't necessary, maybe the old dowagers were right, in time you will learn to love a good man. But then, I don't recall that he ever made a declaration using the word love as Daniel had, but then...Daniel had never declared his intention to marry. Am I a fool chasing after a dream and letting a fine man slip by or what? Tolya's intensions are certain. He is steady, direct and dependable, not a composer of dreams.*

When the coachman stopped in front of her home, he lifted her chin and kissed her lips. "Thank you for a wonderful afternoon," he said.

That night, Jeniya slid deep into her fluffy down bedding and assessed all that had transpired over the past weeks. Tolya had been an absolute prince in dress, manners, looks, everything a girl could hope for in a husband, but something was missing, something which she could not put her finger on. When Daniel entered her life, he was mysterious, flirtatious, and quick witted. Just to be in his presence sent a rush of passion through her body and caused her whole world to blossom.

She smiled thinking of the time she spent with Daniel on the carousel. She missed the lively discussions on their differences of opinion. Anatole did not seem to have an opinion. His conversation would eventually drift to the Tsar, the aristocracy, and his elite regiment; a nobleman to the core. Even Vadim, a born military man, did not see life through the narrow lens of his service. Maybe the problem with Anatole was that he viewed a wife simply as an appendage, an extension of his own ordered universe.

Jeniya could still see her aunt, who was married to an officer in the elite Chevalier Guards, running to her sister with tears flowing from her eyes begging for a loan to buy groceries. "Only in Russia, only in Russia," she exclaimed brandishing her hands in the air. "Can a man watch his family sink into ruin because he cannot refuse a comrade when he asks for money to pay his gambling debts. I can understand esprit-de-corps. I can understand why man wants to defend the uniform he wears after a comrade-in arms has dishonored it by his despicable actions. But to put his comrade above his family? Only in Russia!" She'd cock her elegant head to the side and with her hands on her hips, said, "A Russian may be a bad husband, a bad son, and a bad brother, but never, ever a bad comrade." And then she would ask for the loan.

Jeniya understood that to be a good and faithful comrade is the highest ideal to which an officer can attain. He had been indoctrinated to be a good comrade in school, in the military academy, and the cadet corps. Once a member of the regiment, he discovers that a good comrade never refuses to endorse his buddy's gambling IOU. To do so is a crime against the corps, even at the liability of his wife, his mother, and his home! She knew of noble families who took pride in seeing their sons wear the elegant uniform of an elite regiment only to see their fortunes vanish when they had to sell estates and jewels to pay for their son's debts. She had great confidence in Tolya's moral virtues but could she trust him in his duty to his comrades?

The next morning at breakfast, Jeniya told her mother she needed to talk.

"Certainly dear, come upstairs to my room where we can be alone. I'll dismiss the servants." Zinaida led Jeniya to her petit salon in which a warm fire was burning in the porcelain stove. Vases filled with fresh flowers from their greenhouses scented the air. Zinaida sat in her reading chair by the tall windows which looked out over neatly trimmed boxwoods in the courtyard gardens making interesting shapes beneath the snow. Jeniya sat in an inlaid rosewood chair by a matching tea table gazing at the new impressionist paintings her mother bought at the auction in Kiev hanging on the blue damask walls. She loved the Monet best of all.

"Now tell me, what is troubling you. I've noticed you moping around here lately with a frown on your face. You are about to marry a fine young man. You should be ecstatic with joy in making you wedding plans."

"I know mama, but..." She gazed at the birds twittering between the evergreen branches shaking up a fine spray of snow which sparkled like diamond dust in the morning sunlight. "I don't love him."

Zinaida laughed. "Is that it? Anatole is a good man and will be good to you. That's what counts. The love will come in time. Besides, in marriage, it is better for a man to love a woman more than she loves him. You should be grateful you have a man that doesn't gamble, treats everyone with respect, is sure footed..."

"And predictable," Jeniya interrupted.

"What's wrong with predictable? Would you want someone who runs out on you and gambles away your fortune without you knowing?"

"No but...he is almost too good, too accommodating, there is no spark, no mystery, no adventure, no...I don't know." She sighed thinking of the times he kissed and caressed her. She felt nothing. "When we walk together, he talks mostly about the regiment. It was interesting at first but it's not what I want to hear. I want...I want to do something exciting, fun."

"All men talk about themselves and their work, you should be grateful that he shares with you. I know many women who wished they had any kind of conversation with their husbands. You are looking for life in a fantasy world that doesn't exist. Once trouble sets in and you discover your Mr. perfect is not Mr. perfection, you will be happy to have a devoted man, with security and position in society. These things are what matter to people in our class, not an infatuation that will not last and more than likely bring on hardship."

"But mother." She jumped up and stood shaking her out stretched arms and open palms in frustration, trying to make her mother see her dilemma. "You just don't understand!"

Zinaida sat like a spectator staring at her daughter carrying on with childlike gestures, waiting for her to settle down and come to reason like an adult. "No," she said. "I don't understand how you could turn down one of the finest young men in the Tsar's service, a man with a brilliant future. You go to balls, receptions, parties, decked out in gowns and gems. What more do you want?"

"I want love!"

"Love? Love! What do you call love? You have a man who has adored you since you were a child. Now you are telling me you are looking for some dandy to flatter you with lies and promises of love. Is this what you call love?" Zinaida shouted with her own frustration. "Too many girls like you from fine families get involved with these arrogant, self-absorbed Don Juan's who ignore them and cheat or gamble away their fortunes. Many are used up before their time and wind up bitter lonely women going from one lover to the next looking for anyone who will give them a little attention. You know who they are and so do I. You have the finest and you are turning him down because he does not excite you?" She put her hand to her forehead. Her diamond rings sparkled in the morning sunlight streaming in the windows. "*Mon Dieu!* What is wrong with this girl?"

"But mother, you have to love a man, I mean in a sexual way to want to have his children."

"Sex? Sex! In my day sex was not even considered in the marriage arrangement. A suitor came to visit and was seen by the family. If he met their expectations, an aunt would act as a liaison between the two families, until a proposal was made and granted by the parents. It was as simple as that. When a man is solid and good, you will learn to love him."

"But I don't want to learn. I want to feel love."

Zinaida shook her head and frowned in frustration. "*Bosha, moi dobre!* To speak sense into this girl's head is impossible. I can't seem to get through to you. The truth is you have not grown up yet. You are spoiled and you don't know what you want. If you keep on being so choosy you will wind up with no one. All you have done is criticize this man. If you do not love him, then don't string him along. Don't trifle with his feelings. Let him go!"

Jeniya pressed her lips together in an obstinate gesture. Her argument had run out of steam, not only with her mother but with herself. Now she began to think something was wrong with her attitude and began to hate herself for not being able to love Anatole.

She wanted to run away, somewhere where she could find peace and think...Belozerkovka. That's it. Belozerkovka.

Just then Boris pushed the door open. "What's all the commotion in here. I can hear you women ranting all the way down the hall. The servants must have gotten an ear full!"

"Boris, please speak to your daughter and drum some sense into her head!"

"It seems, my dear, you have stated you case perfectly." He turned and slammed the door behind him.

Jeniya stood and gaped. Her mother got up and left the room.

Maybe the spark was not necessary, maybe in time it would come. When she received no word from Daniel, Jeniya decided to reassess her relationship with Anatole and try to fit herself into his life and into his arms. After all they did have some fun times together. She would try to love him. She would go to all the receptions, the balls, the dinners, and frequent all the salons and...then what? Look for romance?

Her elder sister, Yelizaveta, was happily married and a baby was on the way. This delighted her mother, who now focused all her attention on the first grandchild. This also delighted the hearts of the society matrons and bearers of etiquette when they saw that knowing smile of true marital happiness on the faces of the young couple. This was not to say that their elders were all happy in their marriages, most were not, but still, they too had their dreams which they lived out through their sons and daughters.

While Zinaida had lectured on her daughter's fantasy world, she was creating one of her own. Everyone knew she was not only looking for the arrival of the new baby but was anticipating a wedding announcement would be made soon. Everyone was happy except Jeniya. Her aunts chided, saying, "if you let a good man go you may not find another." Not that there was no lack of available suitors. There were many. But most of them were enjoying their liberty with women now that the old ways of courtship and tradition were yielding to the new European style of enlightenment.

One afternoon, Jeniya and Anatole were strolling arm and arm through the summer gardens with its many beautiful marble figures standing like ice sculptors. Snow was falling, sometimes slow and drifting, sometimes whirling around in a spiral. In the distance they heard the muffled sounds of children's laughter and of skaters playing ice hockey on hardened snow. Jeniya held out her arm and let the flakes settle on her jacket. "Look," she said. "Did you ever notice the lacey designs on each flake?"

"Yes," he said. "Each one is different."

Suddenly, she bent over and sprayed him with arms full of snow and ran kicking up more snow with her toes. He looked on and laughed and threw a snowball. "Look," she said lying down in the snow on her back making angel's wings with her arms and legs. "Can you make snow angels?" He smiled but did not join her. She stood up. "Tolya?" she hesitated for a moment to gain courage. "I have been thinking."

He gazed at her with questioning eyes. "Yes?" he said cautiously, sensing that something was wrong by the change in her tone.

"I need to go home to Belozerkovka. I need to think...to be alone."

He remained quiet, waiting for her explanation.

His silence made it all the more difficult to express her feelings. The last thing in the world she wanted was to hurt him or drive him away, but she needed to reveal the burden she had hidden in her heart. "Tolya, you are the most wonderful friend I ever had but...I don't know if I really love you enough to make you a good wife...the kind of wife you deserve."

He took both her hands in his and gazed down at the snow on her muff and her clothing. "You know Jenka, I have always cared for you deeply. I have always idolized you for your free spirit. Something I know I do not possess. I wish I did, but I cannot live with that kind of uncertainty. Maybe that is why I chose the regimental life of the military. Everything is ordered. We do what we are told." He laughed. "Remember how you would always order me around. You didn't know it but even then I adored you for it."

"Like the time I told you to go and hunt for rabbits on the island while I took off with my two sisters in the rowboat. I shall never forget the expression on your face when we came back to get you. I never saw you look so angry."

If it weren't for their laughter at a silly memory, she would have felt lower that a worm after his eloquent comments.

He nodded with a smile on his face, "I remember that. You ran off with our snacks in the boat." He looked away for a moment to find his own words of parting. His bright eyes were glistening; she couldn't tell if it were tears or the falling snow. "I hope you will find your answers in the peaceful beauty of Belozerkovka and I hope"…he paused. "I hope your decision will be for me."

Jeniya did not take dinner that evening but sat in her room watching the darkness settle over the city. The snow that once brought her happiness now became a landscape of loneliness. Nor did she find the answers to her dilemma for which she so desperately sought at Belozerkovka. She continued to comb the mail each day hoping to find a letter from Daniel, but nothing. Her sister Yelizaveta and Anatole wrote often and she looked forward to reading the news.

Moya draha,

Have you made up your mind as to whether you will take Anatole as your husband. You two have always been so perfect together. Remember, ma chere, that so called passion has little to do with a good marriage. Take it from your old married sister, when you have a good man love grows. If you do decide to make this marriage, which I hope you do, then you may want to return to Petersburg, tout de suite. Our dear little sister Katiya has quite latched herself on to Anatole. They have been working together side by side to raise money for the famine victims.

All of society, led by the Empress Marie herself, is working hard to mobilize a great fundraising campaign to deliver grain in the hardest hit areas along the Volga. Our own dear *batiushka* has donated millions from his own personal account to relieve hunger among his people.
Kissing your hands,
Vetka

Moya draha Jenka,

How are you doing? Have you made your decision yet? Since I hear from you less frequently these days, I am beginning to feel in my heart that you do not love me. When you told me of the uncertainty of your feelings toward me, I continued to hope that you would decide in my favor but I sense that is not coming as our letters have been mostly of the news and not of the necessary commitment. I am writing you to tell you that I am releasing you from this relationship. But I want to warn you as one of my dearest friends, and as a brother. And I say this in love. At the barracks several of the officers are asking if we still intend to marry. I know they are thinking of contacting you. Beware! And I cannot emphasis this enough. As you know our endearing customs of etiquette in which we were raised are yielding to the new laissez-faire attitude from the west. Girls are seen out on the streets without chaperones. They mingle with men freely. You see how easy it is for young men who have no intention of marriage to steal the girl's hearts and run on to the next affair. So again I am warning you - be careful!

Please know that I am still here for you but if you wish to go your own way then I wish you well, and in good health.
Tolya

Anatole's letter struck a Panic in Jeniya's heart. She never dreamed he would not always be there for her as a last resort. This relationship could not be drawn out any longer. With Daniel fading from the picture, she had decided to marry him. She sat down at her writing desk, penned a letter to him and sealed it. She was ready to give it to the footman to mail, when Galina presented her with another letter from Yelizaveta.

Moya draha,
    Just a note to let you know you have been dragging your feet for too long. Ekatrina and Anatole are engaged. A good man gets snatched off the market quickly these days.
Toya sestra,
Vetka

Well, how do you like that. She had always been the quiet backward one. What a clever manipulating little devil she turned out to be and right under my nose! I guess he is as unremarkable as his chosen bride after all. They deserve one another.

Instead of ringing the servant to bring afternoon tea, she went to the kitchen. She needed the comfort of someone older and wiser. Someone maternal and domestic like Suska, the cook. She sat down at the long wooden prep table where a maid servant brought tea and a plate full of apricot and prune filled cakes. She devoured one after the other while Suska recounted tales of everyone in the province.

After the marriage of Ekatrina and Anatole, Jeniya was miserable. She couldn't blame Anatole. He made his mind up he wanted a wife and she turned him down. He was not a fool; he was a man. In retrospect she wished she had married him. The security of having a notable husband, however boring, a name in society, and the invitations which she never thought she would so desperately miss were better than living alone even in her beloved Belozerkovka. She used to pride herself into thinking these pretentious things were not important but now that they were gone she realized that they meant everything in her life. They were a part of her upbringing and she could not deny them.

Chapter 27

"Someone here has been asking for you." Yelizaveta's wrote in her last letter. Jeniya's heart leaped. Daniel? But why, she wondered, if he wanted to see her did he not inquire at Belozerkovka? He knew the way there. She read on. "You remember what mama always told us? If you reach twenty-five summers and have not married, you will never have a husband. You don't want to be a spinster and be labeled "Old Maid, never been married" do you? Aren't you just about there now? You need to come stay with us and be seen again in society, while you still have an ounce of beauty left, if you haven't already dried up in the Ukrainian sun!"

If Vetka's words meant to prick her into action, then her sister had succeeded. She gazed at herself in the hall mirror, she was rather resembling a *moujika*. She quickly ran to her room, took the hand mirror from her vanity and went to the window by the sunlight to examine her skin. She felt ill when she saw fine lines beginning to appear on her forehead. She decided to take her sister's offer. Besides, she was anxious to know who was asking for her, as Vetka insisted that it must be a surprise.

The big evening finally arrived and it seemed when she wanted to look her best, she imagined she looked her worst. Her prettiest dresses were all too small and out of fashion. The bustles had vanished into hip slimming skirts and the sleeves had grown into enormous puffs. If it weren't for the mounting excitement and anticipation of this mysterious gentleman caller, she would make an excuse not to be seen.

When Galina announced her visitor, she combed out the creases in her dark skirt with her hands hoping to make herself appear thinner. Her heart was beating rapidly as she entered the drawing room.

"You?" she gasped when she encountered "the gentleman" sitting comfortably in an easy chair as if uncovering a slimy creature from under a rock.

He cocked his head. "Yes it is I. Were you expecting someone else?" he chuckled with a roguish grin, the detective in him reading her thoughts.

She made no apology for her rude greeting and was irritated by his response as well as the arrogant manner in which he crossed one leg over the other, sinking deeper into the chair. He wore a blue tunic with a black belt and high black boots over loosely fitting trousers.

Vadim smiled. "Don't tell me you are still carrying the torch for that Jew, what's his name?"

"You are the crude, uncivilized, savage…"

"I wouldn't consider your reception exactly gracious and lady-like. What did you expect of me?"

She turned her face away.

"What a pity." He shook his head admiring her voluptuous beauty. Now that she put on a few pounds, her corset accentuated a full bosom beneath her white shirt with billowy sleeves. Her dark hair was swept up in front and braided in back with a ribbon.

"What did you say?"

"Such a pity, a rapturous female like you going to waste."

She glared at him and tactfully changed the subject. "So, are you still in the Emperor's *Konvoi*?" she said with a cool politeness.

"Da, I am. And proud to be." He uncrossed his legs, leaned forward, took some sunflower seeds from a dish on the table and popped them into his mouth. "I heard your friend has latched himself onto some count or other, or is it a prince, yes, I think it is a prince, sure knows how to pick *em*."

"Prince? What prince? What are you talking about?"

"I don't know."

She eyed him skeptically. "You're playing games with me."

"I would like to." He grinned, took some more seeds and winked slyly from the corner of his eye.

"I was going to ask you to stay for dinner. I thought you had become a civilized human being after joining the Tsar's Imperial guard, but I see differently and changed my mind."

"Oh you did. Well it so...happens your sister invited me, so...I stay." He crossed his arms, swung one booted foot over his knee and leaned back in his chair. "And you thought I came to see you, didn't you?"

"I can't believe this. You're nothing but an animal."

"Evidently you prefer animals over gentleman. You had the best man in the Tsar's regiments and turned him down. He wasn't good enough for you."

"I don't have to put up with you!" She turned and started to leave the room.

"Don't go. I enjoy watching your face when you get angry. Your cheeks get so rosy and your eyes so big and green."

She wheeled around. "You beast!"

"From an animal to a beast." He laughed. "Actually, I did come to see you. A soldier whose regiment is his mistress needs the refreshment of a pretty woman once in a while. To me you are like spring flowers growing on a battlefield."

"I can't stand you!" She turned and left the room

He smiled and called, "I know. But you are stuck with me through dinner tonight."

"Jenka, *ma chere*," Yelizaveta said one morning. "You can't sit around here day after day reading and getting fatter."

Jeniya peered up from her book. "Why did you do that to me?" She was lying on a sofa near a sunny window. A tray with tea and little cakes sat beside her on the table.

"Do what dear?"

"Vadim."

"I thought you liked each other. He had been asking for you."

Jeniya turned her face away and moaned.

"Well I'm sorry. I only had your welfare in mind."

"I know." Jeniya got up, went to the window and gazed over the city block. In spring, Petersburg came alive with a passion for life. People took in the warm sun which rarely shines in winter, sitting on benches along the pleasant tree lined streets reading newspapers, eating lunch or just chatting.

"I'm thinking about returning to Belozerkovka," she said. "There is nothing here for me." She turned, went back to her sofa, and continued to read the "Prisoner of Zanda".

"What are you talking about? If you would get off your derriere and get out of the house maybe you would find something that would interest you. Look, Papa has invited Cyril and I to the Yacht Club for lunch. He wants to talk to Cyril about a position opening up at court, would you like to join us?"

"Thank you for asking, but no."

"You are behaving like an old spinster; you'll never find a husband if you lay around the house all day moping. You need to be seen in society."

"I am not looking for a husband! Besides that's an old men's club. All the Tsar's men," she mocked.

"It's not an old men's club anymore. We have a new young Tsar and Tsaritsa. It is the beginning of a new era in the Empire. I should think you would want to be a part of it."

"A part of what? Ever since his disastrous coronation a few years ago, the clairvoyants have been saying that new Tsaritsa has entered

Russian land behind a coffin and brings misfortunes with her. Who wants to be a part of that?"

"Oh, you don't believe the tales of silly old women, do you?"

Jeniya thought about the coronation of Nicholas II. It began as a dream, a perfect day in May, 1896, under clear blue skies with the pealing of thousands of church bells. When the news of the event reached the farthest parts of the Empire that souvenir gifts would be distributed to all the people along with unlimited free beer, bread, sausages, and pastries, thousands of men, women and children poured into the city of Moscow. They came by boat up the great rivers and by rail to witness the oriental glory of the grand pageantry which had never before been seen in modern history nor would ever be seen again.

Following the coronation, Nicholas II gave a great festival for the common people, just outside the city limits on Khodynka field, a vast area used by the Imperial army to hold summer military drills and to practice constructing entrenchments.

City authorities under the direction of the Tsar's uncle, the Grand Duke Sergei Alexandrovich, had not bothered to level the deep trenches before they set up tents and tables. When the time came to distribute the free food and beer, the people stampeded toward the tables, surging and billowing and then vanishing into the ditches, trampling one another to death. Many more died of suffocation under the weight of the dead bodies. The fatalities were estimated between eight and twenty-thousand souls. There was no accurate count as the bodies were hastily loaded onto hundreds of wagons and carried to the nearest cemeteries to be buried in mass graves. No one even bothered to cover the bloodied arms and contorted legs dangling over the sides of the wagons.

When the Tsar arrived to address a select group of dignitaries at Khodynka field, all evidence of this tragedy had been cleaned up. Although the illustrious guests were shielded from learning of the event, they were aware that something was wrong when Nicholas stood up and spoke in a halting voice; his face stricken with grief. After the ceremony, news of the catastrophe quickly spread through the crowd. Everyone wondered if the Emperor would cancel the lavish ball given by the French embassy at the Moscow hunt club in favor of a solemn service for the dead. Many in his entourage warned him not to let enemies of the regime say that the young Tsar danced while his murdered victims were taken to Potter's field. Others advised him not to slight his gracious host and faithful ally and let this unfortunate calamity cast a shadow over the joyous celebration. That evening Nicholas and Aleksandra decided to dance at the ball. To add insult to injury, eight days later the Tsar saluted 40,000 troops in a grand military review on the same field stained with the blood of his people.

Count Pahlen, grand master of the coronation ceremonies and arbiter over the dispute as to whom was to blame, made a dire prophesy. "Such catastrophes as this must repeat themselves so long as your majesty will entrust responsible posts to irresponsible men." As a result, Count Pahlen fell out of favor with the Emperor and was dismissed.

All the compensation in the world given by the sovereigns to the grieving families could not erase the stigma of insensitivity. All the money received by the orphanages was soon forgotten. Only the horror remained. "The Emperor and Empress danced while Russians died" became a mantra of the *narod*.

"Jenka!" Yelizaveta insisted. "Close that book and come along with us, it will do you good to get some fresh air. It's a beautiful morning, we can walk to the club. You do need to walk more and loose some of that weight you've gained."

Jeniya reconsidered her situation. A walk might do her good. "All right," she said.

Pink and violet clouds rising over the waters of the Neva River billowed above the buildings along the canals. Salty breezes coming off the Gulf of Finland still had the faint smell of winter musk. They strolled down the fashionable Morskaya past luxury shops and fine restaurants. Yellow and blue clad Cuirassiers Guards going for a morning walk winked and tipped their hats at the pretty sisters as they passed.

"Now, dear, aren't you glad you got yourself out?" said Vetka. "You would have missed this beautiful morning by laying around reading all day. And maybe a nice husband. These old men do have sons."

Jeniya moaned.

The Yacht Club "thinks" was not simply a pretentious comment. The presence of the Grand Dukes, ministers at court, and other influential persons who spent their evenings at the club gambling and negotiating affairs of state, united its members with one mind. The Emperor had two kinds of subjects, those who were members of the Yacht Club, and those who were not, the latter being a secondary consideration of the realm. Many careers were made by these favored beings and many reputations were broken.

Jeniya and her sister ascended the wide red carpeted staircase past the tall handsome Chevaliers Guards standing like statues looking down their arrogant noses. An officer of the Guards stood at the registry where they signed their names as visiting guests. They walked through the gambling rooms elaborately decorated with crystal chandeliers, high gold leaf mirrors and huge paintings by Russian artists. She noticed a few members standing with their noses glued against the window panes looking down on those lesser beings passing through Morskaya, no doubt persuading themselves of their own self-importance and superiority above all other mortals. Many longing souls strolling by would raise their envious eyes to this Holy of Holies as the object of their innermost desires. If these ordinary folk only knew the aristocrats, she thought, they would be surprised to discover what simpletons they are.

The count sat at a table near a high arched window. He smiled broadly revealing his dimples when he saw his girls join the others at the table. They were enjoying a glass of vodka and blini topped with Beluga caviar and sour cream, the specialty of the house for which the Chef was celebrated. After everyone was seated he clapped his neatly groomed hands drawing the attention of the waiters. An *offeeshyat* advanced immediately. The sommelier opened an iced bottle of wine and handed the count a glass to taste. "I thought we would try the Baron de Rothschild this afternoon." he said.

When the attendants disappeared, he lifted his crystal glass with the Tsar's insignia, and said, "I propose a toast to Cyril, may he be successful in his new post. *Za zdaroviye.*" They all repeated after his lead and drank to Cyril.

Zinaida looked around at everyone and announced proudly. "And I would like to propose another toast." All eyes gazed upon her inquisitively. "To our own Katiya who has been chosen to be a lady in waiting to our new Empress Aleksandra Feodorovna." Everyone grinned with surprise and delight. They lifted their glasses as Zinaida proposed a toast to Katia.

"*Za zdaroviye,*" they repeated and drank.

"What does she have to do?" asked Yelizaveta, always anxious to hear the latest society gossip.

Zinaida beamed. "All the lovely things she was taught to do, painting, horseback riding, music, embroidery. She may be asked to read the Empress's correspondence or write her letters, or to inform her of the activities and personages at court, or relay a message upon command."

"Oh," Yelizaveta sighed wishing it could be herself. "Will she live at court?"

"Only for one month at a time as she will rotate with her Majesty's other ladies."

"Did she get a diamond broach with a portrait of the Empress?"

"Not yet, that will come in time with faithful service." Zinaida said smiling.

The count sat up straight with the pride of a lion, his wavy dark hair gleaming with auburn highlights in the sunlight streaming through the tall windows. He wore his dark blue court uniform with all the gold trim and decorations in the tradition of the Yacht Club and the ladies were always pleased to have another opportunity to display their jewels.

Jeniya looked around the room to see if there were any men younger than fifty sitting at the elegantly set tables. Although she adopted a fatalistic attitude toward marriage, she still kept an eye out for any possibility. Suddenly an icy chill darted through her body and her eyes widened as she ogled a young man sitting with Prince Dmitrievich Militsyn and the new Minister of Finance, Sergei Witte. She stared intently, blotting out the family's lively exchange. The stranger strongly resembled Daniel, only he was more mature than she had remembered, but the likeness was striking.

No, it can't be, it's impossible. No one has ever come from such circumstances as his to be invited as a guest at the Imperial Yacht Club, especially a Jew. She knew with absolute certainty that no Jews, under any circumstances, were even allowed to breath near the fierce anti-Semites in the Imperial Court. But the likeness was uncanny.

Occasionally the young man's gaze drifted her way and caught her staring. She quickly averted her gaze, embarrassed. She tried not to be conspicuous, but she couldn't help herself. His wavy dark hair had barely touched his high, white starched collar, just as Daniel's had. His attire was impeccable, the wide white shirt cuffs which shown below his jacket sleeves were in elegantly good taste.

"Jenka?" Her father's voice punctured her thoughts. "Cyril is addressing you...What are you staring at over there?" He turned and squinted his eyes at the three men chatting. "Isn't that Prince Militsyn over there with the Sergei Witte?"

Zinaida also glanced in their direction and nodded.

"I wonder what they're cooking up? Some kind of an important government contract with the railroad no doubt. He turned and faced his wife. "I heard Prince Militsyn made a good deal with his steel plant in the Urals. I have to contact him for a chat one day." He took another glance. "Who is that young man sitting with them? Face looks familiar."

When the handsome prince of small stature and large brown eyes caught the count looking in his direction, he exchanged a nod and a friendly smile. The two men not only knew each other as members of the state council, but they were also both provincial governors. Rostovsky also knew Witte from the Tsar's Council of Ministers.

Jeniya put her hand to her chest and began to fidget with her locket, hoping her father would not get up, walk over there to greet his colleagues, and then inquire if the young stranger were single. It would be just like him to be so rash, so impulsive, and even insensitive to her feelings on the marriage issue. She turned her face in the opposite direction the incident would evaporate. To her relief, the count quickly lost interest in the three men and continued his conversation with Cyril.

Jeniya became increasingly uncomfortable and excused herself from the table. With her gaze fixed on the red oriental carpets, she headed to the grand staircase.

"Jenka" She heard someone call here name in a familiar voice. She turned around. Her heartbeat swelled and dropped. She gasped. It was the handsome young man. She stared at his face, both puzzled and frightened. How did he know her familiar name? She immediately wanted to get her dowdy fat self away from his sight and continued walking towards the stairway pretending not to hear.

"Jenka, you don't remember me?" he said trailing her and smiling good-naturedly.

She turned and stared at him speechless, like a dumb woman.

"Danya?" she said weakly, her voice quivering with uncertainly.

He smiled and nodded.

"Is it really you?" She wanted to throw her arms around his neck and hug him out of joy in finding him again and knowing that he was doing well but hesitated for fear that he had a wife and children. She couldn't bear the thought. She tried not to show her anxiety nor did he make any attempt to step forward and embrace her. Not only was she dying to know if he was married, but how did he get himself into the Imperial Yacht Club. Only those who did business with the Tsar and the state council were invited to lunch here, and never, ever Jews, not even the bankers.

"You look well," she said. He had matured and looked more attractive than ever. He had acquired strength in his body and in his facial expression. Not the raw strength of a warrior like Vadim, but a strength that came from deep inside. By the fine gabardine suit and the impeccable trim on his mustache, he must be doing extremely well.

"And you?" he replied politely, "are as lovely as ever."

This almost made her feel better although she knew he said it out of courtesy. Since she gained weight, she had neglected herself and did not feel inclined toward fashion. She stood humbled, even humiliated by a princely phoenix, a man beaten down and rejected, now resurrected with honor. He revealed nothing of his thoughts or his availability, neither by his expression nor his words. He made no advance toward her nor gave any indication of interest. He simply stood and politely gazed at her somewhat detached like a man who was securely married and bound by a swarm of children. A hot flash of embarrassment rushed to her face. She wanted to ask a million questions but her thoughts evaporated in his presence. Finally, she said somewhat coolly, "what are you doing here?"

"We are discussing the expansion of the railroad with the Sergei Witte.

"Oh?" She wondered how he got a railroad contract with the government, but only wanted to know one thing. Did he have a wife? *They always do.* More than once she had been talking to a fine looking gentleman and out of nowhere a wife would materialize with that knowing smirk, embarrassing her to death.

She could feel her face flushing again. He was so cool, so composed. *Mon Dieu*, he must be married. She looked at the diamond time peace which she wore as a locket around her neck. "I must go...it was so nice to see you again, Daniel." She turned and quickly rushed back to the dining room, sat down and brushed away a strand of hair which fell over her eyes. In those brief moments she felt humiliated, unwanted, rejected, and fat. At the moment none of these things troubled her, except fat. She couldn't remember if she smiled when she left him. *Oh how he must have thought I was horrible.*

She glanced around the table, as far as Daniel knew, Cyril, her sister's husband, might have been her own husband.

She recalled Vadim's words, "he latched himself onto some prince or other." *Prince Militsyn? So it was true.* Now, she was more curious than ever. She didn't want to believe he was an opportunist, of which there were many in this town.

"Jenka, you have been behaving oddly all afternoon. Is something wrong?" asked her mother.

"No." Her heart was still pounding. She could think of nothing else but her horrific encounter with the one man she had been longing to see again.

Zinaida and Yelizaveta gave each other a puzzled look.

She had to find out more about him. She couldn't ask Prince Militsyn or Sergei Witte and make a bigger fool of herself. Who then? Cyril! She would ask Cyril who frequents the English Club where government intrigues and policy making contracts were always discussed.

Chapter 28

DANIEL'S FEELINGS TOWARD Evgeniya were as mixed and confused as were hers. He was dismayed by her blunt, cool demeanor, after all the lofty words of love and the undying vows of commitment. She acted nervous, anxious, disconcerted, so unlike herself. What happened five years ago was not the fault of either one of them. He had intended to look her up and visit but his business had advanced so rapidly that he failed to notice he had neglected his social life. Maybe if he didn't drag his feet they could have renewed the old flame, if that was possible.. He decided that he had two choices, to forget the past or to visit her and find out if she still felt anything for him. He noticed she wasn't wearing a wedding ring.

When the Galina brought Daniel's calling card, Jeniya told her she did not want to see the visitor. She felt unprepared to deal with the tension of rejection, not from him but from her own low self-esteem.

"My lady countess," said Galina. "Isn't that the same Daniel Mendelev you knew a few years back?"

"Yes, Galina. But I don't know if I can manage this visit, when I know nothing about him. If he were married, I would be devastated in facing him again."

"If he were married, I shouldn't think he would come to see you."

"No, maybe not. But look at me, I can't go downstairs looking like this."

"You look fine, my lady countess. "We just need to find you something appropriate to wear and brush out your hair."

She rummaged through the closet and pulled out a slim skirt with black vertical strips to minimized Jeniya's buttocks and a starched white blouse with enormous puffed sleeves and narrow pleats down the front. A black and white cameo pinned at the collar completed the look.

Jeniya went to the mirror to assess herself. When she was satisfied, she went downstairs to see her visitor.

Daniel jumped up when he saw her enter the drawing room.

She smiled. "Daniel. How good to see you," She said, forcing herself to be pleasant. "Won't you please sit back down?"

"Thank you," he said.

They rigidly faced each other; she on the sofa, and he on an opposite chair with a round table between them. He glanced around the room taking in the knickknacks on the tables and family portraits on the walls mixed with priceless works of art. Jeniya toyed with the pearls around her neck groping for words.

"Would you like something to drink?" she said. "Tea? Brandy?"

"No thank you."

"So...what have you been doing all this time?" She said with a certain reserve in order to shield herself from the dreaded but inevitable words, "I got married."

"Well," he said "It's a long story." He saw the pictures of brides and happy babies. "Are these your children?" he asked.

She shook her head and gazed downward at her hands clutched in the folds of her skirt. "No," she said.

Reading her gestures, he said, "I take it you are not married, then?"

"No, and you?" She looked at him. Her hands grew clammy from nervous anxiety.

"No," he smiled.

Her jaw dropped open with a smile of delight. She wanted to run, laugh, cry, celebrate. She put her hands to her face and laughed.

"What's the matter with that?" he said chuckling.

She jumped up. "Let's go for a walk!" She had to remind herself that this time, although he was available, he was not in the habit of making marriage proposals. She just wanted to be with him.

He took her hand and they strolled into the beautiful summer gardens built by Peter the Great on the Neva. A sweet fragrance filled the balmy salt air from the many daffodil beds and blossoming trees just as they did when they first met. "When I am here strolling by your side," he said. It is as though time had stood still all these years. Nothing has really changed much, has it?"

"I've gained weight."

He laughed. "You can be as round as a *matryoshka* doll, it would not matter to me."

They entered the summer cottage of Peter the Great and marveled at his leather boots made for a giant and the imprint of his enormous hand in contrast to the small furniture. They examined the first boat he built as a youth before returning to walk in the gardens.

A company of soldiers passed by, marching with vigor to their regimental band. When the music ceased, they continued singing in a rousing chorus. When she saw them, she was thankful she did not consent to a marriage with Anatole and miss this blessing.

"Daniel? How come you never looked me up or wrote to me. I worried so much about you."

"I am sorry. No amount of apologies could make up for that, but I went through some very bad times, times when I thought I would not make it in the land of the living and I didn't want you to know."

"But why? I could have helped you."

"No, your world and mine were as distant as the sun and the moon. You were about to make you debut and did not need to worry about my burdens when nothing could be done."

She thought about his words and felt an ache in her heart in remembering his suffering due to her insensitive self-absorbent behavior. "And now?" she asked."

"Now?" he said. I thought for sure you were married and happy, then there was the issue of your father."

"Oh, he has changed a lot." She frowned. "I am curious about one thing, if I may ask. How did you go from prison to a guest of Prince Militsyn at the yacht club?"

He laughed. "God was merciful to me."

She looked into his eyes puzzled. "But?"

"Let's sit down over here." He extended his hand to a bench. "And I will explain everything to you. Or would you like to go somewhere and get a bit to eat?"

"No," she said. "Let's stay here, it's a beautiful afternoon."

"I was on my way to Amerika, to leave Russia forever, when the famine struck, and claimed victims among the poor in every corner of the Empire. I was one. I thought I had died and when I awoke I saw the face of an angel shining down on me from heaven, giving me cool water to drink and I knew then that Christ is real and had saved me. Then I suddenly realized I was still on earth, still in the stinking Pale, and the angel bending over me was one of the volunteers at the *hekdesh*, a sort of hospital-triage-poorhouse in Odessa.

Once I became strong again I saw a man passing out leaflets. It was a decree from Alexander III, ordering the building of a continuous railway across Siberia to connect the far eastern regions of the Empire, rich in natural resources, with the rest of the Russian railway system. It called for all able-bodied men to work in building the new Trans-Siberian railroad. Thousands were needed to set railroad ties, most were convicts and peasant soldiers. The work was grueling in the sub-zero temperatures of winter. We blasted rocks to make tunnels and build bridges with primitive axes, saws, and shovels. We had no roads. We transported all our materials by river.

The Tsar had given Sergei Witte complete control of the Trans-Siberian project. Witte hired managers based on their performance rather than political appointments and I got my lucky break. I quickly advanced from laborer to lineman to foreman and then manager. I learned on the job training in these various positions, which gave me a practical understanding of railroad operations. Under my management, the railroad line increased in efficiency and profitability and caught the attention of Sergei Witte. He introduced me to Prince Militsyn who wanted to sell his iron works plant which had gone bankrupt. He was a provincial governor at the time and wanted to get rid of this burdensome drain on his pocketbook. Since I did not have the money or collateral, I could not buy it, so he offered to give me the plant."

"You mean just hand it over, give his factory to you for nothing?"

"That's right, but in order to give me the plant, he had to make me a legal heir by adopting me."

She gaped at him speechless. "This sounds like a fairytale. Does that make you a prince?"

Daniel laughed.

"You are joking with me," she said laughing with him.

"No, it's all true. God did a miracle in my life and as I look back I am overwhelmed and filled with thankfulness to our Lord and Savior."

She stared into the beautiful blue eyes she fell in love with all those years ago when they met at Khishniakov's party, still amazed that they found each other again. "What did his family say?"

"Naturally, they were not happy, but when they looked over the books they wanted to get rid of it too. Before the deal was consummated they made me sign off all titles and inheritances."

"I can't believe Prince Militsyn just gave you the factory," she said shaking her head.

"You're right. It wasn't as simple as that. Because of my success with the railroad, Witte was able to secure a small loan for me to improve the plant. At first it seemed like a tremendous undertaking and I was not certain I wanted it. I had a good job and was advancing in a new career, but as I thought it over, I decided to take the challenge. I made some simple changes, like reduce the men's working hours and gave them better food. Working at hard labor myself I understood that tired malnourished men do not produce. Along with the loan, Prince

Militsyn and I were able to work out an investment plan where I gave him shares in the new business. Now he is our biggest shareholder. From there we went on to produce steel for locomotives and now I am here about to sign a contract to supply the steel for the new railroad through Manchuria to Vladivostok."

She stared at him speechless and astonished. "A prince, you were at one time a prince!" She wanted to announce this to her crazy father, to her whole crazy family, but they would never understand. "I always believed in you, I always knew you would find a way. That was one of the reasons I've love you all these years." Her eyes glistened with tears as she spoke with happiness for him.

"You...loved me through the years?"

She nodded. He put his arms around her and they held each other tightly, shedding tears of happiness and laughter together.

They stared at each other, their thirsty souls drinking in the beauty of each other's soul with longing in their eyes and a hungering to be merged in an enchanted union of body, mind, and spirit. That moment could have been a minute or a thousand minutes, it didn't matter.

"Jenka, let's get married."

"Of course we will."

"No, I mean now."

"But what about a wedding?"

"Frankly, I don't know if I could handle a ceremony in the Orthodox church. But," he added graciously. "If you really want a wedding we shall have a wedding."

Like every little girl, she dreamed of the day when she would wear a beautiful wedding dress and carry a bouquet of sweet scented lilies as family and friends gathered to honor and celebrate her new life. But somehow it wasn't important now. They gazed at each other in a happy haze, all she wanted was him.

"Well, what is your problem today?" said the count. "Is it a new suitor or a new dress?" His brows were knit in deep concentration over his work. She could tell he wasn't prepared to listen but she was sure her news would peak his interest.

"Papa," she said trying to retrieve his attention. A woman needs a man who can protect her in this changing environment," she said. "One who is advancing in his profession, don't you think?"

"I've always thought that," he said without looking at her. "Don't tell me you are planning on marrying that renegade, Vadim."

"Vadim?"

"He would be a good catch for you, he has advanced to an officer in the *Konvoi* of Tsar's Imperial guard. That should give you plenty of excitement. How many summers have you now? Twenty-five. Thirty? It's time you get hooked up."

"No papa, it's not Vadim. It's Daniel."

"Daniel?" He looked up at her. "Who is Daniel? What kind of a name is that?"

"He was the young gentleman who sat with Prince Militsyn and Sergei Witte at the Yacht club, remember?"

"Nikolai? Nikolai Dimitrievich Militsyn?" He stared at her in astonishment for a few moments, tossing the events over in his mind, trying to remember.

"Yes!" She gazed at him with her green eyes, wide and bright. "He and Prince Militsyn signed a contract with Witte to provide steel to expand the Trans-Siberian railway through Manchuria which would shorten the route of transportation to Vladivostok."

"That so? This is the first time I heard this news. Daniel, eh? Daniel who? Where did you get this news?"

"Daniel Mendelev."

"Daniel Mendelev?"

She watched his every move, listened to his every word, hoping he would not bring up the past.

"Oh yes, now I remember. Daniel Mendelev...that Jew!" He frowned as the dangling pieces of information congealed in his mind. "You mean to tell me that Jew has bedeviled Nikolai Dmitrievich? What kind of preposterous talk is this from my daughter?" He stared at her, his sharp mind taking in what she had to say and then going right back to his business. "Leave me now with this nonsense, I have a lot of work to do before tomorrow's State Council meeting."

Boris Vasilevich Rostovsky lived in his own reality and sometimes it was impossible to get through to him. Jeniya looked him in the eye. "No papa it's different this time. He has worked hard to get to where he is now. No one gave him anything. I always knew he would succeed no matter how the odds were stacked against him. He has also embraced the Christian faith. He tells me things about God I never knew. Wonderful things, stories from his people and their prophets. I feel we have lost something very valuable in Russia by not tolerating others who have something different to offer. We have not only become bland and myopic, but lost a certain flavor, a splash of color."

"A splash of color?" Her father dropped his pen in his papers splattering the ink. "So you think we have lost a splash of color by not absorbing those Jewish dogs? How do you know he is not beguiling you? You and Prince Militsyn? He did it once before."

"Papa don't say things like that, it hurts me."

"I think I'll pay Prince Militsyn a visit after the State Council meeting tomorrow."

———

Count Rostovsky invited Prince Militsyn for a little card game one evening at the yacht club. They sat at Vasilivich's favorite table by the tall windows in the evening sunlight. Twilight descended later and later until at the end of June, St. Petersburg's nights were transformed into a mystical pearly white. The count clapped his hands for the *offeeshyat* to bring two brandies and a deck of cards. After the two men wagered their bets, he wasted no time in bringing up the matter on his mind; the subject of Daniel.

"I saw you and Sergei Witte with a young man at the club several weeks ago. Who was he? I'm curious because he resembled someone I once knew in the Ukraine."

"His name is Daniel Mendelev…a fine young man. I am a shareholder in his steel mill." Although the prince was up in years, he held his handsome head like a true aristocrat, as well as one with a true heart.

"He owns a steel mill? Don't you own a steel mill?"

"Yes, one in the same. You could say, I bequeathed it to him."

"Bequeathed it, what are you talking about?"

Prince Militsyn told him the whole story of how they met through Sergei Witte and the deal he made in giving Daniel the factory for a percentage of the ownership. "It was going bankrupt and I was about to lose it. My children didn't want it so thanks to this brilliant young man who was willing to take it over, I had an opportunity to save my interest in it."

"Has he told you he is a Jew?"

Stunned, the Prince's wide brown eyes grew larger. "No…? I believe he is a Christian. What makes you think he is a Jew? Why are you telling me this?"

"I knew him back several years ago when he was a student at Kiev University. He has a brother who is a revolutionary, one of those "uprooters of foundations" and this Daniel was believed to have been working with them at the time to infiltrate the homes of land owners in the province of Kiev. My estate was one of those that were targeted. He got in by wooing my daughter, Jeniya."

"Are you sure this was the same man you saw at the club."

"Absolutely. Because my daughter has been seeing him again. She wants to marry him. We have tried introducing her to every decent bachelor in the Empire and she has refused them all. Seems she still carries a torch for this...Daniel."

The prince silently stared at his brandy for a long moment, twisting the stem of the glass. "Was he proven guilty?"

"No, but what else could he have been?"

Prince Militsyn took out his ruby and diamond studded cigarette case and offered a cigarette to Rostovsky who declined with a wave of his well-manicured hand. "Has your family ever come to any harm?" He took out a cigarette and tapped it on the table.

"No. Not that I am aware of."

"Have you been shown the evidence that he was part of that revolutionary cell?"

"No."

"Then he was never found guilty."

"No...I'll admit it."

"Then he could have been innocent of the crime for which he was accused. You cannot blame a man for the actions of his brother."

"True...but he studied law and is very clever." Rostovsky squinted his eyes. "How do you know this Jew has not bewitched you?"

"No. Of that I am certain. I can testify that he is a good and honest man. I should say...an exceptional young man, well-liked by all who know him, including the workers. He has been fair in all his negotiations, loyal to me and dedicated in building his business. Whatever he was in his past, he is a Christian now who takes his faith seriously and knows more about the bible than anyone of us. I believe he would make a faithful husband to your daughter and a most treasured addition to your family. I only wished one of my daughters had married a man like this."

"That so?" The count stared at his friend, startled. "Come to think of it," he said putting a finger to his chin and gazing across the room, weighing his words. "I rather liked him in the beginning. He was polite, intelligent...but as a convert from Judaism, he will never have any standing at court."

"Boris. Boris. Who cares what the mediocres at court think. It is your daughter's happiness that is at stake. Think of it this way. No matter what you say or do, your daughter will find a way to marry him if she loves him the way you say she does...you might as well accept it and have peace in the family. Anyway, sometimes I think that we nobles have become a bit too narrow-minded, bored and boring. Haven't you found that?"

Rostovsky looked at him with an oblique glance.

Prince Militsyn picked up the deck of cards. "Now what was your bet?"

Prince Militsyn had given Daniel advice on how to pick a valet. "He must be a man who has given you impeccable service. It is imperative that he be honorable in character since he will be the one person closest to you next to your wife. Do not show him too much preference. Your servants, no matter how close they are to you are not your equals...to make them so, would be dangerous. And do not dismiss him and tell him you are doing for yourself. You must always be master over your household of servants."

Daniel had always done for himself and had great difficulty in yielding his personal habits to another man. The valet did more than dress him in the morning and prepare his toilette, he was his personal attendant, and it was unthinkable for a gentleman to do without his valet.

However, today, on the morning of his wedding, he was grateful for Savva's services in attending to the formal attire.

"Today is your big day, sir. You must be excited," he said helping him on with his shirt and tying his cravat.

"Excited yes, but mostly nervous about going through with this ceremony."

Daniel had abhorrent memories from his childhood which he attributed to the regime's Orthodoxy, and had difficulty in coming to grips with the ritual. But out of honor to the Rostovsky family and friends, and his love for Jeniya, even though she didn't insist, he could see that she longed to be a bride and agreed to a simple ceremony. His only desire was for his bride's happiness and he knew her family and friends were looking forward to sharing this special day of joy which only comes once in a girl's lifetime.

"Don't worry, sir. You will do splendidly." Savva brought in his shoes, newly shined by the servants, slipped them on Daniel's feet and tied the laces. Lastly, he helped him on with his jacket, and brushed off any tiny speck of lint. Everything must be perfect.

Jeniya radiated with happiness on her wedding day. Her magnificent dress was fashioned of white slipper satin with seed pearls and trimmed in French Chantilly lace at the sleeves and down the long train. She wore a matching lace veil adorned with sprigs of white orange blossoms amidst the folds held in place by a jeweled tiara, and carried a cascading bouquet of fragrant white lilacs interlaced with sweet peas.

A coach drawn by four white horses brought her to Prince Militsyn's palace where the ceremony and the reception were to be held. On the arm of her father, she passed through several rooms filled with guests into a small chapel. Everyone whispered that they could not remember when they saw a bride so radiant with joy. They marveled over her new slim figure and predicted that she would be the next celebrated beauty in St Petersburg society.

Daniel stood near the lectern in the center of the chapel, smiling. She saw in his eyes something she had not seen before, that of a man filled with a gladness he never thought would come to him, and she gave thanks to God for His amazing blessing.

Her father led the bride to stand beside Daniel as Yelizaveta arranged her long train. Eight bridesmaids stood in two rows behind them and the service began. Daniel took her hand and they stepped forward to the priest who approach the lectern and faced the couple, wearing his sacerdotal robe under a chasuble of gold cloth and a gold cross. He lit two candles decorated with flowers and handed one to each, then opened the missal and repeated prayers of blessings. After each invocation, the choir mirrored the blessings with a chant. Then he read the rites of the marriage ceremony after which the young couple exchanged rings.

As the ceremony drew to a close, they repeated their vows, and more prayers, after which the priest threw back his chasuble, took the young couple by the hand and led them around the lectern to introduce them to the wedding guests after which the bride and groom shared red wine from a single cup. Then the priest said to Daniel, "you may kiss the bride." How one day, one hour, a simple ceremony could magically unite two separate souls into one was nothing short of a miracle to Jeniya, especially after she had longed for so many years to be wrapped in Daniel's loving arms as his wife. Her heart overflowed with joy and happiness.

The officiating clergyman spread a rose-colored carpet of silk cloth in front of the newly married couple as the choir chanted a Psalm. Daniel and Jeniya looked at each other and grinned, having made a pact that they would both step on the silk cloth in unison to confuse the on-looking guests as to who would become the head of the household.

Everyone watched and held their breaths to see who would be the first to step on the pink cloth, especially Zinaida. Just as the newlyweds approached the silk cloth, Jeniya caught the heel of her shoe in the train of her dress and Daniel christened the marriage with the first step. The women moaned and the men cheered. Daniel would rule the household. Then the bridal procession proceeded to the reception rooms where the new couple received their guests.

When they departed, Jeniya's parents, Prince and Princess Militsyn who became like surrogate parents to Daniel, stood at the bottom of the stairs and offered the newly-weds a large loaf of bread with a small dish of salt, a symbolic gift of love, happiness and prosperity. Whoever broke off the largest piece would be the boss for the next twenty-four hours. Not by accident Jeniya broke off the largest piece, dipped in the salt and fed a bite to Daniel. This time she would be the head of the household if only for twenty-four hours. Everyone laughed.

Zinaida watched them stepping off together in the enthusiastic gate of two lovers on their way to new adventures, remembering her own fleeting youth. There was something wonderful in the energy of young lovers. The way their garments swing as they move swiftly, chattering, laughing, carefree and successful, along with absolute bonding, and she sighed.

At the train station they were met with more friends and well-wishers before they boarded Daniel's private coach to honeymoon at Prince Militsyn'a villa in the Crimea. Daniel's valet had prepared the table set with fruit, smoked salmon and a variety of salads and Jeniya's favorite, apricot and prune kolache. A bottle of champagne was chilling in a silver bucket of ice.

There are some pleasures that cannot be explained like the soft caressing breezes on a summers day or the warm pleasure from the early autumn sun. Jeniya thought she knew how it would be, but she could not have imagined the anxious anticipation or the hesitant uncertainty in experiencing something new and unknown, as the mystery between a man and a woman.

Daniel approached her with two glasses of the bubbly wine, and they beheld each other's eyes. His sensual gaze reflected a mature depth that not only comes with life's experience but an understanding that comes with suffering. She also saw there a mirror of herself and in that transcendental instant she knew him to the depth of his soul. They were truly of one mind and there was nothing that could be hidden.

He unbuttoned her blouse and pealed her clothing letting it fall to the oriental carpet. All the while she kept her eyes fixed on his; until at his gentle touch, she bucked, overcome with passion and want. He carried her to the bed. When he came to her, she cried out in surprise for a moment, not comprehending what had happened. Then she relaxed and marveled at the expansion of his strong masculine chest, giving her unimaginable pleasure. She sighed with pure happiness, and rolled over into his arms, her head nestled in the curve of his shoulder and melted into a serene happiness. Now they were truly one, and nothing else in the world mattered.

As they lay together, his hand stroking her temple, entwining her long hair in his fingers, she began to get a glimpse of the deep abiding love that would be theirs until the end of their days together.

Chapter 29

1903

THE NEW CENTURY began with the organization of labor unions, workers strikes, the assassination of the minister of internal affairs, Dmitrii Sipiagin, and the last spectacular ball in the history of the Empire. In January of 1903, Nicholas II sent invitations demanding that all guests wear the costume of the seventeenth century court since he desired to relive those glorious days when the authority of his ancestors reigned supreme, if only for one magical night. He and the Empress, Aleksandra Feodorovna, looked magnificent wearing the jeweled attire of the first Romanov Tsar and Tsarina. Every guest glittered in precious gems from the crowns of their haughty heads to the tips of their sparkling slippers.

In the days that followed, the salons and reception rooms of St. Petersburg's haut monde swirled with exuberant praises about the remarkable ball. Everyone enjoyed such a glowing evening in the magical palace, that count Alexander Sheremetev replicated to reproduce the ball in all its details at his mansion.

While the myopic aristocrats danced, a new and hostile Russia began to emerge from the city's labor mills. The Russian Social Democratic Labor Party was formed to liberate the working class, crush capitalism and establish a socialist society. Vladimir Ilyich Ulyanov, known by the pseudonym Lenin, called for a united revolutionary front with strong leadership, violent insurrection and mass terror to achieve this end.

His colleague, Julius Martov opposed this idea, saying that party members should be free to express themselves independently of party leadership. Martov leaned toward a definitive socialist structure working within a parliamentary government to spearhead a successful revolution among the non-partisan proletariat. However, Lenin's supporters were in the majority and called themselves Bolsheviks, and Martov called his minority Mensheviks.

In 1904, the minister of the interior, Pleve, declared. "We must do something to suppress the masses from revolution." General Kouropatkin, suggested "a small but victorious war with the little short-tailed monkeys," in order to expand the Trans-Siberian railroad into the vast mining opportunities of central Asia and secure Port Arthur, a warm water harbor on the Yellow sea, leased to them by China.

Japan offered to accept Russian presence in Manchuria in exchange for their cooperation in recognizing Korea as part of the Japanese sphere of influence. However, Nicholas refused Japan's offer and send Russian troops to fight the "yellow peril" in the Far East, demanding that Korea be a neutral buffer zone. This move delighted his cousin, German Kaiser Wilhelm, who wanted to advance his own military presence in Europe, but Japan perceived it as a threat to its strategic interests. On February 8th, in a surprise attack, they torpedoed and sank three Russian cruisers anchored in Port Arthur in one hour. Weeks later Pleve, like his predecessor, Sigiapin, was assassinated.

As circumstances became shaky within Nicholas's ministry, the Russian Social Democratic Labor Party urged their followers to take an active role in the unfolding of civil unrest and Ezra jumped at the opportunity. His job was to distribute socialist propaganda, agitate political demonstrations and strikes, and perpetuate these uprisings by using current political controversy. Next, he had to convince the workers that the liberal sympathizers helping to promote the socialist agenda, or the useful idiots as they were called by Lenin, were anti-proletariat. These well-meaning individuals had to be prevented at all cost, from taking control of the labor movement and becoming its champion.

Once the fire was lit, the laborers already simmering with pent up rage, would ignite into a revolution for which they had to be armed. The final step was to infiltrate all aspects of the proletariat, degenerate the army and topple the government laying the foundation for an eventual civil war.

Now he needed to get a job inside a factory, and he set his sight on one, Daniel's metallurgical works. In his eyes, Daniel had abandon his family, his father and his faith. Although faith was not an issue to Ezra, he had long ago abandoned his own religion when he became a rebel. His loathed his brother for selling out to the anti-Semitic aristocrats in order to pursue the easy life of wealth instead of taking on the job as an arbitrator for the poor working class and plea their cause against the oppressors.

Getting employment at the Mendelev Metallurgical works wasn't easy. A long line of applicants waited to get a ground level job in the steel mill. The grueling labor did not suit him but he would persist.

St. Petersburg had two main haunts, one for the destitute, and the other for the working poor. Haven field, a refuse dump, was also a gathering place for the outcast, the homeless, the jobless, and the thieves. During the day they would wallow in squalor and pour any kind of fiery liquid they could find into their blotched and bruised faces. These hopeless individuals were not Ezra's targets but the working poor who lived in Maiden Field. He observed these ashen faced individuals lumbering home to their tenements after standing on their feet for fourteen or fifteen hours a day in their sweat shops. Men, women and even girls had to work overtime because their wages were so low. He rented a bed for a few kopeks a day in a flat that housed several families packed like caviar in one apartment. When the bread winner came home from work and saw his listless wife and children surviving in one squalid corner of the room, he went to the local dive and obliterated his senses on cheap vodka. If a man was not a drunkard it was because he had not enough money. The sanitary conditions in these tenements were so deplorable and the air so foul that the tenants would say, "we can cut it with an axe."

Ezra befriended these people and genuinely empathized with them. They would gather around and listen to his words of hope and liberation. To his surprise, he discovered that not all the people who lived here were of the working class. Many were born into the upper classes; officers, barristers, society women who had lost their virtue, and even those from aristocratic families who lost everything to gambling.

When his money ran low, he worked piecemeal at several mills, all the while spreading Bolshevik propaganda. With cheap labor flooding into the cities from impoverished villages, factory owners could expand their wealth on the backs of greenhorn workers. In order to add greater profits, they convinced themselves that the *moujik* had a child-like mind and had to be cared for by suppling his basic needs of housing, meals, and medicine on factory premises. In effect they were the new barons of labor who owned the souls of their workers as the land barons once did in the days of the patriarchal system of serfdom. For the miserable peasant there was no way out of slavery. When one worker was spent, dozens more stood outside the factory gates eagerly waiting to take his place and the selected one had to pay the foreman a bribe.

Finally, Ezra's patience paid off. A bottom line job opened up in Daniel's plant. Hoping not to be discovered by his brother, he adopted the pseudonym name of Samsky in honor of his ancestor Samson who brought down the temple of the Philistines.

He found the barracks were meticulously maintained. The dormitory for single men was airy and neat, with a double row of iron framed beds and comfortable mattresses. The bedding was clean. Families who chose to live on the premises had roomy quarters larger than most apartments. When the factory whistle blew, the workers orderly proceeded to the cafeteria, and meals, he had to admit were tasty. The workers were allowed to take brakes and the wages were among the highest in the city, including double pay for overtime. Everything was not as he imagined. The workers seemed loyal, despite the hard and oftentimes grueling work in the steel plant, especially in the heat of summer. But with public sentiment in his favor, he would attempt to arouse class hatred and enmity toward their boss. He arranged meetings with the employees and explained to them the extent to which they were being exploited. "You need to make higher wages for the back breaking work you are doing. Look at how your *barin* lives in luxury, with servants, horses and homes. His wife is wrapped in jewels and furs. They party continually on the wages that are due to you."

Daniel made it a priority to treat his workers as he wished to be treated, the bottom line was not his concern so much as the welfare of his employees. He understood the grave conditions under which so many men and women, and even children labored since he worked at back breaking labor himself, living in drafty rat infested barracks eating watery cabbage soup and moldy bread, trying to gain strength for another day's work.

He kept his equipment up to date and saw to it that his employee's wages were more than sufficient to eat well and obtain a decent apartment for their families in the city. He maintained an immaculate infirmary and held classes for those who wished to learn to read and write believing this would make them more responsible workers, with a better future.

Ezra invited a priest called Father Gapon to speak at some of his meetings. Gapon's huge power of verbal persuasion and fiery passion more than offset his slight build. His charisma had inspired the working masses with hope and rallied them to unite. It also ingratiated him with the St. Petersburg police captain who gave him the liberty to organize an Association of Russian Workingmen in different factories. But Ezra knew better. The Okhrana never gave anyone suspected of collaborating with the worker's unions liberty unless they had their net ready, not only to catch him, but his followers.

At first, the young priest had one objective, to lift the workingmen and women from dire poverty, but later he abandoned his idealistic views when he received money from the socialist revolutionary groups in order to agitate the workers. Now the heart of his talks went from encouragement to changing the entire social structure through revolution. As a first step in achieving his goal, he would organize a mass labor march to petition the Tsar on behalf of the workingmen of Petersburg.

A young man called Vluddy Bogdanovich, with a broad powerful chest, carrot red hair, and freckles was asked to lead their factory procession in the march. He always displayed a pleasant disposition and his fellow employees respected him. Daniel also recognized his talents as a diligent worker with a strong forward vision and had plans to promote him as manager.

On the morning of Epiphany in January, 1905, Evgeniya telephoned Daniel at his office crying hysterically, "Danya, please come home quickly!" When the footman opened the door, she rushed to meet her husband. "Oh my darling, I'm afraid a revolution is starting. We are no longer safe on the streets. An assassination here, a bomb there, our ministers Pleve and Sipiagin, the strikes."

Daniel put his arm around her trembling shoulders and escorted her to the sofa. "Come sit down." He rang for Yaroslav. "Please bring us some sherry, quickly. He held her in his arms as one who soothes a child. "What happened?" he said in a quiet voice to calm her.

Yaroslav presented two glasses of sherry on a silver platter and gave the platter to a tending footman while he stood by to oversee the needs of the family. He had served Count Rostovsky as first footman and is now in service as butler to Daniel's household. He had watched Jeniya grow up and his serene manner had a calming effect on her.

Daniel took a glass and put it to her lips. "Here drink this. This will sooth your nerves."

"They tried to kill Nicholas. They tried to kill all of us!"

Daniel could not absorb her words. He heard that something had happened during the ceremony of Epiphany this morning, but no one had any details. He generally avoided attending the Emperor's frivolous ceremonies, the one duty of state Nicholas enjoyed and the one obligation in which he had succeeded; employing the entire Imperial Court in a pageantry of which the Roman Emperors could only dream.

The privileged courtiers who took part in this ceremony at the Winter Palace were arranged in pairs and stood between two lines of Imperial guards to form the Emperor's grand procession. The masters of ceremonies then walked along both sides of the line to the Malachite room where they announced the Emperor and Empress with the tapping of their long ebony staffs. The sovereigns entered the hall with the Imperial family behind them in order of rank. Then the masters of ceremonies led the entire procession to the house chapel in step to the lively anthem played by the Preobrazhensky Regimental marching band. The jewels in the arched crowns and necklaces of Aleksandra's ladies in waiting sparkled in the sunlight as they marched through the great palace halls wearing elaborately embroidered court gowns with long trains.

When the chapel mass ended the procession descended the palace's great Jordan staircase to the quay on the icy Neva where they were joined by more military units, church processions and choirs from all over St. Petersburg singing the sacred liturgy. Ornate iconic banners fluttered above their heads. The courtiers followed the Metropolitan and his clergy to a canopy built on the frozen river where they stood shivering in sub-zero temperatures as the Metropolitan lowered a cross through a hole cut in the ice to bless the waters of the Neva. The sacred rite ended with the salute of cannons firing blanks from the fortress of St. Peter and Paul across the river while everyone chanted to the rolling drums and regal trumpets of the "Te Deum".

"What do you mean they tried to kill you?" Daniel asked. "Who?"

"After the metropolitan blessed the waters of the Neva, the cannons fired real ammunition…on the second or third round…I can't remember which…we heard the windows of the Palace shatter. Hundreds of aids to the ministry and persons of the diplomatic corps were up there…watching from those windows. We looked up and saw canon holes in the building around the windows. A guard was killed and a broken banner nearly fell on the Tsar. I don't know how many were wounded. …it was horrible!" She began to tremble in remembering the direful event.

He gave her the glass of wine. "Be calm, you are safe now."

"Then someone shouted. 'They are firing live ammunition. They exchanged the blanks with real cannon fire.' We Panicked. We didn't know what to do. We didn't know who was in the streets. So we stood there like quarry on the icy river bank…it was so cold."

Daniel vacuously stared at the four gold and white French provincial chairs with a pink floral pattern woven in emerald silk, given to them as a wedding present from Prince and Princess Militsyn and the large Monet painting Jeniya loved so much hanging above the fire place, also a wedding present from her mother. He hoped he was mistaken, but he believed revolutionary forces were not only behind the organization of Sunday's march, but today's events in order to aggravate hostility between the government and the thousands who were preparing to march. The rebels knew the Tsar would react and order his troops to crush the demonstrations. They were aware that innocent men, woman and children might be marching to a possible slaughter. He worried about Vluddy leading many of his own workers.

"That means the police will be on high alert," he said. "God only knows what will happen on Sunday when the workers and their families march."

"What? What march?" Jeniya shouted in alarm.

"The workers and their families are gathering at the winter palace on Sunday to present a petition to Nicholas asking for an eight-hour work day, health care…a list of things that are only fair."

"Oh no! Nicholas immediately issued an order forbidding all demonstrations in the city. They will be ignoring the Tsar's Imperial order!" Tears came to her eyes. "Oh, those poor children, those poor innocent women and children." Her hands trembled as she reached toward the end table for her glass of wine.

The governess came in with their two sons, Alexei who was six and Gavriil, three. They ran to their mother's arms. Gavriil was crying.

"Mama," said Alexei. "We heard you shouting and we were afraid." She took them both in her arms and hugged and kissed them. "Don't be afraid my darlings. Everything is all right. Our family is all together now. Don't cry, Gavriil, everything is all right."

She stood up and put her hand affectionately on Daniel's shoulder. "Darling, I am not coming to the dining room tonight. I will be taking dinner with our sons," she said and dismissed the governess.

Samsky was already on his next mission. He waited in the tavern with the others for Father Gapon to arrive and give the facilitators of the event their marching orders. Excitement was escalating and the dense air smelled of tobacco smoke and burning pine logs.

When the young priest appeared in his long flowing black cassock and rectangular hat, all eyes turned upon him and all ears were eager to hear what he had to say. He raised a hand and gazed around at the crowd with large penetrating dark eyes. "On Sunday, January 9th, we will march to the Winter Palace and give the Tsar our petition," he said.

"What if the Tsar does not come out to see us for a long time?" someone said. "I was told he may not even be in Petersburg."

"Then we will wait. His residence is only an hour's journey from here. Be prepared and bring bread for your families."

"What if he will not listen to us?"

"If he does not listen or if innocent blood is shed, then we have no Tsar! You will carry two flags, one white and one red. If he hears our petition, raise the white flag. If he refuses, then raise the red. In that case, do what you think necessary, but no hostility and no gun fire. We are to march without weapons in our hands, not so much as a pocket knife…and do not carry revolutionary banners. We don't want the aristocracy to have any cause for accusations. We will carry Church banners and those of our Emperor and Empress. Bring your women and children to show we still believe in the monarchy. Tell them to wear their Sunday best out of respect to our Tsar.

I have sent a letter to the Tsar ahead of our march. In it I begged him to accept the petition from the workers of St Petersburg, who were to gather from all quarters of the city. I summarized the desires and hopes of these workers as stated in our petition, and assured him that to receive his people would be a gesture of good will because it shows he sincerely wants to help them. It would also renew his people's confidence in the monarchy. I told him that if you do not show yourself to your people and if innocent blood be shed, then your people's confidence will be broken and the trust which they have in you as their *Batiushka* will disappear forever." Then he gave out copies of the petition to distribute among revolutionaries inviting them to join the march. Ezra took a bundle.

The day before the march tension began to mount in the city. On the streets workers cheered and waved white flags whenever Father Gapon passed by. Little children ran out and kissed his hands. Many people had tears in their eyes. They wondered if those excellent men with him carrying banners in front of the crowd may be walking to their death should the police open fire. "We know you are going to the Tsar tomorrow to speak for the people," they said. "May God help you!"

The night before the march, the young priest met with the men who organized the event from every factory in the city; upstanding men respected among their fellow workers, men who would march proudly at the head of their divisions to present their petitions to Nicholas.

"The great labor movement has begun, said the priest. "Each branch leader will be in charge of his own procession. Our goal is to reach the Winter Palace and present our petition to the Tsar. Do not grieve if there are victims. Remember, if blood is spilt, it will prepare the ground for revolt against the aristocracy. Show the workers of Russia that you, their leaders, are willing to lay down your lives for the people who labor in our factories and mills, and for the noble and worthy cause of freedom from Imperial tyranny."

The men nodded and quietly shook each other's hand, encouraging one another, speaking solemn words of farewell, with heads bowed. Some of the men wiped tears from their eyes. They wrote down the addresses of family members and embraced in long tearful hugs, wishing one another God's blessings. "Take courage, *tovareeshee*," said the priest. "May God be with you."

On January 9, 1905, the northern sun blazed on an icy horizon and the temperature plummeted below zero in a city under siege. Infantry and cavalry set up barricades around the palace and on the broad avenues that extended into the worker's districts. They laid out bivouacs where camp fires burned under black iron kettles of soup. Soldiers were told to use fire if necessary because the workers intended to storm the Winter Palace and murder the Tsar and his family. Ambulances waited to carry the wounded.

Some thirty-thousand working men, women, their children and their elderly were ready to converge in the Winter Palace square from every avenue of the city; their ranks increased by the participation of many ordinary citizens in empathy with the cause. Excitement and anticipation mounted. Children dressed in colorful peasant costumes, with rosy faces scrubbed clean, jaunted happily by their parents thinking they were participating in a parade. The procession penetrated the vicinity of the Winter Palace, in denial that the troops would seriously hurt them. Military units intercepted the marchers and repeatedly warned them to turn back or they would fire.

Vluddy, the strong idealistic leader, marched at the head of his processions proudly holding a banner of the Tsar's portrait. He lifted his voice with the others and sang, "How glorious is our Lord in Zion" and "Save us, O Lord" with enough fervor to ascend the gates of heaven, and hopefully, to reach the ears of their *Batiushka*.

Father Gapon was advancing from another part of the city. He stood at the head of his column in front of the Narva triumphal arch holding his arms in the air. When the troops fired, he urged the workers onward toward the Palace square. "If the Tsar refuses to see us then we have no Tsar." He shouted. "So let us defend our rights." Like a powerful tidal wave, determined and without understanding, lost in some kind of holy euphoria, they surged forward into the firing line of the soldiers.

Near the winter palace square, Ezra and his cronies began their work among the demonstrators. Large red flags appeared here and there in the hands of the rebels between the church banners and portraits of the Tsar. Again the soldiers ordered the marchers to disperse, but they continued to press toward their sacred mission, incited by the revolutionaries. Suddenly, four rounds of fire ripped into the Panicking marchers in the gardens near the entrance of the palace square. People fell to the ground. Blood curdling screams mingled with more gunfire. Vluddy felt a sharp sting in his abdomen. In a faint haze, he watched men, women and children fall and hundreds more scatter, running in every direction followed by horses with heads and manes waving, their riders charging into the frenzied crowd wildly swinging sabers, slashing them down on the ice, pounding them beneath the grinding hoofs of their horses. The young man fell forward and his face hit the icy pavement. Everything went black.

Daniel stood on his balcony watching the workers moving through the streets, anxiously worrying about his own men and their families who were participating. "Get my horse," He said to a footman when he heard the first round of gun fire. He threw on his overcoat and rode to the Alexander gardens. Men and women were running in every direction carrying their wounded. A few hundred bodies were strewn over the blood red ice. The eyes of one elderly man once lifted in hope, now stared skyward, hollow and cold.

"Oh Lord God! Massacred. Trampled. Children." Daniel staggered like a drunkard stumbling over human beings, his vision blurred with tears, his boots stained with blood, hoping he would not find what he was looking for. "Oh God! No!"

When Vluddy regained consciousness, he saw buildings whirling around in a circle. In his disoriented mind he saw someone kneeling over him and began to recognize Daniel tearing the crumpled banner of the Tsar, making a tourniquet to stop the blood pouring from his wound.

Vluddy put his hand to his face and wiped blood. His gloves were wet. "Sir? What happened to me?"

"Quiet, don't speak," Daniel said wiping his face with a cool handkerchief dampened from the snow. "I am going to get the ambulance."

"No, don't." He coughed up blood. "Don't leave me. I want you to do something for me, if you will, sir."

Daniel feared that his friend had only moments to live, "I will," he said.

His lips turned into a faint smile and he said weakly. "Please take care of Maria, and my Children."

"I will, you do not need to worry."

The young man's face contorted in pain for a brief moment and then took on an angelic glow.

Daniel rose to his feet and gazed at him for the last time. He hadn't noticed a spirited black stallion nervously shifting beside him or the bloodstained greatcoat worn by his rider.

An officer stared down at him through cold grey eyes and lifted the blade of his saber still dripping in blood to Daniel's neck. "Move on, I said."

Daniel became enraged with indignation. "What kind of beast are you?"

The rider eyed the clean shaven face, the neatly trimmed mustache, the fine cashmere coat with beaver-fur lining and the matching hat. He put his weapon back in its shield, pulled his horse's rein and turned away, signaling his men to clean the bodies from the park.

With tears still standing in his eyes, Daniel looked out over the bloody battlefield. *This day we have witnessed the beginning of the end of the Romanov Empire. It will live on in the people's hearts as bloody Sunday, the day of the red snow and I am afraid it may be the harbinger of a bloody year.*

Nicholas continued to lose credibility and favor among his people. A delegation of provincial councilmen took the opportunity to call upon the Emperor asking for constitutional reform, but he rebuked them. "This is a senseless dream. I shall maintain the principle of autocracy just as firmly and unflinchingly as my unforgettable late father."

However, to the surprise of his Imperial Ministry, Nicholas issued an ukase on February 18, 1905 granting individuals and institutions the right to address him with their grievances. He was even willing to consider an advisory legislative board elected by the people if it did not infringe on his complete autocratic principles. He had no intention of giving an inch of his sovereignty.

The public misinterpreted his ukase thinking he had granted them the right to public assembly. Now the Tsar had to make an unexpected compromise between the throne and the people. His minister of the interior, Bulygin, nominated a commission to construct a national assembly of elected delegates. The commission welcomed suggestions from all classes of the citizenry, except the Jews, citing that, "The Jew is the enemy of our house. A fusion with him is impossible owing to his religion and other disturbing causes. He is an active propagandist of Western European socialism and is a growing danger of a most serious nature to our Empire in two of its most vulnerable points of attack, the Austria and German frontiers. For these reasons, we cannot admit to him equal rights. Furthermore, we claim the right to resort to our own measures to safeguard the peace of the realm. We will not permit anyone to coerce us into admitting this race to the common right of Russian citizenship. Socialism is synonymous with the Jew and both are unwelcome intruders. For this reason, he must go to any country who will admit him and is ruled by another system."

Added to his woes, Nicholas' small victorious war which was supposed to divert the unrest of the dark masses and renew their patriotic faith in their Batiushka, had turned into a catastrophe for the Russian navy. After Port Author had fallen, Japan with its superior military strategy now took command of the eastern seas.

Within weeks after the shock of defeat, Nicholas' uncle, the Grand Duke Sergei Alexandrovich, governor of Moscow who drove the Jews out thirteen years before, was assassinated.

Three months later, on May 14, the Japanese decimated the entire fleet of antiquated ships sent from the Baltic sea to replace the torpedoed ships. The Emperor was just about to play a game of tennis when a telegram came announcing the disaster. He simply said, "what a horrible catastrophe," and without another word, asked for his racket.

Nicholas II was defeated. By that time nothing could have mattered. The glory of his reign for which he so desperately desired was smashed along with his fleet. From then on, he treated both good and bad news with indifference, as a man who had lost his heart.

Daniel discovered that Ezra had anchored himself in the city's revolutionary movement. He wasn't hard to find because he wrote editorials for the city's radical newspapers. Ezra, like Lenin, was a Bolshevik. He held the Marxist view of a single objective vision for the world and promoted the continual escalation of violent confrontation to achieve that end.

For his dedicated work in committing the workers at the impenetrable Mendelev works to the revolution, he was elected to the newly formed St. Petersburg Soviet Council of Workers Deputies, a non-party revolutionary organization which became a testing ground for the opinions and tactics of all revolutionary groups. "By placing many disconnected organizations under its control," Lev Davidovich Bronshtein, who called himself Trotsky, wrote. "The soviet united the revolution around itself."

Daniel knew that as long as Ezra was in town, trouble could break out in his factory at any time. He alerted his plant managers to be on the look-out for strangers entering the premises, unusual looking objects, and other signs of a possible terror attack.

Chapter 30

SERGEI WITTE, NOW bestowed with the title of Count Witte, after returning victoriously from America and having successfully negotiated a peace treaty between the Tsar and Japan to end the war. He took advantage of his popularity among the common people to bargain with Nicholas in granting his subjects civil liberties. First he organized meetings with labor delegations to gain support of the working men. He told them to address one another with the common title of "citizen" a term which would be used again after the soviet revolution to denote equality. Then he urged several influential men including the Tsar's uncle, the Grand-Duke Nicholas Nicholaiovich, to persuade the Emperor that the only way to avert an armed revolution was to give labor representation in the government.

Inspired by Count Witte, the workers took the liberty to speed up matters and staged one of the greatest strikes in the history of labor. About one million railway workers from Siberia to the Crimea walked off their jobs and paralyzed the entire Empire. In solidarity, factory workers, postal clerks, telegraph operators, bank tellers, shop keepers, government employees, doctors, lawyers, teachers, professors, janitors and cabbies, even the ballet troupe of the Imperial *Marinski* theater went on strike. Industry ground to a halt, fuel deliveries ceased, street lights went dark, trolley cars stopped, banks fixed iron bars on doors and windows, and stores lowered metal screens and boarded windows. Kazak patrols and mounted police were powerless to stop the thousands of workers from organizing meetings in the streets.

Workers in the provincial towns as well as in every city marched down the avenues waving red banners above their heads. They sang the Marseillaise, the French national anthem and standard for revolution, shouting, "Freedom. Life or death. Down with the Autocracy. Long Live the Revolution." Their battle cry shook the foundations of the Empire.

Sailors on the battleship Potemkin mutinied and killed their officers. Revolutionaries smuggled pistols and Browning automatic rifles across Russia's borders with the aid of foreign revolutionary sympathizers and made ammunition from materials stolen from the munitions factories. Russia was churning with strikes and violence.

Lenin wrote; "The uprising has begun. Force against force. Street fighting is raging, barricades are being thrown up, rifles are cracking, guns are booming. Rivers of blood are flowing, the civil war for freedom is blazing up. Moscow, the Caucasus to the south and Poland to the north, are ready to join the proletariat of St. Petersburg."

Ezra wrote inflammatory editorials in the paper of the St. Petersburg Soviet of Workers Deputies, demanding that Nicholas grant political concessions to everyone. Instead of taking immediate action, the Emperor's bungling ministers and advisors sat around and cackled like frightened hens.

Count Witte, who had drawn up a constitutional manifesto, positioned himself to offer the Tsar an ultimatum. "Either grant civil rights to all the Russian people, including freedom of speech, and agree to establish a national assembly of elected delegates to confirm all laws...or find someone to crush the rebellion by force. Then we should be back to where we started within months."

The Emperor lived in a constant state of torturing anxiety, between riots, revolution, and the pressure to introduce a constitutional assembly. Papus, a famous diviner, was summoned to the palace to call up the spirit of Alexander III for help. When the spirit appeared, Nicholas asked his father whether or not he should resist the wave of liberalism. The spirit replied, "at any cost you must crush the rebellion that is now beginning, but it will spring up again one day and its violence will be proportionate to the severity with which it is put down today. So be brave, my son and do not give up the struggle."

Nicholas chose to ignore the pleas of his subjects. He consulted with his old Jesuit teacher, Pobedonostzev who said, "the continuation of the regime depends on our ability to keep Russia in a frozen state. The slightest warm breath of life would be certain to cause the whole thing to rot." The Tsar found the arrogant and cruel General Trepov, his chief of police to put down the rebellion in the capital.

Trepov ordered his garrison to crush the street protests. "Should the people resist, spare no bullets," he said to his troops. He threatened the workers that further disorder would be met with unlimited gun fire. This brought calm to the city for one week until workers embolden by rebel leaders poured back into the streets to meet General Trepov's infantry bullets.

Revolutionaries ready to spill blood for the revolution occupied the universities with machine guns. Panic struck the citizens. They besieged shops snatching up provisions before shopkeepers shut their doors. Nicholas and his family took cover in the Peterhof Palace where the imperial yacht, Polar Star, remained under full steam ready to take them aboard and flee to Denmark.

Finally, the Dowager Empress Marie put an end to her son's indecision and convinced him to take the council of Count Witte. On October 17, the Emperor granted a manifesto to the people giving them freedom to assemble and speak, and to establish a state Duma in which no law should go into force without the approval of its representatives; under one condition. Nicholas reserved the right to have the sovereign word above all matters and retain, "that authority which my ancestors bequeath to me."

When the manifesto was declared, St. Petersburg celebrated, all except the revolutionary forces who saw the new constitutional assembly as a hindrance in spreading their socialist revolution. Trotsky, declared. "Everything is given and nothing is given. A constitution is given but the aristocracy remains." He urged workers to purchase more weapons. "Stand guard over our freedom. We must not abandon our battle stations. We must continue the struggle for freedom."

Small shop keepers, tradesmen, petty government officials and soldiers loyal to the Tsar formed their own reactionary organization called the Black Hundreds. These two polarized groups continued the struggle with more bloodshed and murder.

Nicholas hated Witte and hated to call upon him for help, but he was the only man in the Empire who had the strength of character and the audacity to quench the revolution. Witte acted promptly and decisively. "We must fight terror with terror," he declared and advised the Tsar to dispatch the Sememovsky guards to bombard the armed defenders of the revolution in Moscow with artillery fire and burn every building occupied by the rebels. In St. Petersburg, the police surrounded the headquarters of the Petersburg Soviet Workers of Deputies and arrested over three hundred members, including Ezra, ending Daniel's fear of a terror attack on his family and the bloody revolution of 1905.

Chapter 31

IN SUMMER, ARISTOCRATS vacationed in Paris, on the Rivera, in Biarritz on the Atlantic, or on their vast estates in the country. At Daniel's insistence, Jeniya took the children to Belozerkovka to get away from the unrest in St. Petersburg, although she would worry about her husband who needed to remain behind in the city during these turbulent times of change. "A holiday in the country will give the children an opportunity to experience life on the estate now that they are getting old enough to appreciate it," he assured her.

Alexei and Gavriil loved the country, running in the fields, discovering baby rabbit nests, watching the deer graze on the meadows in the predawn, riding the ponies, and rowing on the lake with their English tutor. Their laughter and innocent, carefree spirit reminded Jeniya of her own childhood and the happy days she spent with her grandmother.

She missed her grandmother's wise council and wished she were still here to guide her through these difficult days of uncertainty in managing the country estate, especially concerning the changing policies toward the working masses including the peasants who served on the grounds.

At the village fair, she met the one man she hoped to see, her liberal neighbor, Khishniakov who invited her to a soirée at his home. Alexeivich would be there. Over the years, he had embraced many new and liberal ideas in granting his peasants civil liberties and privileges, and she wanted to know more about how well it was going for him.

She knew his progressive policies caused constant dissention with the conservative provincial governor and his deputy officials who insisted that his course of action would create a rebellion among the peasants serving on other estates.

"The peasants are in no way your equals," her grandmother would say. "You cannot let them get a foothold. They will try, the cunning devils that they are, but you must always maintain your position of authority over them as mistress of this manor. Our neighbor Alexeivich has had some success with his peasants and I admire him for that. But he is treading on thin ice with our governor. One day he will go too far for his own good."

The old man Khishniakov met Jeniya on the veranda and escorted her inside. He was still the intriguing character she remembered always supporting the liberal view. She found the many photographs and trinkets from his world travels decorating the walls of the drawing room a reflection of his own interesting personality.

"Now, my dear countess," said Khishniakov. "You remember my wife Anna Vanyova," Jeniya smiled and the two women exchanged friendly greetings.

"Countess Borisovna," Alexei Alexeivich called when he saw Jeniya. "It's been a long time since we've seen each other. What brings you here to our meetings? Are you interested in getting more instruction on how to conduct your peasant affairs over at Belozerkovka? Or in government reform?" He laughed.

She smiled cordially. "Yes, as a matter of fact," she said. "I am interested in…" a large gentleman came over to meet her.

"I would like to introduce you to Vladimir Korolenko, publisher and author."

The gentleman slowly bowed his head of thick grey-flecked hair and kissed her hand. "My lady countess."

She already recognized the great man, both in stature and in brilliance. "I am very happy to meet you," she said. "I am greatly impressed by the intensity and passion by which you championed human rights."

"If one is to make a difference in this world, one must do it with passion," he said.

"This is Piotr Struve," Korolenko said of the man standing next to him. "Nice to meet you," my lady countess. He was a man of unkempt appearance with brows that slashed across hardened eyes, and a vehement critic of the Tsarist regime. He also edited several Marxist journals and wrote the manifesto for the Russian Socialist Democratic Labor Party.

"How do you do," she said with reserve in her voice.

He bowed. "My lady countess. No doubt you see me as a dangerous Socialist radical," he said detecting resistance in her voice.

She shook her head. "No, not really."

"Socialism, to tell the truth, never aroused the slightest emotion in me and still less attraction... Socialism interests me mainly as an ideological force...which could be directed either to the conquest of civil and political freedoms or against them."

She stared at him.

He bowed and turned to Vassily Mukhanov. "May I present countess Borisovna."

Mukhanov was a small man with large eyes and the fine wide cheek bones evident of a Mongolian heritage. She remembered him as the chamberlain of the court before he was dismissed and sent into exile after he led the delegation of provincial councilmen who dared to ask Nicholas for a national constitutional assembly after the Emperor granted his subjects the right to address him with their grievances.

Anna invited Jeniya and Alexeivich's wife to sit at a round table near the open window. A maid placed a platter of little sandwiches and one of assorted cakes on a white embroidered table cloth. The hostess served the tea from a porcelain teapot. Jeniya tried to be polite and contribute to the conversation but her attention kept drifting to the men's conversation.

"I have heard a rumor that Nicholas and his cousin Wilhelm signed a treaty to become allies," said Korolenko stroking his great white beard. "Did you hear anything about this from your sources in Germany, Piotr?" His eyes reflected much insight into life having spent time as a political exile in Siberia.

"Yes, they did," replied Struve. "But there is talk that Nicholas broke the treaty. His minister of foreign affairs, Count Lamsdorf took it upon himself to send a diplomatic envoy to tell the Kaiser that it is impossible for Russia to enter into a treaty with Germany due to her previous treaty with France. Wilhelm was humiliated and called on God to witness this treachery of the Russian Emperor. He swore he would never believe his cousin again."

A servant came in carrying a hand-carved wooden tray of brandy and vodka and served the men with drinks. He opened a box of cigars and one of cigarettes and offered each man a choice. Jeniya noticed that he did not wear the traditional white gloves, a mandatory attire for footmen.

"If the Kaiser offered his hand in good will, shouldn't we have taken it? In the past we were united with Germany against the superpowers of the west." said Khishniakov.

Struve sipped a little brandy and drew a puff on his cigarette. "Wilhelm is far too clever to offer a hand in good will," he said. "Germany is collapsing under debt, colonial scandal and internal struggle with the Social Democrats. He regards English supremacy of the seas as a threat to the expansion of his empire and fears that in case of conflict, their superior fleet would attack his ports and cripple his own fledgling fleet. An alliance with Russia would be of great benefit to him."

"I would think it would benefit both nations," said Khishnaikov.

"Except for one thing," said Struve. "Nicholas would never break his pledge to France, and the Kaiser is aware of this. He persuaded Nicholas to keep the treaty quiet until it became effective, thus insuring that should France become offended, she would not unite with England and start a war against Germany. In any case, France would never agree to those terms and it would come to nothing,"

"How did these two leaders get away with this farce?" asked Korolenko, who gained notoriety writing harsh descriptions of the Emperor and his injustice toward the people. Surely there were witnesses to such a paramount treaty?"

"Evidently the Tsar ordered his witness not to read what he was signing." Struve took another sip of brandy.

"And he obeyed?"

"Of course," said Struve. "Or he would be in exile like us." He laughed as he sipped his brandy.

"The Tsar needs to be removed," said Korolenko. "Along with his clique of ministers, whose utter stupidity and irresponsibility are persisting in bringing about the downfall of Russia. This nation can survive a fool but she cannot survive a multitude of fools."

Struve nodded in agreement. "I also feel there can be no intermediary position between autocracy and constitution," he said. "We need to establish a national constitutional democratic government, and the cultural and political liberation of Russia must become a national cause."

The men sat quietly contemplating one another's opinions, sipping their drinks and puffing on their cigars and cigarettes.

Gossip spread through the peasant villages faster than a fire in a drought. Workers on leave from factories in the North told their families that their *Batiushka* had granted them "civil liberties," and the right to assemble before him. The peasants did not understand civil liberties. In their minds it meant that the huge estates belonging to the *barins* would be broken up and distributed to them. It also meant the opportunity to pillage and take a well-deserved bonus from their landlords.

A delegation of the eldest and most respected peasants from the village came to visit Evgeniya. Their spokesmen, a broadly built *moujik*, approached her on the veranda with his head bowed and holding his cap in both hands. The others stood in the yard while he addressed his Panii. "My lady countess," he hesitated for a moment. "At a meeting with the elders of our village we decided to protect our *Panii* and not permit the ransacking of her property. But if it were at all necessary to be ransacked then she and her family were to be allowed to go free while we would loot her estate with our own hands and keep all outsiders away." He did not look up and spoke one long stream. He had served the family for over thirty years and believed that by his faithful service he had gained the right to freely express his opinion to his *Panii*.

"Kusma, I am surprised at you after all these years. Why must you do such a thing?" She chided him like a child to humor him.

"We promise it won't be bad, my lady countess. If we don't do it then the *moujikii* from other villages will. They may even ransack our *isbys*." This was not true but he wanted to justify himself.

"When are you planning this raid, my dear man?"

He scratched his head and looked at her from the corner of his eye. "Humm...ah...we don't know exactly but we will tell you in advance so you can be away."

"Thank you Kusma, it is good of you to bring me the news."

He bowed profusely without looking up, and backed down the steps. "Yes, my lady countess."

The peasants are in no way your equals and you cannot let them get a foothold, her grandmother's admonition ran through her mind. "Kusma!" she called. "Before you go, I have here twenty rubbles. Do you want to earn them?" She had the money in her hand and his eyes widened. The money could buy a lot of liquor but not nearly as much as the count had stored away in his wine cellar. He squinted at the rubles shining in the sunlight, scratching his beard.

"You can take the twenty rubbles now, and if no damage has been done on this estate, I will give you fifty more at the end of the summer, and twenty for everyone in your delegation." He smiled and took the money in his big hand. "Yes my lady countess! Someday, the souls of the *barins* will shine as big stars in the sky but ours only as little ones," he said bowing again.

Late that night Jeniya awoke in a Panic. From her window, she saw flames blazing on the horizon. She jumped out of bed and rushed downstairs. The servants followed terrified, repeatedly crossing themselves.

"It's coming from the direction of Alexeivich's estate!" said one. "He was on the friendliest terms with his peasants."

A rooster crowed. The sun rose casting a heat mist in the meadows and the air smelled with smoke from smoldering ashes. Belozerkovka remained intact. Jeniya decided to take a ride around the countryside to assess the damage. Most of the pillaging had been done to the storage houses and distilleries where the peasants carried off grain and liquor, sometimes they burned a barn or stole timber.

When she rode by Alexeivich's estate, a horrific sight met her eyes. His beautiful empire style home was burned to the ground. Nothing but charred rafters and beams remained. His large library and important archaeological collection, the music room with the Steinway piano, everything chopped, burned and destroyed. As she rode closer she became sick to her stomach. The carcasses of his beautiful thoroughbreds were brutally killed and lying about everywhere. *Could this be the work of the village peasants or someone else,* she wondered? *Would the moujikii slaughter useful animals that could till the soil or pull a cart, or had Alexeivich gone too far bucking the governor and the system?* She came to one conclusion, her grandmother was right, "one day he will go too far."

On the way home, she heard a roar coming from the village. Normally she had no fear of the villagers, but today she was cautious. A boy approached leading an ox with tree branches tied to the animal's horns to brush away the flies. She stopped and asked about the commotion.

"I don't know, madam. I think they are going to beat a man."

Beating someone sometimes meant beating him to death, she thought, even though that may not be the intent.

"Beat him for what?"

"I don't know, madam. I've never seen him before."

As she rode into town she noticed scythes, rakes, and a wagon left half filled with grain in the fields. Past the tree line road and wooden huts, she saw a crowd gathered in the middle of town.

Young men with big hands and broad ruddy faces in sweaty home spun *rubashkas* stared with stone faces, not revealing their thoughts, neither in word nor in expression. They stank from perspiration. Old men with toothless tobacco stained mouths grunted and smelled of vodka.

"Untie that man!" she shouted. "Is there no end to brutality?"

"But Panii, we only wanted to help you punish the man who tried to plunder Belozerkovaka last night," said Kusma. Before the law sent the Kazaks to ride through the villages and punish the perpetrators of last night's pillaging, the peasants decided to be good citizens and punish the offenders themselves in order to save their own hides from the many stinging ends of Kazak knouts.

"The law will judge responsible individuals, not a lynch mob," she said.

Kusma took off his cap and scratched his head with dirt stained fingernails. "We only wanted to help," he said obligingly.

Several *starushkii* moved in close to Jeniya and silently stared. She could tell by their sober gazes and pondering eyes that they were doing a lot of thinking, but said nothing. When she acknowledged them with kind words they lowered their heads and giggled like school girls putting hard working knotted fingers over their semi-toothless grins. They had strong steely bodies with sinewy arms extending from puffed sleeved blouses. One, tiny babushka with the slender figure of an adolescent dared to touch Jeniya's skirt. She hummed a pleasurable sound upon feeling the soft silky material slide between her fingers.

In the distance Jeniya heard the rhythmically clanging bells on the cows coming home from pasture to be milked. She turned her horse and slowly guided him through the crowd. Chickens picking in the road scattered.

She could not comprehend what was hidden in the soul of the docile Russian peasant, raging one moment and obsequious the next. They may be outwardly humble and submissive and physically close by, but their thoughts were as far away as the stars and as incomprehensible. They were not the dull witted beasts the gentry would like to have believed, but cunning pretenders. The words of Turgenev came to her mind, "the soul of the *moujik* is a dark forest". She had not known anyone who understood the Russian *moujik*...although everyone tries.

Until now she was unaware of the resentment which lay below the demeanor of the docile peasant and for the first time even her own peasants caused her to fear. *Can a landowner win the peasant's trust, no matter what he does, when he has so much and the moujik so little? When he amuses himself with ostentatious pleasures while the tiller of the soil slaves in the summer heat?* She had a premonition that the sleeping giant of peasantry would one day awaken and become infected with revolutionary fever, demanding his share of the land on which he labored.

Terrorism and brutal murders continued throughout the summer of 1906 until the police and militia rounded up over one thousand people and sentenced them to death. It wasn't until 1908 when order was restored to the Empire by the outstanding statesmen, Prime Minister Stolypin. He abolished the village commune and initiated a new law granting peasants their own land. Under his reforms, industry, banks, and small peasant farms flourished and Russia was on her way to join the modern world with a prosperity which it would not see again for some sixty years later. However, his belief that the government and parliament must work together to unite the right and center factions while weakening the antagonizing far left, earned him many political enemies.

Chapter 32

THE FIRST DUMA opened on April 27th 1906 in the throne room of the Winter Palace. An enormous image of the Imperial double headed eagle rose behind the scarlet throne and above it, a bas-relief of St. George slaying the dragon. Jeniya imagined the dragon's blood dripping over the red throne as the young Emperor had been dubbed "Nicholas the Bloody".

Members of the council stood on one side of the throne in a symphony of gold braids embroidered on their Imperial uniforms with numerous metals hanging across their breast like ornaments on a Christmas tree. The Grand Dukes stood on the bottom step of the throne's red carpeted platform with long chains studded in enormous diamonds around their necks, according to the order of St. Andrew. Jeniya spotted her sister, Ekatrina standing behind them with the ladies of the court, in all her haughty red-headed glory wearing an embroidered gown and arched tiara embedded with precious stones.

On the other side of the throne, stood the archimandrites ablaze in jeweled robes and crowns and behind them the bishops in red robes. The ladies in the congregation had not left one bauble behind in their jewel cabinets. Jeniya could hardly tell the style of their dresses beneath the accumulation of pearls and diamonds glittering under the lights of the great tiered chandeliers. She looked up at Daniel, the dark hair and blue eyes, so handsome in his formal wear.

Two erect officers of noble birth flanked the throne, one bearing the Imperial flag and the other an upright sword. Nicholas wore his usual stoic expression and stood before the assembly of representatives. The Imperial mantle of ermine was draped over the throne behind him. He delivered his address in perfect control of his emotions and concluded with these words of welcome. "I sincerely hope that you will commence your work in an atmosphere of pious diligence, inspired by a sincere desire to justify the confidence of your sovereign and of our great nation. May God's blessing be with me and with you."

The Kadety, members of the newly elected liberal party, held the majority of seats and stood in one block. Jeniya was disheartened to see these men, some of the most brilliant and capable professionals in the Empire, dressed in colorless common suits, almost in a deliberate affront to the monarchy. Fear etched on the faces of many council members and hatred blazed in the eyes of many in the liberal wing as they glared at one another across the aisle. The grand-dukes and many of the nobles wiped tears from their eyes as if they were witnessing the funeral dirge of the Romanov Empire.

"I understand the animosity the Kadety must feel towards the court," Jeniya said later. "But I would think that the newly elected members of the Duma would have the good manners to dress in formal wear out of respect to their sovereign and to our country. After all they have to work together now for the good of the people."

"That is why Russia is in revolt. The people have had their fill of this oriental display of arrogance in empty suits," Daniel replied.

"Danya, that's unfair. The noble classes are the only people who have the experience to deal with state problems."

"That's because they are the problem."

Jeniya frowned and changed the subject. "I didn't see your old mentor, Count Witte there, did you?"

"He was there, among the spectators. He was dismissed from service last night."

"What? But why? He created the Duma?"

"He was accused of being a rebel in conservative clothing, and would you believe, because his "artless" speech was too direct and not flowery enough to please the state council members."

Jeniya shook her head. "Well," she said thoughtfully. "Alexander III had great respect for Witte's ability. How I miss the old Tsar, how we all miss him. He died too young."

"In all due respect to the old Tsar," Daniel said. "If it weren't for the foresight of those two men, we would still not have the railroad and I would not be where I am today." He gazed at her flimsy dress blowing in the breeze revealing her form. "And I wouldn't have found you again." He whirled her into his arms and showered her with kisses.

She laughed and put her arms around his neck, and felt a flush of desire.

Nicholas had no intention of limiting his power or finalizing the new Russian parliament. And the Kadety, confident by their electoral mandate, had no intention of justifying themselves to their sovereign. They boldly demanded freedom of speech, the right to strike, elimination of class privilege, the abolition of the death penalty, the sale of land to the peasants, and for all barriers between the Tsar and his people to be demolished quickly. But the Jews were not included.

The Black Hundreds endorsed by the Tsar and supported by the Royal family, blamed the Jews for the labor movement and the creation of the Duma. Terrorism broke out with a new wave of pogroms, and counter-terrorism resulting in the assassinations of officers, land owners and bureaucrats.

In Bialystok, an industrial center for the Jewish revolutionary movement, someone killed the chief of police. In retaliation to the murder, the infuriated gendarmes and the enraged populace slaughtered entire families in their homes, hacked arms and legs from bodies, drove nails into hands and ravished women. Eighty souls were killed and hundreds more wounded. When the unbelievably horrible news reached the Duma, an investigative commission immediately left for Bialystok. There in the police department they discovered evidence of a secret printing press which issued a patriotic proclamation to exterminate the Jews.

When the Duma reconvened, the Imperial Ministers conveniently tucked the bill concerning civil rights for Jews into the discussion for petty class discriminations and women's rights. There was no outrage from anyone, except for a few Jewish individuals including Daniel who sat in on the Duma specifically to find out if they would redefine their bold declaration of equality for all Russian citizens including Jews, but there was no mention.

In defense of the persecuted people, Daniel rose to his feet and said. "Gentleman, you may arrange a pogrom on whatever scale you please, be against ten people or ten thousand, but the momentum of this current revolt will not disappear as long as the affairs of state and the destinies of the Empire are subject to the influence of authorities who by their convictions are pogrom makers." He looked into the haughty faces of the Tsar's clique of ministers. "But let it be known that Jews will join the chorus of those voices which say to you imperialists. Go away! We will not be pushed back by fear of the aristocracy but will continue to go forward and declare our rights. We shall only follow that government which represents the will of ALL the people."

Silence came from stony Imperial faces. Someone coughed. He glanced around the entire semicircle of staring eyes. "I believe that the Russian people bear no enmity toward the Jews, our enemy is the ruling elite, which for its own purpose seeks to incite the Russian people against the Jews."

A storm of applause shook the house. The Kadety roared. "Resign, you pogrom fiends. RESIGN!" That day, the majority in the Duma adopted a resolution denouncing government policies of oppression, intimidation, and extermination, citing, "this policy has created a situation unprecedented in the history of civilized countries," and they demanded the immediate resignation of the reactionary ministry.

When the representatives returned two days later, they found the building bolted and an Imperial Manifesto nailed to the door that stated. "The Duma has encroached upon a domain outside its jurisdiction and has engaged in investigating the acts of authorities appointed by us." Nicholas, who still retained control of the army, the police, the autocracy, and one half the national budget, held the Duma in contempt and promptly dismissed it.

With upheaval in the Empire and brutality toward the Jews increasing, Daniel thought constantly of Nathan and Ronnie. He had written them about his success in business and about his marriage to Evgeniya and of the deep love they had for one another. He told them she was a Gentile woman and of his conversion to Christianity. He confided that he truly believed Yeshua was their long awaited Messiah who had come to deliver his people not from the bondage of Gentile nations but from the bondage of sin and despair. He thought his father would celebrate his happiness and asked him and Rochelle to come and live with them in Petersburg.

In his eagerness to share his good fortune, how could he imagine that Nathan, who had been nearly killed in a pogrom and suffered so much pain because of the escapades of both his sons, would understand. Instead Nathan delivered a sharp blow to Daniel's heart when Rochelle wrote in her last letter that his father had declared him dead. However, with their lives in danger, he would not rest until he saw Nathan once more and make an attempt to amend the broken circle of family before it was too late.

On the morning of Daniel's departure, Jeniya handed him her gun which she had tucked into her skirt pocket. "Please take my pistol, she said. "Travel in that part of the country is dangerous now for the gentry. As it is, I shall not sleep at night with worry over the murders taking place there.

He hesitated, looking at the gun and remembering how God had saved him from starvation and death when he was defenseless. Ever since the famine he believed that God would either deliver him from danger or take him home and he was not afraid of anything on this side of heaven or the other, however...

At that moment, Yaroslav came to the door and knocked. "Your carriage is ready to take you to the train, sir," he said.

Daniel and Jeniya embraced for a long emotional moment before they kissed good-by. She made the sign of the cross over him and over herself and followed him to the carriage, waving from the street as he disappeared from view. How empty and cold would be his place beside her in their bed as she lay awake nights with worry for his safety.

When Daniel stepped off the train, he stared at a well-dressed gentleman in a dark suit. The man tipped his black fedora and disappeared into a waiting carriage. *Strange. Nobody like that rides the train here and steps into a waiting black carriage.*

On the way to town, he looked over the lush fields of spring wheat rippling in the early summer breezes and breathed in the fresh country air, something he never appreciated growing up in this little town. People stared, wondering why a gentleman should be walking their streets. He saw no destruction in the square, only deterioration, poverty and fear. He peered through the window of his father's shop and saw empty shelves where bolts of cloth had once risen from floor to ceiling. No one was there. His father's house was still standing but it looked different. Someone had built an addition onto the back. He approached the door and knocked.

Ezra, dirty, shabby and perspiring after working in the factory met him at the door. He eyed his brother's fine gabardine jacket, the meticulous tie, the starched white collar, the hands smooth beneath pressed white cuffs, as those of an aristocrat living in splendor. He looked at his own hands, knurled, calloused and dry like those of an old man. Although he was not yet forty, he looked older.

"Ezra?"

"Didn't expect to see me here did you."

"I thought you were…"

"In prison." Ezra squinted. "What do you want here?"

Daniel was not surprised by his brother's brusk and inhospitable greeting. "I have come to see our father."

"Our father! How dare you call him our father, you greedy bourgeois insect, you lazy grub." His eyes contemptuously raked the fullness of his brother's stature. "You walked out on him, walked out on us, when you became a no-good Christian so you could escape the poverty of the Pale, this *stinkin* overcrowded ghetto forced on us by those Jew-baiting pigs with whom you've cast your lot. And now you have the chutzpa to come here and stand before your father with an open sore on your forehead? *Feh!*" He thrust a dirt stained finger in his brother's face. "You! You have brought disgrace to this family, you and your fictitious messiah, you and your goy god. MY father has been humiliated by you, disgraced, broken and sick. The people in the shtetl call him *mishegas*. And do you want to know why?" he said, waggling his finger, screaming. "Because he asks for you! He worries about you constantly, you no-good goy swine."

Daniel burned with anger toward his brother's ugly rebuke and at the same time felt remorse for what had befallen his father. "I thought you were arrested. How did you get out?"

"You would have liked that, wouldn't you? To see me locked up in a dungeon, or in a Siberian labor camp, or hung! You thought you were rid of me." Ezra made a derisive laugh. "Now why don't you just get out of here!" He shouted and brandished a hand close enough to lay a slap across Daniel's face. "You are not wanted here.

When Rochelle heard Daniel's voice between Ezra's rantings from the kitchen, she rushed out and pulled on his shoulders, but it was like trying to move a beam lodged in cement.

"No Ezra. Let him go see his father. He is on his death bed and calls for him constantly."

Nathan heard the angry shouting at the front door from his bedroom and called. "Ezra what's going on out there?"

When Daniel entered the bedroom, his father came alive for the first time in weeks and received his lost son with great joy. He opened his arms and embraced him pulling him to his breast with all his strength. Tears streamed down his face into his white hair. "My son... my son," he cried. He affectionately put his trembling hands on each side of Daniel's head and studied his face, the generous wavy hair, the blue eyes glittering, and saw his beloved Este. Tears spilled out onto his beard. "For too long we are separated," he said.

Ezra's wife Leinha crept in the room silently like a feline, her shrunken heart filled with loathing and envy. "How can you come in here like a prince!" she sneered. "When we sweat every day for bread and a few potatoes." The old man silenced her with a flick of his hand. "Go Leinha."

"My soul could not rest in its eternal peace until I knew what had happened to you," Nathan said.

"I had written you so many times, *tahtuh,* but my letters were returned unanswered. Why?"

"*Ny.* So what was there to write? Lootings, beatings, the usual."

Daniel looked down at his father's rumpled bed clothes and tears began to fill his own eyes. "*Tahtuh,*" he said and took his hand. No words could express the remorse he felt in his heart for those barren years that separated them when there could have been so much happiness.

"Nathan gazed at his son as if to read his thoughts. "Do not take the past with you." He smiled and his eyes shone with love. "An evil has come between us, but that is over now. Our God has delivered us." Daniel smiled and squeezed his father's hand. "So tell me, my son, how is life by you. Tell me everything I've waited so long to hear."

Daniel sat down on the bed beside his father, his heart heavy and yearning not so much for those lost years but that he could not bring his father to Petersburg where he could live out his years in comfort. "I have a picture of my family," he said and gave it to Nathan.

His father took the picture in a trembling hand. "Please," he said and pointed to the dresser. "Over there you will find my glasses. Bring them."

The elderly man twisted the wires around his ears and gazed intently at the picture as one trying to live out the lost years with Daniel and his family.

"This is my youngest son, Gavriil, who will be four and this is Alexei, my first born. He is seven now, and already he is a little book worm."

"Like you. I remember how you would always ask so many questions. And this must be Jeniya, your wife," he said pointing to her image. "She is very beautiful." He nodded his head in approval. "And she is good to you?"

"I am very fortunate and blessed," Daniel said.

Nathan ran a hand over the fine cloth jacket and stared as an old man who sees as in a dream. "I am happy you are doing well. I am proud of you. You are the jewel in the crown of my old age and have brought much happiness to my dying days. Now I can go to the bosom of my fathers in peace." He gazed out the bedroom window, grey clouds began to move in over the blue sky. "Tell me this one thing," he said. "Have you found peace in your heart living in the gentile world?"

"Not only peace but even through sadness and difficult times, I have a certain joy that fills my heart with thankfulness to our God... *tahtuh?*, I want you to understand that because I believe Yeshua is the Messiah, it does not mean I am a gentile. I am a Jew. I will always be a Jew."

Nathan stared at him for a long time trying to fit together the pieces of this enigmatic statement. "How ever God has brought you peace then it is his blessing and I am happy for you." Then he raised his hand and blessed Daniel, his family and his marriage. "May you all live a long life and prosper as you walk with Yeshua."

Tears came again to Daniel's eyes, a great burden and a terrible hurt, deeper than he knew had been lifted. Nathan patted his arm affectionately and the two men held each other, each liberated from a long dark journey into light and joy.

"You and Ronnie don't have to worry about eating or keeping warm ever again. I have taken care of you."

"You don't have to do for us. No... I won't hear of it." Nathan flicked his hand.

He still prided himself as the all capable head of the household. Daniel smiled.

"Ronnie planted a garden," he laughed. "Go and see. How she manages to get so much from a little patch, I don't know."

"How is Sholem?"

"He and Golda left for America with two of the children and their families. Two are still here in Kiev."

"I am glad to hear that. Now, I have a surprise for all of you." He called the family in and took out gifts for Nathan and Ronnie and even something for Leinha and her children. Ronnie squealed in delight when she unwrapped her gifts and saw the fashionable dresses and a warm winter coat. Daniel laughed with her but he was saddened to see her become a timid little mouse with her hair tied back in a bun under a scarf. He asked her to come back to Petersburg with him but she would not leave her father. "Maybe someday," she said

The day before he left, Ronnie called him aside and said, "I have discovered some individuals tailing you. I am certain they are making plans to harm you when you get to the train station. I am afraid for you, Danya. Brutal murders of land owners and government officials are happening every day now. They could attack you and leave you somewhere in a forsaken field and no one would ever find you. Please, don't get on that train. I have made arrangements from that livestock dealer to fix you up with a horse and carriage. You can drive to Kiev and get on the train there. The dealer's brother who lives in Kiev, will pick up the carriage. But you must leave now, before Ezra and Leinha get home from work. Don't wait until tomorrow when they are expecting you to leave. It's a two days' journey from here and you will be one day ahead of them in case they decide to follow. I've also told father that you must leave immediately."

"Is Ezra behind this?"

"I don't know, but he has been telling everyone about your visit. No one from your class is safe here. Anyone who is not in sympathy with the revolution is safe."

Daniel looked at her in amazement, not because of what she said but because of what she did. She was not the little mouse he thought but a brave young woman and he was proud of her.

"I have one question for you," he said. "How did Ezra get out of prison? I though he was tried and convicted on charges of supporting an armed rebellion."

"He was, but they sentenced him to internal exile here in the Pale."

Daniel shook his head remembering. "At least he got a trial, that is more than I got."

The sun hung low in the sky when Daniel drove through the industrial outskirts of Kiev past burned out buildings. A bullet whizzed past his head. His heart flipped a beat. He led his horses into a full gallop. More gunfire volleyed in the street. Suddenly a grenade exploded like an umbrella in front of his carriage. The horses reared and rocked the buggy on its side tossing him into the dirt. Everything went black. Images were whirling and unfamiliar. He lifted himself on one arm and tried to remember where he was. In a half conscious stupor, he heard the jingle of a man's spurs advancing toward him. Sweat poured off his body. He had not remembered this kind of fear since the day of the pogrom when he was pinned beneath the rubble, not even when he laid at death's door in Odessa or slept in the Siberian barracks with the rats. The man stopped by the carriage. Daniel could see the dusty boots and the barrel of a rifle still hot from fire. He tried to reach out and take hold of the gun but the killer stepped back. He slid back down and waited for the last shot. "Lord, whatever be your will," he whispered. Peace came over him and there was a long silence.

"Well," he said to his assassin. "Why don't you just go ahead and do what my brother charged you to do."

"Daniel." The man called his name.

Daniel looked up at the stranger's face, puzzled.

"You don't recognize me, do you." The man drew his hand across a clean shaven chin. "I shaved my mustache," he said grinning.

Daniel propped himself up to a sitting position and stared again into the man's face, a face he would never forget. Those chiseled high cheek bones and the cold grey stare. "Vadim?"

"It is I, at your service." He bowed, not in reverence but in a mocking way.

"How? What?"

"Jeniya asked me to keep an eye on you. She had a dream that something terrible was going to happen so she called me...here...let me help you up." He reached down with his hand.

"How did you get here so fast?" Daniel said brushing the dirt off his clothes. He looked at the horse.

"Vadim looked over at his mount. "Him? No, he didn't ride the train with me. I got him from our peace keeping division nearby."

"You were on the train with me?"

"All the way."

"And how did you know...?"

"The attempt at your assassination would be here? I followed them. When you stopped to spend the night and change horses, they continued on to Kiev. They knew you had to pass by these abandon buildings on the way to the train station."

"You were the man in the black suit and fedora?"

"One in the same. Do you feel strong enough to ride back to camp with me?"

"I can make it," Daniel said. He scanned the burned out buildings in case there were more snipers.

"Don't worry," said Vadim. "I got them all."

"You?"

"They were amateurs."

Of course. He's a master sharp-shooter.

Vadim poured some water from his canteen on a scarf and handed it to him. You can wipe the scrape on the side of your head with this. It doesn't look too bad. It's the best we can do until we get back to camp." He unhooked the horses from the overturned carriage and brought his mount over for Daniel. "Here, you can sit in my saddle and I will ride one of your horse."

"He has no saddle."

Vadim laughed and shook his head. He took a few quick steps, leaped onto the animal's bare back and took the reins.

And a master horseman.

"Tell me, what in the devil's name brought you out here in the first place?"

"I had to see my father and my only sister. I hadn't heard from them in years and was concerned when the pogroms broke out. I had to..." He turned his face away. "You understand." This issue was too painful to discuss.

Vadim looked at him. He didn't understand. "Were they all right?"

"Yes," he said staring aimlessly in the distance. He turned and faced Vadim intently. "There has always been one question I had for you."

"What was that?"

"Why did you turn me in to the Okhrana for being a Marxist conspirator?"

"What? Did I do that?"

"Some fifteen years ago when Jeniya invited us to a dinner party."

"Fifteen years ago? Who remembers that far back. How'd you know it was me?"

"It couldn't have been anyone else."

"Then I must have thought you were guilty."

"Then why did you sacrifice your life to save mine?"

"A warrior seeks not to save his own life but to give his life to save others," he said thoughtfully. "But I didn't do it for you. I did it for Jeniya. You are the man she chose to marry and I see now that you are a man of high principle. Every day I encounter brutes. Men who roam in packs and kill. Men who rape, maim and destroy. Mad-men who want to conquer and control. Men filled with anger and hatred. In a way I am like them, filled with anger and hatred toward them. You are an unusual person, without this kind of malice. I don't understand what motivates you."

"I try to believe God, and try to obey his word." He was speaking to himself as much as to Vadim, thinking of Ezra. He had still not reckoned with him or forgiven him in his heart.

"How do you know what he wants you to do? This Empire is filled with religious fanatics who hear God talking to them. He tells each one something different. Russians are always looking for signs from the clairvoyants and the *starz*ii who wander from town to town, giving blessings and warnings for a few kopeks. I don't believe in these predictions."

"Do you believe in God?"

"It's hard to believe in God when I see so much hell."

Daniel reached into his pocket and pulled out a little book. "You asked a question before. Do you want an answer or are you satisfied with your explanation?"

"Which? How do you know what God wants you to do? Well?"

"By his commandments in the Bible. Here take this and read it. See for yourself."

Vadim took it and flipped the pages. "These pages have notes written in them. It is your personal Bible."

"That's all right, take it."

He gazed at it for a few moments and put it inside the breast pocket of his brown uniform. He glanced at Daniel but said nothing, nor was there any detectible expression on his face. His eyes were as inscrutable as when they first met.

"Civilian train transportation is perilous. A new terror attack can flair up anytime, anywhere. A division of Kazaks is leaving tomorrow aboard a military train for Petersburg. If you ride with them, you will get there safely."

His demeanor was again distant, as a warrior who considers life and death without passion. If there was a man on the earth to be feared, it was Vadim's kind. He stopped at nothing to achieve his dutiful end, right or wrong. But he was not a beast. For the first time Daniel began to respect the Kazaks for what they were, hard drinking, leather smelling rough riders, loyal to their Tsar. Sometime a man can't help what he is. It is when a man doesn't know another man that he conjures up prejudices, fear and even hatred. Daniel asked him candidly. "Why are you so intent on delivering me back to my wife?"

"Because she needs a good husband. If you had died out there, she would be alone."

"If I died out there, you could marry her."

"No, a professional soldier does not make a good husband. I would have brought her unhappiness. Always fighting wars, traveling from one assignment to another, long extended periods of duty. No, it wouldn't work out. And then of course, she loves you. She always has."

Chapter 33

Slander tore through the fashionable salons that a strange relationship had developed between the Empress Aleksandra and a certain sorcerer called Rasputin who possessed secret powers. When the Tsaritsa had canceled all receptions and balls given at the palace and was only seen at official ceremonies, people began to whisper that she had joined a cult and participated in orgies of black magic with the devil.

The sensational new mystic from Siberia began to gather a following of socialites who knew the Empress, including her closest confidant, Anna Vyroubova. Ekatrina was part of Aleksandra's entourage and Jeniya wondered if her simple minded sister had joined this holy man's clique of fanatical female admirers who had fallen under his spell of deception.

"Tell me something Katiya," Jeniya said to her sister one afternoon at the women's weekly Bridge game. "Do you know this…holy man… everyone is talking about?"

"What do you mean?" Katiya raised her blue eyes cautiously.

"I mean…" Jeniya searched for a diplomatic way to phrase her fears which would not offend her sister.

"You mean," Katiya finished Jeniya's statement. "Am I involved in these so called orgies with Rasputin you are hearing about."

The animated chatter that filled the room ceased at once and all eyes focused on Katiya.

"No, I…just wondered if you knew him."

"Yes. I know Rasputin. So what?"

"You know Rasputin?" said one of the women. The diamonds traveling up her arm sparkled in rainbow colors as she threw down her card with a quick flip of her hand. "Does he really practice black magic?"

"I resent that! There is no truth to these horrid accusations you are hearing about "our friend".

"Well, I'm sorry."

"Rasputin is not just any man. He has been sent of God to save and protect the life of our future Tsar. This is worth the world to their majesties."

"No one meant to offend you," said Jeniya. "We were just curious about this mysterious faith healer. "Actually, I would feel better if you did not associate with this controversial man."

"You would feel better? How do you think I feel listening to all this slander against our Empress? This plebeian attitude of yours and your friends is making a wreck out of her and out of me." She threw her cards on the table and got up. "If you will excuse me, I think I will take my leave."

"Well!" said the woman. She picked up another card and said examining her hand. "Does anyone really believe that Rasputin has the power to heal the tsarevich?"

"It maybe so," said Yelizaveta. "The doctors couldn't help him but this Rasputin supposedly did. We cannot imagine what it is like to be in the shoes of the Empress…and the pain she must bear fearing that her only son might not live another day…knowing she must give Russia an heir and an Emperor. Maybe these vicious rumors about the Empress are untrue?"

"Every woman wants to see her sons grow up strong and healthy," said Jeniya. "I would be heartbroken if one of my boys were growing into an invalid, especially if he is my only son and is expected to become the future Tsar. It is no wonder she shrinks from the public."

"Had the old Tsar lived and saw that she had a history of hemophilia in her family, I don't think he would have allowed the marriage, and there would be no Rasputin," said another woman with dyed red hair and flashing diamond ear bobs as big as quail's eggs.

"When she renounced the right to give the Imperial monogram to our daughters," said another woman who used to be a lady in waiting to the dowager Empress Marie Feodorovna, "she has denied them the honor of taking a position at court. Many of us would have kept our loyalty to the new Empress had she simply acknowledged our families with this honor. Now our daughters have nothing to look forward to, not even an invitation to an Imperial ball. I don't care if Aleksandra has crossed us off her social list."

"She should have reached out for the people's sympathy and understanding long ago, when they first discovered the tsarevich's affliction." said Yelizaveta. "Instead of trying to hide it behind a shroud of mystery."

"It is her German pride that makes her shrink from public," said the redhead. "She has always impressed me as an arrogant and distant woman, even before Alexi was born. She never has a pleasant word to say to anyone and she freezes out everyone who approaches her."

"No one really knows her," said Yelizaveta. "She goes about in a kind of mystical haze…she's hard to understand. No wonder everyone is talking."

Jeniya did some investigation and discovered that Rasputin was the son of a horse thief and a notorious womanizer. His unbridled passion led him to join the licentious cult called the *Khlisty* which combined the Christian religion with primitive pagan rites. These mystics sought to communicate directly with God by calling down an incarnation of "the Christ". Deep in the night forest, they would gather in a circle and sway to demonic incantations inducing a dizzying erotic ecstasy. They swirled around and around, spinning faster and faster into a frenzy invoking an influx of spirits, until they fell to the ground rolling in convulsions, giving themselves to abominable orgies and sadistic practices. If someone's energy would slacken, the leader of the dance would whip them. The adherents believed that anyone possessed by these spirits belongs not to himself but to a controlling divine spirit.

Rasputin left his village in Tobolsk at the age of thirty-three, under the disguise of a pilgrim in search of saintliness. He walked the entire way with irons on his body in order to demonstrate that his repentance was painful, difficult and sincere. He possessed a prodigious memory, memorizing long passages from the Bible which his vulgar mind was incapable of understanding, but with which he managed to bluff the religious scholars in the monasteries. He arranged to be seen in the company of archpriests, abbots, bishops and archimandrites who all agreed that he possessed a spark from God.

Soon he acquired a reputation for holiness which spread throughout the countryside. He delivered evangelical addresses and told parables. He developed a sense of mysticism and began to prophecy. Simple peasants knelt in the streets as he passed, kissed his hands and touched the hem of his robes, calling out "Our Christ, our Savior, pray for us miserable sinners."

"God will hear you," he said making the sign of the cross over their bowed heads. "In the name of the Father, the Son and the Holy Ghost, I bless you, little brothers... Fear not. Christ will come again soon. Possess your souls in patient memory of His agony. For love of Him, mortify your flesh."

But Rasputin had no inclination to mortify his own flesh. It was reported that he raped a nun, pushed a naked woman out of a brothel whipping her with a belt, and mesmerized married women with such extravagant passion that they felt honored to be seduced by "the Saint from God". He chicaned his hapless female victims by convincing them that that they must yield their base nature to him before they can be purified of their sins. "We must sin in order to have an opportunity for repentance," he told them. "When God places temptation in our way, it is our duty to yield. How can we repent if we have not yet first sinned, for it is by repentance that we will win our salvation. Was not the first word of life and truth which Christ uttered to mankind...repent."

The Archimandrite Theophanes, Rector of the Theological College at Petersburg and personal Confessor to Their Majesties was touched by Rasputin's simple faith and introduced him to the Grand Duke Nicholas Nicolaievich, his brother the Grand Duke Peter, and their wives Anastasia and Militza, daughters of the King of Montenegro. The two sisters, sometimes called the black crows or the black spiders, held séances to consult with spirits at the winter residence of Grand Duke Nicholas. Rasputin fascinated this group of idlers already given to the practices of occultism and necromancy, with his extraordinary gift to foresee future events. The two Grand Duchesses talked everywhere about their wonderful discovery, and Grigory soon gathered a devoted clique of unbalanced socialites, some seeking excitement in spiritual experiences and others looking to escape abusive and philandering husbands. All were looking for loving attention.

The two princesses spoke of nothing but him, and thought of nothing but him. They introduced the man of God to the Tsar and Tsaritsa telling them that Rasputin had the power to heal their only son from hemophilia, a disease that caused the boy's blood to hemorrhage inside his body after an injury until the inflammation would painfully press against his bones.

"Grigory is marvelous," said the two Montenegrin spiders to the Empress. "He can cure all illnesses...a simple peasant from Siberia. You know, Alix, God never entrusts his power to the spoiled children of sophistication."

But before their Majesties would grant him an audience, they sought the council of Theophanes who reassured them, "Grigory Efimovich is a peasant, a man of the people. Your Majesties will do well to hear him, for it is the voice of the Russian soil which speaks through him. I know his sins which are numberless and most of them heinous. But there dwells in him so deep a passion of repentance and so implicit a trust in divine pity that I would all but guarantee his eternal salvation.

Every time he repents he is as pure as the child washed in the waters of baptism. Manifestly God has called him to be one of His chosen."

Theophanes, their trusted spiritual guide, was a man of solid religious convictions with an unshakeable devotion to true Orthodoxy, and from that moment, Rasputin gained extraordinary ascendancy into the guarded family life of the Tsar and Tsaritsa.

Aleksandra had a natural tendency toward exalted mysticism. Her constant plea to the Almighty to spare her son from morbid hemophilia, made her an easy prey for this holy charlatan who dazzled their Majesties with his exceptional powers of healing. When he demonstrated that he could deliver the tsarevich from his horrible pain, the empress became a passive tool in his hands. She was convinced that Rasputin was sent of God to be the savior of her child and the guardian of his health. Nothing and no one could persuade her otherwise, not even the bold and disingenuous familiarity with which he treated the royal family.

As the child grew, the people saw that he was fragile and retarded in size and needed to be carried by a strong Kazak. When he did walk by himself, he was at first lame and the people began to speculate that he may not live. "What?" they said. "Is this our future Tsar? Is the future of Russia to be in the hands of that little cripple?"

To ease the doubts of his people, the Tsar made a public statement that the Tsaritsa believed in Rasputin's sincerity and his power of prayers for their family. Almost immediately the *staretz* gained a new circle of admirers, this time from the grand dames of society. His influence soon spread to political circles, high officials and fashionable socialites. Petitioners from all walks of life sought his spiritual guidance, financial help, and most of all, recommendations to high office within the Tsar's ministry.

As Rasputin's star arose over the court, the Tsar's council of ministers, and even members of the Duma, Jeniya began to wonder if she had wrongly judged this man. She heard conflicting reports about him. Many people reported that they have never known him to be anything other than good-hearted. When his clients gave him an offering, he never kept the money for himself but distributed it to the poor and gave it freely to anyone who asked. He was a saint in the eyes of the *moujikii* and the poor. He was always there when someone called on him to heal their sick child. He comforted the Imperial family and gave them hope for their son. Those who attend the tsarevich said he was always happy when the *staretz* would visit him.

Jeniya wondered who was this Rasputin. An agent of God sent to cure the tsarevich and help the poor, or a devil? She decided to call Ekatrina and find out for herself.

Chapter 34

"I would like to meet Rasputin," Jeniya said to her sister with some hesitation. "Can you arrange it?" There was silence on the other end of the phone and then…"You really want to meet him?"

"I do."

"Do you think you could handle it?" Katiya said mockingly.

"I don't see any reason to fear. After all, he does so much good for people."

"Yes he does," she replied thoughtfully. "Well…tomorrow he is having a party at his apartment…do you really want to do this?"

"I really do." She knew she might be compromising her own welfare with something evil beyond her power, but she had to know how much her sister was involved with what may be a dangerously growing cult. That night she prayed before the icons for strength, protection and understanding.

The next day Ekatrina's driver pulled up to Rasputin's apartment on Gorokhovaia street behind a line of autos, coaches, and carriages. Secret service agents stood by the gates and three more on the main staircase leading to his flat.

"You will see for yourself that "our friend" is not the evil person the gossiping idlers make him out to be," said Katiya. "But an apostle who devotes himself to prayer and the healing and purifying of souls,"

Inside, people from all spheres of society besieged the stairwell and hallway outside his flat. Body odors, stale cabbage, fish soup and the smell of baking bread permeated the stale air. Mothers with crying children, peasants, workers, petty officials, and even bishops, stepped aside when they saw the two well dressed women disguised under large hats with black veils hiding their faces. They immediately knew these women were aristocrats.

"Our friend gives all his money to these needy people, he never keeps a penny for himself. You will see how poorly he lives."

"Did it occur to you that by claiming poverty and contrition, he arouses the sympathy and admiration of the public and especially in those he wants to impress."

"No! Never! He would never do that."

A kindly woman immediately approached them. "Are you here for intercourse with the holy man?" she said smiling.

"What?"

"Do not be afraid," Katiya assured her sister. "It is not a sin to sacrifice your body to the holy one. It will purify your soul and this is pleasing to God."

Jeniya gasped in horror wondering what went on with her sister.

Katiya gave Rasputin's elderly attendant, Attila, a note of admittance. Jeniya grabbed her sisters arm and said, "Katiya! What is this?"

"Don't worry, it's not what you think. No one will touch you here." Katiya tugged her sister toward the door.

Attila led them to wait in the reception room where elegant, exquisitely dressed ladies, a general, and a few civil officials sat on the leather sofa and chairs waiting for the *staretz* to appear. Jeniya curiously gazed at the bits of dirty paper littering a writing desk and saw notes on which the illiterate peasant had scrawled a line demanding appointments for his stooges in the Tsar's ministry. Someone crept in stealthy behind them wearing bedroom slippers and a long white kaftan. Everyone in the room arose and approached him, kissing his hands and his sleeves.

Jeniya turned around, shocked by the repugnant appearance of Rasputin. He hugged Katiya and planted a wet, slobbering kiss on her lips. Jeniya looked on in shock.

"And who is your charming guest?" he said reaching with disproportionately long arms to take Jeniya's hands in his. He leaned forward in an attempt to kiss her but she drew back and grimaced. He reeked of cheap perfume.

His face was long and thin and pale; his features coarse with a Neanderthal forehead and a big bulbous nose like the beak of a raptor. Stringy dark hair fell over his ears and a forelock in his face. His dark auburn beard was stiff and unkempt. His thin form gave him the impression of being much taller than his medium height. Jeniya sensed his lecherous gaze feasting on her bosom. He raised his greenish grey eyes and held her gaze, remote and yet piercing like needles into her innermost being stirring a feeling within her of both repugnance, uneasiness and intrigue. She saw in him as something more than a simple Russian peasant or a holy man, but something dark and unworldly.

"This is my sister Countess Borisovna Mendelevna.

The beady eyes sunken under thick dark brows lit up. "Ah, you must be the wife of Daniel Mendelev, the notable industrialist." He was immediately captivated by her statuesque beauty and voluptuous figure and could not keep his eyes from her.

Without shifting his gaze, he put his arm around Katiya's waist and said something about her that struck Jeniya as odd. "You have a very wise sister here. She speaks well of you…you should listen to her…she will be your spiritual guide." The sweet and insipid smile on his thin lips almost repulsed her as much as the expression in his eyes.

Katiya smiled in delight.

"A *staretz* is one who takes your soul, your will, into his soul and will." Dostoyevsky's words from the brothers Karamazov popped into Jeniya's mind and made her think of a false christ who comes as a wolf in sheep's clothing performing magic and uttering strange prophecies to dupe the gullible flock.

Jeniya could hear laughter and high pitched chatter resonating from the dining room as their host escorted them through the kitchen into a small, simply furnished bedroom. A narrow iron bed was pushed against one corner of the room covered by a red fox bedspread, a gift from the Tsaritsa's close friend, Anna Vyroubova. Sly and foxy were terms too benevolent for him, Jeniya thought looking at the covering. Near the bed was a crude wardrobe of painted wood, a wash stand, and in the opposite corner a small lamp burned before some icons. A portrait of the Tsar and Tsaritsa hung on the wall along with primitive engravings of biblical scenes.

The dining room was filled to capacity with a few dozen women. Someone put a record on the gramophone and played a popular jazz tune. In the middle of the dining room table stood a great basket of fresh flowers, a teapot on top of a samovar humming with boiling water. Plates filled with biscuits, cakes and nuts sat on small tables.

Katiya admired the flowers. She took the gift card in her hand and read it. It said, from your fondest admirer, Anna.

"Do you like the flowers?" Rasputin crept up from behind and put his hand on Katiya's backside drawing her to his side.

"Grishka, you are given flowers like a prima donna," she said.

"Silly creatures, these women who spoil me. They send me flowers every day. They know I like them."

Jeniya looked on in horror, sickened by Rasputin's obscene gesture especially on the heels of her sister's remark about sacrificing one's body to the holy one. She turned and saw the notorious Anna Vyroubova she had heard so much about. Anna was a dumpy woman with a round head, fleshy lips, voluptuous hips and ample thighs, which would exude sex appeal to the Slavic peasant if it were not for her colorless face and personality to match. She gazed through large limpid eyes. People thought of her as dull-witted and infantile, but Jeniya had a feeling that beneath the facade, she was anything but. She saw Anna as an innately crafty woman who used this pretext to manipulate political intrigues in Petersburg society. But a curious intriguer. She sought no honors or rewards, appeared at no ceremonies, wore plain unassuming dresses and no jewelry. She seemed to derive a certain pleasure in perpetual self-effacement, that of a servile, inferior being, but there-in lies her power over equally neurotic beings like the Empress. She devoted herself, body and soul, to the perniciously ailing Aleksandra, a victim to all sorts of imaginary illness and terrors, with a premonition that some terrible fate is hanging over the throne. Anna had no friends other than the Empress and she jealously guarded her relationship as her mistress's confidant from those who could have been her friend by inspiring her to distrust them. She fed her own pride and low self-esteem by betraying her sovereigns intimated secrets to Rasputin who used this information for his own advancement in circles of power. Since the shy Aleksandra Feodorovna secluded herself from society, she became an easy prey for cunning wiles of Rasputin and the devoted madam Vyroubova who stuck on her like a wart.

Anna had connections to the imperial family through her sister who was the daughter-in-law of the Emperor's uncle, the Grand Duke Paul Alexandrovich. Her father, director of the Emperor's Own Chancellery and a classical composer, Taniyev, was probably one of the most intelligent and cunning men at court, and Jeniya surmised that the apple did not fall far from the tree. Everyone knew the power and influence of Taniyev and about the relationship between Anna and the Empress. They also knew father and daughter were heavily involved in the current vogue of religious mysticism. They were the first to invite *staretz* to join their intimate society. They taught him to dress properly, comb his hair, and wash. Her father's acceptance of Rasputin made him a much sought after man in the fashionable Petersburg salons. It also enabled Anna to gather a clique of socialites who were given over to occultism and necromancy.

At first the gatherings with Rasputin were purely religious, but in time it drew unscrupulous individuals desiring to use the holy man's influence for personal gain. Soon he lost interest in his first feminine admirers and dropped them, one by one. These ladies of the cult soon became jealous of the growing friendship between Anna and the

Empress. In retribution, they devised some extraordinary slanderous tales about them to spread around the salons of the capital. This petty gossip did not affect Rasputin. He had already moved on to entertain only the very great ladies of court. Jeniya pitied the Empress for having to endure this slander and yet, she like everyone else who did not see the whole picture, wondered if these tales were not built on some truth.

Speaking of air-headed socialites, Jeniya heard a boisterous laughter break out from the two black crows the Grand-Duchesses, Militza and Anastasia, both chattering at the same time. She wondered how the forceful, decisive Grand Duke Nicholas Nicholaievich, standing six foot six in his stocking feet could tolerate his flighty wife, Anastasia. The two swarthy, square faced sisters were talking to Madame Golovina, the sister of the Grand Duke Paul's morganatic wife, Olga.

"Evgeniya, so nice to see you," said an acquaintance from the court gliding over to greet her. She swept an air kiss, brushing her cheek. "Your sister is such a dear girl…we all love her." She glanced admiringly at Rasputin. "Our friend here is so generous, don't you think. Just look at all those poor souls standing out there in the hallway, waiting for his favor. Not one will be turned away. Our friend never refuses anyone who asks of him. When my dear daughter laid dying, I called just about every doctor in Petersburg and no one could help. I was desperate. Then at the advice of the empress, I called on our friend and he immediately came to our home and healed her."

"How did he heal your daughter?" Jeniya asked.

"Well, I can't tell you what happened exactly, but it was a miracle. He took my hand… She stared across the room as though she saw a vision. "His face changed…he appeared like a corpse…yellowy…waxy, and dreadfully still. He rolled his eyes back in his head until I only saw the whites and then he said in a low dull voice, 'she won't die.' He let my hand go and the blood flowed back into his cheeks again and he continued talking as if nothing had happened."

Her story made Jeniya's skin crawl, all she could think of was a devilish trance. But at the same time she was intrigued. If it were one of her children, would she not be tempted to do the same? "And your daughter became well?" she said.

"She is the picture of health, to this day." The woman gave a little chuckle glancing again at Rasputin as though he were an apostle sent from heaven.

Jeniya found an empty seat on a high-back chair behind the group next to a bulky break-front filled with crockery. She gazed at a few badly painted pictures on the wall. A brass chandelier hung from the ceiling and lit the dining room table.

Someone turned off the gramophone and the women gathered around their apostle in silent reverence. They trembled in anticipation when he placed a tidbit of half-eaten cake from his plate and placed it in each of their mouths like a communion wafer. Then he took a porcelain tea pot off the samovar and poured tea into their uplifted cups like a holy atonement. They looked upon him as a god-like figure coming from heavenly realms. He plunged his long talon like fingers into a bowl of raspberry jam and allowed each one to suck from them. "Humble yourself, daughter," he said in the manner of a benediction. "Lick it clean, lick it clean." Jeniya turned her face away when he approached her sister, Katiya. She could not bear to watch.

Rasputin moved like a shadow around the table with quick nervous steps and launched into some kind of continuous incoherent speech about God and brotherly love, quoting at random from the Bible. His voice sounded hollow, his pronunciation indistinct. His hands moved constantly in rapid impatient gestures, his eyes always roving. At times they grew round, like little white bulbs popping from dark sockets beneath thick low brows and for an instant blazed into a kind of phosphoric flame as if he were stealing into the souls of his listeners. Jeniya tried to make sense of his speech but the more she listened the more obvious it became that he himself did not understand what he was saying. His admirers listened with an attitude of pious veneration and clung to his every word believing he was revealing some profound mystical meaning from the divine. She could feel the cold magnetic gaze settle on her resistant spirit like a searchlight. She became frightfully uneasy and looked away to avoid coming under his power. From the corner of her eye she saw that he turned his face away and began to talk to someone but the moment she returned her gaze upon him, she was square in his view, as though he had eyes around his head under his thin stringy hair, anticipating her every move.

Suddenly one of the woman had descended into a trance and declared. "A great prophet is among you. It is his mission to reveal the will of Providence to the Tsar and to lead him into glorious paths."

A reverent silence descended over the guests, until gradually they began whispering to one another in awe, "did you hear that?"

Rasputin could see immediately that Jeniya was not the usual simple minded society woman who fawned around him, and her strong spirit challenged his vanity and power. He drew up an empty chair, sat beside her and put his arm around her shoulders. "Are you enjoying the afternoon with us, my dear girl," he said in a caressing voice.

"It's a lovely party," she said pulling herself from under his long arm. She tried to appear pleasant but everything about him repulsed her. She gripped her hands in the folds of her skirt.

"Ah…I see you are frightened of me," he said inclining his head toward her. "You needn't be. You'll see what kind of man I am when you know me better." A forelock persisted over one eye and his nervous long fingers fidgeted in his beard. His patronizing tone was agitating. It made her blood turn to ice. "You are worried. I will cure you of your worries. I work with divine remedies…not with ordinary drugs."

"Drugs?" She wondered if he had not offered drugs to the Tsar and Tsaritsa.

"Do you know Dr. Badmaiev? He makes remedies from herbs that grow in the forests and on the mountains. God makes them grow, that's why they have divine properties."

"Is the tsarevich treated with these herbs?"

"Most certainly he is, and papka too. Mamka and Annushka see to it that papka is given a tea which causes divine grace to descend on him. His heart is filled with peace, everything looks good and cheerful to him…anyway, what kind of Tsar is he? He was not cut out to rule an Empire…that is beyond his strength. He is just a child of God…a simple soul. He should be down there in Livadia with his flowers where he'll be closer to God." "There are a lot of bad people around him who whisper in his ears that Gregory Efimovich is a wicked man who works for your downfall. It's ridiculous. Why should I want to ruin them? They are good and pious." He put his creepy hand on her thigh. She pushed it off.

"I am powerful. Papka and mamka listen to me and so you should listen to me too.

I stand on no ceremony with them. The other day I talked to papka about someone who should be given a post. But he keeps on postponing the appointment so I threaten to leave them. I'll go to Siberia, I announced. And you'll stay here and rot all by yourselves. When you lose your son it will be through your own fault because you have turned away from God…and then you'll fall into the clutches of the devil." An insipid smile crossed his lips which sent peals of ice down her spine. "That's the way I speak to them…don't go Gregory Efimovich," they say. Don't go…and they run after me. We will do anything you wish, so long as you don't forsake us…they would have all died if I hadn't been there. And that is why, my dear girl, they love and respect me."

As he prattled in a continuous stream, his colorless little eyes morphed into flaming orbs of phosphorescent light merging into one luminous ring. At times the orb drew nearer and then moved farther away. She was only semi-aware that he was making strange motions in the air, commanding some kind of malevolent energy to overcome her will. It was then she realized she was gradually falling under his power. She fought with all her strength to resist until it became a merciless struggle between her personality and his. Gradually, her determination to resist formed a protective shield and she was able to distinguish his form again. The terrifying ring of light in his eyes disappeared and she saw a satisfied smile cross his lips. She knew then that he could not read her thoughts or perceive the power in her own strength.

Rasputin left her and addressed the group again with the ingenious jargon in which he clothed his erotic appetites. "It is not the horror of sin which prevents us from yielding to temptation, for if sin was really a horror to us then we should not be tempted to commit it. What really stops us from tasting is the hurt to our pride because it involves repentance. Absolute contrition implies absolute humility and no one likes to humble himself. Even before God. When we are in the valley of Jehoshaphat, God will know how to remind us of all the chances for salvation he has offered us which we have rejected."

Jeniya rose and told Katiya she wanted to leave.

"Why?"

"I don't feel well."

"If you insist." Katiya said and gave her a funny look. "You are acting strange."

Rasputin suddenly appeared beside them. "I am sorry you have to leave so soon, my dear children." He put his arm around Ekatrina and drew her to his side. "Your sister is a very intelligent young woman," he said fixing a craving gaze on Jeniya, thinking he had succeeded in his hypnotic power. "If she continues to obey me everything will be all right. Isn't that so my child," he looked into Ekatrina's face. "Make it clear to her, so she'll understand."

"Well, good-by, girls. Come see me again." He embraced them both and Jeniya froze like an ice cube.

On their way out the door, Katiya said, "there's such a comfortable easy atmosphere around Gregory Efimovich, don't you think? In his presence all the worries and troubles of this world are forgotten. He has a gift of making one feel serene and peaceful…and loved."

Jeniya winced at her sister's words. She worried about Katiya's marriage and Anatole's obvious detachment. Her fears were compounded when she thought of how Rasputin may have twisted her simple mind. She wondered if he put something in her tea to make her feel so... peaceful? She said nothing but kept her gaze downward on the pavement. She wanted to tell her sister never to darken this door again, but she knew Katiya wouldn't receive her rebuke, not at the moment.

There must be a million sorcerers in Russia, how has this one come to have such power? She didn't know which alarmed her more, the acquiescence of the sovereigns to Rasputin's will or that of the Russian ruling classes, who could do something to stop this, but walked around in a stupor seeking after his favors.

Chapter 35

RASPUTIN'S CONTROL OF the Empress, his insolent speech concerning their majesties, and his debaucherous escapades in fine hotels and restaurants roused a storm of indignation from decent citizens. The press tried to suppress the scandals and spare the sovereigns, but the public read between the lines. Everyone who had the slightest contact with the *staretz* added his own version to the torrid tales, from the coachmen who waited on him during his drunken nocturnal orgies to the secret police who gathered information on his shady dealings with dubious individuals and state officials.

Prime minister Stolypin was the only man in the Empire who had the courage to defy the Empress when he handed Nicholas a condemnatory police report on "her friend's" involvement with an underground network to undermine the monarchy through questionable appointments to the Tsar's Council of Ministers. Because Nicholas depended on Stolypin's reforms to restore his crumbling Empire, he agreed to draw up an order to banish Rasputin from the capital but the Tsaritsa rescinded the order before the ink was dry.

Scandal after scandal continued to rocket out of control and Stolypin commissioned another police investigation hoping to convince the Tsar of the satyr's unscrupulous atrocities. Public outrage finally forced the Tsar to take action. He allowed Stolypin to take the initiative and order Rasputin to once more leave the city. Aleksandra was furious.

However, Rasputin took it upon himself to disappear from the capital for a while and make a pilgrimage to Jerusalem. This move filled the emotionally empty society women with both grief and veneration. The Empress began to cave into a series of nervous spasms and fainting spells. "The tsarevich's hemorrhaging is becoming more frequent," she constantly complained to her husband. "Suppose my child dies."

Never-the-less, Aleksandra managed to keep in touch with her holy confidant through letters. When copies of these letters mysteriously surfaced and began to circulate all over Russia, the people were appalled as well as intrigued when they read the Tsaritsa's words to her guru, "I only wish one thing, I want to lie with you, my arms around you...to fall asleep forever on your shoulders and in your arms...where are you? Oh, where have you gone? I am so sad and my heart is longing...will you soon be again close to me? Come quickly... I love you forever. Mamka."

The people expressed even greater shock when they read the letters from her young daughters indicating that Rasputin had given them evening baths. When the police questioned Rasputin after his return several months later, he insisted that he was attacked and letters were stolen. Whether he made up lies or boastfully brandished them in front of someone he wanted to impress, the damage was complete. Pornographic lampoons illustrating Rasputin as an erotomaniac cavorting with a naked Empress and her daughters quickly passed from hand to hand through the clubs, drawing rooms and salons, along with photographs that showed the satyr in depraved sexual exploits with several ladies of high society.

In September of 1911, Stolypin was assassinated. Both Nicholas and Aleksandra greeted his death with cool indifference. People were aghast at his funeral when they overheard the red-headed Empress with white marbled skin and icy blue eyes making frigid remarks concerning the one man who had done so much to save her husband's reign from revolution. "Those who have offended God in the person of "our friend" may no longer count on divine protection...the prime minister's role in the world was ended. One must not feel sorry for those who are no more." Aleksandra never forgave the prime minister, even on his death bed. Stolypin, a man of great courage was Russia's last hope for advancement from an oppressive autocracy into a modern democratic state.

Neither could the Archimandrite Theophanes forgive himself for introducing Rasputin to the Empress. He spoke out against the *staretz*' unscrupulous lifestyle with great courage. Rasputin denied the charges and Theophanes, once the trusted confessor to their majesties, found himself exiled to Taurida.

When the Siberian *moujik* was elevated to be ordained as a priest in the Holy Orthodox Synod under the orders of a puppet Procurator, a violent controversy broke out in the Church. The giant Hermogenes, Bishop of Saratov, lured the *staretz* into a trap with a beautiful prostitute. Several priests barged into the bedroom holding the pectoral cross and beat Rasputin mercilessly, cursing him with each blow. "Accursed...Sacrilegious...Devil's viper." Then in a fit of rage, Hermogenes slammed the cross into the culprit's head several times and shouted. "Limb of Satan...Sacrilegious scoundrel...Fornicator...Foul beast...Down on your knees before the holy icon and ask God's forgiveness for your foul sins. Swear that you will never again dare to pollute the palace of our beloved Tsar with your filthy presence." Terror-stricken and bloodied, Rasputin beat his breast and swore to obey. But as soon as he was well enough to walk again, he ran to their majesties and complained. Bishop Hermogenes lost his position and was exiled to a monastery in Lithuania.

Representative Purishkevich denounced Rasputin before the Duma in a prophetic outburst. "I would gladly sacrifice myself and kill that scoundrel."

One of the few honest and courageous men in Nicholas' Council of Ministers, Khvostov, begged the Tsar to send Grigory Efimovich back to Siberia. "This man has obtained your majesty's confidence by false pretenses," he said. "He is a charlatan of the worst description. The newspapers…"

The Emperor interrupted him, "You mean to say you take notice of what the newspapers say?"

"Yes, sire, when they attack my sovereign and the prestige of the dynasty."

"These criticisms are ridiculous. I hardly know Rasputin."

"Sire, in the name of the dynasty…of your heir, I beg you to let me take the necessary steps to secure the return of Rasputin to his village and prevent him from coming back again."

The Tsar replied coldly, "I shall tell him myself to go and never to return. Good-bye Vladimir Nicolaievich, I need not detain you any longer."

Upon his departure, the *staretz* left their majesties with a threatening portend. "I know evil people are lying in wait for me. Don't listen to them. If you forsake me, you will lose your son and your crown within six months."

Within several months, the lascivious satyr finagled his way back to Petersburg. In 1912, at a hunting lodge in Spala, a Russian territory in Poland, the tsarevich suffered a nearly fatal attack of hemophilia from a slight fall. A large swelling developed in the groin. His temperature rose alarmingly. Inflammation pressed on all the nerves of his thigh, causing the leg to bend until his knee pressed against his chest in excruciating pain. For days he shrieked in constant agony and begged to die. He took no food. Priests prayed. The people prayed. Doctors told the Tsaritsa they could do nothing more. In frantic desperation, she summoned Rasputin with whom she secretly remained in touch. He telegraphed her back. "God had seen your tears and heard your prayers. Do not grieve, your son will live." In the few days the boy's temperature decreased and he was out of danger.

Aleksandra's faith in the mystic became as solid as an iron wall. She was convinced that she had chosen the right way and that all the criticisms were only thorns on the path of those who follow after righteousness. Rasputin now cemented himself in the trust of the Emperor and in the seat of political power by playing on the feelings of a mother and father who were racked by anxiety for their son's well-being and for the future of the dynasty.

Soon, the debauched spirit of Rasputin engulfed the capital city like a whirlwind. In the few short years before the declaration of war, people lived from thrill to thrill, seeking pleasure and eager for new excitement. They gambled on the stock market, danced the tango, explored the depths of every conceivable vice and every hedonistic practice. Modern forms of music and art were discordant, mysticism was fashionable, sodomy was in the open, and gay marriage was approved. Prostitutes paraded in furs and more diamonds than the Dowager Empress wore at her last palace ball.

Three powerful industrialist formed a tobacco trust manipulating the commodities trade and consolidating privately owned banks. They dictated the financial destiny of the nation as well as the political careers of the men who played in their game by granting their operations leniency from laws and regulations. These men loved big government and corporate power. They hated to see competition from individuals. They sent underhanded vultures to persuade small entrepreneurs to put their companies up as IPO's on the market, causing their stock prices to rise astronomically. "Why," they said to these small factory owners, "do you want to slave six days a week when you can sit back and make more money on the stock market?"

Everyone went money mad; clerks, clerics, and coachman all owned a share of stock and discussed the rising prices of his investment, not knowing the difference between a stock and a bond. Fashionable hostesses featured stock gurus at their salons. Furs, jewels, troikas, carnivals, operas, ballet and balls, once only enjoyed by the families of the aristocracy and the industrialists were now available to the city's ostentatious nouveau rich. Even the liveries of these newbies wore emerald frock coats with scarlet collars and gold braids complete with tri-cornered hats.

Hysteria reigned as the shadow of war loomed on the western horizon.

Chapter 36

WHILE PETERSBURG PARTIED, Kaiser Wilhelm II was building a strong navy to rival that of England. His factories were feverishly producing high caliber weapons and heavy artillery to expand his Empire on the European continent and build colonel territories in mineral rich Africa and Asia. Russian citizens traveling through Prussia had reported that his empire's northern border was beginning to look like an armed camp.

At the same time, hostility was mounting in the sovereign nation of Serbia over the annexation of their Bosnian neighbors into the Austro-Hungarian Empire. The Serbs were fighting to free Bosnia-Herzegovina and unite them into a single nation of South Slavs. Then, on June 28, 1914, a Bosnian rebel and member of the black hand, the revolutionary wing of the Serbian-Bosnian freedom-fighters, assassinated the heir to the Austrian throne, Arch-Duke Ferdinand. These liberators had hoped this daring move would bring their Russian comrades to the aid of the Slav brotherhood's struggle for liberation against Austro-Hungarian rule.

Within days of the assassination of the Arch-Duke, Rasputin was stabbed in the stomach several times by a prostitute. "I've killed the devil," she announced. The Tsar received the news of both assassinations while on a summer cruise with his family aboard the imperial yacht, the Standart. When he learned that Rasputin lay at death's door, it caused him more immediate distress than the assassination of the Arch-Duke. After a few weeks, Rasputin miraculously recovered and was venerated more than ever by his followers for his super-human power. However, there was to be no recovery from conflict in Serbia as she fought against her Austrian-Hungarian oppressors.

"Depose of Serbia," said Kaiser Wilhelm to his Austrian-Hungarian ally. "I will stand behind you."

With Germany at her back, Austria audaciously issued Serbia an ultimatum of ten demands, knowing that some of these orders would be impossible for them to keep and would lead to an open armed conflict. They ordered the Serbs to cease inciting rebellion with her sister nations and agree to accept Austrian domination in Bosnia and commit to neighborly relations with their oppressors. They also demanded that the Austrian army conduct an investigation into the assassination of the Grand Duke in Serbian sovereign territory. The Serbs were willing to consider everything except they refused to allow Austrian boots on their soil.

The mood in the capital became tense as the press relentlessly pursued Russia's foreign minister, Sazonov for information on a possible war with Austria. To ease the tension, Zinaida Rostovsky gave a small garden party for the family and a few friends. The evening sun still shed a soft light over the walkways lined with French tea roses and boughs of English floribunda, filling the balmy air with a delicate perfume. A white clothed table was set with hors d'oeuvres of stuffed eggs in spiced sauce, caviar stuffed blini, smoked salmon, button mushrooms in hot sherry cream sauce, ham, cocktail sausages in wine sauce, and cucumber salad. Footmen in formal livery and white gloves poured iced vodka from frosty bottles into crystal glasses as the butler stood attentively to see that everything went smoothly.

"My chef makes blini every bit as good as the chef at the yacht club. Don't you think?" said the Count after he took the first bit of his favorite delicacy and washed it down with the cold vodka.

"They are better...his aren't stuffed." said Prince Militsyn leaning toward his host and smiling. But food was not the subject of interest tonight, it was the impending war.

"I feel the Kaiser and the Tsar are playing a game for a supreme stake," Prince Militsyn said. "This would not be a political war so much as a duel between Slavism and Germanism. One of the two would have to succumb. I have spoken with many people lately and no one has any illusions about the nature of the conflict. In case such a conflict should arise, we should not shrink from any sacrifice, even if our beginning should be unfortunate. Russia must hold fast. Remember the great struggle against Napoleon."

"I would agree," said the count. "Any war with Germany is a duel to the death between the two ideologies and every Russian knows it."

"I beg to differ with you, sir," said Daniel. "But that is demagoguery. A romantic notion to justify an insane war. Wars are never fought over ideals but for land, wealth and power."

Both the count and the prince flinched. It was in their inherent nature to romanticize momentous events with imaginations of great drama and heroic feats.

The guests moved to a formal table and sat down under the canopy set with fine china. The footmen set before each guest a bowl of cold borsch with sour cream and hot pastries. After the first course, they brought jeweled tobacco boxes and offered each guest cigars or slim yellow cigarettes. Ekatrina took a cigarette.

"There is one thing that concerns me if we are to go to war," said Zinaida. "I have long been convinced that the Emperor is plagued by bad luck and is doomed to misfortune. He seems to fail in everything he undertakes. I heard it said that the lines of his hand are terrifying."

"Don't tell me you believe that foolishness," said Yelivaveta's husband, Cyril.

"Well, isn't it obvious?" she said. "I mean about his bad luck...the tsarevich, the Japanese war, the coronation."

"The emperor himself believes it," said Princess Militsyn. "He was born on Job's name day, May 6th. My husband has overheard him say that everything he fears comes to pass and all the evils he foresees descends upon his head. He has some kind of conviction that fate has destined him for some terrible trial."

The Prince shifted somewhat annoyed.

"Does fate control us or do we control fate?" asked Cyril.

"And is there such a thing as fate?" said Daniel. "Is it not God who ultimately knows the course of lives and of nations?"

"God?" said Princess Militsyn. "Although the Tsar exhibits all the outward signs of piety, he does not behave as a man guided by God. He's very underhanded. Just look at the way he dismisses his ministers. When he is determined to get rid of them, he gives them the friendliest of receptions showing them special confidence and kindness, and then one fine day they open the morning newspaper to find that their health obliges them to take a long rest. Have you ever heard of such a thing?"

Ekatrina took a drag on her cigarette from a long holder, the latest in style for fashionable women and said. "One of the ladies in waiting to the Empress went to see Madame de Thebes, the famous clairvoyant in Paris, to have her future read and the madam turned her away saying that she received such a terrible headache she could not read. She said, that when the Tsar entered Paris that morning and passed by her window she saw a terrible black fate in his face. I will never forget those words and I pray to the Virgin for our sovereigns daily." She lifted her head and looked away into the garden, conscious of her superior position at court.

"This is poppycock," said the count.

"In defense of our Emperor," said Anatole. "He is devoted to his wife beyond the call of duty, and he adores his children." Though he was not looking admirably at his wife, Ekatrina, but stared longingly at Jeniya. She took an uneasy breath and turned toward her husband. Ekatrina did not miss a move.

"That kind of love is neurotic if you ask me," said countess Zinaida. "He wouldn't dare to behave any other way with that German woman, Aleksandra Feodorovna. He's scared to death of her and incapable of doing anything without her, while she and that mad charlatan, Rasputin, are ruling behind the throne."

"Nicholas told his Prime Minister, better ten Rasputins than one of the Empress's hysterical fits," said Princess Militsyn.

"*Mon Dieu*, women," said the count. "Doesn't anyone have anything positive to say? To listen to you, Russia is already marching to its doom and war hasn't even been declared."

"Bravo, your excellency," said Cyril clapping his hands. "Actually, I don't understand why Russia must become involved in this Serbian conflict at all?" said Cyril. "Let the Serbs and the Austrians settle their own disputes. Why should they drag all of Europe into their madness?"

"The Serbs are of the Slavic brotherhood," said Anatole. "If we don't back them, then Austria along with Germany will turn Serbia and all of the southern Slavic nations into a blood bath. We cannot accept the threats of Austria and her ally Germany and allow the sovereign Serbian nation to be crushed." Ekatrina kept a jealous eye on her husband causing him to feel uneasy as he spoke.

"Why that's a romantic, old-fashion notion," Cyril said. "What did they care about the Slav brotherhood when their king put Serbia under Austrian dominion? We ought to let the Serbs suffer the chastisement they deserve. Besides, the they have nothing Slav about them. They are only Turks christened by the wrong name."

"In the long run ideology does not matter," Daniel said graciously. "I have tried to make some sense of all this insanity, and have concluded that what this boils down to, is a conflict between England and Germany for naval and economic power. England wants to halt the expansion of German colonization into ports of trade in both the Baltic and Mediterranean seas. The conflict between Austria and Serbia is secondary."

"So you think Great Britain is drawing Russia into a war?" said the count.

"But England has not committed to our alliance with France," said Anatole.

"No, but she will," said Daniel. "When Germany shows her hand. England's aim is to destroy Germany's growing Navel power and her colonies but she alone cannot cope with Germany. She needs Russia and France to crush German aggression before she makes her move. Several months ago I met with ex-minister of the interior, Durnovo, and I was impressed by his foresight. He stressed the danger of adding England as a third member of the alliance as Germany regards England the greater adversary in this sphere. Under such circumstances, a war between Germany and England with the participation of Russia and France as allies, would be but a question of time. He believes Germany would make the decisive first strike and engage in war at the moment she considered most favorable for herself, the moment when Russia had not yet fully mobilized and equipped her military forces. At a moment such as now. Already the Kaiser is provoking conflict with Russia. If you recall, less than a week ago workers at the Russian munitions plants declared a strike and several agitators with German accents were caught at their meetings and arrested.

Moreover, I have it from a very reliable source that England and France intend to use our Russian armies as their mammoth shock-absorber against Germany on the Austrian-Polish front should war break out. As the first order of business, our commanders have been advised to save Paris from German attack, no matter what the cost to our troops."

"That is a preposterous assumption," said the count. "France has committed to defend the interests of Russia as we have committed to her. This is not the time to ascertain as to whether a war could or could not be avoided and who is the blame, but to win the victory for Russia. Should our ambassadors fail to negotiate a resolution to this conflict with Austria, our imminent duty is to preserve the integrity and unity of our country, and to inspire our soldiers with faith in the rightness of our cause. To give them hope for victory. Anything less would mean a triumph for Germany."

"I would agree with you that we must support our troops in case of war, by all means. Which reminds me of another point Durnovo made which I found even more alarming considering the agitation I have recently experienced between my workers and these German provocateurs. No matter who won the war, he said, its immediate results would be a socialist revolution in Russia and Germany, beginning in the country which was the loser and spreading to the one which was the victor. Even in a successful war, Russia would gain nothing, since France and England would cast her aside as soon as the great might of Germany had been crushed."

"Positively speaking," said Cyril "Let's hope that the great powers of Europe can come to some kind of an agreement and stop this conflict between Austria and Serbia."

The footmen served the main course of sturgeon in horseradish sauce and roasted partridge a la Kiev. For dessert they had ice cream over orange sponge cake topped with raspberry sauce and fresh peaches accompanied by an assortment of fresh fruit. After dinner coffee was served in the garden.

The three Rovstovsky sisters sat down by the fountain under the rose floribunda. Jeniya cupped a bouquet in her hands and drank in the delicious perfume.

"Katiya," said Yelizaveta. "You are not still a part of that Rasputin gang, are you?"

"Well…," Katiya hesitated for a moment. "And why not, anybody who is anyone attends his gatherings these days. He is truly a miracle worker. Instead of being so critical and narrow-minded, why don't you join us," she said to Yelizaveta, making a jab at Jeniya and avoiding her critical gaze.

All the arguments to drive her sister away from this charlatan only bounced off her stubborn head. "Have you thought about what your behavior is doing to your marriage?" Jeniya asked.

"My marriage? My marriage has never been better," Katiya retorted. "My husband completely supports me!"

"That's because Anatole never puts his foot down. Haven't you noticed that he is becoming more and more resigned?"

Ekatrina gave her sister a hard cold stare; a look so forceful that Jeniya could feel the daggers piercing her heart. Until recently, she was unaware of Katiya's growing jealously and Anatole's unhappiness. She didn't mean to accuse her sister, but to open her eyes to the faltering marriage.

Katiya stood up abruptly. "Excuse me," she said. "I have better things to attend to than to sit here and listen to your idiotic prattle," and she stomped away to find Anatole.

Jeniya and Yelizaveta both shook their heads. "I'm worried about her," said Yelizaveta. "She can't breathe without Anatole."

Jeniya said. "I'm worried about them both." She not only worried about Katiya's involvement with the Rasputin gang and the harmful toll it had taken on her sister's marriage, but her son Alexei, who would be graduating from the Corps de Pages as an officer in the Emperor's elite guards.

Chapter 37

As Daniel predicted, English Ambassador, Buchanan, explained to Sazanov that should a war break out, his government would prefer to remain neutral because he was apprehensive that France and Russia could be crushed by Germany and Austria.

Sazonov protested, "England's neutrality would be tantamount to her suicide!"

"I'm certain of that," said Buchanan. "But I'm afraid public opinion with us is still far from realizing what our national interests so urgently require. English opinion will only accept the idea of intervening in the war if Germany is indubitably the aggressor."

The next day, on July 25th German ambassadors in Paris and London warned Russia and her ally, France, not to interfere in the Austrian-Serbian conflict citing; "the German government is extremely anxious that the conflict shall be localized as any intervention by a third power may, by the natural operation of alliances, have incalculable consequences."

France had only an entente cordial with England in an agreement to end the squabbling over colonial expansion, and Russian armies were not equipped for modern combat. Not only did the Russian troops hopelessly lack the necessary artillery, but their stock of boots and overcoats were inadequate to clothe the millions of men needed to fight a battle which could explode into a major conflict. Minister of war, General Souklomlinov, who resembled porky pig, chose to ignore the deplorable conditions of his army. Rather than prepare his troops with ample supplies of rifles and ammunition, he challenged Germany by writing an editorial in the newspaper announcing, "We are ready."

These threats of war did not alarm the money-crazed society of St. Petersburg. Their only concern was that a conflict may cause a crash in the stock market. But brokers were quick to assure their clients that, "blood always makes the market rise!"

On July 20th 1914, French president, Poincare, sailed into St. Petersburg with great fanfare. At a diplomatic reception that evening Poincare inquired of the Austro-Hungarian foreign ambassador, Count Szapary, if there had been any further developments concerning the Austrian-Serbian conflict.

"*Monsieur le Président*, we cannot suffer a foreign government to allow plots against our sovereignty to be hatched on its territory," Szapary warned.

"With a little good will this Serbian business is easy to settle. But it can just as easily become acute. Serbia has some very warm friends in the Russian people. And Russia has an ally, France. There are plenty of complications to be feared!"

Szapary bowed and left without a word.

Poincare later told his French Ambassador to Russia, Paleologue, "I'm not satisfied with this conversation. The ambassador had obviously been instructed to say nothing. Austria has a *coup de théâtre* in store for us. Sazonov must be firm and we must back him up. "

"If we had only Austria to deal with I should be hopeful," said Paleologue. "But there is Germany. She has promised her ally (Austria) a great personal triumph. She is convinced that we dare not resist her to the bitter end and that we will give way as we have always given way. But this time we cannot give way, on pain of ceasing to exist. We shall not avert this war!"

Sazonov pleaded to Buchanan for help, "England should hesitate no longer to arrange herself on the side of Russia and France in a crisis which the stake is not merely the European balance of power but the very liberties of Europe itself."

At seven o'clock that evening, the Tsar sent his generals preliminary orders for mobilization.

On July 28th Count Leopold declared war on Serbia. Almost simultaneously, the German ambassador to Russia, Pourtales, warned Sazonov that as Austria's ally she naturally supported the legitimate claims of the Vienna cabinet against Serbia."

Paleologue beseeched the German ambassador to intervene in the conflict. "Don't ask Russia to let Serbia be crushed," he warned. "It would be to ask the impossible and would lead to a catastrophe such as the world has never known. This calamity may still be averted as the Russian Government is peace-loving, the British government is peace-loving, and your government claims to be peace-loving."

"Yes, indeed, I call God to witness!" Pourtales replied. "Germany is peace-loving! For forty-three years we have preserved the peace of Europe! For forty-three years we have pledged our honor not to abuse our strength! And it is we who are now accused of desiring to precipitate war! History will prove we have the right on our side! We cannot... we will not abandon our ally...No, we will not abandon her!"

When Paleologue informed Sazonov of Pourtales resolve, the Russian minister said, "things are very bad. It is clear that Austria is refusing to negotiate with us and Germany is secretly egging her on."

Paleologue agreed. "I'm afraid Pourtales has helped to drive his government into this terrible abyss by asserting that Russia would not face a conflict in Austria and that if she did yield to Germany's demands, which is unthinkable, France would denounce the Russian alliance.

Only yesterday Pourtales assured the Dutch minister that Russia would give way and it would be a great triumph for the German Triple Alliance. I have this from the best source. But...I do ask you to not resort to military measures on the German front until Germany has definitely shown her hand."

"Our generals are getting restless," Sazanov protested. "And even now I am having great difficulty in holding them in."

"You understand my responsibility in this is enormous," Paleologue replied. "And that is why I ask you to pledge yourself henceforth to accept all the proposals France and England may make to you to save peace."

The next day, Pourtales threatened Sazonov. "If you do not stop your military preparations at once Germany also would mobilize her army."

Sazonov replied, "the preparations of the Russian General staff were the result of the uncompromising obstinacy of the Vienna cabinet. The Austro-Hungarian army corps are already on a war footing with us. If today we stopped at mobilizing the thirteen corps destined for operation against Austria and tomorrow Germany decided to give her ally military support, we should be powerless to defend ourselves on the frontiers of Poland and West Prussia."

That same afternoon, Tsar Nicholas II received a telegram from his cousin, the Kaiser advising him to halt mobilization as he is doing everything in his power to bring about a direct understanding between Austria and Russia. Despite the opposition of his Russian generals who have continuously insisted on the dangers of a partial mobilization, the Tsar heeded the Kaiser's advice and immediately called his chief of staff ordering him to halt mobilization. The chief of staff replied, "I am frightfully sorry, but I am unable to do anything whatsoever." In desperation, the Tsar telegrammed the Kaiser with a proposal to refer the Austro-Serbian dispute to The Hague Tribunal. The Kaiser had only to accept this suggestion and the war would have been averted. But he did not even attempt to reply to the Tsar's request.

On July 30th Austria-Hungary bombarded Belgrade.

The Kaiser then sent a threatening telegram to the Tsar, "If Russia mobilizes against Austria-Hungary the role of mediator which I have undertaken at your urgent request will be compromised, if not made impossible. The whole weight of the decision to be taken now rest on your shoulders and you will have to bear the responsibility for war or peace."

When Sazonov found out about the exchange between the two Emperors, he said to Nicholas. "We shall not escape war now! Germany is obviously evading the mediatorial intervention for which we asked her. All she is after is to gain time to complete her military preparation in secret. In these circumstances I don't think your majesty can postpone the order for general mobilization any longer."

The Tsar said, "just think of the responsibility you're advising me to assume! Remember it's a question of sending thousands and thousands of men to their death!"

Sazonov predicted. "The war will break out just the same at Germany's appointed time and will catch us in hopeless confusion."

"Sergei Dimitrievich, the Tsar replied. "Ring up the chief of staff and tell him I order a general mobilization."

The mobilization decree was issued at dawn. Still hopeful, the Tsar wired the Kaiser, "It is technically impossible for me to suspend my military preparations. But as long as conversations with Austria are not broken off my troops will refrain from taking the offensive anywhere. I give you my word of honor on that."

The Kaiser wired back, "I have gone to the utmost limits possible in my efforts to save the peace. It is not I who will bear the responsibility for the terrible disaster which now threatens the civilized world. My friendship to you is still sacred and I have been loyal to Russia during your last war with Japan. Even now you and you alone can still avert a war. You can still save the peace of Europe by stopping your military measures."

That afternoon, German ambassador Pourtales requested an audience with the Tsar to expand on the Kaiser's proposal. "Germany has always been Russia's best friend," he said. "Let the Emperor Nicholas consent to revoke his military measures and the peace of the world would be saved." But the Tsar stood his position.

At eleven o'clock in the evening, Pourtales announced to Sazonov, that if within twelve hours Russia did not suspend her mobilization on both the German and Austro-Hungarian frontiers, the whole German army would be mobilized. "Agree to demobilize! Agree to demobilize!" he said with a trembling voice.

Sazonov replied, "But it's technically impossible for us to demobilize without dislocating our entire military organization."

The next day, Kaiser Wilhelm proclaimed Germany in danger of war and immediately called up the reserves and closed the frontiers.

The Tsar immediately wired Wilhelm, "I understand that you are compelled to mobilize but I should like to have the same guarantee from you that I gave you myself, that these measures do not mean war and that we shall continue our negotiation to save the general peace so dear to our hearts. With God's help, our long and tried friendship should be able to prevent bloodshed."

Before the ink was dry, Pourtales handed Sazonov the declaration of war. "His Majesty the Emperor, my August Sovereign, in the name of the Empire accepts the challenge and considers himself in a state of war with Russia." When Sazonov finished reading the declaration of war, he was amazed to see there were two versions and that one was written hastily in brackets. "This is a criminal act!" he declared to the German ambassador.

Pourtales replied, "we are defending our honor. We are defending our honor!"

"Your honor was not involved," Sazanov said. "You could have prevented the war by one word. You didn't want to. But there is divine justice."

"That's true...there is divine justice...a divine justice!" Pourtales staggered toward the window and burst into tears. "So this is the result of my mission," he muttered.

The events that led to war continued to play on the Tsar's mind. "Wilhelm was never sincere...not for a moment," he told Paleologue the next morning. "In the end he was hopelessly entangled in the net of his own perfidy and lies. At 2AM in the morning, a servant informed me he had a very important telegram from Emperor Wilhelm. I read and reread his last telegram, but I couldn't understand a word...pretending that it depended on me whether war was averted or not! He implored me not to let my troops cross the frontier. Have I suddenly gone mad? Didn't the German ambassador hand Sazonov the declaration of war just six hours before? There's no doubt that the object of his strange telegram was to shake my resolution, to disconcert me and inspire me to make some absurd dishonorable step."

Paleologue said, "I have, Sire, a somewhat different explanation. I think the Kaiser is a braggart. He has frightened himself by his own undertakings. The part played by reason in the government of nations is so small that it has only taken a week to let loose a world of madness."

Chapter 38

"War...just look at those poor souls out there, so filled with passion and patriotism and for what? Do they know what they are fighting for? Does anyone know?" Daniel said watching the people gathering in the street below the balcony of the drawing room. We give our bright eyed youth a uniform, a flag, and a marching band and send them off to war to defend the honor of their country, while the technocrats who control industry and finance grow richer."

Again, true to Daniel's predictions, on August 3rd Germany declared war on France and two days later, ambassador Buchanan announced that he had received a telegram from the Foreign Office declaring England's participation in the war. "My ally! My dear ally!" he said to ambassador Paleologue with great emotion.

Jeniya stood beside Daniel wearing a frilly pale lavender summer gown with ruffles adorning the neckline, sleeves and hem. A distant sadness reflected in her eyes. "Our son is already seventeen," she said. "I am so afraid that if this war should drag on..."

Daniel put his arm around her shoulders and drew her close to his heart. "They tell us this war should be decided by the end of the year."

She took a large picture hat decorated with lilac-colored plumes and adjusted it on her head looking in an elaborately carved gilded floor mirror. Then she slipped her hands into long white gloves.

On the way to the palace, they saw a wondering *starista* wearing a tattered white dress trimmed with dozens of scarlet ribbons. The woman cried out in a loud voice. "Red is the color of blood. Blood will soon be as plentiful as these scarlet ribbons." These were not the words the people wanted to hear on this day of solidarity and patriotic celebration. But never-the-less people stopped and dropped a few coins into the hands of the holy woman.

Many of these *starzii* were deformed and outcast of society. Others led debased lives in their youth and have renounced the world and its ways, separating themselves to live as ascetics. But all had struggled against human frailty and sin and had crossed over into a pious lifestyle. Educated Russians held them in higher esteem than those who lived good and blameless lives because of their battle against temptation and treated them with great respect. To the simple minded peasants, they were prophets sent of God, speaking the words of God. They prayed for the sick, comforted the troubled, ministered to people's spiritual needs, and with their great imaginations entertained people with stories of the miraculous deeds of saints. And some, as this woman, claimed to foresee the future.

Jeniya put a few rubbles into her hand and said to Daniel. "I am frightened," she said. "I have a strange presentiment that something terrible is going to happen as a result of this war."

"Terrible things always happen in war."

"No," she said. "It's something else. Something more disastrous and it troubles me. I fear for our family and especially for our sons."

"Do you think it will rekindle the revolution?"

"We have survived a revolution. If it were just revolution, but no… According to my sister, Rasputin said that a terrible storm cloud hangs over Russia. Disaster, grief, murky darkness and no light. A whole ocean of tears, there is no counting them, and so much blood…Russia is drowning in blood. The disaster is great. The misery is infinite. The war must be stopped. It will mean the end of all things."

"You don't place credence in the babblings of that charlatan or your hysterical sister, do you? Don't allow yourself to be brainwashed by these wondering soothsayers making dire proclamations. There will always be bloodshed in war. They do not profess to know anything more than what reason would have it."

"And reason says..."

"I don't know," he said with a sudden faraway stare in his eyes. But he did know. He also had his apprehensions of the future. He worried over the lack of guns and ammunition. He worried about the incompetence of the men who were leading the troops into this war. When he asked the artillery administrator if there would be a need to increase the production of weapons and shells, the officer replied, "there is no need."

He worried about the moral decay of the capital city spreading throughout the empire, and the sleazy influence of Rasputin in high places. How long would a righteous God tolerate this moral rebellion in a nation? He knew from history that the lust for power, pleasure, greed, corruption, dissension, and open sodomy were always the last chapter in the fall of nations. But on the positive side, he saw that this crisis had inspired people to unite despite their differences and work together for victory over the enemy. Factory workers halted their strikes and rebels silenced their protests. Workers in almost all parties enrolled in various military regiments and took up arms alongside the sons of the noblesse. He prayed that through this trial the Russian people would somehow emerge with a renewed purpose and rebuild their nation.

Alexander Square was thronged with people; their faces a strange mix of sobriety and anticipation, as the significance of the unfolding events began to enter their consciousness. Flags waved lightly overhead, catching what there was of a breeze. Church banners and portraits of the Tsar embellished with golden cords gleamed in the sunlight. The crowd began to part and make way for the Imperial motorcade of shinny open Victoria automobiles crawling across the square, stopping and starting as they made their way to the palace entrance. Blessings began to well up from the voices of the people. "Long live the Tsar! Long live the Tsar!"

About five or six thousand invited guests had gathered inside the great Nicholas hall. The whole court dazzled in a resplendent display of majestic pomp, men in meticulously clipped beards and elaborate court uniforms and women in light summer dresses under great plumed hats showered in diamonds, pearls, rubies, sapphires, and emeralds; a spectacle which no court in the world could rival. The open windows along the Neva could not freshen the heavy perfumed air from so many people packed into the ballroom.

Jeniya gazed at the great chandeliers lit up with countless lights and remembered the magnificent state balls that were once held in this room in a world that was only yesterday, but now seemed so long ago. The hall had been dark ever since Rasputin entered the lives of the sovereigns almost ten years ago.

She and Daniel stood with the Rostovsky clan around her father looking elegant with his thick wavy hair, the meticulously groomed mustache, and his formal uniform with the gold braids decorated with metals of valor. He had the distinction of serving in the Preobrazhensky Guards, the first regiment of the Russian guards initiated by Peter the Great as proof of loyalty to the Empire and to the Tsar. Alexander I was its first commander. Membership was only assigned to sons of the nobility by birth on their maternal side and of considerable height.

Ekatrina wiped tears from her eyes as she gazed at Anatole standing in his brown field uniform with the Tsar's officers of the elite Guards. He stared straight ahead; his soft brown eyes cold and inscrutable. No doubt he had apprehension concerning the war, but also must have been subconsciously affected by the underlying tension in the marriage ever since his wife had become a part of the Rasputin clique.

Yelizavetka's husband, Cyril, had just slipped over the age of forty-eight, the cut-off for recruits. Jeniya looked up into Daniel's discerning eyes and he smiled down at her more mature and handsome than ever. Although he was younger than Cyril, she was grateful that he also did not have to serve in the military, but she worried for her eldest son, Alexei. He had already been in the Corp de Pages for five years and had decided that when he graduated he wanted to join the Preobrazhenski Guards like his grandfather and uncle Anatole.

The Imperial family entered the great Nicholas hall, headed by the Emperor, the dowager Empress, Maria Feodorovna, and the Empress Aleksandra Feodorovna, followed by the Grand Dukes who stood a head taller than most everyone else. Men with expressions of loyalty and women with tears in their eyes dropped to their knees kissing the hands of their sovereigns as they slowly passed by. Everyone present raised their voices and sang the "Te Deum" a cappella.

The miraculous ikon of the Virgin of Kazan was brought to the palace for this occasion from the national sanctuary of the Kazan cathedral and placed in the center of the room. It had always been a symbol of unity and hope before which the Russian people prayed in the crucial hours of a national crisis including Field Marshall Prince Kutuzov who knelt before it in prayer before he joined his army at Smolensk in the battle against Napoleon.

A tense silence settle over the hall when the imperial cortege ceremoniously crossed the room and stood by the altar. Women with tear swollen eyes nervously crumpled handkerchiefs in white gloved hands, and men frowning with uncertainty, shifted from foot to foot, readjusting their swords to find relief from standing so long at attention. The aged old walrus, Goremykin, president of the Tsar's council of ministers and his most trusted advisor, stood tottering, drawing deep exhausted breaths and looking like he was about to expire. Jeniya felt sorry for the old man but more so for Russia whose government depended on his archaic consultation.

The clergy appeared ablaze in flame radiating from their red jewel studded robes. They led the solemn mass and a chorus chanted the Orthodox liturgy in majestic harmonies of varied a cappella tones. Nicholas's pale face took on a mystical expression as he prayed with fervor. The Empress stood rigidly next to him, nervously working her hands, her blue eyes fixed in a glassy stare, her bosom heaving from uneven jerky breathing; her fair complexion veined like marble. Every now and then when she closed her eyes, her face reminded Jeniya of a death mask framed in red hair and she thought of the morbid grip Rasputin held on the Imperial family. In contrast, her mother-in-law, the dowager Empress Maria Feodorovna stood motionless; her head raised in regal dignity as a last reminder of a once glorious empire that was now crumbling.

The Tsar raised his right hand toward the gospel held out to him and declared in a slow, low voice. "Officers of my guard, here present, I greet in you my entire army united as it is in body and spirit, standing firm as a wall of granite, and give it my blessing. I solemnly swear that I will never make peace so long as one of the enemy is on the soil of the fatherland."

A frantic tumult of hurrahs burst forth and was soon intensified by cheering crowd standing in the palace square in answer to this oath once declared by the Emperor Alexander I in 1812.

"The man who puts on his armor should not boast like the one who takes it off," Daniel whispered to Jeniya.

The Emperor and Empress proceeded from the ball room to the balcony overlooking their subjects who were standing shoulder to shoulder. The people dropped to their knees as one body when they saw their sovereigns. Flags dipped in honor and there arose a surging harmonious chorus from thousands of voices singing the moving strains of the Russian national anthem. Each time their Majesties left the balcony the people clamored for their reappearance with more hurrahs, the waiving of hats in the air, and singing of "God Save the Tsar".

"The Emperor played his role with perfection today," Daniel said to Jeniya on the way home. "The undisputed autocrat over all the Russias, a being somewhere between God and mortal; the military, political and religious leader of his people. The absolute master of our body and soul."

"Don't be so down on the Tsar," said Jeniya. "One good thing to come out of this is that the country is uniting around the Tsar for the first time since the war with Japan. It was a glorious thing to see our people out there today. It brought tears to my eyes and made me proud to be Russian."

"Yes, glorious. Speaking of Japan, do you remember what happened to the glory after the war ended?"

Jeniya looked at him, thinking about the words of the *starista*, thinking about her sons.

Chapter 39

Anatole stood ram-rod tall at the head of his regiment, noble and devoted to his Tsar, his country, and most of all to his men. This is the life he had chosen and they were his family. The young men stood shoulder to shoulder in a square formation around a pulpit placed in front of the Preobrazhensky cathedral for a solemn mass. They were wearing new brown field uniforms with brown caps trimmed in red bands. A bright sun painted the onion domes of the basilica in gold and the classic portico in white. Barrels of three black cannons stood upright on each side of black iron gates, the tallest surmounted with the double headed golden eagle.

The ceremony began with the regal trumpets and rolling of drums of the Te Deum. The immediate families invited to the service knelt and prayed when the regimental men's choir sang the mass. The emotions of many were so stirred up with in them, that they shed tears listening to the rich harmonies of the base and baritone voices.

The priest delivered a brief address, cathedral bells tolled, and the ceremony ended. Anatole mounted his horse at the head of the column and gave a sharp command. His regiment closed into ranks with their heads held high. The choir master struck up the first chords to the lively allegro of the Preobrazhensky Anthem and the squadron joined in song as they marched through the yard. Anatole made no recognition of his wife as he passed by and Jeniya feared that their marriage was deteriorating more than she realized. She worried for Anatole going off to war in such a state.

The Rostovsky family was standing outside the gates to encourage the troops with a rousing send-off. Jeniya gazed into the profile of her father standing next to her, the old soldier, with shoulders square in his summer white tunic, and head held high. He had lost his slim waste but great pride still shown in his face. He saluted his son-in-law and grinned broadly as he past, but Anatole only looked ruefully into Jeniya's eyes.

She lowered her head. She couldn't help but wonder how many of these brave young men who were obediently willing to throw themselves into battle without questioning would return to worship in this cathedral with their families and how many more would return laid out in coffins. She worried for Anatole, for Katiya and Irina, his daughter.

Crowds lined the streets along the parade route, tossing hats in the air, waving small flags and saluting the regiments of the Empire with roaring cheers as they marched in firm rhythmical steps with grave and determined faces.

Ekatrina, along with the sweethearts and wives of the men, some with small children in their arms, joined the columns, striding out as best they could to keep pace with their men before they said their last good byes at the barracks. Inside the camp, soldiers trampled about, officers shouted orders, pack horses neighed and chafed as ammunition wagons, baggage carts, arms service corps trucks, ambulances, field kitchens, and peasant carts cut across fields in a picture of resolute disorder. The women stood beside their men exchanging loving glances and heroically trying to hold back tears as they attempted to leave them with cheerful, encouraging words. The men did not try to hide the tenderness that shone in their eyes before they had to pile into wagons and be driven to the Warsaw railway station where they crowded onto the waiting trains.

For Ekatrina and Anatole, their conversation lagged into awkward silences. The officers were last to leave and board their private cars. Once at the station, they thrust their heads from the windows and gave the command. The trumpeter blew his final signal, threw his trumpet over his back and jumped on board the moving train.

"Paris for lunch, Petersburg for dinner," the Kaiser announced when he launched the full force of the German army on France. In a Panic, the French ambassador, Paleologue ran to the Tsar and begged, "Sire, order your troops to take the offensive immediately. If they do not, there is a risk that the French army will be crushed. Then the whole German mass will turn *en bloc* against Russia."

""I shall order the advance when the mobilization is complete," Nicholas replied. I have already sent half my men to fight the Austrians, and the rest of my army is not prepared to fight the Germans. But Nicholas did not stand firm in his decision. With the advice of his northwest army group commander, Zhilinski, and to accommodate the urgent request of the French ambassador, he changed his strategy and sent eight hundred thousand troops to invade East Prussia, including his finest, the troops of the elite guards who were normally kept in reserve and sent into battle only after all else had failed.

The Russian army rolled into combat covering hundreds of miles on muddy roads, or no roads at all, using horse carts to pull the artillery through the wilderness. They had limited rail service, an antiquated communication system and no parts for reconnaissance planes. Some soldiers went into battle with nineteenth century rifles since there were not enough guns to supply entire divisions. Shells had to be rationed.

Group commander Yakov Zhilinski was a dull looking person, a reckless braggart, a courtier and a paper pushing soldier with little experience on the battlefield. From the first day of the campaign he had frittered away manpower, weapons, and precious shells on borderline skirmishes. He failed to modernize his communications between headquarters and the two armies under his command.

Commander of the first army, the debonair General Paul Von Rennenkampf, looked down through haughty eyes and sported a brush mustache that extended well beyond his face. Anatole joked that he had the widest mustache in the army. The portly old aristocrat had distinguished himself as a cavalryman in past wars but did not have experience in modern warfare. He still believed he could use nineteenth century war tactics by throwing a wall of human bodies headlong into battle against twentieth century machine guns and heavy artillery to defeat the Germans within a few weeks. Britain's military attaché, General Knox observed that in retrospect he was an anachronism and a danger to his army.

These obstacles were further complicated by Rennenkampf's feud with Zhilinski, as well as an on-going battle of animosity with General Samsonov, his counterpart and second army commander, making it impossible to carry out a precision military campaign.

Again, true to the prediction of Daniel's informant, the Russian army's first assignment was to attack the Germans with nearly a million men in order to draw their troops away from the western front before they could reach Paris.

The plan was to move Rennenkampf's first army in two divisions, west and southwest toward Tannenburg in East Prussia and simultaneously attack Prittwitz's German eighth army in a pincer movement. General Samsonov would advance his second army toward the northwest to engulf the enemy and attack from the rear.

German commander Herman Von Francois, an elegant portrait of the German ideal Arian, who fought under Prittwitz, discovered the plan. To counter the threat, he gathered every man and every gun from the French border to engage Rennenkampf's right flank in a surprise attack before he had to face Samsonov's assault coming from the south.

Anatole commanded the first army's right flank division. He laid awake, sweating in the oppressive heat from the nearby swampy marshes and from fear. Not only did his troops have a limited number of shells to fight the German infantry, but this was his first major command and he was responsible for the lives of thousands of his countrymen. An eerie quiet pervaded the blackness of the night, as if all of nature had sensed a terrible shaking was about to take place.

In the deadly pre-dawn silence of August 7th he heard a wrestling movement in the distance. He knew this was not the ordinary sounds of nature, but of enemy troops moving in and around the forests surrounding the potato fields which expanded between the two opposing armies. Sensing that German troops were maneuvering into an attack position, he vigorously summoned his troops into battle, but it was too late. Herman Von Francois had already ordered a murderous barrage of artillery fire that caught the Anatole's infantry by surprise. Russian light artillery tried to reply but the Germans had already entrenched their guns. When the first division of Anatole's brave troops rose from their trenches and hurled themselves onto the battlefield to meet enemy fire with bayonets, German machine guns mowed them down by the hundreds. By sunrise, twelve more batteries of Germans had slipped behind the Russian lines and opened with heavy artillery fire, raining a storm of high explosives on the Russian positions. When Anatole realized what had happened, he jotted in his log. "Our communications have been intercepted and we have been set up for a catastrophe. Who the hell is in charge?"

By 8AM Francois had unleashed his infantry division. Waves of warriors in spiked helmets and gray uniforms surged like a swarm of locusts onto the potato fields to meet the enormous Russian army. Riflemen assembled on the battlefield returned German shells in volley after volley until the culmination of battery fire sounded like dynamite exploding in a gigantic cauldron. The ground shook beneath their feet and the air filled with the acrid odor of chemical explosives and blinding smoke. More Germans poured over the fields like a mindless firing machine. They dodged around the dead and wounded and fell beside their comrades until the fields turned grey with German corpses. With triumph in sight, Anatole's heart raced with a mounting rush of adrenaline and he ran to the head of his troops to rally them on to victory. "Hurrah. Hurrah." He shouted. The men fought with the strength of titans until suddenly their batteries began to fire sporadically.

"Our guns fell silent." Anatole jotted in his log in a state of furry. "We had no more shells left to shoot. I was helpless. The opposition had the opportunity to inch forward unhindered from prone positions and fire only 5 or 6 paces from our batteries slaughtering men in entire companies like sitting ducks. I have lost almost three-quarters of my army. Why, in God's name did England not share in this campaign and send her troops to save Paris? Why did they leave the entire burden to fall on us when we were not yet prepared? Why did they betray us?"

When the smoke lifted, he stepped onto the battlefield to assess the carnage, and saw his men fallen in the rows where they stood with their officers and battalion commanders, his friends and comrades, frozen into grisly contortions. In a wave of blinding emotion and grief, he did the unthinkable and put his hands to his face trying bravely to hold back an uncontrollable rain of tears, tears he had not experienced since he was a boy.

With victory in the German camp, commander Mackensen moved against Rennenkampf's left flank, but his army was caught in a quagmire which gave Rennenkampf the advantage to prepare for the offensive. The Russian infantry bombarded Mackensen's men with a wall of fire nearly wiping out several units and sending the remainder into flight. Prittwitz feared another attack from Samsonov's army closing in on them from the rear and ordered his men to retreat. This was unacceptable to the German Chief of Staff, Moltke. He replaced him and his deputy with the ruthless Ludendorff and summoned the seasoned old general Hindenburg from retirement, who immediately counter-ordered the retreat. Rennnenkamph, arrogantly thinking that his armies sent the German army in flight, rested to replenish his troops in the nearby town of Gumbinnen.

Paul Von Hindenburg, a large boned man with a frighteningly icy stare in his blue eyes, wore a handlebar mustache around his wide jowls. When he learned that Rennenkampf's army was resting rather than preparing for another attack, he launched a long shot maneuver on a hunch that his enemy thought the worst of the battle was over and would not move quickly to aid Samsonov's men. He set up a decoy cavalry at the Vistula river and spread the rest of his troops loosely along Rennenkampf's path to confuse him as to the location of the Germany armies and to keep him from coming to the aid of his comrade. At the same time, German General Francois transported troops with legendary speed by non-stop rail from the French theater to meet Samsonov's second army advancing northward.

Group commander Zhilinski, also certain that enemy troops were in retreat, wired Samsonov through the Warsaw office ordering him to cut off what he believed to be the Germany cavalry gathered at the Vistula river. Hindenburg intercepted the uuencoded wire and learned that Samsonov was moving his entire army of twelve divisions and three corps toward the Vistula. Chief of staff, Grand Duke Nicholas Nicholaevich, frantically hurried to Zhilinski's headquarters to warn of a massive German advance moving southward toward Tannenberg, but the myopic group commander ignored the warnings and directed Rennenkampf to defend the border towns instead of rushing to aid his comrade. Hindenburg intercepted two more uuencoded wires and discovered Samsonov's detailed route in pursuit of the delusive retreating forces, and that Rennenkampf would not march to reinforce him. The experienced old Teutonic warrior made a daring move and ordered all his troops to intercept Samsonov at Tannenberg.

Confused by Zhilinski's orders to defend the border towns, Rennenkampf spread his armies out thinly across the eastern front while the Germans were hastily moving heavy artillery by train to Tannenburg for a massive offensive against Samsonov.

On August 14th Francois opened fire on the second army's left flank with two hundred heavy artillery weapons and battled the Russian infantry who had less than fifty big guns. The intrepid Russian warriors fought the German bombardment with the bravery and veracity of lions as fire and steel rained death upon their heads. Rennenkampf did not even attempt to discover Samsonov's location or come to his aid because of their continuing feud as well as the confusing orders from Zhilinsky. When General Francois surveyed the battlefield later that day he said, "It was one of the most tragic sights I saw during the entire war. Trenches over six feet deep were piled with dead and seriously wounded Russians soldiers."

The following day, the battle continued to rage as German troops moved in on the remainder of Samsonov's army. On the morning of August 16th, Francois's cavalry joined General Von Mackensen's army to close the trap and deliver the final blow.

By evening, Samsonov knew he was trapped and without relief. He ordered his exhausted, hungry men to withdraw. But it was too late, German columns had already deeply penetrated Russian flanks. What was left of his army marched directly into a slaughter from all sides by the encircling enemy forces. Only a few thousand men managed to escape from the ring of fire. The victors took ninety-five thousand Russian prisoners, confiscated over five hundred precious field guns, and thousands of horses.

As night fell, Samsonov, accompanied by five other staff officers fled from the battlefield on horseback but a party of German infantry armed with machine guns spotted them. Amidst a hail of bullets, the party dismounted and continued their way on foot into the blackness of the forest. From time to time a halt was called and all drew closer to make sure that nobody was missing. General Samsonov, who suffered from heart trouble found his breathing increasingly difficult and lagged behind. On the last roll call he did not answer, but a few of the men heard a shot. The party searched in vain for the missing general and soon realized he had taken his life.

The carnage from the first thirty days of war cost the Russian Empire over three quarters of a million men, including prisoners. In retrospect Hindenburg reminisced, "Why did Rennenkampf not use the time of our greatest weakness to fall on us, when the troops were exhausted and crowded together on the battlefield of Tannenberg? Why did he give us time to disentangle our units, concentrate afresh, rest and bring up reinforcements?"

The battle of Tannenberg was celebrated as Germany's greatest victory of the Great War. The fields and marshes of Eastern Prussia drenched in the sacrificial blood of Russian soldiers would soon be forgotten, but their tragic loss allowed French General Joffre to win his celebrated battle of the Marne and move on to save Paris, a French victory Russia would never forget.

Chapter 40

No one could have imagined that the opening days of the war would take so many lives or inflict so many casualties. Due to the shortage of field hospitals, trains brought causalities from the northern front to St Petersburg. Emergency care units were set up in the palaces at Tsarskoe Selo and the Winter Palace, the first of many hospitals to be organized by the Empress Aleksandra Feodorovna from one end of Russia to the other.

Evgeniya and her sisters volunteered with other upper-class women for a Red Cross crash-course in nurses training. While they trained they attended the large influx of wounded arriving each day. Katiya worked mornings with the Empress and her daughters at Tsarskoe Selo and Jeniya and Yelizaveta worked at the Winter Palace. Their assignment was to remove the blood soaked bandages and filthy clothing taken to be burned.

Jeniya's first patient arrived with a severely injured leg and her heart went out to him. He couldn't have been much older than Alexei. She began to peal the stiff, dark blood-stained bandage when she saw maggots in the puss filled wound. The stench of rotting flesh, perspiration, heavy antibiotic preparations, and agonizing shrieks of pain caused her to swoon. She sank to the floor and fought with all her strength to maintain consciousness. With the same determination of will she used to fight against Rasputin's evil spell, she would fight these emotions. She pushed up, steeling herself to perform her duties and placed a cool compress on the soldier's sweating face before she continued to peal the filthy bandages from his leg. The young man stared at her with both fear and pain in his eyes.

"You're going to make it through this," she said trying to comfort him. "You will soon be fine." She stroked his face again with another cool compress.

Suddenly they heard screaming sirens. Staff and volunteers raced down the long corridor beneath the palace where they set up their make-shift triage before they moved the men to beds upstairs in the palace halls.

Medics shouted. Wounded men cursed. Shrieks of pain filled the corridor. Volunteers rushed to reach the wounded in ambulances and remove them onto stretchers and gurneys where they rapidly rolled them down the wide corridor past dozens more wounded who were able to sit. Nurses and doctors scurried about in an organized bedlam to treat men with gaping wounds; abdomens torn open, lacerations to heads exposing bone and brain, parts of faces blown away, and raw burnt flesh. Jeniya's hands dripped with blood as she quickly unrolled bandages where arms and legs had once been. The odor of rotting dead flesh overpowered all antiseptic odors and became intolerable. She heard the head surgeon pass by pronouncing a life or death sentence over the mutilated bodies, "this one is hopeless…as good as dead…both lungs shot through…this one may recover."

Her next victim was obviously a man of high rank. He lay unconscious with dirty wrappings around his head. She carefully began to unwind the bandages and screamed, "Tolya! *Mon Dieu.*" She quickly removed the bandage and washed his face. "Tolya," she called again. But he lay still, like a dead man. "Doctor," she screamed hysterical with fear.

One of the doctors rushed over to examine him. "He is in a coma from a head wound," he said. "He could remain this way for days, maybe weeks, or maybe only hours."

"Will he recover?

"If there is a chance, it will mostly depend on his will to live. Is he a relative?"

"My brother-in-law."

"I'm sorry," he said and touched her shoulder in empathy.

After she cleaned him and removed his dirty clothing, she summoned for the orderlies and called Katiya to come at once to the palace. She ordered a chamber in one of the rooms set aside for families of the wounded and knelt before an icon to pray.

Katiya arrived looking anxious and lost. Jeniya tried to comfort her sister as she ushered her to her husband's bedside.

Katiya flung herself onto Anatole's breast sobbing and calling his name. Suddenly Anatole opened his eyes. She laughed in relief and showered his face with kisses but when she looked into his eyes, they were staring like those of a corpse. "Tolya?" she said. "Tolya, can you hear me?" But he made no motion.

The doctor on duty tried to comfort her. "Do not be alarmed," he said. "It is a good sign that he opens his eyes. Sometimes he will respond and sometimes he may not. We have to be patient."

She looked at the doctor and nodded gratefully wiping tears from her face. "Thank you," she said.

Katiya stayed with Anatole late into the night. Every so often, between short naps, Jeniya would check on them. When she saw her sister dozing with her head awkwardly thrust backward, she shook her and said, "Katiya darling, why don't you go to your room and get some sleep. I will stay here with him." Katiya nodded in a daze and Jeniya helped her to the room to lie down. Immediately she slept, overcome with emotional exhaustion and heartache.

The great ballroom once bright with sparkling chandeliers was now lit by a lonely lamp at the nurse's station. Suffering and pain had replaced laughter and rhythmic snoring and heavy breathing had replaced the gay waltzes. A month ago victory was proclaimed in this room with pageantry and pomp. Now an eerie darkness and a morbid presence hung over the great hall. Jeniya wondered if the beautiful palace would ever see happy days again. She thought of the time when Anatole escorted her to her first ball and she said "I will always remember this night. Suddenly, a gurgling moan pierced the darkness and sent a chill through her bones; her first experience with death as it began to strike the living in the pre-dawn hours when the victim was least prepared to struggle for life. She fearfully gazed at Anatole for a long time, wondering and hoping, waiting. She drew closer and detected movement in his solemn face. He opened his eyes and immediately recognized her.

"Tolya!" she exclaimed smiling and took his hand to comfort him. "You are going to be all right!"

He clasped her hand to his breast and smiled, "Jenka?"

She nodded. "Katiya has been sitting here beside you since you arrived. I will get her," she said pulling her hand from his and rising from her chair.

"No," he responded in a weak voice, "You stay."

"But?"

"Please...stay here with me." He gripped her hand tighter. She was happy to see he still had strength in his body and that was a good sign.

She sat back down and looked into his eyes waiting for him to say something more. He stared at her with the mournful yearning and questioning eyes as one stares when he is about to pass from this world. They gazed at each other for a long moment in silence and tears began to well up in Jeniya's eyes. Then he turned his face away and said, "before I went to battle I had a terrible premonition that it would not go well and I was afraid. That night, I laid awake unable to sleep until finally I drifted off into a dream and heard a great chorus. The melody was so intensely beautiful I wished I could remember it so I could hear it again in my memory. Then I saw a magnificent land shimmering in iridescent colors, like the sky when the sun sets over the Neva. I got up from my bed and went towards a great procession, so great in number, I could not count them, moving toward a great light, singing praises to God. They were dressed in garments of jewel-like colors more brilliant than the jeweled garments worn by our bishops. I heard the angel voices singing with them and I was drawn like a magnet to join the procession when I saw the cross of our savior barring the entrance." He gazed back into her eyes and saw his pain.

"The cross is the symbol of suffering and resurrection. It must mean that God has sent you back from this trial to live out your life. You will not die yet!"

"No, I am letting go of all that is my life, like sand slipping through my fingers. I must let it all go."

"But you can't let go. You have Katiya and your daughter, Irina."

He did not respond but looked away, his dark browns knitted in intense pain. Pain from what, she wondered, pain that he suffered in his broken body, pain from losing his men in battle, fear that he would not return home to his family or…that he did not want to. "I will get Katiya," she said wiping the tears falling from her cheeks with the sleeve of her free arm.

He gripped her hand tighter. "No," he said. "Please stay a little longer. You will take care of them for me. He gazed again into her eyes with the familiar softness she had remembered. "I was just thinking of the happy times we had at Belozerkovka, the times we laughed rowing on the lake to the island, the wild raspberry picking, the long boat cruises on the river at night under the sliver of a moon. The stars shone so brilliantly we could almost reach up and touch them. We were so happy and carefree then." He smiled. "I used to follow you around everywhere, remember?"

Jeniya nodded unable to hold back her tears. "I remember." Her emotions were in a jumble, guilt that he wanted to spend his last conscious hours with her and not with his wife, hurt that he did not find the happiness he so deserved.

"There will be happy, carefree days again for you, you will make it through this crisis, we all do. You'll see. Tolya?"

He smiled again and his grip began to weaken. He closed his eyes and whispered, "Yea, though I walk through the valley of death, I will fear no evil," and his voice began to drift off.

She replied anxiously, "Thou anointest my head with oil, my cup runneth over, surely goodness and mercy shall follow me all the days of my life. Tolya?"

He slipped back into the coma. She released her hand from his and ran to get Ekatrina.

"Katiya, Katiya! Wake up!" She shook her sister, dead as a stone. "Wake up. Katiya's eyes flew open in alarm. "What? Is Tolya all right?"

"Yes, but go at once."

Katiya jumped up and rushed out of the room. Jeniya knelt before the icon and made the sign of the cross over her breast. She prayed that God would heal Anatole's broken body and give him strength to go on and face life with his family, but defeatism was in his character. In the past few days she noticed this sentiment in many of the wounded who chose to see their future without hope. The fight seemed too difficult for them and they feared that to go on living would only bring more misfortunes. *Why is this fatalism so prevalent in our people? Was it because of the constant struggle to work the land through hostile winters and unforgiving summer droughts, or the routine drudgery in jobs that offered no future? But this was not the case with Anatole, his struggle was within himself, something no amount of encouragement could overcome.*

She thought of Tourgueniev's words; "We start out to climb to the sky. But no sooner are we off than we discover that the sky is a very long way up. Then our only thought is to tumble down as soon as possible, incidentally hurting ourselves as much as possible."

The next morning Aleksandra had entered the ward with her two eldest daughters to check on the operations of her hospital and offer a word of solace to the patients. Jeniya noticed that the men did not receive her good will in gratitude. When they saw their Empress dressed in the common grey nurse's uniform and a white apron with the insignia of the red cross sewn on the front, surprise and disappointment crossed their faces. The white kerchief tied around her head in the style of a nun diminished the beauty in her face and accentuated the austere German features and the narrow lips tightly pressed together, almost into an ill-tempered scorn. The men watched with anxious and fearful eyes as she moved about the room and their expression did not change even after she spoke with them.

Poor woman, Jeniya thought as she gazed into Aleksandra's melancholy blue eyes, no matter what she does she is not received by her people. Even in acts of kindness and mercy she fails to radiate genuine warmth and concern, no matter how sincere she may have been.

"Pretty lady," said a lad staring at Jeniya.

She smiled down at him.

"I have never seen the inside of a palace. Is it in order that the nobles may live in these great homes and eat fine dinners that we must toil in the factories and fight the wars?"

With the death of Anatole and the heavy losses of so many brave young fighting men in the elite regiments of the guards, Jeniya grew to despise the war and all those individuals who initiated it, whom she regarded as psychopaths, starting with the Kaiser. She wondered if any one of these madmen know why they were fighting? "Yes, of course they did. The French knew. They had to defend their land against the German invaders and they wanted Alsace Loraine back. The Serbs knew for the same reason. The Austrians who had lost their future Emperor could not think reasonably and the Hungarians were in their usual state of rage. England knew the Germans intended to expand their Empire across Europe from the Balkans to the Dardanelles and were threatening their colonial supremacy. The Turks were in it to re-conquer the nations they had lost and defend Constantinople. But what did Russia stand to gain?

To save their honor with France. To liberate Serbia? To gain back Constantinople, the ancient capital of Byzantium?"

She was not alone in her sentiment. With a lightening swing in mood for which the Slavic people are capable, their enthusiasm for victory had degenerated into pessimism and worse, into a romance with fatalism. The same words were heard in the drawings rooms and clubs, as among the *muzjikii* on the streets. "When will this dreadful war end. This war is way too long and way too terrible. We were told it would end by Christmas. Besides, we shall never beat the Germans. The French may be victorious but we Russians have lost in the game. Why in God's name let our finest fighting men go on to be massacred. Why not be done with it at once." They did not see a contradiction in their behavior but on the contrary, they found an argument to justify it and one notable statesmen came from retirement to champion their cause, Count Witte.

Chapter 41

SOMEONE ELSE HELD Witte's view. Ezra aka Samsky arrived in Petrograd on a mission. His objective was to incite riots against the industrialists and their war. The time was at hand with strife among the nation's leaders, the demoralization of the country from the great war, and peasant soldiers returning from the front, maimed and embittered. These events revived the hopes of the revolutionaries and injected new blood into their veins.

Ezra now had forty-four summers, an old man as far as the new crop of radical students were concerned. He, like Lenin, was a father of the movement and greatly respected for his knowledge and leadership and he wanted to do what he could to encourage this new breed of rebels. The Bolsheviks who had infiltrated the ranks of peasant soldiers, wanted revolution now to overthrow the whole system, but the Mensheviks who represented the voice of the workers, wanted a gradual socialist takeover. Ezra understood that these two factions had to unite in order to establish the new socialist regime and he wanted to contribute his part.

He had heard about the peasant from Siberia, who helped the poor and granted key bureaucratic appointments to those who found his favor. When he inquired where he could meet this man, everyone said, "just go to his flat, he never turns anyone away."

Inside the door at 64 Gorokhovaia street human bodies, emitting the heavy stench of body odor, pressed against each other and lined up the stairs to Rasputin's third floor flat. His apartment was besieged day and night by palace hunters, aspirants for titles, generals, officials, bishops, councilors of the empire, aides-de-camp, chamberlains, maids of honor, socialites, members of the duma as well as peasants and workers. Every sort of social intriguer who wanted to prey on the Emperor and his ministry tried to enlist Rasputin's support. Many tried to bribe him with money, which he took and distributed to the poor. In turn, he gave them notes of recommendation. After waiting ten minutes, gaping over and around the backs of heads to see if the line was moving, Ezra began to fidget. He looked at his watch. It was already getting late, he would have a better chance at Rasputin if he arrived early in the morning, that is, if people didn't sleep on the stairwells.

On his way down to Gorokhovaia street, he bumped into Manassievich Manuilov, a Jew who worked with him and father Gapon to instigate the march on Bloody Sunday. Ezra didn't know it at the time but both Manuilov and Gapon were double agents working with the Okhrana as well as with the revolutionaries. He only discovered it later when Gapon was murdered. Gapon believed that by working with the Okhrana, he could better serve the revolutionary cause. Some said the revolutionaries killed Gapon for betrayal, others believed Manuilov had murdered the priest because his double dealing began to compromise the Okhrana.

"Samsky?" he said. "How are you?" Manuilov never knew Ezra's real name.

Ezra stared at the stranger in an expensive tight-fitting frock-coat and slicked down oiled hair which made his head look like that of a black ant. The short man had grown chunkier, his countenance darker and he wore a sinister downturned mustache. But the stony countenance and the hard, sometimes frightening stare in his eyes which betrayed an evil genius, had not changed. "Manuilov?" he said.

Manuilov nodded. "So where have you been keeping yourself all this time?"

"Around." Ezra eyed Manuilov imagining himself in a new suit and slicked down oiled hair. "You're *lookin'* well these days," he said.

Manuilov puffed himself out drawing attention to his corpulent girth. "Life is good by me. So what have you been up to these days? Still working the unions?"

"*Nothin'* much." Ezra guarded his words, remembering that he was speaking to a treacherous man, a provocateur and peddler of crooked deals, an insider who sold favors to anyone for a price.

During the war with Japan in 1905, he was accredited for stealing the Japanese cryptographic cipher, an act for which Nicholas II decorated him with a metal of the Order of Saint Vladimir. This enabled the sly Manuilov to start on the road of power as a protégé of prince Meshchersky, a homosexual who groomed him to be a police spy. The prince sent his young apprentice to Paris to assist Rachkosky, the international head of Russian espionage, but he was soon dismissed for spying on Rachkovsky. The prince called Manuilov back to Russia to work under Plehve, head of the Okhrana, who directed him to spy on the minister of interior, Count Witte. Manuilov, a master schemer, first betrayed Witte to Plehve, then betrayed Plehve to Witte. His conspiracies and treacheries became so complicated that even his supervisors had difficulty in determining exactly who Maniulov was betraying at any particular time. "I am a vicious man," he once said. "I love money and I love life."

"Well." Manuilov offered his hand. "Good to see you again, Samsky."

When Ezra shook his hand he noticed the diamonds sparkling on his fingers. "By the way," he said. "Do you know a man called Rasputin?"

"I know him. Why? Do you want to meet him?"

"Yes."

"Have you been to his flat?"

Ezra nodded. "It was impossible," he said.

Manuilov made a slight nod in agreement and thought for a moment. "I could give you a note of recommendation…it might help…" He stared at Ezra with the sharp eye of an interrogator, perceiving the soul of another cunning, manipulating devil. "No," he said, reconsidering. "I have a better idea. A friend of mine gives a dinner party at his salon every Wednesday night. Rasputin will be there. I can get you an invitation."

A possible invitation into a Petrograd salon stunned Ezra. His imagination ran away with him and his face flushed with excitement. He took on a new persona for this occasion discarding his rumpled shirts for a frock-coat he found in the second hand shop, and colored his grey hair black making himself look younger in a freaky sort of way. On the eve of his debut into society, he dumped oil on his unruly mane, smoothed it down with his hand, and puffed himself up in the mirror. *Now, I can pass for a gentleman.* He would have loved to flaunt himself in front of his brother. He wondered if Daniel frequented the salons. He wondered if he had grey hair.

Ezra stood by the tall double entrance doors and awkwardly watched the guests file in. Men and women stood or sat in small groups conversing. Evidently they all knew one another. He felt conspicuous and wanted to leave but his curiosity held him back. He glanced around the room, planning his exit strategy, when a ravishingly beautiful young woman glided toward him wearing a long clinging white silk-satin sheath with a flowing train of black velvet.

"And who are you?" she asked in a soft compelling voice. Her intriguing almond shaped eyes moved over his face and body.

He stood taller, squared his broad shoulders, and put a grin on his tanned weathered face, something of an anomaly in a society of white faces who navigated the salons by night and slept by day. Subconsciously he ran a hand over his oiled dyed black hair and said, "I'm...ah...Ezra..."

"Ezra? What a lovely name."

He stared at her graceful form, paralyzed and out of his mind. Before she slipped away like an oriental queen through a cloud of sweet fragrance, he tried to speak, but instead, stood like a klutz and grinned.

He adjusted his annoying black cravat and looked around the large reception room absorbing every little detail. Paintings in ornate frames crawled up walls of gold patterned damask and long gold velvet curtains tied with scarlet cords fell from scalloped valences. A table was set with a lavish presentation of delicacies, the likes of which he had never seen; platters of smoked and salted fish, hot and cold appetizers, elaborately decorated salads, blini and caviar.

This aristocratic business ain't hard to take. He wondered why he wanted to work with the ragged radicals. He had completely lost sight of his motives now that he had it within his reach to climb the ladder of society and was beside himself; his mind racing with imaginations. He never dreamed he would eat caviar one day. He took a canapé, popped it into his mouth with one bite and grimaced. It had a raw fishy flavor, sort of like pond scum, a taste which didn't sit well on his pallet. A few dozen glasses of ice cold vodka sat at the end of the table. He belted one down. The fiery white liquid burned away the disagreeable taste. He wondered why everyone raved about caviar and decided to go for the little stuffed sausages instead.

Manuilov appeared by his side with his soft, diamond studded fingers wrapped around a goblet of brandy and greeted him. "Come," he said. "I would like you to meet our host and some of the guests." He introduced him to Burdukov, the Imperial master of the Tsar's stables at Tsarskoe Selo, Nikolai Radtig, the Tsar's trusted valet, Admiral Nilov, commander of the imperial yacht and aid-de-camp to the Emperor, Bielitzsky, director of police, General Voyeikov, his best informer, and one time crony of General Sukhomlinov, Andronikov, a high living crook who called himself Prince Andronikov and gathered intrigues at his own salon that he published in his gossip tabloid, and Aaron Simanovich, organizer of cabarets, brothels and gambling halls for the purpose of blackmail.

1905, when Rasputin had cured Simanovich's son of an uncontrollable facial twitch and a jerking motion of the hands and feet, he immediately saw in Rasputin an opportunity for advancement into the palace where he soon became jeweler to the Empress and the grand dames at court. He and Manasevich Maniulov gradually moved themselves into a close position with Rasputin where they could make high government appointments using him as their stooge. When the public learned that the court began to swarm with spies, cheats, thieves, and swindlers, they blamed the mad monk for being the power behind the throne.

All the cunning, underhanded geniuses were present at Manus's party to meet Rasputin, except for the old Admiral Nilov with twinkling blue eyes and a bushy handle-bar mustache which slashed a white line across his thin wrinkled face. Manus personally invited him because he had a loose tongue when fired up with wine. These shady characters had one end in mind, not revolution, but to seize power from a weak and impotent Emperor, make themselves rich and manipulate state policy through Rasputin's intimacy with Tsar and Tsaritsa. Ezra instinctively knew he was in good company and his brain worked wildly.

"Ignati Porfirievich," Manuilov said to the host of the Wednesday night gatherings. "I want to introduce you to Ezra Samsky. He works the Austrian front." He made that up to impress Manus.

Ezra didn't catch on at first. He wondered what Manuilov meant by working the Austrian front. He tried his best to twist the minds of the embittered soldiers against the regime, but that was not on the front.

With a pleasant smile, Manus scrutinized Ezra. "I want to talk to you later. Meanwhile, make yourself comfortable." He made a brisk gesture toward the buffet.

With a little investigation, Ezra discovered that Manus was an influential Jewish banker. He operated this salon to glean inside information from investment bankers and venture capitalists in order to manipulate the stock market. He also learned that Manus was a defender of the Imperial throne and cozied up to the champion of orthodox absolutism, the old homosexual Prince Mestchersky. Ezra's shrewd and cunning mind told him something did not fit together here. What he could not discover was that beneath the surface Manus and his banking colleague, Rubinshtein, maneuvered a far shadier operation of espionage, obtaining sensitive information from Rasputin and his contacts within the palace for which they rewarded Rasputin generously. These two bankers also manipulated Rasputin into recommending servile incompetents to Nicholas through Aleksandra.

Of all the puppet masters that revolved around Rasputin, Rubinshtein, was probably the darkest. Unscrupulous bankers and industrialists paid him to make deals in obtaining reinsurance contracts for managing their foreign risks, in order to pass on military secrets to Berlin by way of agents in Stockholm.

Rasputin entered the room and Manus snapped his attention toward the guest of honor. Everyone swirled and gushed around the *staretz*. There was no end to flatteries. Ezra stared at this man of medium build with a puffy face and grey pasty skin given to debauchery and drunkenness. He wore a white silk *rubashka* with blue embroidery, belted by a black satin sash trimmed with a gold braid, and wide black velvet trousers tucked into brand new top boots. He arrived in the company of two candidates chosen by Manuilov to be groomed for prime minister of the Empire, Sturmer and Protopopov. The latter being treated by Rasputin's buddy, the Tibetan quack, Badmaev, for sudden feelings of heightened imaginative excitement.

So this is the man about whom all Europe was talking, the man who held the Emperor and Empress in the grip of superstition. In spite of his initial repulsive physical appearance, he exuded an incredible personal magnetism and conducted himself as a man in possession of great power, albeit a strange, almost inhuman force. What impressed Ezra most was that no one who met him could escape this power, and it made him a dangerous being to all but the strongest of souls.

Ezra watched as everyone fawned around him, anxious for his attention, wanting to buy favors. He glanced around the room looking for Manuilov, hoping for an introduction when he saw Rasputin turn his attention on the famous gypsy singer, Nastia Polakova, who just entered the room. His eyes were barely detectable under the heavy low brows and watery pouches, but when he widened them to ogle the voluptuous woman, Ezra noticed a strange metallic expression. The *staretz* left the group of fawners and put his arm around Nastia, giving her a resounding kiss on the lips. She pulled away and grimaced.

Disappointed, Ezra headed back to the *zakusky* table. Food was always comforting. He ate a half dozen sausages and smoked salmon canapes with his fingers, and belted down another glass of vodka. The footman stood by with a jeweled box of cigars and cigarettes. He took a cigar, the servant lit it and he took a long drag. "Not bad," he said to himself examining the smooth body between his fingers pretending to be a gentleman. He went back into the drawing room and stood at the far end of the room. Two maids crept in and stood beside him in the shadows of the doors hoping to hear Rasputin speak.

"Enough of this war," said the guest of honor standing before the group. A footman filled his goblet with wine. "Enough bloodshed. It's time to end this slaughter. Isn't Germany our brother too? The lord said thou shalt love thine enemy as thine own brother."

Ezra glanced at Manus. He was fidgeting with the corners of his napkin. Ezra wondered what his game was and what he wanted to talk to him about.

"This war is an offense to God," continued Rasputin. "Russia entered this war against the will of God. Evil be to those who still refuse to believe it! There are too many dead and wounded…too many widows and orphans…I know of villages where everybody's in mourning… and what about those who come back! What are they like? Legless, armless, blind. When people suffer too much they get bad…they may even become dangerous." He paced in quick steps about the room, his eyes mercurial, avoiding contact with anyone, his hands moving in jumpy gestures.

"To hear the voice of God…it is necessary to listen humbly. But when men are strong they are puffed up with pride. They think themselves clever and despise the simple until one day the judgement of God falls upon them like a thunderclap!

But what do they care, the generals, about having *moujikii* killed. Does it prevent them from eating and drinking or getting rich...Alas!" He raised his voice and his hands. "The blood of the victims will not bespatter them alone, it will bespatter the Tsar himself for he is the father of the *moujikii*...I tell you, the vengeance of God will be terrible! For more than twenty years we shall harvest nothing but sorrow on Russian soil!"

Madam Golvenova, sister-in-law to the grand duke Paul Alexandrovich, sat in a chair near Ezra and repeatedly crossed herself, uttering mantras, "God help us. God help Russia."

"That is why the war must end," Rasputin said. "But papka constantly opposes this. Mamka won't hear of it either. Someone is giving them bad advice. But what does it matter, if I give the order, they'll have to do as I say." All I have to do to enforce my will is to bang my fist on the table," he said banging a clenched fist on the table with great force." The tableware jumped.

"But I haven't finished my work with them...Now, this is what's going to happen." Manus, Manuilov and the other dealers of treachery snapped their heads to attention and followed the staretz with their eyes. Manus snapped his fingers for the footman to fill Rasputin's glass with more madeira. Rasputin drank it up and rattled along. "Papka ordered me to make myself scarce...I reminded mamka that I need neither her nor the Emperor. If they abandon me to my enemies, it will not worry me. I'm quite able to cope with them...the demons themselves are helpless against me," he made a low growling laugh. "But I tell her that neither the Emperor nor you can do without me... If I am not there to protect you, your son will come to harm.

Mamka promised to send away all those chatterboxes at the Duma. They spend all their time slandering me, and that distresses mamka. But they won't do it much longer. I'll soon have the Duma dissolved and send its representatives packing, then they'll see where their gossiping has led them and they'll remember me. I'll have their necks...I'll send them to the front!" His cold eyes became frightening and his features dark and cragged like a madman possessed. "I can do it! All those who have found fault with Gregory Efimovich will come to a bad end." He emptied another glass of wine, and made a creepy grin at the gypsy singer.

"Mamka's been running things lately. Did you know? And the more she does, the better things will be. As for him...we'll come to his rescue and send him to Livadia for a rest. He'll be glad to go. He's worn out and needs a rest...down there...at Livadia...with his flowers. It's for the best. He'll be closer to God. He has enough sins on his conscience to atone for. A whole life of prayer wouldn't be enough to atone for this war." He stopped abruptly and went over to talk to the gypsy girl.

Madam Golvenova, whose husband holds an important post in the Ministry of the interior, was an ambitious woman addicted to intrigue. She leaned toward Ezra and said, "see that fine looking gentleman over there by the *staretz*? The one with the greying hair and neatly groomed goatee? His name is Boris Sturmer." She pointed to an older man with a proud head and empty stare wearing a curled up brush mustache. "Before long you will see great things from him. Then our country will be in the true path of safety. Boris Vladimirovich will be the first minister to her majesty the Empress."

"Did I hear you right?" Ezra said.

"Why yes. I said her majesty the Empress. You will see."

She gave Ezra her arm to escort her to one of the tables for supper and placed him next to a nun and sat on the other side. He groaned. The opportunity of his lifetime was not turning out as he expected. The nun told him her name was Akilina Laptinsky, and artfully grilled him as to his profession. She said that she only posed as a sister of mercy, but did not reveal that she coerced Rasputin into playing her well-planned game of passing military secrets to her revolutionary contacts working in the Empress' hospitals. However, Ezra began to suspect her angle because he detected the underlying meaning in her camouflaged language when she grilled him. It appeared the deck may be falling in his favor after all. They artfully danced around one another.

The ravishing woman in white silk-satin was staring at Ezra from across the room and he asked Akilina if she knew the woman's name.

"She goes by the name of madam O," said Akilina. "That's all I know about her."

The *offeeshyat* served a borsht of mushrooms in wine sauce and pirogues.

Astonished, Ezra watched Rasputin pick up his bowl and slurp down the liquid like the hound that he was, dripping red juice on the white table cloth. He lifted his wine goblet and the servant immediately filled his glass with more madeira wine.

"Everybody who comes to me wants something," he said chewing his pirogue. He looked at Ezra with a disturbing all-knowing gaze that caused him to flinch. "Do this for me, do that for me. And how do you fulfill all these requests? I send them to see a minister or some other influential person with a personal note…sometimes I send them directly to Tsarskoe Selo. Every one of them, without exception is afraid of me…they all owe their positions to me!"

The *offeeshyat* came in, picked up the empty dishes, and placed the *staretz*' favorite meal in front of him, a platter with chunks of sturgeon baked in cabbage, and refilled his glass with madeira wine. Roasted venison, cauliflower, peas, roasted potatoes, mimosa salad, and grilled middle-eastern style lamb on skewers rounded out the menu. A musician entertained the guests by playing popular folk tunes on the balalaika.

Rasputin grabbed the food on his plate with long talon like fingers; his nails bitten and pushed it into his mouth worse than an uncivilized savage without regard for the people who sat at his table. The sauce from the sturgeon slid off his fingers and into his beard. He washed everything down with glass after glass of wine. But no one seemed offended or even shocked except Ezra who stared in disbelief.

"How do you propose to get the Tsar to leave Petersburg," asked Manus.

"That's easy," he said wiping his mouth with the sleeve of his white silk *rubashka*. He stood up and swung his long arms around like an ape, showing everyone his new embroidered shirt. "The old girl made this for me, I can do anything I like with her. As for the Tsar, I am the minister of his soul."

Rasputin mystified Ezra, a bundle of contradictions surrounded by enigmas. His tone changed from one moment to the other, jumping from one subject to another, sometimes coherent and profound, and other times, disjointed and rambling. This ignorant peasant who had risen to the pinnacle of power seemed to have confidence in his extraordinary mystical abilities. How could he not, when those he claimed to have healed gave proof after the fact and the Empress trusted him with unhesitating obedience. Was he a crazy man or a twisted genius? Whatever the reason, Ezra could see he was a dangerous man. However, he was not concerned for the Russian throne but happy that the rebels had a powerful, albeit an unwitting ally in the palace.

Rasputin rambled on, emptying glass after glass of wine and Ezra marveled at his capacity for drink. The alcohol just made him more garrulous, and he gave away plenty of information to whom Ezra now suspected were spies in his entourage. Why else would these powerful men who lurk in the shadows of the throne fawn over an obscene peasant magic man. As the picture became clearer, Ezra suspected that Rasputin may have given much of his information more or less deliberately. He remembered reading in a recent headline about lord Kitchener's ship being blown up by the Germans on route to Russia. The British envoy was on his way to convince the Tsar that Rasputin needed to be banished and to stop the Empress from interfering with state affairs. Ezra had no doubt that this story was sent off to Berlin by someone in the Rasputin gang who wanted to keep the deranged Empress in the power of the holy man.

As the wine loosened Rasputin's tongue, words spilled over like a torrent. "I am hunted like an animal by those who want to destroy me because I stand in their way."

"How do you intend to use your power to convince the Emperor to retire to Livadia?" Manus persisted.

"That's easy. I will tell mamka and papka that the Grand Duke Nicholas is conspiring to dispose of him and take over his throne. Then mamka will tell him to get rid of the grand duke and go to Stavka and take charge of his own armies. Papka is not happy to be Tsar…but he will be happy in Livadia with his flowers. We'll keep him happy with some soothing tea. Hashish and henbane…maybe mix in a little pot. Then we will put the tsarevich on the throne and mamma will be his regent. She will listen to me. I have the old lady eating out of the palm of my hand."

Ezra couldn't believe his ears, hearing Rasputin's cavalier attitude towards their majesties, when they trusted him with their most confidential affairs. Without blinking an eye of offense, madam Golvenova leaned toward Ezra and said, "see. I told you. She will one day sit on the throne."

Ezra smiled. "Doesn't it bother you that the *staretz* calls the Empress mamka…or the old lady'?"

"Oh no. Why he calls her that to her face. It makes her feel like a mother to all the Russian *moujikii*."

With sardonic effrontery Rasputin went on to brag about his amorous conquests, explaining how he takes his devotees into his bedroom to have his way with them while his other guests drink tea and listen to their moans of pleasure.

"Yes! And this is how I proceed. I take all the ladies to the public baths and seduce them in the cubicles. I just say, undress now and wash the *moujik*. If they put on airs, I have a good way of convincing them and they soon swallow their pride." He demonstrated his stories with vulgar gyrations.

"Every one of them is a mountain of pride and it's pride that breeds sin. The women are worse than the men. If you wish to please God, you must stifle any feelings of pride."

His disgusting descriptions and crude drunken mannerisms did not concern the guests, not even the women who were present. They did not avert their eyes in shock or make a face of disapproval. Even the most vulgar stories did not bring a blush to the women's cheeks, rather, they found him amusing.

"That's the way the aristocrats should be treated. They are filled with envy because a *moujik* in clumsy boots entered the halls of the palace and trod its marble floors. I make no attempt to make myself look other than a peasant. Mamka and papka call me the voice of the Russian soil…it's the will of God, they say…and so it is. God has given me this power.

After dinner, the party's electric mood began to slacken. At last Ezra had his chance to introduce himself to the powerful, drunken holy man. At the moment he arose from the table five gypsy girls began to dance and sing lively ballads. Nastia Polakova stepped up and sang "Ochii Chorniya". This aroused the *moujik*. His beady eyes grew brighter with delight, his puffy face paler and his wrinkles deeper. He jumped up and whirled around the room, stomping like an ape to the beat of the music. He took a half empty glass of vodka, waved the glass in the air and said to the gypsy girls, "a toast to Russian women."

Before the beautiful Nastia finished her ballad, he clutched at her ample bosom and attempted to slobber her lips with wet drunken kisses. She threw him off like a filthy rag. Rasputin staggered backward bumping into the table, clattering dishes, and cursing her with obscenities. "You arrogant bitch. It's the devil who owns you." He swept his hands through the air like a wild man. "One day, the devil will leave you and you will fall flat like an old shirt thrown on a dunghill."

When the mad monk had his fill of food and drink, he left in his usual manner before any of the other guests.

Ezra looked around for madam O, but she too had disappeared along with some of the others. He didn't see anyone leave or say goodby. He marveled at Manus' untiring energy enduring deep into the night, even after everyone had obliterated themselves with drink. He wondered what Manus wanted to talk to him about.

Chapter 42

DANIEL PAUSED AT the field of mars to watch the new recruits marching in review before their officers who were mounted on horseback. A yellowish haze hung in the misty atmosphere and shed a peculiar morbid gloom over a pitiful sight. One thousand men leaving for the front to be slaughtered and not a rife among them. His son, Alexei, would soon receive a commission when he graduates next spring from the military academy, and this tore at his heart. He ordered his chauffeur to drive him to the English club where he could unwind and relax with a drink. The red and gold lounge decorated with portraits of the Tsars was a popular meeting place for government intriguers and policy makers.

A downcast sentiment prevailed over the members, some sitting at tables talking in low voices making weary gestures, some in comfortable chairs quietly reading, others playing cards, chess or billiards. Several months ago, these same men were jubilant looking forward to a victorious war. Now the defeat of the Russian infantry has turned their enthusiasm into gloom.

Old Prince Karlovsky sat alone gazing at a fire dancing in the fireplace, puffing on a cigar and nursing a brandy; his grey eyes gazing off into another world and maybe another time. His cane rested over one arm of his chair. He was once a dynamic force in the political world but had now confined himself to the pleasures and trivialities of the social world. From his vacuous stare, Daniel perceived that neither pleasure nor triviality was on his mind this afternoon.

"May I join you Prince Kalovsky?" Daniel said.

The old man turned, sat upright and smiled beneath his drooping mustache reaching just above his chin. "Please do," he said. "Like to have you Daniel Nathanievich. Please sit down."

A footman came with a tray of drinks. Daniel took a Remy Martin Louis XIII. Prince Militsyn taught him the elegant life-style and how to choose fine brandy, wine and cigars.

"No good deluding ourselves," said the old prince. Things are going badly...the Grand Duke is incompetent...the battle of Tannenburg... Lotz...madness... disaster...our losses more than a million...we shall never get the better of the Germans again...we must begin to think of peace." He cleared his voice and took a sip of brandy.

Daniel nodded in agreement, thinking again of Alexei and the young men he saw drilling without guns. "If only it were possible," he said with a sinking heart. "But the Emperor has sworn on the Holy Gospel and the ikon of Our Lady of Kazan that he will never sign a peace treaty so long as there is one single enemy soldier on Russian soil."

Prince Karlovsky leaned in, his intelligent eyes penetrated into Daniels perceiving his melancholy and said in a hushed voice, "Oh! The Emperor...the Emperor. At the moment the Emperor is very angry with Germany, but he'll soon realize that he is leading Russia into destruction. He'll be made to realize it! I can hear that low hound Rasputin telling him now, 'Well, how much longer are you going to spill the blood of your people? Don't you see that God is abandoning you?"

Daniel shook his head. "I believe he would rather face death and bring us all down with him rather than break his oath."

The prince drifted off in thought for a few moments and said with sadness in his eyes. "That reminds me of something that happened not so long ago. I had attended a mass with his majesty when he told me something that sent chills down my spine. He said he had given much thought and prayer to the matter of taking supreme command of the armies. 'Perhaps a scapegoat is needed to save Russia. I mean to be the victim. May the will of God be done.' He had an expression of utter resignation on his pale face."

"What? Him take command of the armies? Soon we'll have the Empress and her camarilla commanding at General Headquarters."

"My greatest fear is that if our military fortunes do not improve, the Emperor will find an excuse to slacken his efforts in submission to divine will and resign himself to any and every catastrophe. This idea of predestination to sacrifice is only too consistent with his passive nature. God has entrusted him with the lives of one hundred and sixty million men, women and children. He should move heaven and hell to assure their happiness and save them from the unnecessary suffering of this war."

"I couldn't help but over hear your conversation," said professor Miliukov, a staunch supporter of the war effort. The popular leader of the liberal party in the Duma leaned beside the fireplace with a glass of wine in his hand and stared down at them through a pince-nez. When he lectured in America at the university of Chicago and the Lowell Institute in Boston, people sometimes mistook him for Theodor Roosevelt. "To end the war and yield to Germany would be unthinkable, not to mention treason to our allies and to the few million men who spilled their blood on foreign soil to defeat the enemy." The footman came by with a tray of drinks. Daniel and the prince each took another brandy.

"Pavel Nikolayevich," said Karlovsky turning to look Miliukov in the eye. "Our soldiers go to battle without guns...like animals led to the slaughter...the poor devils sit for weeks at a time in stinking trenches under showers of shrapnel...watching their comrades fall before their very eyes so they can pick up their guns. They do not know what positions they hold or even what is expected of them. They've had enough fighting and war...they do not understand it. I have been told they have become so completely indifferent that when German planes circled over them not one so much as raises his head. How long can men survive such a fiery trial if this war continues? These massacres are perfectly ghastly."

"The military situation bad though it may be, is anything but desperate," said Miliukov.

"Mind if I join you Pavel Nikolayevich; Prince Karlovsky? Nice to see you Daniel Nathanovich."

Daniel looked up at the tall erect figure of his old mentor, Count Witte.

"It would be our honor," said Daniel. The elderly statesman sat down and immediately a footman appeared with refreshments.

Witte did not excel in pleasantries. With his proud head held high, his speech firm, and his eyes fixed in the usual singleness of purpose, he got right to the heart of his business, speaking slowly in his unique, precise manner.

"This war is madness," he said. "It has been forced on the Tsar's prudence by his stupid and short-sighted council and can only have disastrous results for Russia. I am more alarmed every day at the abyss into which the Anglo-French alliance is driving us. I am utterly downhearted."

"Russia stands to profit from this war if there is a victory," said Miliukov.

"All right, let's talk about the profits and rewards a victory would bring us. An increase of territory. Great Heavens. Isn't his Majesty's empire big enough already? Haven't we enormous areas which stretch from Siberia to the Caucasus? Then what are the conquest they dangle before our eyes? East Prussia? Hasn't the Emperor too many Germans among his subjects already? Galicia? It's full of Jews."

Daniel flinched, but Witte took no notice. He wondered if his old mentor was ever aware that he was Jewish.

"Prussia's Polish territories? The moment Poland is united she will want absolute independence. What else have we to hope for? Constantinople, Santa Sophia once again with the cross on its dome, the Bosphorus, the Dardanelles? It's too mad a notion to be worth a moment's consideration...and even if we assume complete victory and reduce the Hohenzollerns and Hapsburgs into begging for peace and submitting to our terms, it would not only mean the end of German domination but the proclamation of republics throughout central Europe and the simultaneous end of Tsarism, only France and England can hope to derive any benefit from victory. And anyhow, a victory for us seems to me highly questionable. Russia is at the end of its rope and Tsarism is on the point of perishing. I prefer to remain silent as to what we may expect on the hypothesis of our defeat."

"Then what practical conclusion do you come to?" said Miliukov

"My practical conclusion is that we must liquidate this stupid adventure as soon as possible. History shows that Russia is never so strong as at the beginning of a war. Now, look at the tragic position we're in. We cannot make peace without dishonoring ourselves and yet if we continue the war we are inevitably heading straight for a catastrophe."

"You astonish me," said Miliukov. "That a seasoned statesman with your intelligence and experience would suggest a liquidation of this conflict. Can't you see that a compromise for peace would mean victory for Germany?"

Looking incredulous, Witte said, "so we've got to go on fighting? We shall require months and months to strengthen our armies and complete our artillery supply. Within weeks the Germans with the help of their railways will return and attack us with new army's superior in numbers and provided with all the munition they require. And this time they will finish us off. That's what the Emperor and his minister have to realize if they are capable of realizing anything. If we do not make peace at once we shall soon be on our way to revolution."

"In my opinion?" said Daniel. "The ship had already gone over the falls."

Witte shrugged his large shoulders. A footman immediately appeared to offer the men cigarettes and cigars.

"Enough of these trifles. I must take my leave." He rose from his chair and awkwardly straightened himself in the manner of a large elderly man. "Nice to see you again, Daniel Nathanovich...Pavel Nikolayevich, Prince Karlovsky," he said towering over them.

"A man, lesser beings love to hate," Miliukov said watching him drop money into the cash box for the poor. "As always, there is much foresight in what he says. Perhaps this war is descending into stupidity...or is it treason?" The men puffed on their cigars and gazed absently at the members of the club.

"I believe the days of Tsarism are numbered." Daniel said reflectively as a cloud of smoke dissipated between them. "Revolution is inevitable. For the first time in modern history, we are witnessing an unparalleled spectacle of revolution being engineered not from below, not by the citizens against their government, but by the government against its own citizens. Their criminal actions and pernicious lies to conceal their atrocities; their arrogant indifference to the voices of the people will eventually force the masses to revolt. This disaster coming on our country will be purely the product of their own efforts. No doubt it will be the intellectuals who give the signal for the revolution, thinking that they're saving Russia. But from there it shall descend into a working class revolution, and soon after to a peasant revolution...and then anarchy."

"Then Russia is lost," said Prince Karlovsky. "All hope is gone."

"You stand to make a fortune on this war? No?" Miliukov said to Daniel.

Suddenly a giant explosion, like the sound of a hundred cannons, rattled the windows of the building and quivered the chandeliers. In a flash, men scattered to find shelter thinking the Germans had bombed the city. Outside, a huge cloud of purple smoke rose from the industrial district.

"Daniel," said Miliukov looking eastward. "Isn't that in the direction of your munitions plant?"

Daniel's heart pounded wildly at the confirmation of what he instinctively feared. He ran downstairs and ordered his chauffeur to get the car and race him to the plant. Flames of the conflagration, enlarging by the minute, illuminated the horizon. Less violent explosions followed consuming nearby apartment buildings and warehouses. His powder plant had been sabotaged. Badly needed explosives, cartridges, propellants, fuses and grenades, all sabotaged.

At the scene he went into shock and watched like a dazed spectator viewing a surreal movie. People were running hysterically in the streets, screaming, carrying the wounded from burning buildings. The rotten smell of sulfur engulfed the vicinity. When he regained his senses, his first thought was casualties. *"My God, I am responsible for the lives of how many people?"* The plant had already shut down for the day but there were the night watchmen and those who stayed on to work overtime.

He fell to his knees, bowed his head in the palm of his hand, and wept. "Oh, God. God help us!" He cried out.

He did not take dinner that evening, nor greet his family but went straight to his room, knelt down and cried out to God. The tragedy in human life and suffering was too much for him to bear.

Jeniya ran upstairs and knocked on the door, but he did not answer. She knew that a munitions plant had been blow-up and now she knew it was Daniel's. She sat by a table outside their room and wept for him. Later when she went in to try and comfort her husband, she found him lying in bed fully clothed staring towards the tall windows with the eyes of a dead man. She laid down next to him, put her arm around him, and rested her head on the back of his shoulder. He took her hand in his and held it tightly.

Professor Miliukov's comment had plagued his thoughts. "You stand to make lots of money from this war." Money. Money for suffering, money for lives, money for blood!

The following day, news of the explosion screamed across the headlines of every newspaper in the city and spread consternation into the heart of every inhabitant. People did not consider a rational cause for this disaster. They worried that an evil omen hung over the city and called it a bad sign from God. The practical left wing publishers, however, seized the opportunity to use the tragedy to spread their propaganda against the industrialists and the Imperial ministers.

Telephone calls from friends and well-meaning acquaintances offering condolences as well as reporters bombarded Daniel and his family.

"Pull those telephone receivers off the hook," he ordered the butler, Yaroslav. He also ordered the servants to keep everyone away except his wife.

The following day, Jeniya slipped quietly into the dining room and said, "Good morning in almost a whisper. Daniel stood by the window gazing at the lumber barges slowly moving up the canal, drinking a cup of coffee. Yaroslav kept watch in his acquired expressionless manner, wearing a black jacket, starched white shirt and white gloves. Daniel did not care for this kind of formal livery but Jeniya insisted on keeping the family tradition alive for her children.

As soon as Jeniya sat down at the table, Yaroslav advanced to pour her coffee. In the intense silence, she felt the heaviness in his spirit.

Daniel knew she needed an explanation and said, "I am ruined... my workers are homeless and I feel responsible for their welfare."

When she saw the deep pain in his expression, she said, "I'm sorry. I don't know what to say. I wish I could do something...think of something...to help you."

"There is nothing you can do. Right now I've got to go to the site and assess the situation. Find out how many died...how many families are without a father or mother. They will need compensation right away." He gazed at her for a few moments and went to the table, wrapped his arms around her shoulders and hugged her tightly. "I love you. And I'm sorry for being so abrupt this morning, but I have a lot on my mind." He kissed her on the forehead.

Dozens were wounded and several had been killed. It didn't take long for the police to find a scapegoat.

When he heard that the perpetrator had been caught, he immediately thought...*Ezra*. But why Ezra? Aren't there many Ezras working with the German underground? He hadn't seen his brother in nine years, since his father died. But he could smell Ezra. He had heard that his brother was back in Petrograd and had hooked up with a pack of notorious double dealing German agents. *So that rotten snake was slithering around in Petrograd.* He had expected to see him show up again sooner or later, but never in this way.

The perpetrator, whoever he was, had specifically chosen the Mendelev plant to execute his dastardly attack. Who knew the workmen and the night watchmen? Ezra. Who else could have slipped in like a roach, but Ezra. It was a simple matter for him to get an infernal machine concealed into the powder factory and deprive the Russian army of the munitions they so desperately needed to carry out their assault against the German armies and ruin his brother, all in one blow.

On his way to work, Daniel picked up a copy of the Volga, a sounding platform for the government, to see if they had identified the terrorist, when he read this inflammatory headline. "No pardon for the Jew!"

"People of Russia, look around and see who is our real enemy. The Jew! From generation to generation this race, the accursed of God, has been hated and despised by all. The blood of the sons of Holy Russia, which they betray every day, cries aloud for vengeance."

It cited a letter written by the Grand Duke Nicholas Nickolaevich that stated. "Our experience has clearly revealed the hostile attitude of the Jewish population. As soon as some substantial change in the locations and movement of our troops occurs, and whenever we temporarily evacuate one district, the enemy because of the intervention of Jews, adopts cruel measures against the loyal non-Jewish population. In order to protect our population and safeguard our troops against the treason which the Jew employs along the front, the supreme commander of the Russian armed forces considers it necessary that Jews be banished as soon as the enemy retreats. It is necessary to take hostages from among the rich and other persons holding important positions and deport them as prisoners to the interior of our country and to the province of Kiev where they are to be held in concentration camps."

Daniel felt a burning anger when he read these words, and he became anxious for his sister, Rochelle. He knew these stories were invented to turn the wrath of the public away from the Emperor's appointments of incompetent generals and the "German Woman" Aleksandra Feodorovna whom they accused of running the government with her lover, Rasputin.

Despite the warning of a massive German-Austrian artillery building on the western front, Stavka persisted in its determination to remain on the offensive sending even more untrained *moujiks* into battle without rifles. They were told only to fire when necessary and then take the guns and ammunition from the men after they had been killed or wounded.

"Our army is drowning in blood," General Beliaev had announced to the War Industrial Council. We have no ammunition. One thousand men are leaving for the front without rifles. Mackensen's brutal artillery assaults are churning our untrained raw recruits into gruel and are literally plowing up the battlefields with metal and shrapnel, leveling our trenches and burying our defenders in the process. Others lay gun-shot and screaming impaled upon barbed wire in no man's land. Whole regiments have been reduced to meager skeletons. They now number less than companies to face another onslaught of German fire. The Germans use up metal and we use up human life. We cannot train men in time to stop the German advance from taking our fortresses in Poland and Belarus. I've pleaded with France for guns and ammunition but they refuse saying they need everyone they can get."

Masses of Russia's peasant soldiers began to defect or surrender at the height of battle, preferring to sit in enemy prison camps rather than return to the filthy rain soaked trenches, stinking like putrid open sewers with the unbearable stench of the rotting human and animal flesh. They had grown tired of fighting for an Emperor who gave them nothing in return. For them, life at the front was all death and no glory. They had lost all hope of victory and they had nothing to fight for. An unimaginable two and a half million men were killed, wounded or taken prisoner.

"Our soldiers are treacherously deprived of shells," said general Denikin. "Either by traitors, ministers, generals, or spies selling our strategic operations."

The commanding officers felt they could not afford to go on fighting and began to retreat from Poland and Western Russia. They believed the German forces were invincible and were forming another pincer movement to trap the remainder of their troops on the northern front.

In the rapid mass retreat, the Russian army burned everything that might be of use to the Germans. Terrified people were driven from their homes by drunken Kazaks wheedling their long multi-pronged *nagaikas*. In horror, villagers watched their houses and stores of food go up in flames. Tens of thousands of peasants and Jews alike were forced to trek like beasts along rutted dirt roads with their children and elderly, toting only what they could carry in a bundle tied up in a sheet slung over their backs. Some families piled their meager worldly goods in one or two carts tied together and drawn by one broken down plow-horse. They trudged along railroad tracks watching as trains sped past them loaded with couches and chairs from officer's clubs, and junk belonging to the mistresses of senior officers, even the quarter master's bird cages filled with canaries. Many fell ill and died from an outbreak of typhus and cholera as well as from starvation. These evacuees were not told of their destination nor where they could find food and rest because the authorities didn't know.

When Daniel heard commanders returning from the front declare that they could not compare this spectacle of human horror to any catastrophe they had witnessed on the bloody battlefields, he knew he had no time to waste in getting to Rochelle, if she was still alive.

Chapter 43

THE MORNING LIGHT shed flickering patterns of sunshine and shadows over the table as the train rhythmically clacked across the wetlands and marshy grasses that surrounded Petrograd. Daniel sat on a cushioned arm chair in his private coach sipping fresh brewed coffee reading the latest news concerning the explosion. The establishment had pointed the finger at Miassoyedov who had served under the minister of war, General Sukhomlinov by spying on the officer's corps. His past record of espionage made it easy to accuse him of colluding with German agents.

The corpulent Sukhomlinov's duplicitous dealings with the army led to his dismissal, but with the recommendation of his friend Rasputin, he managed to squeeze out of his crimes by appealing to the Emperor and blaming all the army's disasters on the Supreme Commander Grand Duke Nicholas Nikolaeivich. When the Emperor could no longer shield Sukhomlinov from his crimes, the general was arrested, placed under high command for investigation, and incarcerated in the fortress of Peter and Paul. Miassoyedov was found guilty and sentenced to execution.

The Grand Duke's military blunders were music to Aleksandra's ears. She despised him because of his great popularity with the army as well as with the people, and she now had the perfect opportunity to dispose of him.

"It seems to me, sir, that the Empress is predestined to ruin Russia," said Savva placing a basket of warm rolls and an assortment of apricot and raspberry jams on the table.

"How so?"

"She has demanded that the Emperor send the grand duke Nicholas Nikolaevich packing to the Caucasus after she learned he wanted to send her to Siberia and lock her up in a nunnery."

"Where did you hear that?"

"Everyone is talking, sir. They say she wants the Emperor to take his place as supreme commander of his armies. She tells him it is his divine duty. Personally," he said with a chuckle. "If I were him, I think I would do it just to get away from her constant brow beating. Why, she even forbids the Emperor to consult with the Duma, says God will not forgive him for failing to execute his divine duty on earth as Tsar Autocrat.

"If what you say is true, it may be good for the Emperor's ego but bad for the country. If she and Rasputin are left alone in the Palace, they will soon be the sole rulers of Russia."

"God forbid, sir. Before long they will be meddling in the Emperor's affairs at Stavka...will that be all, sir?"

"Da, *spaseeba*." Daniel buttered his roll, spooned some apricot jam over it and idly gazed out the window. The news that the saboteur had been executed, did not relieve him, not as long as Ezra was still on the loose somewhere in Petrograd. At the moment, these matters did not concern him. He had to reach Rochelle, living or dead, he had to know.

Little villages clustered around onion domed churches and separated by vast distances, began to pop up here and there. Funny thing, he reminisced, how far he had come from the days when he sat on hard wooden benches packed like a sardine with several other people in a rickety old third class compartment. He had great dreams then. He knew exactly what he wanted...to succeed in the world outside the Pale. But now where was he going? The future looked bleak and without definition, as the Empire was sliding downward at an alarming rate into some kind of an impending disaster. The Emperor's fawning ministers were sinking to new depths of treachery and larceny daily.

The whole world was at war. Everyone had a sense of an apocalypse just ahead, but no one could pinpoint when, although everyone had his own idea of how. All the best ideas put forth by earnest and competent statesmen came to fruition. The prudent men of the Duma were helpless as the Emperor refused to let them take the reins of government. Even decent men, loyal to Tsar feared to contest his authority. To do so would be to stand against God's anointed. One man, one autocrat, one being ordained by God to rule his people, one intermediator between the divine and human was allowed to bring his nation into destruction. The Emperor's only strength was a stubborn will, but instead of using it to demand justice for his people, he yielded to the stronger will of the hopelessly deranged Empress who ordered the dismissal of capable men that dared to question Rasputin's council and in a seemingly unending carousel of appointments, replacing them with one of the holy charlatan's incoherent and dull-witted creatures. Even those with the white hairs of wisdom sat by and watched helplessly as every piece of sound advice to save the staggering Empire was refused by their sovereign.

The poor struggled to eat, building up hatred and bitterness toward anyone who flaunted wealth. The idle rich whirled around aimlessly like dried leaves in the wind, without direction, seeking every kind of pleasure but they could not satisfy their inner longings. Many had abandoned their lives to the anesthesia of drugs, alcohol and sexual exploitations. Others turned to the occult and looked to soothsayers for guidance. Everyone was clamoring for a piece of the Tsar's pie now that he was retreating into his own invisible world. In time, Nicholas became oblivious to everything, like a child seeking to dwell in a garden of delights shielded from all responsibility. He had already abdicated the throne in his mind and spirit to the rantings of his neurotic wife, it was only a question of time until he would be physically removed.

Except for a few loyal statesmen, the majority of officials played the game of power manipulation. Everyone had his hand in someone else's pocket. People longed for the days of tranquility before the war but felt helpless to stop the plunging momentum, as if some invisible force had bound them to a speeding meteorite. A voice would speak out here and there that Russia needed a strong leader, but no one was able to step up, except the fearless leaders of the radical left who had nothing to lose but their poverty. These men and women were bound to one another by an oath of dedication to the revolution, an oath to crush the old order and from its ashes build a new one, an oath to the death. Wickedness had run so deeply through the veins of the Empire that only a national repentance could save her.

"Would you like some lunch, sir?" said his valet popping Daniel's reverie.

"Yes, thank you." Daniel gazed out the window regaining awareness of his surroundings. The landscape had changed from marshland to white birch forests and wooden houses with hand carved window shutters. In the distance he saw a deep blue onion dome painted with white stars rendering a beautiful portrait of the Russian soul. In the morning he arrived in Moscow, the heart of Russia and the seat of the Russian Orthodox Church. From the Moskva River he could see the iconic bell tower of Ivan the Great rising above an ensemble of golden domed cathedrals inside the massive red walls of the Krasnaya Ploshchad, the ancient words for beautiful square, which had somehow evolved over the years to be called the Red Square.

He thought of the first time he saw the immense square expanding before him and he was awestruck. He surmised the whole town of Lensk would fit inside its dark red walls. He remembered an odyssey, whimsical and almost hallowed, that stood at the far end, in direct contrast to the heavy massive walls and towers. He had seen paintings of St Basil's Cathedral, but none of them could do justice to the beautiful frescos and magnificent spiral onion domes of many colors. In its strange way the magical cathedral belonged in the picture and he could understand why this was named the beautiful square.

On the overnight train to Kiev he drifted into a deep sleep that comes after emotional turmoil and awoke with a start when the train pulled into the station with a jerking halt. While he waited for his car to change trains, he saw a group of Kazaks playing a game of Russian roulette to amuse themselves. One placed a glass filled with vodka on his head while another aimed his pistol and fired live ammunition. The loud shot shook the train window. Daniel gasped. To his amazement, the soldier's head remained in tack but the bullet split the glass and vodka rolled down his face onto his tongue while the others stood by laughing and making sharp jesting whistles.

Daniel could not understand this brutality, not only to others but to themselves. He had heard somewhere that drunkenness among the Kazaks was a rite. As he traveled closer to the western border, another horrific spectacle spread out before him; hundreds of Jewish refugees, mothers with crying babes in their arms, children wandering in a daze, trudging along the railroad tracks. *Where were they going? Did they know?*

This heartbreaking sight made an indelible impression on his mind and he remembered his mother's wise council to always remember the poor. How far had he drifted into the world of the wealthy aristocrats, into the world of business and politics since God had blessed him with the desires of his heart. Miliukov's words crossed his mind. *You stand to make a fortune on this war. Money for blood.*

He decided to use his fortune and set up a foundation for the relief of Jewish war victims. Through his foundation he could work with communities to distributed funds, bread, salted meat, warm blankets and clothing to the poor house shelters.

Prince Militsyn had always supported him in all his endeavors. He was the past plenipotentiary of the Red Cross in Moscow and now served in aiding the Russian war prisoners. Nikolai Dimitrievich not only had the expertise but also the necessary connections to purchase food and clothing from Prince Lvov, president of the All-Russian Union of Zemstvo for the relief of sick and wounded soldiers. Daniel decided to ask him for help in establishing a network of aid throughout the Pale. He may not have been able to save the Empire but he had it within his power to make life a little easier for the victims of war.

That raised another question with which he had been wrestling since the explosion; whether to rebuild the munitions plant or turn the building into a mission for the poor families of Petrograd. His tendency was to lean toward the mission as he did not want to contribute any longer to morbid atrocities of war. However, the war would drag on just the same and depriving the infantry of its much needed guns and ammunition would only contribute to more bloodshed. War materials shipped from abroad couldn't begin to supply the shortage of weapons and the zemstvos municipalities were in support of the armies and wanted to cooperate with the manufactures. And as Jeniya suggested, it would put hundreds of skilled people back to work. He decided to build the mission where a large concentration of Petrograd's poor lived, in the mill working district of Vyborg.

The sabotaged munitions plant brought something else to mind, that worm, Ezra. Instead of forgiving him, the animosity only grew in his heart. He knew he had to do the right thing and forgive him but that was not easy. This hatred existed on both sides, as one brother continued to provoke the other.

Green hills, forests and lakes, little villages of thatched roofed houses began to appear between vast tracts of spring wheat as he neared his childhood home. Suddenly, the pleasant scenery transformed into a ghastly sight of revulsion. He shut his eyes to block out the horror and immediately, scenes of the pogrom flashed though his mind. Eiss, Mottel, the screams of women raped. He felt as though he was living again in a twisted, mad world. The pitiful scene of refugees he had just witnessed paled before the brutal savagery which appeared outside the windows of his car. Ropes were wrapped around telephone poles along the railroad tracks and at the end of each rope dangled a Jew by the neck, bloated, dark and hideous from the hot summer sun. Hundreds of Jewish soldiers were on the battlefields at this very moment, shedding their blood for the homeland. What homeland? When the wounded were discharged from hospitals they were told to return immediately to the Pale. And now this. When will the violence against his people end?

Daniel and Savva arrived late at night in Lensk, so they took a room in the local inn. The buildings around the square in the Jewish quarter were in various states of disrepair and the store had turned into a poorhouse and a soup kitchen, but there was little to serve except cabbage and potatoes boiled in water. He almost feared to go home as to what he might find.

In the morning, Ronnie came to the door. Her eyes lit up when she saw her brother but then she lowered her head in shame. Her dress was clean but patched, and hung on her like a bag on a twig and her sparkling dark eyes were dimmed as those which had seen too much pain.

Daniel lifted her chin with his hand. Tears rolled down her pale cheeks. He embraced her and held her tightly to his breast for a long time. He felt the bones in her thin shoulders.

"I'm sorry," she said. "I'm sorry I have not written but…"

"I have seen for myself." He held out his arms and caressed her with his eyes. "You are wearing one of the dresses I sent you!" he said to make her feel better.

"Yes," she forced a smile.

"I see you need some new ones."

She shyly lowered her eyes. "Please. Come in!"

Daniel introduced Ronnie to Savva and she smiled graciously at him. "Come in, she said. "Come in!" She ran to the cupboard to find something to serve them. "I have some bread here and there's cabbage and turnips in the garden."

Daniel smiled. "Ronnie, I want you to come home with me."

"Oh no, I couldn't barge in on you like that."

"This time I am ordering you to come with me!"

"But there is so much to do here, so many in need."

"Ronnie! Enough!" He shook his head, angry and smiling at the same time. *Stubborn, just like her mother thinking she has to be a slave to everyone. She even uses the same words!*

"Leave them your house. We are leaving on the afternoon train and I will not hear any more!"

She stared at him with a tear stained face.

"By the way, Ronnie. Have you seen Ezra lately?" Daniel asked

"No, he left for Petrograd some time ago. Leinha said he has a job working with someone called Manuilov? I forget."

Daniel was not surprised that his brother had sunk to that level of corruption, but that he had wormed his way into the company of those who had a dark hand in manipulating the government and selling military secrets. Now his suspicions about Ezra were confirmed. Miassoyedov was innocent of the crime.

Ronnie gathered a few treasured heirlooms together handed down from her mother, the silver candlesticks, the jewelry, and the little doll she had as a child. Even though she was very young she could still see the beautiful face of her mother smiling down at her when times were happy, before the first wave of pogroms. She looked around the house to see what else she could bring, her father's Torah and books of the prophets. Many things had already been sold for extra rubbles to support the household. Everything else reminded her of sadness. She had no regrets in leaving her childhood homestead.

They sat in silence for a while waiting for the train. Daniel wondered if she knew about the hangings along the railroad track. It was so heinous; he could not speak of it.

In some towns where it was necessary for the troops to evacuate the area," Ronnie said as if reading her brother's thoughts. "Germans have moved in and brutalized the peasants. For this, they accused us as enemy informers and traitors. At first we were all terrified, but now we have grown immune to it."

"How can anyone grow immune to it?" Daniel asked.

"A body can only take so much," she said.

In August of 1915, the Jews finally got compensation for their unspeakable suffering. As much as Daniel disliked Ignati Manus he had to commend him for one thing. Just when the army needed money most to continue its massive offensive on the German front, Manus led the Jewish bankers to withhold loans from the Russian government until they made concessions to the homeless Jews. This action forced the administration to abolish the Pale and allow the Jews to live anywhere they wanted in the Empire. But the government's amnesty came too late. The suffering and death inflicted on the Jewish population over the years would eventually lead to retribution. A retribution which for now would wait patiently in the shadows of the Empire.

Chapter 44

"You must end the time of great indulgence and gentleness." The meddling Aleksandra wrote to Nicholas in her mother language of English, "her soft-hearted child" who needed her guidance in commanding the armies at General Headquarters in Mogilev. "You are an Autocrat and they dare not forget it! All men must submit or else you must crush them all...Russia loves to feel the whip...it's in their nature...tender love and then the iron hand to punish and guide... my darling boysy, how I wish I could pour my blood into your veins!"

Alexei was about to graduate top in his class from the military academy with the rank of junior lieutenant. He met all the requirements for election to the elite Preobrazhensky guards; over six feet tall and a legacy through his maternal grandfather, Count Rostovsky. His parents were extremely proud of his academic achievement but not happy about committing their brilliant young son to serve under the command of Nicholas II.

Traditionally the Emperor always held his prized elite guards in reserve and only committed them to combat with the greatest reluctance under the direst circumstances of battle. However, this did little to ease their fears. The calamitous day when Nicholas sent the guards off to the front before he had completed mobilization still remained fresh in their memories. Especially since the needless death of Anatole leaving Ekatrina to manage on a meager soldier's government pension. Since then, she became increasingly reclusive and refused to share her circumstances with anyone in her family.

They had one small consolation, that Alexei would not be deployed immediately to the front but would train under the newly appointed Minister of War, General Polivanov. Polivanov had recruited over a million man fighting force and prepared them with intense discipline and a high degree of skill in marksmanship, both on the target range and in the field. He drilled them severely in the warfare, transforming them into a superior infantry. Once Stavka had accumulated a sufficient quantity of guns, the Russian army would be ready for a massive offensive against the Germans and Austrians.

But Daniel and Jeniya's hopes of a victorious Russian army soon vanished when Polivanov's retirement was announced. He had committed three unpardonable sins against the crown. He won the independent support of the Duma causing the Minister of the Court, the doddering old walrus, Count Fredricks, whose only claim to fame was that he was a noble nobody, to proclaim, "Polianov is a very intelligent and dangerous man because he is too much inclined to sympathize with parliament."

Secondly, Polianov called the grossly incompetent Minister of the Interior, Boris Sturmer, a favored being of the Empress, into account for his corrupt schemes. Strumer, a sixty-seven-year old debonair gentleman of fine carriage and frequent visitor to Aleksandra's notorious mauve boudoir, knew how to expedite his personal advancement by currying her favor with meaningless flatteries, while she battered him with useless instructions.

Sturmer was a creature of Manassievich Manuilov who maneuvered him into high office through Rasputin for which the evil provocateur was richly rewarded as Sturmer's personal chancellor. After Nicholas took on the supreme command of his armies, he gave Sturmer power over the Duma and his Council of Ministers.

Polianov's third and most egregious offense caused the wrath of the Empress to come down on his head when he offended her venerated holy man, Rasputin, for meddling in military affairs.

"Polivanov is simply treacherous," Aleksandra wrote to her husband at General Headquarters. "How I wish you could get rid of him. Lovy mine...don't dawdle...make up your mind...It's far too serious. Change him at once and cut the wings of the revolutionary party... only be quick about it. Hurry up, Sweetheart...you need Wify to be behind pushing you."

In his place, Nicholas appointed another weak-willed man like himself as Minister of War, General Dmitri Shuvaev. The Emperor's unreasonable decision in the dismissal of Polianov in favor of another incompetent, had all of Petrograd grieving calling it a disaster. The educated public, the allies and the statesmen all agreed that Polianov was the last defender of the Empire.

"Why that weak, mealy-mouthed, cowering little man," screamed an outraged Jeniya. "Can't decide anything without condescending to the demands of his neurotic, hysterical Empress." Her worst fears concerning the increasing insanity of her sovereigns and the treachery of their cohort Rasputin, seemed to be materializing. She worried constantly that Alexei may be trapped in the million man fighting force somewhere on the wastelands of Poland or on the border of Hungry.

The fruit of Polianov's hard work would be executed in the early summer of 1916 by his superbly trained army through General Brusilov's brilliant and daring offensive against the Austria armies despite the fact that Nicholas had appointed two spineless officers to serve under him. General Evert, who commanded the million-man army and controlled two-thirds of the artillery including great stores of heavy shells, desperately tried to avoid undergirding Brusilov's army. He feared the enormous German force building on the northwestern front along with great quantities of heavy artillery. The other genius, General Kuropatkin, had already determined that the offensive had no chance of success and refused to participate.

Brusilov remained alone and undaunted. In preparation for his attack he defied all odds and carefully thought out every possible advancement of the enemy's troops. He planned each move of his armies using a mock theater to train and instill confidence in his men.

On May 22nd, his courageous gunners opened fired on the Austrians. After two days the Russian eighth army totally obliterated the Austrian troops and occupied his first and second lines, leaving only shattered corpses behind. Within another week the victorious eighth army went on to assault Lutsk sending the Austrian defenders into flight. The seventh, ninth and eleventh armies annihilated what was left of their troops and left them with no hope for recovery. Brusilov's four armies captured 3,000 officers, 200,000 men, over 200 field guns and 645 machine guns. The Austrians greatest fear was that the Russians would continue on and capture Budapest, Hungary's capital city, and from there, march on to Austria' s capital, Vienna, less than 200 *versts* from Budapest. These victories alarmed the Germans. They feared this could decide the fate of the war.

The grizzly old battle veteran General Hindenburg stepped in and ordered the Austrians to relinquish the remnant of their armies into German high command. Then he gathered German forces scattered over the western theater to converge on the Austrian front to save their beleaguered ally and the war. Again, as in the opening stages of the war at Tannenburg, this mobilization would take time and Hindenburg had to play the odds that the two Generals, Evert and Kuropatkin, on whom Brusilov depended would not come to his aid and continue the offensive with fresh reinforcements.

Hindenburg's brave and risky hunch to finish the Russian army off turned out to be precise. Kuropatkin lamented that his 420,000 men were no match for the 192,000 Germans assembling on the northwestern front. Not to be out done by his comrade, Evert made every cowardly excuse for not entering combat. "Too many Germans massing on the Austrian front to secure a victory," he said. "I cannot attack on trinity Sunday, and the Pinsk marshes had not yet dried up." Instead of learning from Brusilov's example in separating the troops to pull off the element of surprise, Evert informed his commanding officer that he could only confine his armies to frontal blows.

Brusilov's exhausted army was forced to face German bombardment without reinforcements resulting in heavy losses of his best trained men. Furious, he demanded that Chief-of-staff, Alekseev, order Evert to attack. Now forced into battle, Evert, true to his word, turned his army into a massive nineteenth century battering ram to be decimated by relentless bombardments of German fire. Broken down telephone wires further impeded Evert's communications, outdated maps caused his men to vanish in marshy bogs resulting in unnecessary deaths, and his huge infantry clogged the roadways, further delaying deliveries of badly needed artillery and medical supplies.

"If we had a real supreme commander," Brusilov complained bitterly of Nicholas. "And if all the commanders had acted according to orders, then our armies would have moved so far forward that the enemy's strategic position would have become so desperate that he would have to withdraw to his frontiers without even a battle. The course of the war would have taken a very different turn and its end would have come much more quickly"

Evert not only lost thousands of men but turned Brusilov's victories into debilitating losses. In a last minute effort to save the offensive, the Emperor ordered his elite Imperial guards into battle. As their commander in chief, he selected General Bezobrazov, a man of noble birth with a reputation for bad judgment, incompetence, and insubordination. He then chose "one of the most noble of men," as chief deputy, his uncle, the Grand Duke Paul Alexandrovich to lead Russia's finest fighting brigade, and Alexei's regiment, the Preobrazinsky Guards. Ignorant of military tactics, the Grand Duke sent his armies to attack through a miry swamp where they sank chest deep in the bogs, exposing them to German fighter planes that mowed them down like grass under a rain of shells.

The other chief deputy who passed on in history as a nameless individual, claimed he had to retreat from battle because gunfire shattered his nerves, leaving his confused troops to attack enemy forces without a commander. These three military geniuses lost over 80% of the elite guards in less than two weeks.

After the massacre of the guards, thousands of recruits began to defect. Watching their comrades killed for no reason, separated from their families and fearing for the welfare of their women and children in far- away villages struggling to survive the harvest without fathers and sons, fomented resentment. Every day the number of defectors expanded as the war continued to grind on toward the end of a third disastrous year. "Take us and have us shot," these angry infantrymen wrote to the Tsar. "But we aren't going to fight anymore."

A tall blond lieutenant and class-mate of Alexei, visited the Mendelev home to inquire about his friend. Jeniya's heart flipped in fear when Yaroslav announced the young man's name and the purpose of his visit. She rushed to the drawing room to received him, anxious for good news, and at the same time dreading to hear bad news.

He bowed. "My lady countess."

"Good morning Pavel. Nice to see you." She passed over the pleasantries anxiously drove on to her deepest concern. "Have you heard from Alexei?"

Pavel hesitated. "We were in two different companies..."

"And?"

"And were separated just after we arrived at the front. I..."

"Have you heard from him?" She repeated raising her voice.

"No, my lady countess, I haven't. As soon as I got back to Petersburg, I came straight here to find out if you knew anything."

"What was the outcome of the battle?" she asked, her voice quivering.

"I can't say for Alexei's company but for us it was…" His words choked in his throat, as he tried to appear brave and positive. "I'm sorry, my lady countess."

"It was…what? Bad? How bad? How many casualties? Please tell me. I must know." Her tone elevated to almost a scream.

"We lost nearly all of our company, our friends, our comrades… our brave comrades lying helplessly in bogs." He could not hide his tears.

A cold sweat broke out over Jeniya's body. She felt the blood rushing from her head. She sat down and leaned back into the cushions, her head spinning, her consciousness fading.

The young man rushed to her side. "Are you all right, my lady?"

She nodded.

"It was our commanding officers. We give our lives not for Russia but for the whims of our arrogant and idiot generals." He said in a moment of fury. He bowed his head. "I'm sorry my lady countess, I shouldn't have told you."

"What about Alexei's company?" She said weakly.

"I have not heard the outcome, my lady. It may have gone much better for them."

Jeniya stared at him, rigid and white as a marble statue. A million terrifying thoughts whirled in her head. She was aware that he knew the outcome of Alexei's battle and had concealed the truth to spare her any more torment.

"Try to take courage, my lady. Remember, no new is good news."

No news is torment. Her mind reeled with flashing scenes of past nightmares; battle crazed young men burned and wounded with gaping holes in their bodies, the agonizing screams of pain, the stench of black rotting flesh, the minds gone mad. Anatole and his troops sent into the line of fire before anyone had time to prepare them for combat. The room began to spin before her eyes until everything disappeared into a darkened blur before she blacked out. When she opened her eyes, Ronnie was standing over her like a guardian angel.

Chapter 45

IN THE YEARS following Anatole's death, Ekatrina's world fell apart. In addition to mourning the loss of her husband, she had been agonizing over her teenage daughter and only child, Irina, who moved in with a radical young officer she met at the polytechnic institute. In protest against the disintegrating establishment, she touted herself as a nihilist. In Irina's mind, life no longer had meaning or purpose.

Jeniya felt deeply for her niece, understanding that the war took her father when she needed him most. She remembered how close they were and how much he loved her. She tried to encourage her to put her trust in the fatherly love of God, but Irina brushed it off.

"If there were a God who cares," she reasoned. "Why is there so much suffering in the world? Why does He allow endless wars depriving children of their fathers and let the pigs grow richer, consuming every pleasure known to man on themselves while they ignore the cries of the poor groveling for bread? Why does God even allow the poor to be born? The truth is, there is no God. We live and we die and that's it."

When she admonished the girl to be more thoughtful of her mother, she snapped. "I don't want anything to do with my mother. She makes me sick. Her and that dirt bag, Rasputin."

Rasputin's charlatan in arms, the Tibetan magic man, Badmaiev had been treating Ekatrina's debilitating depression with hashish and barbiturates. She not only lost her husband's salary but also his trust fund. Her father-in-law cut her off because of her regular visits to

Rasputin for drugs. Neither would her family facilitate her dependency on the mad-monk and the quack, Badmaiev, for drugs. They urged her to enroll in the addiction rehabilitation program at Daniel's mission but Katiya would rather break a leg than heed their sound advice and condescend to being seen at a mission for the destitute.

An acquaintance, Madam Trevov, who was both a professing spiritualist and a disciple of Rasputin, encouraged her to attend one of her séances with the old master of necromancy, Prince Kurakin, and consult the ghost of Anatole. Katiya was fearful at first, but in her desperation to survive she would try anything. Anything but submit to the drug program at the mission.

On the eve of the séance, she found men and women sitting around a large table, their faces barely distinguishable in the darkened room. They were engaged in a lively discussion of every imaginable kind of sorcery, exploring the transmigration of souls, ghosts, divination, Ouija boards, writing spirits, telepathy, and even sexual fantasies, topics that would ordinarily interest her, but not tonight. She felt a strange uneasiness in calling up the spirit of her late husband.

In order to prepare for the main event, nearly everyone present told some personal anecdote or incident received from direct communication with the supernatural. A deadly silence enveloped the participants like a thick mist as they waited, anticipating the uncanny sequence of events about to unfold before their eyes.

Prince Kurakin fixed his piercing haggard eyes on Katiya and asked if she were ready. She stared at him without a word or a nod. He reminded her of an emaciated vulture with his boney frame, bald head, and hook nose. In a dark sepulchral voice, he began to call up the ghost of Anatole. An icy chill enveloped the room. Kurakin's sinister expression spooked Katiya but when the table began to levitate her throat tightened in fear and she gasped for air. Someone turned up the lights. Several took her in another room and placed her on a couch until she could breathe normally. The séance proved to be futile.

As Katiya's unpaid bills began to mount, she not only needed more drugs but also a cheap place to live. Her friend Rasputin said he would rent a place for her to live but first he wanted some compensation for which he was willing to wait...he knew it would only be a matter of time.

Katiya knew what he wanted. Some of her friends and acquaintances had been through this so called ritual of purification. Some said they felt a sense of liberation from their sins, even euphoria. Others revealed nothing. But she needed a home. She needed her pills.

Rasputin answered the door and Katiya stood in the hallway for a long time watching him drool like a pig with pasty skin, a big bulbous nose and a puffy face given to drunkenness. Over the years he had become increasingly debaucherous; addicted to sexual exploitations and paranoid, haunted by constant threats on his life. His greenish-grey eyes were no longer hypnotic but evil and nasty, the greasy lock of hair persistently fell over one eye. He led her into his bedroom and locked the door.

She slowly untied her waist sash and unbuttoned her dress letting them fall to the floor. His beady eyes enlarged like viper eggs under the low brows. He untied his breeches and moved slowly toward her. The stench of his unwashed body and liquored breath sickened her. Her venerated holy man, the prophet, suddenly transformed into something odious and fearsome and she could see into his soul for the first time. She cringed watching the long, claw-like fingers as they worked to untie her corset. He pulled down her bloomers and flung her onto his grimy bed like a cow and mounted her.

When he left the room she got up, quickly dressed and wrapped her shawl tightly around her body in an attempt to cover her shame. She had to get out of there. She avoided the people waiting in his study, slipping out through the kitchen entrance, and ran down the back stairs into the street skidding and stumbling over the stone sidewalk, slick from a heavy rain. Her untied red hair swirled behind in the stormy wind. People stopped and stared in concern but she did not see their faces. Finally, she slid down on a bench gasping for breath. People asked if she were all right but she turned her head away and wept, her long hair falling over her face. She did not want to look at anyone or speak a word.

She began to shake, not from the chilly damp air, but from the lack of her afternoon "fix". She searched with trembling hands through her jacket pockets for her purse. It was gone. She must have left it behind when she fled Rasputin's flat.

She walked the streets aimlessly, trying to decide where to go. She had exhausted every possibility. She knew many socialites, people she could not face because of her humiliation, not due to Rasputin's seduction, that was of no matter to them, even celebrated by some, but because of her drug addiction. Her head pained and spun and she began to tremble violently before she passed out on the wet sidewalk.

"Take heart, my darling," said Daniel. "We must believe that Alexei is still alive."

Jeniya smiled and turned her face to the tall windows and looked out at the gloomy grey sky. "*Somewhere up there,*" she said in her heart. "*I know you are there, God. Please, if it be your will, hear the cries of my longing heart.*"

Daniel called the war ministry but Alexei's name was not listed among the living or the dead. Whenever the doorbell rang or a letter came in the mail, Jeniya's heart pounded so hard she thought she might have a heart attack. With each telephone call came the dreadful uncertainty that her son may be missing in action or killed. As the family and servants waited to hear news, the minutes of each day seemed like hours and the hours like days.

In those long tedious moments, Jeniya would remember how Alexei looked on the morning of his departure for the front. She tried to recall every detail, how he stood tall and handsome in his brown field uniform. When she held his arms and looked into his face, she observed that he had the large blue eyes and long lashes of his dad and the proud bearing of his grandfather.

"Don't worry *mamuska*," he said drawing her into his strong young embrace. "Our units are well trained. We are not raw recruits."

She had to quit her volunteer work at the hospital, due to difficulty in breathing from Panic attacks and exhaustion. Although she knew she couldn't allow herself to be debilitated by her fears. She owed it to her family. The mail had to be read, the bills had to be paid, the head cook needed her menus and instructions for both the family and the servants, and the household staff had to be directed. She also knew she had to get away from the house and the torment in sitting by the phone, waiting. Ronnie and the women at the mission needed help due to the huge influx of people arriving from the countryside looking for work. Most of these people were poor unskilled women whose husbands and sons were fighting on the front, and this placed a greater burden on the mission for bread, warm clothing, bedding and medical care. Jeniya decided it would uplift her spirits to work with them a few days a week to relieve this obsession from her mind.

One morning after she had written the new menu for the cook, Galina came into her study with the mail.

"My lady countess," she announced with an anxious expression, handing Jeniya a letter. "I think it's from Mogilev."

"Mogilev? Command headquarters?" Jeniya jumped up and took the letter in trembling hands, dreading those seven words. Your son has been killed in action. She slowly opened the letter and began to read. She screamed. "It's from Alexei!" she said. "He's alive!"

Galina hugged Jeniya in jubilation and he two women laughed and shed tears of joy.

"He's alive!" Jeniya declared. "Galina! He's alive!" She whirled around the room like a girl and sank into her chair to read the rest of the letter, eager to find out what happened to him.

"My dearest mama and papa,

Danya

When we arrived at the front, all of us were required to go through the rigorous drilling program and target practice ordered by General Polianov, as you know. At first I was annoyed, thinking I knew everything about riflery, but now, in retrospect, I will be forever grateful for Polianov's orders. At target practice, I couldn't even hit the white paper around the bull's eye. I was angry with myself, not to mention my embarrassment and frustration over my superior officer who stood behind me silently observing. I missed target after target until finally the officer moved on.

I tossed all night reviewing each detail of target practice, trying to understand what went wrong, knowing that soon I would be in the heat of battle. I thought something had gone wrong with my vision and wondered if I should inform my superiors. And then what? Cry to them like a baby? It was not an option."

Jeniya poured through the rest of the letter, reading it to Galina. She couldn't wait to telephone his father and share the news. "Danya," she said. "Our son is alive. He's in Mogilev, at headquarters."

"Headquarters?" Daniel said chuckling at the good news. "What's he doing there?"

"Showing movies..."

"Movies? What kind of movies?"

"He says..." said Jeniya reading from the letter. "because...he couldn't shoot straight at the target."

"He couldn't shoot straight? Why, he could pick a fly off a teacup and not even chip the cup."

"He says...the sight on the rifle...malfunctioned?"

"A rifle malfunction? I wonder who made it?"

"It seems that when his officers saw he couldn't fire a straight bullet, they decided to assign him to the supply wagons. Then someone higher up ordered him to report to Stavka as an adjunct.

"He says...his good fortune was a bittersweet blessing...when...so many of his comrades were needlessly sent to their deaths. Murdered by dastardly commanders, who are totally incompetent and utterly

445

unconcerned about how many of us they kill. It is something I have to live with every day. Why me? Why them? Why this war? Why? How have these things happened? How have all the good and capable men been forsaken and our best efforts come to fruition?"

Daniel reflected on those words. *Could it be that God has forsaken a nation that has rejected Him?*

"Oh, my darling husband, I am so relieved...so happy!"

"Call Ronnie and Prince Militsyn."

"I will, I will. I'll call everyone and tell them! But first I have to read what he wrote about the Emperor...it so unbelievable, so pathetic."

"He rises at 9 am, goes to Alekseev's office for coffee and a briefing where the old general moves flags around on a map to accommodate his fantasies. Then he skims the newspaper, does crossword puzzles, and smokes one cigarette after the other inspecting his nails while waiting to receive visitors at 11AM. Everyone that is, except members of the Duma and his Council of Ministers. He does not want to trouble himself with his foes or the concerns of state.

At 12:30, he eats a leisurely lunch and at 1:30 returns to his study. No one knows what he does there. We think he reads novels. He tells us reading soothes his brain. He especially likes Little Boy Blue because it brings tears to his eyes. Can you imagine!

At 3PM his chauffeur drives him in his Rolls Royce to the countryside where he stops for a walk through the woods or a stroll by the river.

He eats dinner at 7. Then he takes another stroll or listens to music or plays dominoes with his staff.

At 8 pm each evening, I report for duty to show the Emperor a movie if he so desires. Sometimes he prefers to read novels or relax listening to Wagner's operas. I live through this insanity every day, and when I think of my comrades needlessly slain...It's absolute madness.

And that's not all. He dresses the tsarevich in a little uniform like a Kazak and calls in his battle-weary troops to entertain the boy with a military parade. When his generals meet in the war room to make strategic plans for attack, the Tsar amuses himself by watching his little "sunbeam" crawl around the room investigating everything. And when the boy interrupts the irritated staff with child-like prattle, the Tsar simply replies. 'The presence of a sickly child gives life and light to all of us in a place which issues commands to send thousands of men to their deaths.' I tell you it's madness."

We all long to tell him to open his eyes and see what he is doing to Russia, but of course, it's useless. Many have tried, including the grand dukes and his own mother, the Empress Marie, but he is too arrogant to listen, too weak to lead, and to insecure to negotiate with able statesmen who are struggling to serve him. He only listens to the prattling of the Empress and her charlatan, Rasputin who directs the camarilla of incompetents. Our Empire is being guided by the inmates of an insane asylum."

"May God help us," said Daniel.

"Danya, this part is for you," Jeniya said.

"Pop, at first I was disappointed when you said you might turn the munitions plant into a mission for the poor because we so badly need the ammunition, but now I think you were not so wrong in considering it. All the bullets and guns in the world could not save our army from bumbling generals, an Emperor living in fantasy land, and an Empress breathing fire down his Imperial throat."

Ekatrina opened her eyes and saw Ronnie standing over her wiping the cold sweat from her face with a warm cloth. Next to her stood a peasant in a sheep-skin cloak with his cap in his hands. He smiled and said, "I picked you up off the sidewalk, miss, and carried you here. This kind lady here will help you get well. I was here myself, not too long ago. May God bless you." He bowed and left. She stared at Ronnie. She recognized her as Daniel's sister but never bothered to learn her name.

"I need my pills," she said. "Please...bring me my pills!"

Ronnie understood that addicts needed to be weaned off of the habit. She already sent notice to Daniel, that his sister-in-law was at the mission and asked a volunteer to get her a sedative. "I'm going to give you something to make you sleep."

Katiya closed her eyes wanting to block out the filthy dirt bag-beast who had violated her, wanting to block out her life. Tears began to trickle down her cheeks. "I need a bath," she said. "Please get me a bath."

Over the next several weeks and through many more tears, Katiya began to confide in Ronnie on her long road to recovery. Jeniya was anxious to see her sister but Ronnie asked her to stay away. "Jenka," she said. I love you but it would be best if you didn't see your sister, not just yet." She understood that Katiya had been building jealousy towards her sister over the years. She knew its manifestations because she had experience it vicariously through Ezra's hatred for Daniel. She believed that this kind of intense feeling could only truly be healed through divine intervention.

Rochelle looked older than her thirty-nine summers. Her hair started to turn grey but her kind dark eyes still sparkled brightly. Katiya would gaze at her intently when she sat peacefully by her side reading from the Psalms. In the soft light, she appeared more beautiful than many women she knew half her age, women who lived a pampered life of wealth and privilege. Her beauty radiated from a pure soul which had found contentment. This is what Katiya longed for in her own turbulent life.

Ekatrina grew stronger each day through Ronnie's loving patience and devoted companionship. Soon she wanted to go with her and meet the people who came to the mission. She actually took pleasure in helping the needy women and children as she did years ago when she worked with the Empress Maria Fedorovna in her famine relief effort, and soon she began to find purpose in her own broken life.

Katiya came to love Ronnie for her goodness and for her wisdom. She read the scriptures and shared them with the women and children who came to the mission for bible studies. She told them how God loved them and supplied all their needs if they would trust in His love, using her own life story as an example to encourage them. Many of these women revered her as they would a *starista*, crossing themselves and blessing her. Most of those who attended the bible studies were women who already had a deep faith, not in the scriptures but in the mystical power of religious traditions and the prophecies of the wandering *starzii*, and they were eager to learn biblical truths. She thought of how far she had come from the days when she too revered the so called "holy men and women", not because they spoke with Godly wisdom but because they practiced mysticism, prophesied from visions and dreams, read the signs in the stars, the tarot cards, the tea leaves, and every other tool of their imaginations. She went from a hysterical drug induced mystic to the understanding of God's word and she was grateful not only to Ronnie, but to Daniel who had the foresight to make a refuge for the needy, and the dedicated men and women who worked there.

"How is Katiya?" said Yelizaveta to her sister, Jeniya, as they strolled down the Nevsky Prospeckt shopping for Christmas gifts.

"Doing great, I hear. Rochelle advises me not to see her yet."

They stopped in front of a shop window and admired the rows of pink pearls, sparkling green emerald necklaces and ruby red brooches decorating a spray of frosty white spruce branches.

"Let's go in and have a look," said Jeniya.

While they were browsing over the displays admiring the gems, the old countess Ignatiev came gliding toward them. "*Bon matin, mesdemoiselles.* Have you heard the latest?" she said. The countess was a highly influential matron of the ecclesiastical society whose salon was patronized by the autocratic champions of the Orthodox theocracy.

Both sisters turned their heads. "No? What?" They said.

The old countess dressed stylishly, but in yesterday's fashions with a tightly laced corset accenting her ample bosom. "Why, everyone's been talking. Papus, the magician died."

"Papus?" said Jeniya. "Wasn't he the one who came here about ten years ago to advise the Tsar by calling up the ghost of his father?"

"Yes, that one. At that time, he told their majesties that he had the power to avert a future catastrophe but that his power would end the moment he ceased to be on this physical plane. Well, he passed on the 27th of October."

"So...?" asked Jeniya.

"So...that means we are headed for..." A vague transfixed gaze passed over the eyes of the old countess for a few moments. "Well... Papus has not always been right in every prediction. Several times he tried to persuade their majesties that Rasputin's influence on them was evil because he got it from the devil. The healing of our poor little tsarevich is certainly not the work of the devil...don't you agree?"

"Ten years ago...wasn't that just about the time Rasputin came into the lives of our majesties?" asked Yelizaveta.

"*Mais oui,* my dears, and aren't we grateful to have a man of God with us." Rasputin frequently visited the salon of the old countess to glean information concerning the church.

"That reminds me of something else he said. Something more troubling." She paused and reflected for a moment in the same transfixed gaze. "Papus wrote in a letter to the Emperor that from a cabalistic point of view, Rasputin is a vessel similar to Pandora's box. This vessel contains all the vices, all the crimes, all the faults of the Russian people. If it were ever to be broken, its frightful contents would immediately spill out all over Russia." She let out a vexing sigh. "Well, let's hope and pray that Papus is mistaken about this prophecy too."

"That's weird," said Yelizaveta.

People celebrated Christmas that year with the minimum of festivities or none at all. The winter brought an onslaught of brutally frigid weather. Although the homes were heated, no one could escape from the cold. Firewood and food became scarce, especially white flour and meat. Daniel did manage to get some smoked salmon and white flour for the pastry chef to bake cakes for Jeniya's Christmas party when she and Katiya would be reunited. Jeniya invited the family and all their close friends to share the happy reunion.

Yaroslav had a broad smile on his face when he announced Katiya's arrival with Ronnie. Jeniya was standing beside a tall Christmas tree in the middle of the drawing room decorated with candles and all the cherished ornaments she saved from their childhood. The two women awkwardly gazed at each other for a few seconds, each not knowing who would make the first move, then Jeniya held out her arms. When they embraced, tears flowed, tears of joy, tears of laughter, tears of bonding.

Chapter 46

THE SITUATION AT the front deteriorated rapidly. The Tsar grew weaker under the influence of drugs administered to him daily by order of Rasputin whose power had reached its zenith. Not content with dismissing and appointing ministers and generals, the mad monk now made plans to remove Nicholas II from the throne, replace him by the sick little tsarevich, and proclaim the tsaritsa as regent. He met with the Empress almost daily and their conferences were not only transmitted to General Headquarters but to German Headquarters.

In a last minute effort to save the dynasty, Grand Duke Alexander Mikhailovich visited the Empress in her notorious mauve bedroom.

"Your interference with affairs of state is causing harm both to Nicky's prestige and to the popular conception of a sovereign," he said. "All classes of the population are opposed to your policies. Please Alix, leave the cares of state to your husband, do not let your revenge dominate your better judgment. Grant a government acceptable to the Duma and provide an outlet for the nation's wrath."

She looked at Nicky who was sitting on the side of their large double bed smoking one cigarette after the other in resigned silence. "That's ridiculous. Nicky is an autocrat. How could he share his divine rights with a parliament?"

"You are mistaken, he ceased to be an autocrat on Oct 17th 1905. I realize that you are willing to perish and that your husband feels the same way, but must we all suffer for your blind stubbornness. No, Alix, you have no right to drag your relatives with you down a precipice. You are incredibly selfish."

The Imperial family were convinced that the drugs administered to Nicholas were given with the intention of paralyzing his judgment. Someone had to take charge and eliminate Rasputin to save Russia and the dynasty from ruin.

"But what can one do when all the ministers and most of the people in close contact with His Majesty are the tools of Rasputin?" said Duma President, Rodzianko. "The only solution is to kill the scoundrel, but there's not a man in Russia who has the guts to do it. If I weren't so old, I would do it myself."

Rasputin had not shown up at his apartment in three days nor in any of his haunts. Since no one produced a corpse, the Grand Dukes denied any foul play and said. "We've had Rasputin's death announced too often before. Each time he has come back to life, and more powerful than ever!" But that didn't stop anyone from speculating on the mad monk's frightening predictions. "I know I shall die amidst horrible sufferings," he reportedly told the Empress. "My corpse will be torn in pieces…and when I die, Russia will perish. Not individuals but whole crowds…masses…clouds of bodies…several Grand Dukes and hundreds of counts. The Neva will be red with blood."

Grand duke Dmitri, the twenty-five-year old son of the Grand Duke Paul and cousin to the Tsar, confessed that the idea of killing Rasputin had haunted him for months, but he had not yet found a way of doing it until he met co-conspirators Prince Felix Yussupov, the twenty-nine-year old husband of the Tsar's niece, and Purishkevich, the leader of the extreme right in the Duma.

Prince Felix planned to lure the *staretz* to the basement room of his family's palace promising that his beautiful wife, princess Irina Alexandrovna, would be there waiting for him to perform the ritual of purification. There he would be poisoned with cyanide sprinkled on his favorite cakes and in his wine by two more conspirators, Dr. Stanislaw

Lazovert, and army officer Sergei Sukhotin. Prince Yussupov would act alone to entice the satyr while the four others played "Yankee Doodle Dandy" on the gramophone upstairs, pretending to be Irina's guests.

"Protopopov made me swear not to go out for a few days," Rasputin said to his host. "He said there are plots to kill me...but they'd be wasting their time and trouble...they won't succeed. They are not powerful enough. They tried to kill me before, but the lord has always frustrated their plots...disaster will come to anyone who lifts a finger against me!"

Yussupov read a challenge into these words and a feeling of dread crept over him knowing of the staretz claim to read into a man's mind. Certainly with his power of clairvoyance he must have known something.

The prince loved to dress up in costumes and take on the persona of different characters, but tonight he would have to give his greatest performance. Determined to complete the plan, he ignored his emotions and offered the monk some tea and cakes sprinkled with cyanide. Rasputin sat down, ate one, then another and continued to talk calmly and unaffected. He drank one glass after the other of Madeira wine containing cyanide, slowly sipping like a connoisseur, causing Yussupov to become anxious that a man could ingest so much cyanide and not be affected.

"Madeira is good. Give me some more," he said. But the malicious gaze in his eyes said something else." You see...you are wasting your time. You can't do anything to me."

Suddenly, Rasputin took on a fiendish stare. Under the spell of the master's colorless eyes, Yussupov began to feel a power coming against his will. In a contest for dominance, the prince struggled to regained his self-control. The oppression lifted and he saw that Rasputin had lowered his head into his hands. When he looked up, the satyr's eyes had become dull. The prince gave him a cup of tea that revived him. Rasputin got up and started to look around the room at the beautiful objects. He became fascinated by an ebony cabinet, exploring it inside and out, opening and shutting doors. He saw a guitar and said to the prince, "Play something cheerful for me."

Then he sat back down to listen when his head drooped and his eyes closed. The prince watched anxiously unable to continue his song.

"My head is heavy," Rasputin said. "I have a burning sensation in my stomach…give me another glass of wine…it will do me good." The drink revived his spirit and he suggested that they go see the gypsies together.

"It's late, said the prince."

"That doesn't matter. They're quite used to that."

"Sing me another song," said the *staretz*.

After two hours of waiting, the men in the room above began to move about with agitation.

"What's that noise I hear upstairs?" he said

"Probably Irina's friends getting ready to go home, I'll go up and see. The shaken prince ran upstairs. "He's still alive," he said astonishing his friends. "He's not dead!" After conferring with his cohorts, he took Dmitri's revolver and returned to the basement.

Rasputin was admiring a crystal crucifix. "This is beautiful," he said. "It must have cost a lot…but I prefer the ebony cabinet."

The prince wondered how a man who claimed to know everything and see into the future seemed unaware that he was holding a revolver behind his back. "Gregory Efimovitch, you'd better look at the crucifix and say a prayer."

At first Rasputin looked startled, almost frightened. Then he moved closer to the prince, intently looked him in the eyes, and stood motionless. Yussupov slowly raised the revolver, aimed at the heart and shot. Rasputin screamed and collapsed backward onto a bearskin. Blood spattered on his silk *rubashka*. His face twitched and twisted into grizzly spasms, his talon fingers clenched, and his frightening eyes closed. He lay motionless.

Grand Duke Dmitri and Purishkevich rushed downstairs when they heard the shot. The doctor followed and pronounced the *staretz* dead. Satisfied that the ordeal was over, the four men went back upstairs to make preparations for the disposal of the body when the prince had a sudden impulse to go back to the basement and check on the body. He bent over and shook the corpse to be sure it was dead. It leaned to one side and fell back. Assured, Yussupov was about to leave, when suddenly, one of the dead man's eyelids quivered and opened, then the other. The green eyes of a viper stared at the paralyzed prince with diabolical hatred. With a hellish roar rising from his throat, Rasputin lunged to his feet with an abrupt violent motion, foaming at the mouth, hands convulsively thrashing in the air, reaching for the prince's throat. He sank his claw like fingers into the Yussupov's shoulder and held him in a grip of iron. Blood oozed from his lips and his eyes bulged from their sockets. "Yussupov," he growled in a low sepulchral voice. "Felix Yussupov…"

The terrified prince struggled to free himself but was powerless against the devil's steel clutches.

A mortal battle ensued until in a sudden rush of superhuman adrenaline, the prince released himself. Rasputin fell backward motionless. Then he began to move again. Horror struck, Prince Yussupov ran upstairs screaming, "He's still alive! Come down! Quick! He's alive." He turned back to check and saw Rasputin climbing the stairs on hands and knees to the door that led to the courtyard. With a monstrous roar, the mad monk leaped toward the bolted entrance, tore it open and disappeared.

The Okhrana discovered the corpse frozen in the ice of the little Nevka, alongside an outlying Island. When the Empress heard the news, she summoned the arrest of the Grand Duke Dimitri and Prince Yussupov and ordered Rasputin's body to be taken in a metal coffin to a small Chapel on the Vyrubova estate. There Anna Vyrubova, Aleksandra, and her four daughters prayed over the corpse. They smothered 'their friend' with flowers, ikons and tears and buried him in the park at Tsarkoe Selo near their majesties summer palace.

Meanwhile, the citizens of Petrograd received the news of Rasputin's demise with great rejoicing. People kissed each other in the streets. When they learned that one of the assassins was the Grand Duke Dimitri, they rushed to light candles before the ikons of Saint Dimitri. Long lines of women waiting at the doors of the bakeries, butcher shops and grocery stores to buy their ration of bread, meat, tea, and sugar, discussed the murder in all its aspects. "Rasputin was poisoned. He was shot...but he sat up and opened his eyes...he tried to strangle the prince. They threw him in the Nevka alive. He was still breathing when he sank under the ice. Now he can never become a saint...a dog dies like a dog!" They even made up salacious stories concerning the Tsar's daughter, the grand duchess Tatiana. "She witnessed the murder disguised as a lieutenant of the Chevaliers-Guards," they said. "So that she could revenge herself on Rasputin when he tried to rape her. She had the dying Grigori castrated before her very eyes to satisfy her thirst for vengeance."

But Rasputin had become martyr to the poor who came from the villages to labor in the mills. They believed the enemies of the common folk killed Rasputin because he was the only voice who could plead their cause. "He was a *moujik* like ourselves," they said to the women who volunteered at the mission. "A friend to the poor like you. *Vwi dobrayii gensiini.* You work with good hearts day and night and give yourselves to the *moujikii.*

It was right and good for the Tsar to open his palace doors to our saint," they said. "He defended us against the Court folk, the *pridvorny*. So *pridvorny* killed him! That's what's being said in all the *isbee*.

Someone else grieved the death of Rasputin. Rasputin's corpse was not yet cold and already the new Minister of the Interior, Protopopov and his minister of Justice, Dobrovolski, were running to the old Prince Kurakin, to call up his ghost. The three of them would sit in secret conclaves for hours on end as the emaciated old vulture sought the council of the dead monk.

The winter dragged on relentlessly. Grain and wood could not be moved because more than twelve hundred engines had burst their boiler tubes due to sub-zero temperatures and there were no tubs to spare as a result of railroad strikes. Exceptionally heavy snows halted fifty-seven thousand more railway cars which could not be moved because the men fighting on the front created a shortage of labor in the villages.

With the cost of bread rising 2% daily, many of the women who worked in the mills were too poor to buy bread from payday to payday. Their families suffered from hunger for two and three days at a time. Meat, eggs and cheese were now prohibited to all but the highest paid workers.

Jeniya took on the job of supervising activities at the mission which was located across the Neva in the Vyborg mill workers district. They distributed food and warm blankets and set up bivouacs to dish out hot soup to tired working women and their children, many of them abused by husbands drunken on cheap vodka. She hired several more bakers and cooks, in an effort to reach out to these needy families. Some of the women who came for help found employment at the mission, baking bread, preparing meals, sorting clothing, tending the sick and caring for children who lived in unheated flats while their mother's went to work in the mills.

While the workers of Petrograd felt the pain of hunger and cold, the myopic rich immersed themselves in every kind of self-seeking passion in an attempt to squeeze the last drop of pleasure from the crumbling empire. They accumulated furs and dazzling jewels to show off at fashionable salons, receptions and gambling casinos. Stakes upward of twenty thousand rubbles passed hands in hectic activity from dusk to dawn. Corks popped from bottles of Monton de Rothechild and Brut Imperial and champagne flowed like water. Painted prostitutes wrapped in diamonds, sable and ermine prowled the casinos and gypsies sang.

Gentlemen bathing in the scent of Moet and Chandon gathered in supper clubs to discuss which regiment of the guard could be relied on in the coming revolution and the most favorable moment for the outbreak. Since the death of Rasputin they knew it was coming, they could feel it, but they didn't know when, or how bad it might be. They waited like clay pigeons in a trap shoot or buried their heads like ostriches avoiding the need to act. They raised glasses in toast after toast to the salvation of Holy Russia. Conspiracy theories dominated their conversations.

Chapter 47

ON THURSDAY, MARCH 8th 1917, the day before international women's day, Daniel was struck by the sinister expressions on the tired faces of the women who lined up outside bakeries for hours to buy bread, only to be turned away when that bakers put a sign up in the window, "no more bread'. Many had risen in the middle of the night weathering sub-zero temperatures, falling snow and biting winds to assure a place in line the next morning.

Daniel rarely became anxious about anything but today he had an uneasy feeling, especially when he saw Kazaks patrolling the streets. He was scheduled to meet Prince Militsyn for brunch at the English club to order more grain shipments from the All-Russian Union of Zemstva. The Moscow merchants had wisely stored stock piles of reserve grain to supply their charities.

"It's a gloomy afternoon," said the prince. "Why don't we relax with a good glass of brandy and a game of cards." The footman brought a deck of cards to the table and two goblets of Remy Martin. The Prince took the pack, shuffled the cards and dealt them out.

"If all the capable men in Russia would only take a stand," Daniel said picking up his cards. "And confront the Emperor...firmly impressing on him...with force if necessary...for the sake of sanity, that he is leading Russia straight into disaster by abdicating power to the Empress and her stooge du jour, Protopopov."

"Take heart," said the Prince pondering over his hand. "Several Grand Dukes are talking of a plan to save Tsarism by force. Four regiments of the guards would march at night on Tsarskoe Selo, and seize the monarchs. The Grand dukes will show Nicholas the papers of abdication, shut the Empress in a nunnery, and proclaim the accession of the tsarevich Alexis under the regency of the Grand Duke Nicholas Nicolaievich."

Daniel fanned out his cards, looked at his hand and arranged the cards, moving them around. "Then instead of vexing the personnel at Mogilev with his trivialities," he said throwing out the first card. "Nicholas can go to Lavidia, where he can cry over little boy blue, listen to Wagner, watch movies, play dominoes, and take naps."

"What are you talking about?" The prince frowned, his dark brows knit with concern. He knew the Tsar was incompetent but not to that extent.

"From Alexei. He describes in detail everything that goes on at headquarters.

Militsyn's, large brown eyes widened in surprise. "We may indeed be headed for a tremendous catastrophe," he said. "More than I imagined."

When Daniel arrived home from the club, Jeniya was not there. The streets were already dark at 4PM and Daniel began to Panic. She never remained at the mission later than 3 o'clock in the afternoon, and was always home before sundown. He dialed the mission to see if she was still there. "She left over an hour ago," said Ronnie. Is everything all right...Danya?"

Daniel hung up the phone. A cold sweat broke out over his forehead. He called the police station to ask them to send out the Okhrana, but hung up. He had to remain calm. He had to think clearly. He summoned his chauffeur to get the car. He had to find her.

Because of the heavy snowfall during the night, Jeniya took the sleigh to the mission early in the morning to deliver the badly needed flour before breakfast. On the way home, she had run head long into an unruly mob of workers waving red flags and banners, blocking the snowy streets, singing the Marseillaise and shouting. "Bread and peace. Bread and peace!" Some of the women recognized her as the good lady from the mission and pleaded with the agitators to back away, but they were pushed aside in the commotion.

Jeniya stood up in the sleigh holding the horses' reins. "What right have you to monopolize the streets!" She demanded.

"You are *bourgeoise*. Your kind must be eliminated."

"I run the Petrograd mission," she said. Let me pass!" She appeared to them as a wall of strength and courage but inside she shook like a trapped rabbit.

A few backed away out of respect. "Go back to where you came from," they told her. "We can't guarantee your safety." Others surged forward and tried to grab the horses' reins.

A surge of anger rushed over her. She lashed into the mob to the left and to the right with her knout. The rioters reached for her whip, trying to pull it from her hand and force her from the sleigh, but the horses reared and bucked, thrashing their legs in the air over the men's heads. "Let me pass!" She shouted. "If you want to kill me, have at it. What difference does it make if you take me here or in my home!" Finally, the men backed away and she snapped the whip over the horses and tore wildly through the mob, amazing both herself and the men. She did not look back to see that many of them had tipped their caps in amazement.

Within hours the news of the event circulated throughout the Vyborg district and in the city center. She not only earned the workers respect but their protection.

Daniel was just about to step into his car when Jeniya pulled her horses alongside the curb. "Jenka!" He threw his arms around her and held her close in a strong enduring hug. "Thank God you are all right…What happened? We were all so worried."

"It's been a frustrating afternoon," she said. "I was delayed by some demonstrations. I'll tell you later at dinner," she said. "Right now I have to relax in a hot bath.

Before she got to the staircase, Yaroslav approached. "My lady countess, Yelizaveta is calling. She says it's important."

"Oh, she always says it's important," Jeniya said and went to pick up the phone.

"Jenka, ma *chere*. Are you and Daniel going to Princess Leon Radziwill's party on Sunday?"

"No, I hadn't planned on it. Actually, I don't think so. Things are getting pretty tense around the mission. We fear there may be food riots."

"Food riots?" Why Protopopov told the council members that the situation is not as tragic as all that, and everything is fine. The ministry is going to pass out leaflets assuring everyone that large reserves of flour are still available in the city and that more food is on the way."

"He is lying. But what can you do with an insane man who has lost touch with reality and spends his time with that creepy old prince Kurakin calling up the ghost of Rasputin when he should be minding the city. Someone needs to put a stop to this before it's too late."

There was silence on the other end of the phone. "No. I don't believe it."

"Believe it! How could you forget the time when the old lunatic gazed at the corpse of Count Witte and demanded. "We compel you to come to us to-night!" She made a deep hollow voice.

"I wonder who would want to communicate with the ghost of count Witte?" said Yelizaveta. "Well, let's not be morbid about this. Princess Radziwill's party promises to be large and brilliant. Everyone is hoping there will be music and dancing."

"Isn't it a curious time to arrange a banquet."

"And why not? What a better time to arrange a banquet and bring a bit of gaiety before we all go down...by the way which ballerina do you think will be awarded the palm of excellence this year? Pavlova, Kchechinskaya or Karsavina?"

"Vetka! Of all things! Sometimes I think you are as nutty as the rest of them...I haven't time to think about such things!"

"Well, I do hope you and Daniel will reconsider. *Au revoir, ma chere.*"

While the Emperor escaped from his troublesome ministers to the solace of his cloister at Mogilev "to rest his brain" and Princess Radziwill planned her extravaganza, impoverished mothers with hungry children working in the mills were busy organizing their own brilliant affair, one which would eclipse Princess Radziwill's party.

———◆———

Friday, March 9th appeared to be another ordinary day. Petrograd citizens went to their jobs in the morning clam unaware that unrest was brewing in the working quarters. Daniel forbade Jeniya to go to work despite her protests.

"Look," she said. "It's beginning to snow again. Nobody will be marching on the streets today. I'll have the chauffeur drive me."

"No! Ronnie and Katiya can take care of things. A full blown revolution can break out in that district at any moment!"

Again, Daniel was right in his foresight. In the mill district, hundreds of women were gathering in the snowy streets. Hardly anyone was waiting outside to get a hot meal, or to take their children to a warm place to stay while they went to work. The women who toiled for unimaginable low wages in the cotton mills could not tolerate another day of suffering. Their frustration over longer working hours without overtime pay for wages that bought less food, the pain of hunger, and the burden of trying to support their families while their menfolk were away at the front brought them to the tipping point. Several thousand abandoned their positions of servitude at the looms in order to set an example for all their sisters to join them in the streets and force their bosses to take action. The *metallisty* workers from the neighboring Petrograd Island joined their cause and by noon more than fifty-thousand men and women were on the march for bread.

The women surged forward and cried, "Bread" in shrill voices piercing through the men's deep baritone voices shouting, "Down with the war. Down with the Tsar." Red banners waved above their heads in the wind, with "bread" written in big black letters. They sang the Marseillaise. The anthem of the French revolution became their marching order; *liberté, égalité, fraternité;* their mantra.

When the workers approached the Aleksandrovsky bridge leading to the city center, they found a few hundred Kazaks lined up along the palace embankment waiting to disburse the mob. The marchers hesitated to go forward fearing the sting of the flesh-tearing, multi-pronged *nagaikas*. In desperation, a few brave and hungry women stepped out from the crowd of protestors and took hold of the soldier's bayonets, beseeching them. "You also have mothers, wives, sisters and children. We are only asking for bread and an end to the war...Put down your rifles...join us." Several Kazaks took the initiative and grinned. One slyly winked. Cheers rang up from the working men and women, "Hurrah for the Kazaks." The horsemen bowed in reply.

The marchers surged ahead, like the dark waves of the sea, swelling over the Aleksandrovsky bridge onto the shores of the Palace quay. Hundreds more workers slid down the Petrograd embankment and crossed the Neva, stepping over huge blocks of ice. Some daring souls slid beneath the bellies of the horses while their riders stood at attention. Trotsky later commented that, "the revolution made its first steps to victory under the belly of a Kazak horse."

By late afternoon, women and youth in the Vyborg Quarter broke into food shops and looted bakeries. At several points around the city Kazaks charged the crowd brandishing their *nagaikas* to disperse the demonstrators. By nightfall some 90,000 workers had taken to the streets.

Saturday, March 10th thousands of workers from the immense Putilov steel works were on the march. "*Putilovtsy idut*," they proclaimed to the frightened inhabitants of Petrograd. One leader rose up and declared to his comrades. "We must go ahead and solve our problems by force. Only this way will we be able to get bread for ourselves. Arm yourselves with bolts, screws and rocks and start smashing the first shops you find."

About one hundred-thousand workers marched to the city center where five hundred Kazaks and mounted police waited for them. When the police saw the Kazaks bow to the demonstrators, they feared a bloody confrontation and did not interfere.

The demonstrators were for the most part peaceful under the watchful eyes of the law. They assured the authorities that they were only asking for bread and an end to the war. Around 5PM in the evening, some of the workers became unruly with drink and implored the soldiers to join their revolution. They sang the Marseillaise and paraded with red banners that declared, "Down with the Government! Down with Protopopov. Down with the war! Down with Germany!" and began to throw rocks and bolts at the police. Three demonstrators and three officers were killed and about a hundred persons wounded.

The ministers called an "Extraordinary Council," to investigate the desperate need for food supplies. Everyone attended, including the President of the Council of Empire, the President of the Duma and the Mayor of Petrograd. Everyone except the mad Minister of the Interior, Protopopov, who was still conferring with the ghost of Rasputin, seeking his council.

Order was restored by evening. Encouraged by the Kazaks and police patrolling the streets, Daniel and Jeniya took advantage of the situation and attended a private concert at the home of Prince Militsyn.

Sunday, March 11th the Extraordinary Council discussed ways to halt the revolt until five o'clock in the morning. Protopopov finally showed up with a plan extracted from the apparition of Rasputin or more likely from the hallucinations in his own unstable mind. Instead of sending more workers to move the grain sitting in snow drifts and distributing food, he directed the chief of police to preserve order at any cost. Posters were around the city as a warning to the people.

"All meetings or gatherings are forbidden. I notify the civil population that I have given the troops fresh authority to use their weapons and stop at nothing to maintain order!" In response, the shopkeepers and restauranteurs shut down their business in fear that violence could break out at any moment.

The working men and women spit on Protopopov's placards signaling that the peaceful march for bread would transform into a rebellion against the government of Nicholas II. They padded rags and towels beneath their coats to protect themselves from the vicious *nagaikas* and ventured out against a bitter cold wind and driving snowstorm, vowing to struggle unto death. This time when they encountered the mounted police on the Aleksandrovsky bridge, they pulled the division chief from his horse, seized his revolver and shot him. They pushed onto the Nevsky Prospekt where waiting troops blasted the mob several times with machine gun-fire, scattering them in the streets. Scores were left dead and wounded bleeding in the snow.

Several workers dared to approach the Kazaks. With caps held respectively in their hands, they said. "Good sirs, you see how the Pharaohs treat us hungry workers. Help Us!"

The Kazaks charged, swinging their swords in reply, not at the workers but at the police. The troops of Pavlovsky regiment also rebelled against their authorities and sympathized with the workers. They slung their rifles over their shoulders and walked away. Another regiment, the Volhynian of the Guard hesitated to slaughter any more workers and fired into the air. Some of the workingmen gave up protesting and returned to the industrial quarters. "We have had enough of this going to the Nevsky Prospekt to be killed," they said. But others persuaded their comrades not to be naive any longer. "In the arsenals and weapons factories we shall find revolvers, rifles and cartridges," they said and raised their fists. "*Tovareeshee*! It's now or never!"

Daniel had locked the doors of his munitions plant and placed his most loyal employees on guard until the riots in the area settled down, but the mission was serving huge crowds with food and medical assistance.

That evening the revolt had been successfully put down. The clamor of the day's mayhem had been hushed beneath a thick blanket of freshly fallen snow and transformed the city of chaos and blood into a magical wonderland. Daniel and Jeniya ventured out in the snowy streets to get some air after being cooped up with tension and worry.

Despite the revolution and heavy snow fall Princess Radziwill's house was ablaze with lights. A long line of cars and sleighs were parked along the quay, including the limousine of the Grand Duke Boris.

"Maybe we should have gone and celebrated the last grand party," said Jeniya.

"No, that would not have been a good idea. We are fortunate today's demonstrations were quelled. This evening could have turned very ugly and they could have been sitting ducks for an attack."

"We can still go," said Jeniya.

Daniel shook his head.

"Do you think we are witnessing the last night of the regime?" she asked.

Daniel stared off into the distance lost in thought. "The final catastrophe has been brought about by the willful obstinacy of a mad woman and an emasculated sovereign," he said. "And swept us all away with one stroke."

While Princess Radziwill and her guests partied, a young sergeant in the Volynski regiment of the guard stood up in his barracks and cried. "*Tovareeshee*. Listen to me! Fathers, mothers, sisters, and brothers are begging for bread. Should we continue to strike down our labor force? Haven't you seen the blood running through the streets? I propose that we not march against them tomorrow. Enough blood has been shed. Now it is time we must all die for freedom." When his commanding officer walked in the barracks to put down the disorder, the rebel soldiers shot him.

From Mogilev, Nicholas took time from his leisurely afternoon and ordered commander Khabalov to put a stop to the disorders, to which the General replied, "How? Should we open fire if the soldiers decide to join the workers. It will be a revolution!"

———

Monday, March 12th dawned sunny and bitter cold. Commander Khabalov had placed extra military units on alert throughout the city and moved armored cars into position. Machine-gunners had taken up positions where their guns could sweep strategic intersections. Infantry platoons guarded key buildings and Kazak squadrons patrolled the streets. Specially trained non-commissioned officers of the guard chosen for their bravery and loyalty were stationed to protect the intersections. Stores, restaurants and cafes had shut down and the streets were emptied of traffic, even trolley cars. The Troitsky bridge, usually busy with Monday morning traffic, was deserted.

While Daniel was eating breakfast he heard an explosion. He grabbed his coat and ran out to the river embankment to see what happened. A disorderly mob carrying red flags materialized around the Fortress of St. Peter and Paul directly across the Neva. He squinted and saw that in their hands they carried shiny new steel weapons gleaming in the morning sun. An armory had been bombed and raided. An image of Ezra flashed in his mind. He wondered if his faithful employees he left to guard the factory had defected to the revolution and given arms to the rebels. He turned to get his chauffeur and drive to the plant, when he saw a regiment of Volynsky guards moving across the Troitsky bridge towards the armed mob ready for a violent confrontation. But to his amazement, the two groups united with much singing, hooting and cheering. They marched together with red ribbons tied to their bayonets in the direction of the Kresty Prison.

Suddenly a crack of machine-gun fire split the air. Confusion rang out on every corner of the city. Soldiers struggled tirelessly to help the civilians erect barricades on the main thoroughfares against raging mobs. The gates of the Arsenal on Liteïny Prospekt burst open with a crash. Flames engulfed the Ministry of the Interior, the Military Government building, the Minister of the Courts' offices, the headquarters of the Okhrana, and the police-stations. The Law Courts had become an enormous inferno. Rebels sieged the Fortress of St. Peter and Paul and occupied the Winter Palace. They victoriously stormed the military prison and the women's transit prison, liberating the revolutionary leaders. Fighting broke out in every part of the city. Over a quarter of Petrograd' population now stood against Nicholas' government.

The Volynsky regiment paraded throughout the city calling on the people to take part in the revolution. They tried to win over the troops who still remained loyal to the throne and succeeded in persuading the Tsar's prestigious Imperial Preobrazhenski guards as well as three more elite army units. Nicholas' loyal troops now recognized no leadership and were spreading terror throughout the city. By night fall the rebels had seized the armored cars.

Duma President, Rodzianko hastily telegraphed the Tsar. "Your majesty, the capital is in a state of anarchy. It is necessary that some person who enjoys the confidence of the country be entrusted at once with the formation of a new government. There must be no delay! Any procrastination is fatal."

Nicholas brushed Rodzianko's urgent request off like a noisome fly, preferring the flatteries of men who painted a rosy picture. "This fat Rodzianko has written me lots of nonsense to which I shall not even deign to reply. I already know everything that I need to know, and his information contradicts the facts as I know them."

"When Aleksandra learned of Rodzianko's warning, she called it "high treason. "Send Miliukov, Gochkov, Polivanov, and Prince Lvov to Siberia," she said. "My soul and brain tell me it would be the saving of Russia. Go forth like a lion and crush them all!"

Throughout the night, gun fire continued in the streets with cheering and rebel rousing. No one could sleep. Daniel got up and looked out over the balcony. The street and canal below were barely detectable in the mist from the falling snow. He thought of his family, his business, his workers, and he felt helpless. After experiencing God's mercy through the years, he still had to learn to trust Him for another uncertain day. *It seen that we must go from faith to faith.*

A group of drunken soldiers staggering in the street looked up and saw him. "Are you for the revolution?" they shouted.

"I sympathize with the revolution," he said.

"Well then welcome, *tovareesh*. Welcome to the revolution." They saluted him and went off cheering and singing.

Dawn was already beginning to creep over the eastern horizon. He bundled up against the bitter cold of the early morning hours before the household came alive with chatter over yesterday's events and walked the streets to be alone with himself. The swift and complete defection of the army came as a shock to everyone. Daniel felt pity for the oppressed populace because they did not understand that their socialist leaders had not their freedom in mind but confiscation of freedom. He saw the Socialist revolution as a tyrannical beast rising to conquer and rob, not only of material goods and land, but to rob individuals of the freedom to pursue their own dreams. The freedom they so desperately wanted.

At different points along the Nevsky Prospekt, the glow from burning fires was still evident. He stopped to comfort one of the great black Ethiopians who used to guard the Emperor's doors, now just another civilian wandering aimlessly. The servant's eyes filled with tears when he recounted his memories at the palace. Daniel listened and shook his hand as they parted, watching him disappear in the snowy mist with the last splendors of the monarchy.

Across the Neva he saw another symbol of the old Imperial order being ransacked with vengeance from top to bottom, the town house of world famous ballerina, Kchechinskaya. She danced at the Mariensky theater for 27 years. In her younger days she was the paramour of Nicholas II when he was tsarevich and romanced two of the Grand Dukes. Her dinner parties were celebrated. At her last party she displayed her precious collection of Faberge eggs, flowers made of precious stones and small golden trees with branches shimmering with diamonds.

Last winter in the intense cold when the British embassy could not get coal to fire their central furnace, Kchechinskaya managed to obtain four military truckloads of coal and a squad of soldiers to unload it into her furnaces. *Retribution!*

An armored car displaying red flags streaming from machineguns passed him on the street. A thick-set burly student brandishing another red flag, brawled down in his face. "Pay your respects to the Russian Revolution! The red flag is Russia's flag. now."

———◆———

Tuesday March 13th the Council of Ministers met in the Marinsky Palace and formally submitted their resignation to the Tsar. When the Provisional Committee of the State Duma ordered their arrest, these trusted men in Nicholas' cabinet, handpicked by the Empress, fled like rats abandoning a sinking ship and went into hiding.

Chapter 48

AT DAWN, THE rebels stormed the Admiralty, where the war minister, the naval minister and several high officials had taken refuge and arrested them along with members of Tsar's Council of Ministers, including Protopopov, and Boris Sturmer.

"The final hour is beginning to strike," Rodzianko frantically telegraphed Nicholas again. "Position serious. Anarchy in the capital. Government paralyzed. Arrangement for transport, supply and fuel in complete disorder. Immediate steps must be taken. Tomorrow will be too late. The final hour has come when the fate of the country and the dynasty must be decided. I pray to God in this hour the responsibility does not fall on the wearer of the crown."

General Alekseev took the telegram to an Emperor. Because of his intense dislike for Rodzianko and the Duma, Nicholas would not relent and grant the people a responsible government as Rodzianko so desperately requested. Instead, he ordered General Ivanov to put down the rebellion in the city. Four infantry units, four cavalry units, and four batteries of artillery from the front would meet the commander at Tsarskoe Selo outside Petrograd. General Brusilov held more forces in reserve on the southeastern front to be ready at a moment's notice.

The order came too late. With unexpected speed, revolutionary forces besieged Stavka. In the turmoil, the discombobulated high command issued confusing orders to the troops waiting to join up with Ivanov's company, enabling rebel forces to take control of the government and demand Nicholas' abdication.

Recruits hunted down their officers with a vengeance. Marauding gangs mercilessly gunned down the police and tossed their mutilate bodies into canals or threw them into fires, burning them alive. The fortress of St Peter and Paul where leaders of the insurrection had been incarcerated became the headquarters of the revolution.

Daniel tried to telegraphed Alexei, and discovered that rebels had infiltrated the telegraph office and refused to transmit wires to Stavka.

The Tsar left Stavka at Mogilev by Imperial train at 4:30 in the morning for Tsarskoe-selo at the urgent request of the Empress who was nursing their four daughters with the measles. Halfway there he learned that the revolutionaries had closed the Petrograd railway line and seized the palace grounds. In a sudden outburst of emotional vexation, he became anxious for his family, but quickly settled into his usual detached manner and politely said, "Moscow will remain faithful to me. We will go to Moscow."

Moscow had also gone over to the revolution. Nicholas then decided to take refuge at General Russky's headquarters in the northern city of Pskov where he arrived around eight o'clock in the evening. General Russky advised his sovereign to abdicate. "Don't you see you can do nothing else?" He said. "And if you don't abdicate, I cannot answer for your life. You should have realized long ago that you needed to surround yourself with Russian advisors and not those German Baltic barons." He telegrammed Generals Evert, Brussilov, Alekseev, and the Grand Duke Nicholas Nicholaievich to get their opinion. They all unanimously agreed.

Thursday, March 15th Nicholas II had made the decision to abdicate shortly before mid-night. No one knew what could have gone through his mind through those long sleepless hours. Reluctance to give up the divine authority bequeathed to him by his ancestors? Determination to save the oath he made to the Romanov dynasty at his coronation? His son? The future of the dynasty?

Unaware of his decision, two emissaries from the Duma arrived in the morning to advise the Tsar. "Nothing but the abdication of your Majesty in favor of your son can still save the Russian fatherland and preserve the dynasty," they said.

Nicholas hesitated. The Emperor understood that the accession of the tsarevich to the throne under the regency of his younger brother, the Grand Duke Mikhail Alexandrovich would immediately fill the vacancy and probably halt the revolution, at least until a constitutional reform could be drafted. More importantly, he felt the nation's compassion and good-will would favor the boy. However, if he proclaimed the accession of his brother, the Grand Duke Mikhail Alexandrovich, second in line to the throne, it may cause controversy, a risk he would have to take. He must also have been aware that should he delete his son's name from the proclamation and chose his brother, Russia could plunge into a terrible fate. Before he named his heir, Nicholas asked to consult with his physician about his son's prognoses.

Outside the window, snowflakes whirled under a darkened sky while the representatives from the Duma waited for Nicholas' decision.

"I decided to abdicate yesterday." He later told the two men. "But I cannot be separated from my son. That is more than I could bear…his health is too delicate…his disease is incurable. You must realize what I feel…I shall therefor abdicate in favor of my brother, Michael Alexandrovich."

Nicholas compliantly went into his study with two leaders of the Duma and returned ten minutes later with the act of abdication signed.

"By the grace of God, We, Nicholas II, Emperor of all the Russias, Tsar of Poland, Grand Duke of Finland, etc., etc., to all our faithful subjects make known:

In these days of terrible struggle against the foreign enemy who has been trying for three years to impose his will upon Our Fatherland, God has willed that Russia should be faced with a new and formidable trial. Troubles at home threaten to have a fatal effect on the ultimate course of this hard-fought war. The destinies of Russia, the honor of Our heroic army, the welfare of the nation and the whole future of our dear country require that the war shall be continued, cost what it may, to a victorious end.

Our cruel enemy is making his final effort and the day is at hand when our brave army, with the help of our glorious allies, will overthrow him once and for all.

At this moment, a moment so decisive for the existence of Russia, our conscience bids Us to facilitate the closest union of Our subjects and the organization of all their forces for the speedy attainment of victory.

For that reason, we think it right - and the Imperial Duma shares Our view - to abdicate the crown of the Russian State and resign the supreme power.

As We do not desire to be separated from Our beloved son. We bequeath Our inheritance to Our brother, the Grand Duke Michael Alexandrovich, and give him Our blessing on his accession to the throne. We ask him to govern in the closest concert with the representatives of the nation who sit in the legislative assemblies and to pledge them his inviolable oath in the name of the beloved country.

We appeal to all the loyal sons of Russia and ask them to do their patriotic and sacred duty by obeying their Tsar at this moment of painful national crisis and to help him and the representatives of the nation to guide the Russian State into the path of prosperity and glory.

May God help Russia! NICHOLAS."

The accession of the Grand Duke Michael to the throne aroused the fury of the rebels. "No more Romanovs! We want a republic!"

The same terrifying spirit that drove the peasants to plunder and destroy with a vicious frenzy was at work in the capital. Within minutes, they chopped apart the Imperial double-headed eagle with its great wings spread out over the Winter Palace entrance and unfurled a massive red flag in its place. They ransacked the city, sweeping away every oppressive emblem of the Tsar and burned them in the fire that had gutted the district court building. "Death to the two headed eagle," they chanted, waving red flags. "Sever its long neck with a stroke. The people have triumphed! Glory to us all!"

All the regiments of the Tsar had gone over to the revolution. Celebrating soldiers jammed the streets, jostling one another to get in front of newsreels. Bands of revelers with rifles in their hands motored about, cheering and being cheered by shouting civilians. Trucks were thronged with joy-riding soldiers yelling "hurrah!" Everyone turned out for the people's victory on that sunny cold day, believing they had turned a new corner of hope, unaware that their moment of jubilation would one day turn to mourning, beyond anyone's imagination.

The Grand Duke consented to accept the crown only if it should be offered to him by the Russian nation represented by the constituent assembly. Alexander Kerensky, a young progressive lawyer who gained a reputation as an advocate for political justice and spokesman for the Soviets, possessed a gifted tongue for verbal persuasion. He tried to convince the Grand Duke to abdicate the throne and hand his new title over to the government. "No one in the Duma can guarantee you safety," he cajoled.

On the contrary, the leader of the Duma, Miliukov insisted that the brother of the Emperor had no right to evade the responsibility of supreme power. "If you refuse the crown," he said. "It will mean anarchy, chaos, and bloody turmoil. It will lead Russia into ruin. At least take on the title of Protector of the Nation until a constitutional assembly can be established. The Grand Duke concluded that at the risk of controversy or worse, the wrath of the unpredictable masses was not worth the sacrifice.

"Your royal highness," Kerensky said triumphantly. "You have magnanimously entrusted to us the sacred cup of your power. We shall pass it on to the Constituent Assembly without having spilt a single drop from it!" That afternoon, he nailed posters everywhere in the city broadcasting the news. The workers and soldiers fearing the Grand Duke would lead a counter-revolution, put him under the surveillance of the revolutionary army.

Jeniya sat in her bedroom study absently gazing out the window, as if by some magical longing it would produce the living image of her son.

After breakfast, Galina came in and told her mistress that she had a phone call. Her heart flipped a beat. She jumped up and ran downstairs to pick up the phone.

"I woke up this morning to see that damn red flag flying over my house," said a furious Count Rostovsky on the other end. "Who in hell did this?"

Jeniya took a deep breath. "Papa," settle down, it is for your own good…you and mama come for dinner this evening and I will tell you all about it. The streets have quieted down now after the initial reaction to the Grand Dukes resignation. Daniel managed to find some butter, white rolls and smoked fish."

"Have you heard anything from Alexei? Zinaida asked as soon as she stepped in the drawing room that evening.

"No, and it is driving us crazy. The rebels have torn down all communications to Stavka. No telegrams, no wires, no mail, no nothing." She shook her head. "Sometimes I feel like I am going mad…to have to live through this again."

Zinaida puts her arm around her daughter. "You will hear something soon. He is most likely with the Tsar's staff. They still have to direct the men fighting on the front. At least you know he is not on the battlefield."

"I know, mama. Being at Stavka is no comfort. It's so hard not knowing anything for sure."

They sat down on the couch by the warm fire burning in the hearth.

"Have you heard anything about the plant or the mission?" asked Rostovsky, filling a plate with appetizers from a table prepared by the footmen.

"The mission is doing fine, busier than ever, as you can imagine. The plant survived the revolution. I have a skeleton crew on the job still producing shells for the loyal troops fighting on the front. The management is fairly trustworthy, but they never know what to expect of the workers. They show up when they feel like it. They are free now. And there is nothing we can do," he said with a hint of sarcasm. They sat on the couch opposite the women.

"This never would have happened to us if we didn't have that German woman on the throne," said Zinaida. She has cast some kind of evil spell over Russia and uses religion to shield herself from everything in the real world and from whatever thing is living inside her."

"Do you think she is demon possessed?" asked Jeniya.

"Who knows?"

"Zeenah," said the count. "Why do you waste time massaging this subject over and over…it's done…she's gone…get over it." He turned to Jeniya. "What is this you want to tell me about that damn red flag flying over my house. Who put it there?"

"Cyril put them there last night when he first heard about the Tsar's abdication…for our own safety." Daniel said. Consider it a blessing in disguise. Your life is especially at risk since you were once on the Tsar's Council of Ministers. Cyril feels as I do, that allegiance to the monarchy at this point is not prudent…even dangerous. The government is crumbling. The Duma is caving to the demands of the Soviets and giving into the rebellion."

"Papa," said Jeniya. "What will become of Belozerkovka if the Soviets take over, they say they are going to give our land to the peasants?"

Rostovsky shook his head. "I don't know." He signaled the attending footman for another brandy. "Some say that if they confiscate the millions of acres owned by the Emperor, the Grand Dukes and the church, they will not bother us...but I think this thing is not going to stop until they have confiscated everything we own...there is a Russian colony of refugees in Finland, I was toying with the idea of eventually leaving the country."

"Leave the country? Why papa?"

"It's hard to imagine things would go that far," said Daniel. "It will not be the same for sure, but which is worse, living in a foreign land we do not know or remaining here with our family and friends."

Jeniya wondered what she might take with her if it were necessary to flee Russia. She looked around the room at her treasured possessions, not just things but memories of people, of her mother, her grandmother. They embodied the tapestry of her life, the little dolls that once belonged to her great-grandmother reminding her of the happy times she spent at Belozerkovka, gifts from those she loved, the beautiful furniture from Prince and Princess Militsyn, the Monet from her parents which hung above the fireplace, and the family and friends who shared their life from pictures placed on tables around the room.

"We have so many memories here," she said. "The painting you and mama gave us, the wedding present from Prince Militsyn, the small mementos I treasure from nana."

"It may not be a bad idea to start packing and send them on ahead," said her father.

She thought about the family jewels once stored in the hand carved cases in her mother's home, now locked up in the safety deposit box at the bank. Could she trust the bank? Was anything safe anywhere? Was anyone safe?

The revolution inspired everyone to expound on his idea on a new government. Peasants, working men, and students mounted a bench or a heap of snow and preached while passers-by stopped and looked on in dazed silence. Orators shouted in city squares, around monuments, on sidewalks, in front of railway stations, and on into the night. Every neighborhood became a platform for debates. No one could sleep even with the windows closed. Jeniya thought she would go mad listening to the incessant drumming over politics and not being able to contact Stavka. She could hardly eat since this ordeal began. "How can I eat when my stomach is in a jumble," she said to Daniel when he tried to encourage her. "I can't digest anything."

"Look on the good side. He has not been arrested nor is his name on any casualty lists." He said trying to convince himself as well.

"I wish I had your faith. How do I know if those reports are accurate or current for that matter? How can I have peace until I hear something…anything."

Yaroslav entered the dining room in an anomalous state of alarm with the morning paper and said, "Look at this, sir!"

Daniel grabbed the paper. Jeniya jumped up. "Let me see," she said. "Citizen Romanov arrested". "Oh no!" She stumbled backward and grabbed on the arm to brace herself from the shock.

The next morning Jeniya languished in bed when through a daze she thought she heard Alexei calling. "Mama! Papa!" I must be going mad, she thought.

"Is anyone home? Mama?"

"Alexei? ALEXEI!" She jumped out of bed and ran downstairs in her nightgown, crying with tears of joy and relief. She flew into his arms. They hugged and laughed and kissed.

"Where is papa?"

"He's at the office. Let's surprise him and meet him for lunch. I'll go get dressed." She ran back up the stairs like a school girl.

The burned out buildings and the destruction in the beautiful city both astonished and sadden Alexei. *The drunken mobs grew up like animals in huts. Sadly, it's all they knew. They had no regard for art and beauty or the creators of beauty."*

He recalled an encounter with a peasant soldier who said, "What good is an artist. They do not produce food to eat. They are useless." Objects of art and antiques meant no more to the *moujik* than firewood to be chopped and burned in the stove to keep his hut warm.

Three of his majesty's most prized regiments passed by, marching by in perfect order behind a military band. Their officers sported large red cockades in their caps, a knot of red ribbon tied to their epaulettes and red stripes across their sleeves. The old regimental banners, once ornate with icons were now simply red flags.

Kazaks of the Escort, the proud and magnificent horsemen, the privileged élite of the Imperial Guards led the parade, wearing large red scarfs tied across their chests. Following them, the most sacred of his majesty's regiments, sons of high noble birth, those men selected from all the units of the Guards to guarantee the personal safety of their sovereigns. Next came His Majesty's Railway Regiment who had the duty of conducting the imperial trains and watching over the safety of Their Majesties when traveling. Finally, the guards of the Imperial Palaces, who were privy to all the most intimate secrets of their majesties.

"This is a travesty," Alexei said to his mother. "These troops are pledging their loyalty to the new authority, to a name they do not know. But perhaps...the fault is not entirely theirs. Like me, they've seen too many things they ought not to have seen."

Daniel received his son with elation and tears, hugging him in the lobby of the Astoria hotel. They went upstairs to the dining room and sat by a sunny window, anxious to hear the news. After days of gloomy skies, bitter cold and despairing hearts, they welcomed the sun and appropriately so.

"At first I resented the Tsar," Alexei began. "After I had been with him all through these last terrible months, I was exasperated to the point of pulling my hair out. I couldn't stand the sight of his weakness but in time I began to see the man inside, and I came to pity him. He couldn't help himself any more than a soldier without legs could make himself run. He was like that man in his spirit, crippled, beaten down, crushed. On the last day when we had to take an oath to the new government, he remained out of sight, in his room...cast off like a dog. I didn't repeat the oath. I couldn't. My heart was breaking for him. For the first time in three hundred years, the Emperor was not mentioned in the prayer.

He was actually a good man, polite, warm and charming...even to the end. He was terribly shy. He withdrew into himself more and more, unable to make even the smallest decision to go forward. He gave the impression of accepting what he called his doomed fate, but on his face we saw otherwise, the hollow sleepless eyes, the protruding cheek bones, like that of a ghost, a dim reflection of the man that once was. His suffering must have penetrated deeper than even he was willing to admit to himself. The mind altering drugs did not keep him in a state of euphoria but in helpless denial. In his heart he must have known the truth.

I believe he really did have a heart for his people and he was tortured inside. Who could have known what turmoil he suffered in silence through the years with his son...the Empress...the evil presence of Rasputin.

Was he flawed in his ability to judge men, or was he trembling behind his wife's apron strings. Did the scale of problems he had to solve, as many have implied, exceed the measure of his intelligence causing him to be suspicious of those capable statesmen struggling to serve him, or did he simply succumb to the rantings of the Empress in order to survive. We peons called her the German witch. The situation became so bad that several of our officers had to pop valerian pills to steady their nerves when they were in her presence.

The Tsar had no opinion about anything except tennis, horses, books, movies, all the mundane. His mother, the Empress Marie, his uncles, the Grand Dukes all came to Stavka to warn him about the unrest fomenting in the capital, but Nicholas brushed them off like crumbs from the breakfast table, and simply said, "Thanks, I appreciate your interest."

They say Nicholas II was responsible for more blood to be shed on Russian soil than any of the previous Emperors. He became a loathing figure in the eyes of many. But in the long run, I did not hate him, he was too tragic a character to be hated, perhaps one of the most tragic in history.

On the Tsar's last day at Mogilev, everyone assembled in the main hall of General Headquarters to hear Nicholas' farewell address…generals, officers, and persons of all ranks. Nicholas shook the hand of each man in his characteristic calm and reserved bearing. I thought I saw a semblance of a smile on his lips, like he was at last relieved of his burden. He thanked us and asked us to serve our new superior officers with the same loyalty and self-sacrifice we had shown him. He asked us to forget all feuds and to serve Russia in leading our army to victory. Then he said his farewell in terse sentences, avoiding any word that would invoke a feeling of pity. A gentleman to the last. Every man shouted, "hurrah." The elderly generals cried…citizen Romanov bowed and walked out.

The next day General Alekseev invited us to take our oath of allegiance to the Provisional government. Nicholas went to his room like an obedient child during the ceremony. What tortures did he suffer in those hours, what bitterness when he saw the look of elation on General Alekseev's face and the delight in the old man's eyes when the new government promised to appoint him as commander-in-chief of the army in recognition of his cooperation with the revolution.

Everyone lined up behind their new commander. I could not take the oath of allegiance to a combination of schemers who had just broken their own oath to the Emperor. Now, I feel sad for the old Tsar, sad for myself, and especially sad for my comrades who were needlessly blown away in the war. The ceremony broke at four and we were allowed to take leave."

"How did you get away on that first day?" Jeniya said.

Alexei laughed. "The day the rebels invaded headquarters? The big brass ran…like scared rabbits. The rest of us stayed on…they didn't bother us. They wanted Nicholas."

"For the life of me, I cannot understand how Nicholas could have surrendered his Empire to a mob of drunken reservists and rioting workers," said Daniel. "He had an army of fifteen million men at his disposal! A twenty-four-hour battle in the suburbs of Petrograd would have restored order."

"Alexei laughed. "We have a standing joke in the army. Order, counter order, disorder."

Daniel shook his head.

"Are you going back?" Jeniya asked. She stared at her son, an image of his father when she first met him but with a maturity beyond his years. How she was proud. Her eyes glistened with tears of thanksgiving.

"Yes, I have to. As long as I wear this uniform I am bound to my regiment. I simply cannot take it off and walk away, as much as I would like to. That would be worse than an infidel toward my fallen comrades, not to mention desertion.

Chapter 49

LENIN'S SEALED THIRD-CLASS railway car raced across Germany under the protection of armed guards. No windows, no stops for customs, no inspection of visas. The enemy financed the lead-sealed compartment and allowed the train to pass unencumbered as if they were sending a cargo of deadly mustard gas into the heart of Petrograd. The desperate people were longing for someone to rescue them from strife and riots; someone to restore a competent ministry and order in the capital city. They hoped Lenin would be their man.

Thousands of workers and soldiers waited at the Finland station to cheer the arriving train and welcome the triumphant hero of their revolution home from exile. They held red banners above their heads and waved little red flags in their hands. Bands played the Marseillaise. A short, stocky man with a big balding head set squarely on his shoulders stepped onto the platform. "Laynin, Laynin!" The people roared. Suddenly two Kronstadt sailors leaped from the crowd, picked him up, carried him outside, and placed him on top of an armored car.

"*Tovareeshee Soldatii! Tovareeshee Rabowtii! Previit!*" Lenin said to the cheering crowd vigorously pumping their long banners.

"The question of the state system is now the order of the day," Lenin began as the adulations died down. "The capitalists in whose hands the state power now rests, desire a parliamentary bourgeois republic…that is, a state system where there is no Tsar…where power remains in the hands of those who govern by means of the old institutions…namely, the police…the bureaucracy and the standing army."

Lenin bobbed his body toward the crowd as he spoke making wide sweeping gestures with his right hand, exhibiting relentless vigor and charisma. The people went wild and the sailors threw their hats in the air. At five feet, four inches in height, his commanding speech more than made up for what he lacked in stature.

"The Provisional Government offers you sweet speeches and great promises. They are deceiving you just as they are deceiving the entire Russian people. The people need peace. The people need bread. The people need land. They cannot give the peoples of Russia...either peace, bread or full freedom. We must struggle to the very end, to the final victory of the proletariat. We must oppose the bourgeois government...and transfer all power to the Soviet in whose hands all power and authority in Russia must rest. Long live the world wide socialist revolution!"

"Long live the socialist revolution," the people cheered in celebration of their new found freedom from tsarism. They had little understanding that the mastermind of a socialist democratic utopia had something other than their liberation in mind.

A group of school boys stood on the fringe of the crowd shouting, "Lenin is a German spy. He is bought with German money. They sent him back to Russia on purpose. He is a traitor. He will bring unhappiness to Russia. Why do you listen to him!" No one paid any attention.

Ezra advanced from a cosmopolitan gentleman to a member of the Committee of Bolshevik Directors. When the leadership heard that Lenin would be in Petrograd on Easter Sunday, they quickly painted placards announcing his arrival at the Finland Station and gave them to students to parade around the city. People out strolling read the signs and went to see him out of curiosity.

Ezra stood above the crowd and scanned their faces. Among the spectators he spotted remnants of the bourgeois watching the event with haggard faces. He saw some of them wipe tears from their eyes. No doubt they were wondering what would become of their obscene life-style when the rubbles they sucked from peasant labor ran dry. He smiled to himself.

The marching bands followed Lenin's armored car across the bridge to Petrograd Island where thousands more lined up to cheer him. Great red streamers hung from government buildings, little red flags waved in the marble hands of statues, and double headed eagles that had not been destroyed were hastily draped in red. Lenin immediately seized the palace of the dancer Kchechinskaya and established Bolshevik headquarters. He took over the mansion as if private property had already been abolished. Kerensky, the Minister of Justice, and the powerless provisional government made not one peep in protest.

Daniel didn't take Lenin's return lightly but saw him as a very dangerous man. He sat in the courtyard garden thinking of the time when he and Jeniya had taken a holiday to Switzerland. They happened to hear that Lenin had been gaining notoriety in elite European left wing circles and were curious to know his ideas. At an informal talk, Daniel recalled the Mongolian type features and especially the eyes, gleaming like live coals, filled with hatred. After the meeting he approached him and asked him to expound on his views concerning the peasantry, by far the largest population in Russia, and what he intended to do with the vast tracts of land they worked, owned by the gentry.

"Confiscating the land from the nobility and nationalizing it to be shared by all the people in common would not be popular with the peasants," he replied. "Since they all want to own a patch of land. Once I have the power in my hands, I will put socialistic ideals to work, whether or not the peasants...or anyone else...want it"

"How do you intend to gain power in a nation that believes in the benevolence of their Batiushka, the Tsar." Daniel asked.

"We intend to lull the people to sleep by deceit," he said unabashedly, speaking to Daniel as a partisan; all the while scrutinizing him through his squinty dark eyes. "We shall amalgamate with their forces and lead their armies into defeat and at the same time preaching victory. We shall deprive private individuals of their riches by placing them in the possession of the state...thus following the instruction of Marx and Engels. Not one single individual shall have the right of owning were it but a needle or a plough, everything will be socialized...and the people will become our blind weapons."

"But that policy would cause a civil war, especially among the half-civilized peasants, destroying many lives," Daniel replied.

"A sacrifice of thirty or forty millions out of a population of 180 million would be entirely justified if it served to bring humanity a great step nearer to socialism. This would make me very happy. It would be far worse for the socialist revolution to be followed by democracy, which would lead to a new upheaval in favor of socialism."

At the time Daniel felt that Lenin exuded the air of a megalomaniac, like a man obsessed with a grandiose vision of himself, but dismissed him as a potentially inconsequential madman. Never, in his wildest dreams could he ever have imagined that Lenin would one day capture the hearts and imaginations of the Russian masses. *How did this happen? These poor ignoramuses, so desperate to cast off the chains of their wretched existence, had no understanding of Lenin's version of a socialist revolution. They were thinking freedom from bondage under their barons while Lenin thought power, totalitarian power.*

Lenin picked a good day to return, Easter Sunday, the day people were out celebrating the resurrection of the Savior, and on the heels of a colossal city-wide funeral march to bury the defenders of the revolution. A strange sight occurred on that day, for the first time in the history of municipal celebrations, the clergy were conspicuously absent.

"To the peoples of the universe," proclaimed the Soviet leadership. "We, the workmen and soldiers of Russia, announce to you the great event of the Russian revolution and send you greetings of fire. Our victory is a great victory of universal freedom and democracy. Follow our example and shake off the yoke of autocratic power. Refuse to be any longer an instrument of conquest in the hand of your Kings, landlords, and bankers."

The revolution permitted, justified and excused everything. Everyone was free. Cabbies drove anywhere they wanted on the streets, causing collisions. Workers walked off their jobs whenever they felt like it. They were free. Bakers left their dough and truck drivers refused to deliver flour. They were free. Street lights burned day and night. No one bothered to switch them off.

"Comrade truck drivers," said the Soviet leadership. "Unload the flour. Comrade bakers, bake bread. Do not imitate the infamies of the old regime. Do not let your brothers die of hunger."

The workers replied. "We will not unload the wagons. We will not bake the bread because it is not our pleasure to do so. We are free!"

———◆———

When the Bolsheviks, Mensheviks, and Socialists Revolutionaries met to resolve their differences between the radical and moderate wings of the party, Lenin called a closed meeting with the committee of Bolshevik directors to stop the mediation process and redirect their priorities. Compromise was not in his vocabulary.

"*Tovareeshee*," he said. "The conversion of the present imperialist war into a civil war is the only way the proletariat will be able to shake off its dependence on the chauvinist bourgeois...do not use your weapons against your brothers, the wage slaves in other countries... but against the reactionaries and bourgeois governments...in the merciless struggle against chauvinism. There is no escape from barbarism, no possibility of progress in Europe, without a civil war for socialism!

Support for Russia's war effort in any form remains as intolerable as ever. Loyal Bolsheviks must oppose the Provisional Government at every opportunity and dedicate their energies to transferring all power to the Soviet."

Lenin's "April Thesis" drew people into the streets in conflict over the war. Thirteen of the sixteen members of the Bolshevik directors rejected it, calling it Lenin's personal opinion.

The liberal moderates of the socialist party called it the ravings of a madman. "Comrades," they said. "Have you already forgotten our mutilated veterans of war who but a week ago, dragged themselves painfully along the Nevsky Prospekt to protest the pacifism of the Socialists. The blind, the lame, the amputee, some wrapped in bandages and fixed up on trucks, a living embodiment of all the horrors and tortures of war that flesh can endure. Remember their banners. 'Let not our glorious deeds have died in vain. Look at our wounds, they call for victory. War for liberty to our last breath! You took your hats off and saluted these valiant men with tear-filled eyes. How quickly have you forgotten? The pacifists are disgracing Russia. Down with Lenin."

But Lenin pressed on toward his goals and met with the All-Russian congress of Peasant Deputies assembled in Petrograd on the issue of land use. "Land ownership by the squires is the greatest injustice," he said. "All private land ownership must be abolished and lands that lay beyond peasant village boundaries seized. The peasant soviet congress decided that the right to private property must be abolished forever and all privately held land be taken over without compensation as the property of the assemblage. All Russians who desire to cultivate it with their own labor, along with the help of their family or in a cooperative group must have the right to use the land collectively."

Thousands of soldiers, brainwashed by the Bolsheviks who had infiltrated their ranks, deserted the front and wandered over the countryside, scrambling in front of moving trains, stopping the engines and pulling out passengers. They jumped onto the steps, climbed through windows, pushing and shoving their way inside. Everywhere, on the roofs, on the platforms, on the buffers, soldiers swarmed like a cloud of grey locusts, filling every crack, and sat with sacks and rifles taking joy rides to nowhere, anywhere, paralyzing rail traffic.

Mutiny unleashed its fury. When officers tried to maintain order among their troops on the battlefield, drunken mobs murdered them after they refused to take insults from the recruits. In the navy, Kronstadt sailors rounded up their officers, hacked off their arms and legs before killing them and tossing their mutilated bodies into the sea.

Everyone took to the streets. Loiters congested city parks and squares and assaulted pedestrians with verbal obscenities. No one bothered to pick up their litter. Bands played the Marseillaise. The Salvation Army amused the mobs with outdoor gospel meetings. Pontificators deliberated on every street corner with their interpretation of the first principles of revolution. Ungrateful servants rebelled. Jews celebrated their new freedom with boisterous proclamations, "Citizens...Jews! The Jewish people of Russia now celebrate an event which has no parallel in Jewish history for two thousand years! We are citizens with equal rights!" Peasants with greedy eyes on the land belonging to the squires paraded with red banners demanding, "All land to the Peasants. Land and liberty. Peace for the peasant hut. War for the palaces. Rob what has been robbed. Grab all you want, it's rightfully yours. Long live the Soviet."

Peddlers sold pictures with hideous caricatures of the Emperor and his family. Inquisitive seekers of sensationalism took train excursions to Alexander Park hoping to get a glimpse of their disposed Emperor and his family. They stared with a strange indifference, and spoke of him as though he were a monkey in a zoo, unable to understand. Some heartless individuals hurled obscenities at him. Sentries assigned to guard the prisoner Romanov and his family sprawled slovenly on the benches in front of the iron gates in defiance of the old order. Whenever the opportunity arose, these unscrupulous men exploited the public's curiosity by collecting rubbles to show Nicholas II amusing himself for hours with such pitiful tasks as breaking up ice in a fountain with an iron-shod pole. In summer, they bathed naked in the ponds exposing themselves to everyone.

No one bothered to clear the streets of snow or care for the park grounds. Nicholas said nothing, but carried on as if no one was there watching. He considered himself a martyr, the supreme sacrifice offered to God for his nation's transgressions, but people saw him and Aleksandra as the malefactors responsible for the suffering and blood shed of millions. Few could forgive the "German woman" for spawning so much evil with her soothsayer, Rasputin.

Long bread lines, shortages of food, soaring inflation, and hunger was the price paid for freedom from labor. Still the workers continued to demand higher wages for an eight-hour day plus overtime pay. They had found a way to force their will on factory operations by organizing factory management committees which gave them more bargaining power with their bosses, except they didn't understand that higher wage concessions demanded higher production cost.

Ezra found his way back into his brother's factory and wormed through the ranks of workers agitating them into demanding a voice in the management of the plant. "You are the labor force," he said to a group of men gathered in the dining hall. "Without your blood and sweat there would be no production. Your bosses do not understand your needs. They are not sweating over the fires of steel in the heat of summer as you are. They are sitting in cool cafes on the Gulf of Finland or in their fine summer dachas taking tea. Opportunity is now at your door. The opportunity you fought and died for. Don't let it pass. Seize it! Now is the time for every one of you to take the initiative in the production and distribution of goods which you produce. You may have the best working conditions in Petrograd…maybe in the whole county, but you have control of nothing. Your bosses are using your blood and sweat to make themselves richer. And do you think they care. No! When one of you falls, you are quickly replaced by another. You need to demand control of you own daily operations by an elected body of your own comrades!"

Ezra knew he was making progress when he heard a low monotone mutter of agreement rumble through the men's ranks and their numbers grew by the day as did their discontentment.

As factory owner after factory owner was forced to yield to the worker's demands, inflation soared toward the stratosphere, and began to affect even the wealthiest of households. By midsummer many workers began to negotiate their wages for food and clothing to escape starvation. Now the management had a bargaining tool by which they could gain back some lost ground, but the proletariat stood firm. From the elite *metallisty* to shoemaker and laundress, workers took to the streets in protest. "We will have our way," said the *Putilovtsy metallisty*. "Let there be no bourgeois."

Chapter 50

THE BATTLE HARDENED General Kornilov had a small sinewy frame, fiery black eyes and high flat cheekbones denoting a Mongolian heritage; a man of unrelenting courage who defied death. He was wounded, captured and imprisoned for a year by the Austrians, until he managed to slip past his guards disguised as an Austrian soldier. After two weeks walking from village to village under the surveillance of sentries, living only on wild berries, he made it to the allied frontier.

A scholar, historian and author, he spoke several Central Asian languages fluently and surrounded himself with the renowned horsemen of Central Asia. These men known as the Savage Division, sported machine-guns and unsheathed swords and moved with equal resolve and daring.

Alexander Kerensky, elected by the new Soviet coalition as Prime Minister, reluctantly appointed Kornilov Supreme Commander of the Russian armies at the recommendation of his Minister of War.

"It's time to hang that whole bunch of German spies and sympathizers, the chief of whom is Lenin," Kornilov said in an effort to reestablish discipline and authority in the disintegrating army. "The entire Soviet of Workers and Soldier Deputies needs to be broken up… broken up so they'll never be able to meet again."

But the ambitious Kerensky pandered and played into the hands of the Soviets and refused to allow Kornilov to turn his armies on the Bolsheviks. Instead, he asked him to declare martial law in Petrograd.

Then a misunderstanding contrived by one double-talking little nobody, called Vladimir Lvov, who claimed that he was fully empowered to speak for Kerensky, appeared at General Headquarters to inform Kornilov that Kernesky's life was in eminent danger. Korniliv feared that the Bolsheviks may be staging a coup and requested that the prime Minister come to Mogilev for protection.

Lvov immediately went to the winter palace to warned Kerensky that he was doomed and he must leave Petrograd immediately. He said that Kornilov's generous offer to protect him at General Headquarters was a threat against his life because the General planned to take over all military and civilian operations.

Kerensky Panicked. Convinced that Kornilov was hatching a plot to betray him, he sent a wire asking him to confirm his invitation.

"Yes," said the general. "I confirm that I asked Lvov to transmit my urgent request that you come to Mogilev."

Kerensky called on Kornilov to publicly resign as Supreme Commander of the Russian armies and Kornilov accused Kerensky of colluding with the German General Staff to sign a peace treaty.

Kornilov then took his appeal to the army and the people through the press. "I pledge to you my word of honor as an officer and a soldier...I am opposed to all counter-revolutionary schemes, and stand on the liberties we have won, desiring that the great Russian nation should continue independent."

The Soviets immediately pulled the General's appeal from the press and published their own order. "Comrade officers and soldiers. General Kornilov has rebelled against the revolution and the provisional government. He wants to re-establish the old regime and deprive the people of land and liberty."

At the same time the strategic Baltic port of Riga fell into German hands. The enemy now encamped within grasping distance of the Russian capital. Kornilov moved his Savage Division of Caucasian tribesmen to the outskirts of the Petrograd in position to defend it. He also stationed himself in an advantageous position to stage a *coup d'etat*...if he wanted.

The fidgety prime minister's imagination exploded into a mindless frenzy. "*Tovareeshee*," Kerensky cried to his troops. "The hour has arrived when your loyalty to freedom and the revolution is on trial. Let everyone see before them truly revolutionary regiments."

In retaliation, Kornilov ordered the Kazaks of the third cavalry to move in on Petrograd under the command of Krymov, a hard-driving, right-wing General.

The rail-workers of the Soviet immediately answered Kerensky's call and in the dead of night surrounded Krymov's trains, grinding them to a halt. The startled soldiers jumped off the trains and acquiesced to the rail-worker's fabrication. They unanimously rejected Kornilov, fearing that he intended to replace the Soviet democratic assembly with a military junta. Without a moment's hesitation, they announced their alliance to the revolution. "We declare that we are in complete solidarity with the Soviet." They raised their rifles in the air and cheered. "Long live the Soviet of Workers and Soldiers Deputies!"

When Krymov was taken to Petrograd under arrest, he told Kerensky, "I will not deceive you. I had wished to hang the lot of you."

"The last card for saving the homeland had been beaten. Living is not worthwhile any longer." Krymov wrote before he shot himself through the heart.

Lvov wrote Kerensky a complementary letter accrediting himself. "I congratulate you from the bottom of my heart. I am glad that I saved you from Kornilov's hands."

Kornilov underestimated the coordinated power of the Soviet movement and its popular support among the people. On September 7th General Alekseev arrested the General at Mogilev. "The scoundrel, the upstart," said Kornilov. "Can't Kerensky see that his days are numbered. Tomorrow Lenin will have his head and everything will be wrecked."

"Papa? Where are you calling from?" asked Jeniya. "I thought you were at Belozerkovka?"

"No. I'm here in the city. I want to talk to you."

"About what?"

"I can't talk on the phone. I have to see you."

A chill swept over her fearing something calamitous had happened to someone in the family. "Are you...and mama...all right?" she said gazing at the cold September rain slashing against the window pane.

"Yes, we are all fine. May I come over?"

"Certainly." She told Yaroslav to order a footman to prepare the samovar for tea in the drawing room where she would receive her father. "And please be sure the fire is lit in the fireplace," she said.

Count Rostovsky gave his hat, coat and umbrella to the footman at the door and took off his goulashes before he came in and sat down.

"Why did you leave Belozerkovka?" Jeniya asked. "Isn't it dangerous to travel these days." The Count had aged well, his hair a bit whiter and his dimples a little deeper

"Dangerous to travel? It's dangerous to live anywhere in this damn insane asylum. I'm leaving."

"Leaving?"

"I want you and your family to come with us."

"What?" Jeniya's thoughts drew blanks. I...ah...when are you leaving?"

"In about a month, that will give you time to get ready."

"We can't just pick up and leave just like that! Daniel has his businesses, his employees depend on him, he wouldn't leave them. And I have to supervise the mission. What about all the people who depend on us, and Katiya and Ronnie...and Alexei at Stavka...we are still at war...Gavril is still at school. He'll be graduating next spring."

"There won't be a next spring for Russia. You get your sons and let Daniel sell his factory, or whatever he does...or give it to the damn revolution."

"Papa, you're talking like a crazy man."

"It's no wonder."

The footman brought in a tray with warm rolls, butter and jam. He poured two cups of hot tea and served them on the table in front of the sofa along with the rolls. Count Rostovsky took one and buttered it. Jeniya, now in a state of anxiety over this abrupt news, just sipped tea. In back of her mind she felt that her father's sentiments had some validity but she would not allow herself to entertain those thoughts. She had to have hope, if not for her sanity, then for her family.

"What will you do with Belozerkovka when you leave...and your sugar factory...the winery?"

"The winery? There is no winery. That drunken scum we call the army drank it up. And Belozerkovka, there is no Belozerkovka."

"Why? What happened to it?"

"I was forced to move out and give it over. The Socialist government in Kiev passed a resolution to use the great house and its grounds for a school."

Jeniya looked dumbfounded. "I don't believe this!"

The count chuckled. "And you're going to see a lot more if you remain here." He gazed at the family pictures on the table and reflected on the happier times at Belozerkovka. "My peasants were content," he said thoughtfully. "I gave them seed-corn, manure...I allowed their animals to grass in our pastures, even supplied them with amenities from our estate when they had difficulties. Used to be that they just stole some firewood or carried off some grain. Maybe they burned down a barn once in a while. Change didn't enter their minds until those blasted agitators, the Jews, came from the cities and fired them up. This nation survived for hundreds of years in relative peace and harmony until the Jews got their equal rights. Now they're tearing apart the old empire...peasants are on the rampage, seizing manors, thoroughbreds, cattle, swine, fowl, machines, implements, anything they could get their hands on. Drunken soldiers are littering the countryside with filth, honest working men are becoming infected with revolutionary fever.

Everyone is demanding his fair share, that's all I hear...our fair share! They don't understand democracy, don't even know what the word means. The senseless peasants think that free land for everyone means the right to drive us off and take what they can before someone else gets to it. Now that we have no Tsar they can do anything they want and not answer for it. And you wonder why I am half out of my mind!"

Rostovsky rambled on like a man anxious to rid himself of a long pent up rage. Jeniya listened and let him carry on. She looked down at the empty plate on the table. "Would you like more rolls?"

"No thank you. But I will have a shot of brandy...if you don't mind."

Jeniya signaled the footman.

"I blame those idiots in the Provisional Government for having allowed all this talk about social democracy to get about...and freedom. They could have stepped up like men and taken action against the rantings of this rabble long ago when they had the power. Now it is too late."

The footman presented the count a goblet of brandy on a silver platter. He took it and gulped it down. "Do you remember Princess Friedinov?" he said.

Jeniya looked at him with curiosity in her eyes. "Yes, we used to go to her house when we were girls."

"She's been shot. Her country palace taken over by a band of roving scumbag deserters. Do you know they even dug her poor son from his grave, looking for valuables and left his body there to rot?"

Jeniya frowned. "Oh, how horrible!" She remembered Yuri as a boy. He and Anatole were friends.

"It's madness! This sort of thing is going on all over the countryside, digging up graves, brutally murdering land owners. We are living in a lunatic asylum. A jungle of wild animals. He rolled his blue eyes toward the windows and thought for a moment, then quoted from Pushkin, 'We live without power of law, like flocks of ravens they come and sweep the land'...I suggest you convince that husband of yours to use his brain and get out, lord knows he has a good one. I have sent a considerable amount of gold ahead to Sweden. If you would like, I could hold your gold there for you."

"Papa! Can't you wait until after the elections in November. All this will blow over. I have hope that the people will elect a truly democratic government. Then everything will change. We can build a new Russia." She chattered on rapidly hoping to change her father's mind. "If every decent person leaves, who will be around to defend all the good and noble citizens of Russia?"

"Defend it with what, a bandage? You're a dreamer. This criminal, Lenin…this wannabe dictator will not stop until he's corrupted every decent and honorable thing. Already his courtiers, the Bolsheviks, bow to his every word. Heh. And the ignorant proletariat are falling for it…I actually feel sorry for them because they don't understand what he has in store for them."

"And what about becoming a displaced person. A man without a country. Where will you live?"

"As I recall, Jenka, you were never unhappy in Biarritz, we have friends there, a home there. It's not too far from Paris, Madrid, the Rivera…wine country." The count put his brandy goblet down and stood to his full erect height, brushing some bread crumbs from his suit. "Well, what do you say, *dyavushka*, are you coming with us? Yelizavetta, Cyril and the family are joining us. I haven't talked to Katiya or Irina yet."

"I don't know," she said shaking her head. "I have to talk with Daniel. I doubt he will desert his friends, his co-workers, or his factory, when they so desperately need him right now."

"Tell him to shut it all down. In times like these there is nothing noble in foolishness and it is foolish to remain here. Soon there will no longer be an Orthodox Russia. Only a country called revolution."

"You can't mean that?"

"Most certainly. There is no containing this rabble, it is only a matter of time…I'm going to the bank to get you mother's jewels. Do you want to go with me? I would suggest that you send them along with us in case things get out of hand."

"Papa, I'm all so confused right now." She put her hand to her forehead as if to stop the whirling thoughts. "I have to think about all this...and talk with Daniel. When did you say you were leaving?"

"No later than the end of next month. I still have to confirm our reservations and pay for the passage. You have time to get your household in order."

"What about the servants?"

"Well, take them...if they want to leave. Yaroslav has been with you since you were married and before that he served me well."

"I don't think Daniel would ever abandon his work at the mission, feeding the poor and sharing the gospel. If everything will be as bad as you say, their eternity may soon be upon them."

"And upon you...if you remain here. Should this storm blow over and Russia sees blue skies again, we can always return."

Chapter 51

For Ezra and the hard core Bolsheviks it wasn't enough to abolish the monarchy and its parasites. They had to lay the ground work for a complete overthrow of the capitalist bourgeois to the last man.

The masses were ready. The Bolsheviks had gained the majority vote in the Petrograd soviet, the Moscow Soviet and the Ukrainian Soviet in Kiev through armed intimidation. Russia was ripe for the picking.

Lenin hammered for an armed conflict against the government with a blitz of inflaming words in the Bolshevik newspaper, Pravda. "Cowards," he wrote. "Go to the workers in every factory, in every district. Go to the barracks. Be brave...go to the Kazak units. March onward! The moment is urgent! Go to the people in the streets. The pulse of life is there...the source of salvation for our revolution. All who refuse are guilty of betrayal of the revolution." March for... Peace...Land...and Bread."

Not everyone on the Bolshevik's Central Committee received Lenin's sentiments with praise. Most of these men insisted that they, not Lenin, must take the leadership and gradually transfer power from the Provisional Government into the hands of the All-Russian Congress of Soviets when they met at the end of October.

Lenin remained undaunted. He organized a secret meeting where he could convince a few of his most loyal followers to embrace his views on the imminent need of an armed coup. "The present task must be an armed uprising in Petrograd and Moscow, the seizure of power and the over-throw of the government," he told them from a location known only to the attendees. "The time has come for decision and not talk, for action and not resolution. Power is not transferred; it is taken with guns. The success of both the Russian and the world revolution depends on two or three days fighting. Any delay at a time when victory is certain and the chances are ten to one that it will be a bloodless victory would be childish, disgraceful, dangerous, criminal, a betrayal of the revolution, and fatal. The government is tottering. We must deal it the death blow...at any cost...to delay action is the same for us as death."

"Lenin's supporters always felt a surge of strength and resolve when they heard him speak or read his writings," observed Trotsky, the new chairman of the Petrograd Soviet. "Those who experience a certain hesitation set aside their doubts."

The hard liners tirelessly haunted every mill, every barracks, every dive. They launched a blitz on the factory workers stirring up revolutionary fever in such rapid succession that the workers swore they had seen them everywhere at the same time. "The time for words has passed," they said. "The hour has come to deliver the death blow! Denounce Kerensky's government and decide for the revolution. Stand with the Bolsheviks!" The Russian earth quaked beneath the fiery words of these determined men and their cry rolled across Petrograd like a tidal wave.

They whispered in the ears of the impoverished women standing for hours in long lines against the soaking rain and driving winds to buy milk and bread. "The Socialist deputies and the ministers are living in luxury while you starve," they said. "Your generalissimo, Kerensky, even sleeps in the bed of Alexander III!"

At the same time, in rebuttal, the Kazaks galloped furiously throughout the city distributing their own leaflets, exhorting the public to keep calm and support the Provisional Government.

On his way to work one morning in October, Daniel observed small groups of soldiers loitering about on empty streets, grinning with the same silly excitement on their faces that he had seen many times before trouble broke out somewhere in the city. Occasionally he noticed a noisy truck rumble by bouncing a pack of armed soldiers up and down.

By mid-morning the normal flow of daily activities continued as usual and pedestrians went about their business unaware that the *putilovsky* were on their jobs in the steel mill with loaded guns at their sides. The afternoon shoppers had no idea that while they were making purchases, the rebels had taken control of Petrograd's garrisons, or that several hundred sailors burst into the Central Telegraph Office startling the employees and demanding them to surrender in the name of the Revolution. They disarmed the three hundred military academy cadets on guard and kicked them out. They cut off the telephone lines to the Winter Palace where the ministers of the provisional government were meeting. Though not one employee sympathized with the Bolshevik cause, they all responded like zombies whose life-blood of hope had been drained.

The people who filled the theaters that evening were unaffected when the sailors had taken command of the Main Post Office, the Electric Power Stations, the railway stations, and the bridges that led to the center of the city. Patrons eating and drinking at the fashionable supper clubs, immersed in enjoyment and entertainment were totally oblivious to the darkened street lights, and armed workers stealthy moving across the city under the cover of fog and drizzle. Neither did anyone see the Smolny Institute lit up like a beacon on the horizon, stirring with restless machine gunners, nor did they hear the armored car drivers impatiently revving up their engines, waiting for orders to launch their attack on the Winter Palace at midnight.

When Kerensky discovered that the Bolsheviks had seized all the key installations throughout the city and had targeted the ten ministers still in conference at the Winter Palace for annihilation, he frantically searched for troops to defend them, but found empty barracks. A few hundred military academy cadets and several Kazaks volunteered to fight with his own elite forces, the bold and courageous women loyal to the nation, he called the women's death battalion. Commander Kerensky then left these young women and boys to fend for themselves and bolted from the city. With their leader in flight, most of the cadets, the Kazaks and some in the woman's battalion gave up and left. The beleaguered ministers, defended only by a few cadets and what was left of the women's battalion, realized they were sitting ducks for the Bolsheviks. Still, they could not bring themselves to admit defeat. Even after they were given the ultimatum to surrender before the soldiers opened fire, they opted to sit it out until the very end. Now doomed, lonely, and abandon by all, they paced around in what they called a huge mouse trap.

A contingent of about twenty-five sailors thought they could bluff their way past the women without firing a shot. They entered the palace square waiving their rifles in the air and shouting, "hurrah. Hurrah!" The women returned their greeting with a hail of machine gun-fire from behind sand bags barricades stacked around the palace windows.

Like a thunderbolt, a single blast of cannon fire shook the bed and jolted Daniel and Jeniya awake in the middle of the night. Then dead quiet. Yaroslav rushed from the servant's quarters and knocked on the bedroom door.

"Come in," Daniel said putting on his robe.

The butler entered, automatically stood at attention and announced in his direct detached manner, "the servants are frightened to death, sir, and are hiding in the basement. What shall we do?" But he could not disguise his fear through a quivering voice.

Suddenly artillery fire erupted through the incongruous calm. Roar from machine-guns rose above the rattle of rifles and vibrated the windows. Then another long silence pierced by a rumble of cannon fire from the Fortress of St. Peter and Paul across the Neva. Church bells tolled simultaneously with the cannonade in the mortal struggle between Christian Orthodoxy and Bolshevik godlessness. Then the bells went silent. The bombardment continued. Jeniya knelt down on the floor with her head to her knees and her arms over her ears. Since the war, death was always striking at someone's door. It had become so common place that she had almost come to face it with indifference.

Several sailors crawled into the palace through unlocked doors searching for the room where the ministers of the Provisional Government anxiously awaited their fate. At 1:50 AM, they surrendered and were arrested.

More soldiers followed like sniffing hounds following a trail of sent that led to the wine cellars of the Tsars, stocked with rare wines including bottles of Tokay dating back to Catherine the Great. The Bolshevik commander immediately dispatched the Preobrazhensky regiment to guard the national treasure, but it didn't take long before they were all staggering around pie-eyed. The Pavlovsky guards were called and soon they were in the bag. Guards from various other units took their turns and they all got drunk. The armored car gunners guarding the Alexander square drove aimlessly weaving in and out through the amassing crowds who came from everywhere in the city to join their slap-happy comrades. The Bolsheviks barred the entrance of the wine cellars with bricks but the mob smashed through the iron grated windows. "Let's drink to the Romanov's remains," they said in toast after toast as everyone joined in the drunken ecstasy. The firemen arrived to hose the cellars with water, but they got drunk. More troops were rounded up to guard the cellars and they got drunk. Finally, the Bolshevik commander announced the wine cellars would be blown up with dynamite...without warning! The crowds ignored his threat and the party went on for days until finally, the wine was pumped into the Neva.

"Have we survived another day?" Daniel asked when Savva appeared in the morning to assist him in dressing.

"I have not heard the outcome, sir. But I can find out."

Savva went out disguised as a soldier in his old military great-coat to see if the streets were safe amidst the boisterous festivities in the palace square, and after a few hours returned with the news.

"The Winter Palace has fallen in one hour, sir. And the rebels have arrested all the ministers," he said with sadness in his eyes. "It's over. The Empire has fallen."

The Empire fell within one hour? It was all a too easy, all too simple, all too frightening. "It's not over," Daniel said. "Now anything could happen, we are entirely in the power of the ruthless Bolsheviks and nothing but the mercy of God can deliver us."

Tears filled the servant's eyes. "I'm sorry sir." The display of emotion was out of order for his position as valet, but not unwelcome as far as Daniel was concerned.

"Go ahead, Savva. Have a good cry. Don't apologize. Mourning is appropriate in times like these."

"Quite so, sir," he said. "There is more to the story. Something unspeakably horrid has happened last night...our prime minister fled and entrusted the defense of the winter palace to boys and young women, many of them only girls. Their brave commander was the daughter of an admiral and hero of the Russo Turkish war of 1877. I remember meeting him once, a man of the noblest of character...and now..." He took out his handkerchief and wiped his eyes. "All the women were either killed or wounded and the soldiers who invaded the Winter Palace took their still breathing bodies back to the barracks and raped them outright…before killing them. They died in vain for that…that slippery…yellow-bellied dog, Kerensky." The sadness in his eyes turned to anger when he spoke the name. "He thought of no one but himself."

Lenin stepped up to the podium and gripped the edge of the lectern, his twinkling beady eyes surveilling the crowd. He had arrived at the meeting of the Soviet delegates in the ballroom of Smolny Institute, once an elite finishing school for daughters of aristocratic families. He wore a shabby dark suit, and his trousers, much too long for his short legs, hung baggy. However, his intellectual power and audacity to command the masses overrode his unremarkable appearance.

As the morning light seeped through the long windows after the eve of the victorious revolution, many representatives had already left having debated through the night, but none would ever forget that glorious moment when the battleship Aurora fired the first cannon, signaling the commencement of the revolution and the overthrow the provisional government. Those who remained gave Lenin a thunderous applause.

"*Tovareeshee*. We shall now take up the formation of the socialist state," he said. "Private ownership of land shall be abolished forever. All land held as private property shall be confiscated without compensation and become the property of the whole people. Most of all, the peasants should be firmly assured that there are no more landowners in the countryside."

"Hurrah." The people cheered. "To the heroes who first made up the Bolsheviks!"

When the cheers died down, Lenin continued. "The question of peace is a burning question; an immediate peace without annexations and without indemnities." He called on the workers of all nations to join Russia in the pursuit of world peace. "The worker's movement will triumph and it will pave the way to peace and socialism!"

"Hurrah! Hurrah! Under these banners we pledge to achieve a brotherhood of all nations! Long live the Russian Revolution as a prologue to social revolution in Europe! When tyranny falls the people will rise, great and free!"

At the end of his speech, he alluded to the eminent liquidation of about one hundred of the richest millionaires.

"Death to the aristocrats!" shouted the people.

"The fate of the revolution and the fate of the democratic peace is in your hands. Long live the revolution!"

After the meeting, Trotsky and Lenin brainstormed for a name for their new government. Trotsky suggested, "The Soviet of People's Commissars."

"That's brilliant," Lenin said. "It smells strongly of revolution. The main thing is that the people's commissars be those closely tied to the masses...a type born in the fires of revolution." He paused to reflect on their victory. "You know, Trotsky, to pass so quickly from persecutions and living in hiding to power...it makes one's head spin!"

The two Bolshevik leaders selected fourteen commissars and named Lenin as the chairman. But they had one more obstacle standing in the road to power; the Second congress of Soviets were still in control and they were not about to give in to the new radical victors. They joined with the liberals and moderates to form the All-Russian Committee for Salvation of the Motherland and took their case to the citizens. Support poured in. In solidarity with the Committee for Salvation, Petrograd's civil servants and other white-collar workers went on strike, leaving Russia's new People's Commissars to find empty offices when they arrived the following day to take command.

Neither did Kerensky give up when he saw an opportunity to retrieve his empire. He wanted that power over Russia as much as Napoleon wanted power over Europe...and Russia. But when he tried to muster up troops to defend the city from the Bolsheviks, the soldiers refused to fight for him. He finally persuaded several units of loyalist Kazaks stationed outside the city to support his cause. They easily demolished the red stronghold at Tsarskoe Selo, a short distance away from the capital city and prepared the path for victory in Petrograd.

The Committee for Salvation launched the cadets in every military academy to defend the city while they waited for the Kazaks to arrive. But the troops were waylaid by their Supreme Commander in Chief, Kerensky, who continuously intruded with irritating pontifications of victory instead of giving the charging command. After serving under the Prime Minister's constant inconsistency since their commander, Kornilov, was arrested, the fighting men had enough of him. One seasoned solder summed up the attitude of his comrades when he spat in the dirt and said, "everything's so tangled up that I don't understand any of it! To hell with all these orators!" And he rode away.

Kerensky blustering on his soap box gave the Bolsheviks time to drive the cadets back into their schools and assemble a reinforcement of five thousand sailors and soldiers, plus two thousand *putilovsky* to avert Kerensky's attack, about equal in number to those of the Kazak defenders. The troops loyal to the government bravely fought the reds outside at the city limits until they ran out of ammunition and were forced to surrender. In exchange for delivering Kerensky, they bargained for a safe passage home to southern Russia and to the Ukraine.

Jeniya locked her bedroom door and went to work on her project in secret. She had concocted a plan of defense against uncertainty. She dug her oldest coat from the closet and a needle and thread from the sewing table and laid them across her writing desk when someone knocked on the door.

"Who is it?" she said.

"Antonia, madam."

"Just one moment." Jeniya quickly took the coat and put it back in the closet and shoved the needle and thread in the desk drawer.

Antonia had taken on double-duty as head housekeeper and Jeniy's lady's maid since her faithful old servant, Galina, had passed on.

"Come in," she said.

"You have a visitor, madam, Vadim Pavelovich."

"Tell him to meet me in the drawing room…and order a footman to bring some tea, brandy and vodka."

"Yes, madam." Antonia gave Jeniya a hard scrutinizing look from the corner of her eye before she slipped out the door. Since Lenin proclaimed death to aristocrats in his speech at the Smolny institute, she began to notice the servants moving stealthy in the halls; slipping behind doors with malevolent eyes watching to steal and itching ears listening to snitch, or had she imagined it? The line between reality and illusion had begun to blur in what had become a surreal world. Many of her friends had confided that they were living in constant fear that their lady's maids or their husband's valets who were privy to their most intimate secrets might report their activities to the secret police in order to receive special favors.

When Jeniya entered the drawing room, Vadim stood up, bowed and kissed her hand.

"Oh, that isn't necessary anymore, Vadim."

"But isn't it nice to keep some of the old ways alive before we all go mad."

She smiled. "Yes, indeed it is. Please sit down," she said offering a hand of welcome. "Would you like something to warm up?"

"*Pashalusta, hoteil* cognac, if you don't mind." He took a cigarette from a gold case and offered one to Jeniya.

She shook her head and nodded to the footman standing in attendance. "Bring two cognacs, please." She stared at Vadim inquisitively. "So…to what do I owe the pleasure of your visit?"

"So…I came to say goody-by." He said resting one leg over the other.

"Where are you going?"

"To join Generals Alekseev and Kornilov in the Ukraine. We are setting up a counter-revolutionary volunteer army. Whites against reds."

Alousha mentioned that General Dukhonin released Kornilov and was shot because he refused to hand him over to the reds. Is that true?"

"Unfortunately."

Jeniya shook her head. "What terrible things are taking place... did you know they converted Belozerkovka into a school? We have no home there anymore."

"No, I didn't know."

The footman offered two gobbles of cognac on a sliver tray. They in each took one and held it up for a toast. Here's to the days that were," Vadim said. "And to the days that will be. May we find happy days again. *Za zdaroviye*"

She repeated the toast and they drank.

He stared into the distance and made a slight smile of remembrance. "We had some wonderful times at Belozerkovka...didn't we. What's your father up to?"

"He left for Stockholm in September."

"A very smart man. Why didn't you and Daniel go with him?"

"Well...for a number of reasons." Jeniya signaled the footman to bring another brandy to Vadim. "The workers have formed committees to take control of those issues which concern them but they do not have the expertise to run an industry like metallurgy. When the Putilov works were expropriated and the arms industry almost collapsed, Lenin set up a metallurgical trust under the stewardship of a few of the original owners, allowing them to participate in the management.

"You and I both know that will not last long. You should have gone with your father."

"I couldn't leave Alousha." She gazed downward lost in thought.

"Is he still at General Headquarters?"

"She nodded. "He has been committed to the army…" She stopped in the middle of her sentence and looked Vadim in the eye. "Can you take him with you to the Ukraine?"

Vadim chuckled. "I don't know if that's possible."

"Vadim? Suppose your best laid plans don't work out and the reds prevail. Would you surrender to them?"

Vadim frowned. A sudden passion filled his eyes. "Surrender is not in my vocabulary. I'll die with my sword in hand rather than bow down to those dogs. No Bolshevik son-of-bitch will ever make a slave out of me!" He held up his glass. The footman immediately appeared and filled it up. "And I'll drink to that!"

She smiled. *Still the same old Vadim.* She wanted to say me neither, but at the moment, she looked at her future with uncertainty.

Vadim stood up and Jeniya followed his lead and walked him to the door. "Well, Jeniya," he said as he took her hand. "In case we should not meet again, I wish you and Daniel all the best. I hope we all get through this thing in one piece."

"Likewise, *moii droog.*" They gazed into one another eyes, not as lovers, but as parting comrades.

She waited and watched for a long time as he disappeared into the unknown and frightening future, longing for the bygone days of civility and honor, of beauty and social grace, of music.

After Vadim left, she retrieved her coat, the needle and thread and began to sew some of her jewels in the lining. The new constituent assembly hadn't held their first meeting when already the reds announced they would monopolize all private banks and seize stocks, bonds, gold, and jewels. Owners were commanded to open their safe deposit boxes under the watchful eyes of the new All Russian Extraordinary Commission, aka the CHEKA, established to sabotage any counter-revolutionary activity and use whatever means necessary to destroy everything that stood in their way of establishing their totalitarian government.

Most people surrendered their valuable possessions needed for survival like mute sheep led to the slaughter. A few protested but their grievances fell on deaf ears. Alerted by her father, she was happy she went to the safety deposit box and emptied out her Jewels. She sent the gold with her parents when they left for Stockholm, but the jewels she kept, still hoping that normal times would be restored after a new constituent assembly was established and she could wear them again. She had scattered the gems in several convenient hiding places in case the CHEKA should carry out one of its midnight raids for the purpose of instilling terror in in the hearts if the gentry as well as to steal.

Her diamond tiara fit nicely in the lining of an old muskrat hat. She sewed her favorite pieces in the seams of a special vest which she had made and wore everyday under her dresses. She even emptied out a large bottle of ink, removed the diamonds from several pieces, dropped them into the bottom and covered them with paraffin before pouring back the ink. The big wrap around label concealed the valuable treasure sitting in plain sight on her writing table. She also set aside a few pieces in case she had to sell them for emergency money.

She stared at the darkening sky outside the window. A few snowflakes began to drift about, as if they were looking for a secure place to settle. *Funny how when the sun shines and the harvest is plentiful, no one could ever think in their wildest dreams that good times could roll into dark and desperate times.*

Chapter 52

EXCITEMENT AND ANTICIPATION filled the air. Society women turned out in their jewels and sables for the first time since the October revolution. Handsome young guards in gold trimmed tunics and white capes thrown open over their shoulders, and Kazaks wearing their traditional crimson *Cherkesskas* with elaborately carved Caucasian swords tucked in black belts, strutted about in the lobby of the hotel Astoria, waiting to march with their units in the celebration parade. Jeniya took Katiya, Ronnie, Alexei and Gavriil for early morning tea at the hotel to commemorate a new era in Russian history. A Constituent Assembly had been elected in November by a seventy-one per cent majority in favor of a socialistic government working within a capitalistic framework. The Bolsheviks received only twenty-nine percent of the vote.

"*Offeeshyat,*" Jeniya said summing the waiter. "We'll have tea for five, please."

"*Tovareesh offeeshyat,* madam!" the waiter said glaring down from insolent eyes. Jeniya raised her head with an air of indignation. She turned her attention to Alexei. He had deep blue eyes and dark eyelashes like his father, but his wavy raven black hair, unlike anyone in her family, must have been like his grandmother, Este, whom she had heard so much about. Gavriil had favored her people who had dark auburn hair and fair skin.

"So...what's been going on with you at General Headquarters, Alousha?" she said. "You haven't wired or written."

"I've been under a great deal of stress these past few months with this Kornilov affair, the murder, the change of staff. I don't know how much longer they will keep me on. I think the only reason it hasn't been worse is because of the holidays, even though no one celebrated."

The waiter set five cups of tea on the table and Jeniya pulled a jeweled sugar box and a loaf of white bread from her muff. She opened the box and gave each one a sugar cube in their hand for their tea.

"That must have cost an arm and a leg," Katiya said staring in delight. "It's been so long since I've had sugar in my tea, and white bread. I've forgotten what it tastes like."

"Anything can be gotten for a price," Jeniya said, happy to share her precious possessions with those she loved.

"Alousha?" Gavriil said turning to his brother. "Do you think there is a chance that the Germans could take Petrograd now that our army is disintegrating? They are practically on our door-step now."

"I never thought I would say this...but I welcome anything to restore order even German occupation. I still have my doubts that a new assembly can put together what has been lost as long as corrupt and deceitful politicians continued to go through the revolving door." He took out his pocket watch and looked at the time. "If you will excuse me, ladies...and gentleman," he said rising from the table and bowing in the etiquette of the old court, making Jeniya proud he had not forgotten. "It's time for me to join my regiment."

Alexei would be marching with the Preobrazhensky guards in a parade honoring the new government about to assemble in the Tauride Palace. Even though there should have been no need to be concerned over this march, his mother worried. On her way to the hotel, she thought it odd to see cruisers from Kranstadt moving into the Neva River headed toward the Tauride Palace where the new assembly would commence.

"Alousha," Jeniya suddenly jumped up. She had a frightening premonition and wanted to stop him from participating in the parade. "Alousha," she called after him.

"Yes, mama?" He turned around.

She hesitated. "Be careful."

Russia was declared a Democratic Federal Republic, on January 5th 1918. Bands played. Flags waved and banners fluttered in the icy wind. Companies gathered behind their regimental colors ready to begin the parade. People from all classes came out to march with them under the red banners proclaiming their support for the new government.

When the procession turned into the street leading to the Tauride Palace they were met with gunfire from Latvian sharpshooters, the notoriously fierce combat warriors loyal to the Bolsheviks. Gunmen posted around the palace fired into the crowd. Kronstadt sailors stationed on cruisers and battleships were on alert. Alexei was wounded and fell to his knees. When he looked up, he saw the unfamiliar face of a man about his father's age pointing a gun to his head, grinning. He wore a black great coat with the collar turned up against the cold. The graying hair on his hatless head was slicked down with oil, like a devil.

"You are Daniel's son?"

"What business is it of yours? Who are you?"

"You have all the audacity of your father, I see."

"Who are you? What do you want?"

"Where is your father?"

"He is not here."

"You can tell that blood sucking, money grubbing insect, that Samsky will be by to see him…him and his lovely family."

Jeniya heard the gun fire and she pushed frantically through the crowd to Alexei's regiment, calling his name.

When she found him, she knelt at his side. One of his comrades was already tending to a leg wound. "He's going to be all right, madam," the young man assured her. "We are going to bring him to the infirmary at the barracks.

"Alousha?"

"Don't worry about me, mama. It wasn't that bad. Look at it this way, at least I won't be going back to Stavka for a while."

Inside the palace, Kronstadt sailors stood in the balcony with loaded guns looking down on the new assembly in session. After a few hours, they said to one another. "Enough of that. Let's shut this thing down." They aimed their rifles, cocked the triggers and fired. The next day, the red guard barricaded the palace. The Constituent Assembly was stillborn.

The Soviet of People's Commissars bombarded the citizens with a series of imposing new regulations to demolish every resemblance of the old order. Every day, they pasted a list on the buildings throughout the city and every morning, someone would read the new decrees to the illiterate crowds gathered around to hear what was permitted and forbidden.

Only civil marriages are legal. Absolute equality between men and women. Spouses do not lose their identity as free and equal and independent personalities in marriage. Satisfaction of sexual desires and love-making will be as simple and unimportant as drinking a glass of water.

Religious schools will be banned and education is to be nationalized. The state will provide facilities to care for children.

Regional self-governing bodies such as the zemstvo are abolished. Land is confiscated. Houses can no longer be bought and sold.

All banks nationalized. Private bank accounts frozen. Only 125 rubbles will be permitted to be withdrawn per week. Payment of interest and dividends will be halted. In the name of the revolution, criminal speculation by the banking bourgeois will be banned."

The brazen act of seizing power with armed weapons, as well as ending the hopes of the people by running rough-shod over their votes, prompted the infuriated citizens to fight back. The bank clerks threatened to go on strike if the red guard intimated them to burglarize the accounts of their depositors. The communists dared not challenge this capitalistic holy of holies. Not yet. For a while the old ways continued to function side by side with the new order; the old one refusing to yield and the new one unable to tighten its grip.

The people knew something had to be done to stop the encroaching bolshevism but felt helpless against the CHEKA. Most law-abiding citizens wove themselves into a cocoon of denial and went about their lives as though everything would somehow remain normal. Others had lost all hope that the old ways could be restored and sank into debauchery obliterating themselves with an hysteria for sex, pornography, and drugs. "Why deny yourself when life is going to the dogs," they said to justify their actions. "Pleasure, excitement, oblivion. Whatever helps one endure can't be wrong. Live full blast while it's still possible and blow your brains out when you have had enough."

Eventually, the repercussions of the revolution invaded all spectrums of society, from the middle class bourgeois to the desperately poor, as well as the nobles whose property, wealth and titles had been stripped. Everyone had to join the labor force in order to buy coupons for the purchase of food and fuel. Former aristocrats, noblemen and high ranking officers were seen shoveling snow, cleaning streets, and hauling coal. The petty bourgeois cleaned out their homes and sold merchandise from little tables set up on the sidewalk or from the wide stone windowsills of buildings. The poor stood lined up shoulder to shoulder for warmth outside the shops with their wares in hand, selling mostly old clothing, rags and shoes.

Officers who remained alive were assigned a bed in the solders barracks and given entry level salaries, forcing their wives to tramp the city streets in shawls wrapped about their heads, bartering their belongings for food. If a soldier was caught earning a few extra rubbles above his salary, it was confiscated. Even the sun offered little warmth to those who wandered in the streets as it peeked in and out, shedding a thin wintry light. But as long as the Tsar lived, as long as the Romanov family lived, and as long as the counter-revolutionary armies were building in the Ukraine, the people still hoped that Russia could be restored.

Life became increasingly wretched in the city. All consumer goods including firewood had to be shipped in by rail over icy marshes. Trains were often hindered by snowdrifts and sub-freezing temperatures. In addition, the peasants would not cooperate with authorities and ship their grain to the cities, blaming the government for the civil unrest in their provinces. White flour and sugar sold at such a premium that it was illegal to purchase them. If the CHEKA discovered anyone with a loaf of white bread in his possession, he could be slapped with an impossible fine. Should a homemade white roll turn up on someone's table it brought as much delight as a valuable piece of new jewelry.

Now that the capital of the job providers had been stripped and starvation and civil strife threatened the lives of cosmopolitan populations, Lenin became concerned. "It may seem that this is a struggle only for bread," he wrote. "In fact, the very future of socialism is at stake."

Jeniya sat in her study planning meals for the household. She had taken all of their best wines which Yaroslav had hidden, and bartered them on the black market for white flour and sugar from the sailors who worked at the docks. She knew there would be a penalty to pay if she were discovered but it was worth putting something good on the table once in a while. Savva volunteered to venture out and do the bargaining with the longshoremen, this time dressed as a wondering *staretz*. When someone questioned him as to what he carried in his back pack he replied in parables that only peasants could understand, temporarily confusing his inquisitors.

Suddenly the door flew open. Three men pushed into the room, preceded by a rotten stench, as though they had not bathed, shaved or groomed in days. They wore black leather jackets and red bands around their right arms symbolizing members of the CHEKA.

Jeniya sprang up paralyzed in fear.

"Where have you hidden your weapons?" demanded a tall muscular blond.

"There is no law against owning guns." Her fear shifted to enmity, such was her burning hatred toward these marauding brutes.

"The Bolsheviks are the law."

"The Bolsheviks have not been elected by the people. We still have rights as citizens."

"You have no rights. We are the law now and you are the enemy of the people. Now step aside from that dresser." He opened and closed drawers tossing the contents on the floor. "Where have you hidden your jewels?"

Jeniya's blood raced in both angst and anger. She had to think fast. I...I had them in the safety deposit box."

Two of the goons marched into her dressing room and rummaged through her closets. "What are you doing" she screamed following them inside. They ignored her outcries and threw her fur coats in a pile on the floor, the rare sable, the ermine cape, the chinchilla, and the black mink. "Why haven't you surrendered your fur coats to the soldiers who have no coats, greedy bitch." said a tall skinny one with black kinky hair and beard merging into one mass around a thin nose and dark eyes.

"Why should I?" She labored for a breath of clean air against the reeking body odor.

"It's the law. I should lock you up in the fortress prison where you belong to rot with the rest of your kind."

The other one ransacking through her clothes held up a gown. "Hey! Take a look at the gems on this dress," he said to his comrade.

"Take it."

Jeniya's blood boiled in anger when the dirt bag pulled out her fine silken lace underwear with disgusting hands and ogled her, making a salacious seer. The skinny one pulled out her old cloth coat with the jewels sewn in the lining. He held it up and hesitated for a moment trying to decide whether or not to take it. "This one is awfully heavy for an old cloth coat," he said with a bewildered expression on his face. Jeniya's heart pounded so loudly she thought for sure he could detect her secret.

He looked down at the pile of fur coats. "I suppose you need a coat, here keep this one. It's good enough for a greedy bitch like you." He threw it at her and she quickly grabbed it before it fell to the floor.

As the three intruders bent over to pick up the loot, Jeniya saw her vest with the hidden jewels lying on the floor near the door. She gasped for breath, fighting with all her strength to survive the living nightmare swirling around her.

Chapter 53

FOR MOST EVERYONE, regardless of rank or birth, it seemed life had stopped. Their world had degenerated into a struggle for survival. The revolution had over thrown faith, morals, and customs. No one could be trusted.

The new tsars now controlled the farms and the hard working peasants refused to produce food for the urban population resulting in severe food shortages and prohibitive prices for the few available products. The communists confiscated private homes and forced their owners to live in the confinement of a few rooms, like inmates trapped in a concentration camp from which there was no escape, sharing what little they had with crude and often half-civilized strangers who held them hostages in their own houses. In order to avoid such a fate, Daniel moved Ronnie and Katiya into his home, along with many of the widows who faithfully served at the mission.

He reduced his household staff to a few faithful servants, Yaroslav, Savva, and the cook. Jeniya dismissed formal place settings at mealtime and tried to make work as easy as possible for everyone, but the volunteers from the mission were not above pitching in, taking turns as servers and assistants to the cook, trying to make the daily ration of black bread, watery cabbage soup and potatoes more palatable by keeping up the standard of formal meals. The main topic of conversation at dinner time passed from the miserable state of the country to how many creative ways the cook could prepare cabbage and potatoes, and how far he could stretch a little horse meat.

Yaroslav still insisted on wearing his black and white livery everyday as he had for almost forty years even though it now began to hang loose over his shoulders. "Because we are going down with the dogs," he said standing upright and proud even in his old age. "We need not dress like them. We need to maintain some semblance of civility to keep our spirits up."

Prince Militsyn also lived with the family. He had been incarcerated in the Fortress prison of St. Peter and Paul by the provincial government along with the Tsar's Council of Ministers. Upon his release him from prison, the communists ordered him to live within the boundaries of Great Russia and repair shoes for a living. His only son, an officer in the navy had been slaughtered by his own men, and his two daughters left the country with the grandchildren. After her husband had spent over a year in prison, the princess died of a broken heart thinking she would never see him again.

Each morning, Daniel would read from the newspapers to everyone in his household anxious to hear the latest events and about the fate of the Tsar and his family.

"Looks like we have some more decrees from the new masters of the universe," he said looking over the editorials one morning. 'Socialism includes the propaganda of atheism,' says this contributor. 'The people will not propagate religion in any form, but everyone is perfectly free to spread anti-religious propaganda with every means at his disposal. This will result in the complete withering away of religious prejudice, and the liberating of the toiling masses from religious dogma and toward the organizing of a most extensive scientific, educational and anti-religious propaganda'."

"*Ny*, there you are," said Ronnie. "I knew this would happen once the commissar for the poor took over the mission."

"This is an outrage," said Jeniya. "Where are we going in this nation."

Yaroslav refilled everyone's cup with coffee made from dried chickweed. He only felt comfortable when he was serving. It had become so ingrained in his being over the many years.

"Don't feel bad," Daniel said looking around the table at each one. "Many people were helped and many have found an understanding of eternal life through the bible studies. We need to be grateful for the time we had over these past four years." He looked down at the paper still opened to the editorials trying to fight the tears filling his eyes.

"Look here," he said. "Here's something interesting from the Commissar for Public Enlightenment...'educators must refrain from teaching history in a way stimulating the children's national pride. National minority rights, like nationalism in general, serve only as a temporary measure for the prevention of national strife during the era of building a socialist society. Just as the concentration of state power through a dictatorship of the proletariat was intended merely to pave the way for the ultimate withering away of the state, the promotion of national cultures is to be but an intermediate link toward the ultimate submersion of all nationalities in a world nation'."

But the news that swept everyone speechless came a few months later, announcing the execution of Tsar Nicholas II, the Empress, the tsarevich, their four daughters, and their servants on the morning of July 17th 1918 in Yekaterinburg, Siberia, where they lived in exile.

Everyone worried. Their last hope of restoring the Empire had evaporated when the Czech volunteer army failed to reach the Tsar and his family before they fell into the hands of their assassins.

"May God help us," Jeniya said. "Everything is lost. Oh how I wish we had listened to papa and left this horrible place. Papa was right. There is nothing noble in foolishness and it is foolish to remain here. The mission is gone. The business is gone. What's going to happen to us?"

"Do you think the white armies can overturn this terrible regime?" Prince Militsyn asked Daniel.

"Who knows? Right now there is relative peace in the Ukraine since the Germans took occupation. I understand the whites are looking to them for support in their counter-revolution. But..." he said sadly shaking his head. "Civil war would only mean greater bloodshed for us."

"That does it," said Jeniya. She looked Daniel square in the eye. "We've got to get out of here! I'm going to get passports for all of us to leave before it's too late. Hoping that we will be saved by the Germans and the white armies, is like waiting for palm trees to grow in Siberia."

"They would never allow me a passport," said Alexei, still recovering at home from his broken leg. He had been relieved of his duty at Stavka when the reds signed a peace treaty with Germany. They stripped him of his rank and reduced him to the status of common recruit. "I'm a soldier. Sometimes I think I would rather face a firing squad than fight with the red army against my own comrades in the white armies...sometimes..." he turned his face away. "Sometimes I wish I had died on the battlefield with my friends..."

"Alousha!" said Jeniya frowning, more determined than ever to get her family out of Russia.

"No Alousha," said Prince Militsyn. "You must not think that way. You are still young. God has a future for you and a hope. You need to trust him."

"Where is God in this land of hunger and death. God who was on the side of every nation before the war is now on the side of no one."

"Evil is in this world," said the prince. "It is a seed that lives in men's hearts. It has nothing to do with God. You must learn to have faith through these darkest days which will one day pass. There will always be goodness in the world, times of peace and hope because God is still at work bringing love and goodness into people's hearts."

Alexei gazed at the prince, astonished that he had a spirit of serene peace in these tumultuous times, especially after losing his home and family and was forced into poverty.

Ronnie put a comforting hand over Alexei's. "You will get through this, darling. We will all get through this." She turned to Daniel and said, "Jenka is right, Danya. We can't depend on the white armies to defend us. We must go now before the country breaks out in civil war and they will not let us go."

Daniel excused himself from the table and left without a word. Sometimes it was easier to hope against hope rather than leave all that was familiar and settle into another life in some strange country where he didn't understand the culture and the language. Already the reds seized his mission, and requisitioned his auto. They took over his business and reduced him to a worker with a worker's wage. His father-in-law's beautiful mansion had turned into a slum tenement for squatters and Prince Militsyn's palace on the Neva into an exhibition hall trampled by the half-civilized masses. The monstrous machine was grinding and sifting lives as wheat. He saw his days as numbered and running out before his eyes. He looked at everything as if he were seeing it for the last time, the city, the people, the trees, the wide Neva and the blue-green gulf, and felt a sinking in his heart. He was anxious for Jeniya and his sons who had not yet begun their lives. He thought of his many colleagues rotting in the cold damp Fortress of St. Peter and Paul and wondered if he would be next.

Jeniya went to the Commissariat of Foreign Affairs the next morning to find out what she must do to secure passports for the family. After waiting for hours and enduring interrogation and verbal abuse from hardened young Jewish typists, filled with arrogance and vehement loathing toward the Russian bourgeois, she was sent to Solomonovich Uritsky, head of the Petrograd CHEKA, the one man authorized to grant permission for Russian citizens to leave the country. The mere mention of his name brought dread in the hearts of everyone who had to face him. His job was to pursue and persecute members of the nobility, senior officers, and the clergy. Many hundreds of these upright citizens were already sitting on death's row.

Gorochovaya No 2, once the beautiful home of Princess Obolenskaya, was now the home of terror. On the way into the formal ballroom she passed a melancholy elderly man sweeping the floor, dressed in what used to be his footman's livery. He made a nod of recognition towards Jeniya and with tear filled eyes, and said in a hushed voice, "What times. *Mon Dieu.* What times are these."

People of every description with weary troubled faces and frightened eyes fixed like those of dead men, sat on benches and chairs along the walls. Peasants and soldiers caught for bartering prohibited food provisions waited with large bags set at their feet. Jeniya thought of her participation in the black market and wondered how long she would be able to carry on.

She gazed around the room where she had attended many grand parties and receptions. The tables once decorated with white linen, silver place settings, bone china dinnerware and fine Bohemian crystal, were now dirty, scuffed and broken. The sweet air from fresh tropical flowers had been replaced by a heavy and close stink from unwashed bodies. The inlaid parquet floors once shining like mirrors, where dancers waltzed, were covered with disgusting spittle. Her longing heart sank in pain when she remembered those elegant days past.

A handsome young Jew with black wavy hair, sat at a long table covered with a red cloth. Some men approached him with burlap sacks. When they opened their sacks and dumped out the contents, she saw diadems of diamonds, necklaces and brooches of sapphires, rubies, and emeralds tumble onto the red cloth. They emptied another large sack filled with of silver and gold. The young man stood up. His covetous eyes sparkled like the gems set before him. He lifted the golden objects, felt the weight of each one in his hand and placed it into a separate pile.

Periodically groups of people passed through the room driven by dirty looking revolutionary soldiers; pushing them with the butt-ends of their rifles into another room where they awaited interrogation. They were not nobles or aristocrats or even the bourgeois but common people, cooks, peasants, artisans, little shopkeepers. No one was exempt from the red tactics of terror. *Who are these people. And why them? Could it be, that in the red guard's determination to weed out every person hostile to their regime, they had to accuse the common working people of treason by enticing their neighbors, their co-workers, and their customers to snitch on them. May God help us."*

Less than a year ago everyone was free. The toiling masses celebrated their liberation. The Bolsheviks spoke of universal freedom, world peace and unity but in reality these vicious individuals thought only of exterminating everyone who blocked their road to power. The word truth was not in their vocabulary.

The wall clock had ticked off one hour, then two, three...four. Finally, at six o'clock in the evening someone came out of Uritsky's office and called, "Citizen Mendelevna. It's your turn."

Uritsky sat at a table writing. When she entered the room, he raised his head and stared at her intensely through a pince-nez sitting on a banana nose. "You are the wife of citizen Daniel Mendelev, former arms dealer," said the middle aged man.

She nodded.

"Be seated," he said deliberately ignoring her, almost as if he enjoyed seeing the agitation on her face. "I will attend you shortly."

He pushed a button and a man brought out his dinner and placed it in front of him on the writing table. The CHEKA boss threw large chunks of white bread into a steaming bowl of chicken soup and slurped it up, then poured himself a glass of red wine and guzzled it down. He pushed the empty soup bowl aside and started on a plate of roasted veal chops and potatoes, deliberately chewing like a dog, as Jeniya was forced to watch weak from hunger and exhaustion.

"So what brings you here?" he said wiping his lips. "What do you want?"

"I want passports for my family," she said forcing back her rage.

"Why do you want to leave? Haven't we accommodated your husband in every way, allowing him to remain on as a worker managing our factory."

"Management? If that's what you call it. He barely earns a steel worker's wage."

"Your insolence can cost your husband all his wages and possibly his job."

"I haven't come to discuss his wages or his job, but to obtain passports for our family."

"It is denied."

"Why?"

He read from a paper on his desk. "We have a charge from the Central Committee of the Communist Party. Citizen Mendelev is not permitted to leave Russia."

"Why?" For the first time she feared the threat of red terror.

"Don't press the issue...citizen Mendelevna. Good-day."

Jeniya returned home late in the evening. As soon as she entered the foyer, everyone rushed to the door anxious to hear the news. "We are denied passage from Russia," she said in a raised her voice trembling with rage. "As well as the reason why. What have we done? Everyone who isn't a Romanov can get passports to leave but us...and we are not Romanovs!"

"Maybe they are connecting us with our father," said Katiya. "Anyone who served on the Tsar's Council of Ministers is considered an enemy of the state. Maybe they are taking out their revenge on him against us."

"Or..." Daniel said connecting the dots which led to the Central Committee of the Communist Party. "Maybe it is my brother."

"Yes, that's it!" Jeniya said. "It's your brother Ezra. The name communist party hadn't dawned on me; they've changed their name so many times."

"What are we going to do?" said Katiya.

"You are not a Mendelev." Daniel said. "You and Ronnie are fee to go. You or anyone else who wishes to leave." He looked around at everyone in the room with tears filling his eyes.

"But where will we go, sir?" said Yaroslav. "I have nearly sixty-five summers of age."

Early in August, the CHEKA commissar, Uritsky had been assassinated. His murder triggered a reign of terror on the citizens of Petrograd. After another assassination attempt was made, this time on Lenin's life, the search and seizure of homes snowballed into savage executions of hundreds of innocent people. "The bourgeoisie can kill some individuals." A terrorist named Apelbaum proclaimed. "But we can murder a whole class of people. From a population of one hundred million, we must win over ninety million. We have nothing to say to the others. They have to be exterminated."

The new tsars of terror had to purge the land of all harmful insects to save their revolution before the white army, the bourgeois, the liberals and socialists had a chance to unite.

"You think that the path of the proletarian revolution is strewn with roses," Lenin said to drive the hesitant members of the Communist Committee into action. "The revolution is not a pleasure trip. True revolutionaries must be prepared to follow the hardest roads, crawling if need be, through dirt and dung to communism."

No one could sleep at night. Every time they heard an automobile stop outside someone's door or distant screams, they jumped from their beds and ran to the window.

"Danya," Jeniya said one evening at dinnertime. "We have to leave for the Ukraine while we can still get out. I worry constantly about Alexei sitting in that barracks and Gavriil at the university."

"Belozerkovka is gone," said Katiya. "Where will we go?"

"We can find a place somewhere in the Ukraine, said Jeniya. "Or we can get on a ship and sail from the port of Odessa."

"How can we all travel on the same train to Odessa?" said Ronnie. "They will know at once who we are."

"We have to travel separately," said Daniel. "Fortunately we all have different surnames." A sudden cloud of despair crossed his face and cast a shadow over his hopeful thought. "I'm afraid I may not be able to go with you."

"Why?" asked Jeniya.

"Have you forgotten so soon that I am held prisoner here in Russia."

"We can get you another identity."

He laughed. *She's still naive and hopeful after all these years.* "That wouldn't work," he said. "They would discover me sooner or later and I would put all of your lives in danger." The horrific days of the pogroms flashed through his mind. *Once they only came after Jews. This time it is not only Jews, but Christians, capitalists, businessmen, intellectuals, artists, students, and everyone and anyone who would not yield to their demands. We have become less than animals in a regime with no regard for the sacredness of human life…sacrifices to be made to appease gods of tyranny.*

The next morning at breakfast Daniel gathered everyone around the table. "Since the attempted assassination on Lenin's life," he said. "We are now in a reign of terror and our home is targeted. They will hunt down every member of any household they feel is a threat to their power. The border is still open to the Ukraine where the white armies are stationed. Anyone one of you who wishes to go, is free to leave and I would suggest that you make your plans immediately."

"The cook stepped forward. "I would like to go sir."

"Some of the women from the mission said, "We have no means, sir."

"I can provide you," Daniel said. "Anyone else? Savva, Yaroslav?" He turned to his valet. "Savva, I want you to take Katiya and Ronnie to Kiev and look after them. Yaroslav, do you want to go with them?"

"No sir, I will remain with you. I am already old and you will need encouragement."

Then he gazed at Jeniya with tears in his eyes. "And take Jenka and our sons."

She flew into his arms. "My darling. I will never leave you. If you go down, I will go with you."

He pulled her away, thinking of the wives of nobles and high ranking officials whose husbands had been imprisoned, and are now condemned to walk to the streets begging, some engaging in prostitution in order to survive. "No, sweetheart. You must go with Savva," he said.

She collapsed onto the sofa and broke down in tears. Living in an atmosphere of constant hatred, vengeance, and suspicion had drained her fortitude and iron-willed determination. Katiya and Ronnie sat on each side and held her in their arms, weeping with her. Katiya understood her sister's torment. Separation from the man you love in these treacherous times is worse than losing him in death. And she wept for her daughter, Irina, still living with her radical boyfriend; still despising everything her mother stood for.

Daniel fought with his last bit of strength against his own breaking heart. Someone had to stand strong and hold the others up until they could safely leave the country. "Please excuse me," he said. "I must be alone for a while."

He went to his study and fell to his knees. "Oh God," he prayed with tears falling from his eyes. "Lord my God. This burden is more than I can bear. Whatever is your will for me, for my life, I lay it before your throne. But my family, and those faithful ones who have served me...please deliver them, protect them and sustain them." Then his heart began to fill with praise for God. His darkness had turned into light and his tears into joy. He knew his prayer had been heard and his family would make it through this dark night of terror.

He arose, took his bible and returned to the drawing room. "I thought this would be a good time to encourage one another with the word of God." He turned to Psalm 91 and read.

"He who dwells in the shelter of the Most High
will rest in the shadow of the Almighty
I will say of the Lord, "He is my refuge and my fortress,
my God, in whom I trust."
Surely he will save you from the fowler's snare

and from the deadly pestilence.
He will cover you with his feathers,
and under his wings you will find refuge;
His faithfulness will be your shield and rampart.
You will not fear the terror of night
nor the arrow that fillies by day,
nor the pestilence that stalks in the darkness,
nor the plague that destroys at midday."
(Psalm 91:1-5)

"Because he loves me," says the Lord, "I will rescue him;
I will protect him, for he acknowledges my name.
He will call upon me and I will answer him;
I will be with him in trouble,
I will deliver him and honor him."
(Psalm 91:14-15)

As he was reading they heard alarming sounds coming from the front entrance downstairs. A mob was breaking down the door and pushing through the locks, rushing inside, shouting obscenities. Yaroslav quickly ushered everyone from the room to go down the back stairs and hide in the servant's quarters, except Jeniya who would not leave her husband's side.

"Go Jeniya. I insist!" He took her hand, prompting her to move

"No! I will remain here with you, my husband," she said leaning into his arms. He embraced her trembling body.

This break-in did not take Daniel by surprise. He had anticipated it and conditioned his own inner psychological strength. He did not fear for himself or of the possibility of his own execution, but for Jeniya and his sons. He raised his eyes and prayed, "Father, whatever is you will, we surrendered ourselves." The words of St. Paul came to his mind. "The peace of God which transcends all understanding, will guard your hearts and minds in Christ Jesus." (Philippians 4:7)

Though Jeniya was terrified, she felt a supernatural repose settle over her like an invisible shroud.

Several rough men in filthy rumpled brown shirts burst into the drawing room and found Daniel and Jeniya siting peacefully in the drawing room watching as one would watch a movie, without resistance, protest or anguish. The peace that pervaded the room disoriented the assassins for a few moments. They turned to one another, not knowing what to do next when two more men pushed inside. "Shoot them," said the leader. Like trained dogs they lifted their pistols and cocked the triggers.

Daniel's heartbeat dropped for a moment, not so much from fear but from shock at what he was witnessing. Jeniya recognized the second man as the handsome young Jew she saw sitting in Uritsky's chambers collecting gold and precious gems. At that time, he served as Uritsky's deputy and had now become the interim commissar of the all-powerful CHEKA. "Stop!" he shouted. "Put your guns down. Don't kill this man. He is the one we know as the friend to the poor. Do not take his life!"

The men lowered their pistols and looked around at each other. All except one. Ezra. As a member of the Communist Central Committee, he had unlimited power, relentless persistence, and an intense hatred towards his brother. He arranged this little band of thugs to assure his assassination.

Ezra raised his revolver and pointed it at Daniel's head. "This man deserves to die, while women and children were perishing from hunger in the depths of the Pale, he was cavorting at feasts and balls. While husbands and fathers were shot and killed on the front, he was living in obscene luxury off the blood of the men who sweated in his steel mill. Now it is our turn to feed him to the dogs."

"No," said Uritsky's replacement. "This man has used his fortune and set up a foundation for the relief of Jewish war victims. He traveled from town to town, establishing shelters to feed the hungry and cloth those who had lost everything. Our family was among those wandering refugees, lost, not knowing where we were going. My mother was too weak to continue on when he picked us up and carried us in his carriage to a warm place to sleep and provided us with nourishing food."

"This man is a millionaire industrialist and his wife is a member of the nobility," said Ezra. We have sworn not to spare one of these blood sucking insects. Let this man live and he will spread his capitalist disease."

"Will you do this thing to your brother, Ezra? Your own flesh and blood?" For the first time Daniel saw Ezra for what he was, a miserable little man living inside a brutish body, driving him to hate. The anger he had harbored in his heart all these years toward Ezra had given way to pity and most of all, forgiveness.

Even the brutal men were shocked and directed their comments to Ezra.

"This is your bother?"

"What did he do to you?"

"What do you have against him?"

But Ezra was mad with rage. "You call me your brother? You who abandoned your family and your people to marry that Orthodox daughter of the nobility. But that wasn't enough for you, you bled the war ministry of money for shells and weapons. The only thing that kept me alive while I was in exile and in prison was to live to see the day when you were buried with the rest of your bourgeois swine." Ezra glared at his brother with intense loathing; his hand quivering with a finger wrapped around the trigger of his revolver pointing to Daniel's head.

A rush of consternation, dread, and confusion disconcerted Daniel's assurance and he felt his blood turning to ice.

Ezra cocked his gun and fired. Daniel's heart beat stopped the moment the shot blasted from the firearm. Jeniya covered her eyes with her hands and screamed.

At the same time, his young comrade pushed Ezra's arm causing him to stumble. The bullet whizzed across the room and lodged in the wall.

Ezra rose to his feet dazed for a few moments and started towards the door. Before he left, he turned to his brother and said. "I despise the sight of you." The others glanced at one another and put their guns away.

"You will not die at our hand," said the young commissar. "You must leave the country at once. Sell what you can. Take your family and the money and go."

Daniel sat and stared at him in a state of shock before his words began to take hold in his mind. Jeniya gasped in both relief and astonishment.

"We are launching a campaign of mass terror against the bourgeois. They must be taught a cruel lesson until they stop interfering with our plans and leave us in peace to build a new Russia. We will spare no one."

Still rattled, Daniel stood up and thanked him as a gentleman. "Keep all my possessions," he said. "I will take my household and go."

"The seaways are blocked to passenger ships but we will escort you safely past the Kronstadt surveillance station where you can board the next cargo ship bound for Sweden. In the meantime, we will give you the necessary papers and put you under protection until the ship sails."

When the men left, Daniel and Jeniya embraced each other and wept, leaning on each other's trembling shoulders for support. Their ordeal had ended.

They shed tears of relief and tears of joy. They laughed and hugged and cried

"We are free!" Jeniya said looking blissfully into his eyes as she did on her wedding night. "Free to go and start a new life together!"

"I can't believe it." Daniel said. "A bad nightmare has ended." They kissed and gave praise to God for his incredible goodness and mercy.

Downstairs, the family heard the shot. They hesitated to go upstairs for fear of what they might find and what may be in store for them. In the ensuing quietness after the gun shot, Savva slipped up the backway and moved quietly down the hall to listened near the door. Then he heard Daniel and Jeniya burst out with laughter.

"Sir, are you all right?" he said poking his head through a small opening in the door to the room.

"We are fee to go, Savva. Free!" Daniel said.

"Savva opened the door wide and looked at him incredulously. Did you say...free to go, sir?"

"Free! Free to go."

Ronnie and Katiya followed him and ran in the room shrieking with joy. They threw their arms around Daniel and Jeniya, praising God for his answer to their prayers and the miracle of deliverance.

Light summer breezes caressed their faces and they savored the fresh salty smell of the gulf air, it seemed for the first time. As the morning mist lifted from a mirror sea, Daniel and Jeniya recognized the faint outlines of summer mansions sheltered in the pine forests and the yacht club where they spent so many happy afternoons sailing and playing tennis. The Petrograd skyline gleamed in the distance as rays from the rising sun lit the church domes and the iconic spire of the prison fortress of St. Peter and Paul rendering them into a reflection of pure gold.

As the notorious landmark receded on the horizon, a feeling of profound and inexplicable melancholy passed over them, thinking of the people they know; some friends, some acquaintances, and some members of the nobility, including five grand dukes sitting in the damp cold cells at this very moment awaiting their fate. In that bittersweet moment, the times of hardship and privation they experienced could not compare to the tragedy of execution about to befall those good and noble citizens who loved and served their country. They also spoke of Vadim and those who were organizing a counter-revolution and wondered about their fate. All the horrendous events of the past four years now seemed to blur as the Petrograd metropolis became no more than specks on the horizon.

Jeniya also looked forward to the joyful reunion with her parents and her sister, Yelizaveta when they reached Sweden. Most of all she reveled in recapturing the moment of elation she felt upon their release.

Daniel and Jeniya put their arms around Alexei and Gavriil who stood on each side of their parents. Ronnie and Katiya could not keep tears of happiness from their eyes. No one knew what awaited them on the shores of North America, but they knew that the God who had delivered them from so many tribulations was going with them.

Jeniya turned and smiled, sharing the moment of happiness with Prince Militsyn, Yaroslav, and Savva.

Epilogue

MEN HAVE FORGOTTON GOD
From the Templeton address by Aleksandr Solzhenitsyn

MORE THAN HALF a century ago, while I was still a child, I recall hearing a number of older people offer the following explanation for the great disasters that had befallen Russia: Men have forgotten God; that's why all this had happened.

Since then I have spent well-nigh fifty years working on the history of our Revolution; in the process I have read hundreds of books, collected hundreds of personal testimonies, and have already contributed eight volumes of my own toward the effort of clearing away the rubble left by that upheaval. But if I were asked today to formulate as concisely as possible the main cause of the ruinous Revolution that swallowed up some sixty million of our people, I could not put it more accurately than to repeat: Men have forgotten God; that's why all this has happened.

What is more, the events of the Russian Revolution can only be understood now, at the end of the century, against the background of what has since occurred in the rest of the world. What emerges here is a process of universal significance. And if I were called upon to identify briefly the principal trait of the *entire* twentieth century, here too, I would be unable to find anything more precise and pithy than to repeat once again: Men have forgotten God.

Made in the USA
Lexington, KY
08 July 2017